Praise for

'Erica James' sensitive story . . . is as sparklingly fresh as dew on the village's surrounding meadows . . . thoroughly enjoyable and fully deserving of a place in the crowded market of women's fiction' *Sunday Express*

'This book draws you into the lives of these characters, and often makes you want to scream at them to try and make them see reason. Funny, sad and frustrating, but an excellent, compulsive read' *Woman's Realm*

'There is humour and warmth in this engaging story of love's triumphs and disappointments, with two well-realised and intriguing subplots' *Woman & Home*

'Joanna Trollope fans, dismayed by the high gloom factor and complete absence of Agas in her latest books, will turn with relief to James' . . . delightful novel about English village life . . . a blend of emotion and wry social observation'
Daily Mail

'Scandal, fury, accusations and revenge are all included in Erica James' compelling novel . . . this story of village life in Cheshire is told with wit and humour' *Stirling Observer*

'An entertaining read with some wickedly well-painted cameo characters. It's a perfect read if you're in the mood for romance' *Prima*

'An engaging and friendly novel . . . very readable'
Woman's Own

'A bubbling, delightful comedy which is laced with a bittersweet tang . . . a good story, always well observed, and full of wit' *Publishing News*

'James is a seasoned champion of the genre . . . *Promises, Promises* has an extraordinary deftness of touch, coupled with some searing insights into both how relationships fail, and can work' *Daily Mirror*

Erica James is the number one internationally best-selling author of twenty-five novels including *Mothers and Daughters*, *Summer at the Lake*, *Paradise House* and *Gardens of Delight* which won the RNA Novel of the Year award. Her books are loved by readers looking for beautifully drawn relationships, emotionally powerful storylines and evocative settings. A keen gardener, Erica lives in Suffolk and loves to travel, especially to the USA and Japan to visit her sons.

By Erica James

A Breath of Fresh Air
Time for a Change
Airs and Graces
A Sense of Belonging
Act of Faith
The Holiday
Precious Time
Hidden Talents
Paradise House
Love and Devotion
Gardens of Delight
Tell it to the Skies
It's the Little Things
The Queen of New Beginnings
Promises, Promises
The Real Katie Lavender
The Hidden Cottage
Summer at the Lake
The Dandelion Years
Song of the Skylark
Coming Home to Island House
Swallowtail Summer
Letters from the Past
Mothers and Daughters
A Secret Garden Affair

The Holiday

ERICA JAMES

ORION

An Orion paperback

First published in Great Britain in 2000
by Orion Books
This paperback edition published in 2014
by Orion Books,
an imprint of The Orion Publishing Group Ltd,
Carmelite House, 50 Victoria Embankment
London EC4Y 0DZ

An Hachette UK company

Reissued 2023

A CIP catalogue record for this book
is available from the British Library.

ISBN 978 1 3987 1488 5

Typeset by Deltatype Ltd, Birkenhead, Merseyside

Printed and bound in Great Britain by
Clays Ltd, Elcograf S.p.A.

MIX
Paper from
responsible sources
FSC® C104740
www.fsc.org

www.orionbooks.co.uk

To Edward and Samuel
with all my love

And special love and thanks
to Maureen

'Show me a hero and I will write you a tragedy.'

F. Scott Fitzgerald

Chapter One

In the beginning God made man, and when he'd got it completely right, he made Theodore Vlamakis.

This thought, though perhaps lacking in originality, came to Laura Sinclair as she gazed out at the dazzling horizon where a cerulean sky met a sea of aquamarine, and where, closer to the shore, their nearest neighbour and good friend, Theo was swimming. She watched him emerge from the clear blue water and make his way up the pebbly beach. Even by Greek standards he was deeply tanned, and with his strong muscular physique, which he kept in check by swimming at least twice a day and for an hour at a time, he made a striking impression. When he'd finished drying himself off, smoothed back his short wet hair and slipped on a pair of sunglasses, Laura found herself speculating on just how far his tan went up those long legs.

All the way, probably. Theo was not a man who did anything by half.

She sighed nostalgically, recalling a time when her own legs had been lean and firm, when cellulite and thready veins were things her mother worried about.

Banishing such depressing forty-something thoughts, she continued watching Theo as he also took a moment to enjoy the view. He really was in all respects completely and utterly gorgeous. It didn't even matter that he was a vain forty-two-year-old serial romancer; it merely added to his charm.

Beneath the exterior of rich, dark smoothness he was

also a man of considerable kindness. When she and Max had flown over at the weekend, he had arrived within minutes with a picnic basket of freshly baked bread, wafer-thin slices of salami, sun-ripened tomatoes just picked from his own garden and a bottle of chilled champagne. 'To celebrate the start of your summer here in Áyios Nikólaos,' he had said, his thumbs working deftly at the cork as he insisted they leave their unpacking till later.

She watched him turn from the water, sling a towel around his neck, and move along the beach towards the path that meandered up the hillside to his villa. As he did so, he tilted his head and glanced in her direction. She waved down to him and he returned the greeting. She invited him to join her for a drink by raising her arm and making a cup with her hand. He nodded and held up a thumb. She went inside and prepared a Campari and soda for herself, and oúzo with ice for him.

They had met Theo quite by chance, last spring when he'd been on the same flight as them bound for Corfu. Sitting in the window seat next to Max, he had been delighted to learn that they were spending the next three weeks on his beloved island, hoping to buy a holiday home. He claimed to have the very property for them. 'It is newly built and completely perfect. You will fall in love with it, I know you will,' he had enthused. 'I designed it myself, so take it from me, you will not find anything better, other than my own house and you cannot have that, it is mine. It is a part of me.' They soon came to know that this was typical Theo-speak: he was never slow in declaring his feelings or his enthusiasm, or revealing his pride, which in another man would probably have come across as conceit.

He had been right though: both she and Max had fallen in love with Villa Petros the moment they saw it. Tucked into the verdant hillside of cypress trees, and with its easy access to the secluded beach below, it was just as Theo had promised. The deal was struck without any second thoughts, and with Theo's help they had spent most of last year decorating and furnishing the house to make it their own. Now they would be able to enjoy it properly. It would be their first real holiday in Áyios Nikólaos and Laura was looking forward to spending the entire summer there. It was just a shame that Max wouldn't be able to do the same. He would have to make at least one trip home to keep an eye on work, although having organised a little den of *Boy's Own* high-tech wizardry in the villa, there was no worry of him not knowing what was going on at the office.

The running of his own firm – a management consultancy he had set up in the mid-eighties – was a source of pride and satisfaction for Max. In its infancy, it had looked as if the risk he had taken in leaving his then well-paid and secure job would backfire on him, but the business took off and became a major success. So successful that if he wanted to he could sell the company tomorrow, retire, and they would still be able to live as comfortably as they did now. But Max was only forty-nine and Laura couldn't imagine him retiring. Not ever. He was an energetic doer, incapable of sitting still for more than two minutes – unless, of course, he happened to be watching the tennis on telly, and in particular the current coverage of Wimbledon. Tennis was his passion, and since they had arrived, he had been glued to the huge flat-screen television he had bought for his high-tech den. 'Go on, get your racket to the ball!' – was a frequently heard cry that broke the peace and quiet of Villa Petros.

By the time she was back out on the terrace with a tray of drinks, Theo had appeared. He was even better-looking close up, with his instantly engaging smile. In the time it had taken him to climb the hillside, his hair had dried in the baking heat to reveal the streaks of grey running through it, which did nothing to detract from his attractiveness. Not for the first time Laura thought how unfair it was that grey hair didn't do the same for women.

He threw his towel over the arm of a chair in a gesture of easy familiarity and came towards her. '*Kaliméra*, my darling Laura,' he said, giving her a languid kiss on each cheek and a cool touch on the shoulder. 'But look at you, you are turning pink. Why is it that you English women never take proper care of your bodies?'

'Perhaps it's because we live in hope of a devastatingly handsome man doing it for us.'

He laughed, then spied a bottle of sun cream on the table where their drinks lay and guided her to a lounger in the shade. 'In that case, I must not disappoint you. Now, lie down. I will do your back first.' He poured factor fifteen into the palm of his hand and worked it into her skin with slow, sensual movements, starting with her shoulders, his fingers drifting downwards with small circular movements.

'Thank you for dinner last night, by the way,' Laura said, trying to pretend that she wasn't finding the experience quite as pleasurable as she was. 'Max and I really enjoyed it. You're becoming quite a cook.'

'It is the bachelor life. One has to learn to do these things.'

'Well, when the time comes you'll make someone a wonderful husband.'

'Like your Max?'

'Yes, just like my Max. And if I weren't such a happily married woman,' she added, as his fingers slipped beneath the straps of her swimsuit, 'I might feel compromised by what you're doing.' She turned over.

'Ah, Laura, how it hurts me to know that you are immune to my charm.'

'Nonsense! It's good for you to have at least one

4

woman in this world who is a friend and not a jealous lover.'

He poured another dollop of sun cream into his palm and gently rubbed it into her thigh. She hoped he wouldn't pay too much attention to this less than perfect area of her body. 'You think all the women in my life have a jealous spirit?' he asked, his hand lingering on her hip.

'Of course. They must have.'

'But why? I only try to make them happy?'

'Because, you silly vain man, they must hate knowing that they're just one of many.'

'Can I help it if women find me irresistible?'

'Oh, Theo, what a typically arrogant Greek man you are. It would serve you right if one day you fell in love with a woman who had enough sense to tell you to get lost.'

He grinned. 'But I have already, Laura. You.'

She pushed him away with a laugh and crossed the terrace for their drinks. She handed him his oúzo. 'Sorry, but the ice has almost melted to nothing.'

'Like my chance of seducing you,' he said, with a wink. Then changing his tone, as though the game was over, he said, 'When are you expecting Max back from the airport with the first of your houseguests?'

Laura glanced at her watch. 'In about an hour. That's if Izzy's plane has landed on time.'

'And this Easy, whom you mentioned last night during dinner, tell me more. What does she look like? Is she as beautiful as you? Does she have your pretty auburn hair and delicate complexion?'

'Her name's pronounced *Izzy* and she's far prettier than I am. She's younger, slimmer, and with hair that doesn't need to be chemically enhanced as mine does. And I'd appreciate it if you allowed her to settle in before you go offering her the benefit of your charming beachside manner. Just keep your distance.'

He raised one of his thick eyebrows. 'Why must you

continually think the worst of me, Laura? I always respect women. I give them plenty of space. I never crowd them. That isn't my style.'

'Would that be before or after you've broken their hearts?'

Theo took a long sip of his drink and eyed her thoughtfully. 'You are protective towards this friend. Am I right? You think she could come to harm with me?'

'Yes, to both questions.'

'Why? What has happened to this Izzy that you feel the need to wrap her in cotton wool?'

'Oh, the usual. A stupid man who took pleasure in humiliating her.'

'Ah, the cruelty of some men,' he said, with a wry smile. 'She is divorced, then?'

'No. Fortunately for her she wasn't married to the idiot.'

'But there is a new boyfriend on the scene? Or is she still searching for her Mr Right?'

Laura shook her head. 'There's no new boyfriend, and if I know Izzy, she's probably decided that Mr Right is a figment of every young girl's imagination and that—'

'But Max is your Mr Right, isn't he?' Theo interrupted. 'He is far from being a figment of your imagination. He is very real.'

Laura thought of the wonderful man to whom she had been married for twenty-one years and smiled. They had met when she had just turned twenty and was recovering from the break-up of a relationship she should never have got herself into. Stupidly, she had been having an affair with her boss. Always a mistake, that, and especially if he's married. It had been the silliest thing she had ever done, but she'd believed his every word, that his marriage was over, that any day now he would be leaving his wife. In the end, and after he'd tired of her, he had called a halt to their relationship by giving her the sack. With her

6

pride in tatters, she had gone home to her parents for a weepy cry on their shoulders and had met Max at a ball.

From the moment he had asked her to dance there had been an instant attraction between them, but knowing that she was on the rebound she had held off from his advances, not wanting to hurt him any more than she wanted to be hurt again. But his warmth and exuberance won her over, and within the year they were married. The following spring their daughter Francesca was born. Their marriage had been full of love, laughter and happiness, but above all else, it was founded on trust.

'Yes,' she said finally, in answer to Theo's question, 'Max is my Mr Right. But Izzy hasn't been so fortunate. She was landed with Mr Wrong and her outlook has been appropriately coloured.'

'Then I will make a pleasant surprise for her. I will be her Mr Sweep-Me-Off-My-Feet.'

Laura rolled her eyes. 'My goodness, what a self-deprecating man you are.'

'But wouldn't it make her feel better? Wouldn't it lift her jaded spirits?'

'What? Have some Lothario trying to get her into bed and then be waving her goodbye before the sheets are cold the following morning?'

'You are so very cynical, Laura. Did someone do that to you a long time ago? Before the wonderful Max?'

She frowned. 'Most women get that treatment at some stage in their lives.'

'Well, I promise you, I will be more subtle. Much more sensitive.'

'You mean you'd give her breakfast?'

He smiled. 'We shall have to see, won't we?'

Laura was concerned. 'You are joking, aren't you?'

'It is strange, but the more you protect her, the more I feel the need to rise to the challenge.'

'Now, look here, Theo, Izzy's a dear friend. She's coming for a restful holiday, she doesn't need—'

'But a little romance might help her relax even more.'

She watched Theo stretch out his long brown legs as he made himself more comfortable in the chair beside her and wondered if there wasn't an element of truth in what he was suggesting. After what Izzy had gone through this last year, maybe a light-hearted holiday romance would be the very thing to boost her self-confidence. Maybe it was time for Izzy to have a little fun, and if anyone was capable of giving her that, then surely it was Theo.

'By the way,' she said, deciding it was time to change the subject – it didn't do to let Theo bask in his own magnificence for too long – 'when does your guest arrive from England?'

'Tomorrow afternoon.'

'And how long is he staying?'

'Most of the summer, I think. He has the artistic temperament and needs peace and quiet to work on his latest book.'

'He's a writer?'

'Yes. He writes dark tales of death and destruction. His name is Mark St James. You have heard of him, perhaps?'

'I most certainly have. Max is a big fan. How exciting! Will we get to meet him?'

'If you are good to me I will give it some thought.' Then, leaning forward in his seat, he stroked her leg provocatively. 'We could strike a deal: your wounded Izzy for my infamous author. What do you say?'

'And there was me on the verge of asking you to stay for lunch. Suddenly I've changed my mind.'

'As your Max would say, *no problemo*. I have an appointment for lunch anyway. But I could come for dinner tonight. I will dress myself up ready to make the big impression on the lovely Izzy.'

8

Chapter Two

Izzy had spent the last three hours sitting next to a hyperactive child, who had divided his time between pushing past her to go and play with the gadgets in the toilet and bouncing in his seat so that he could spill his foil-wrapped meal more effectively than any muck-spreader. 'He's so excited about the holiday,' his mother kept saying, and showing no sign of restraining him as his trainer-clad feet kicked at the seat in front. 'He's never flown before.' And hopefully never will again in my company, Izzy had thought.

But now, and having retrieved her luggage from the carousel, she was scanning the arrivals hall for a familiar face. She wasn't used to travelling alone, and though it wasn't a large airport, it still made her feel lost and unsure. But Max was easy to spot in the crowd of chatting holiday reps and taxi drivers, and not just because he was waving madly at her and wearing a brightly coloured shirt, but because he had such silvery-white hair. Laura often joked that he had started going grey while he was still in his twenties due to a misspent youth, but Max insisted that it was because he had fallen in love with Laura so unexpectedly that the shock had nearly killed him.

He greeted Izzy with one of his cheery bear hugs, which lifted her off her feet and made her think, as it had the first time she had met him, how like Steve Martin he was. It was a game she played: when she met someone for the first time, she matched them up with a celebrity lookalike. In Max's case it had come to her in a flash. He was Steve Martin in appearance, with his twinkling eyes and short white hair, and he was certainly Steve Martin in manner, with his quirky, self-effacing sense of humour. 'The good thing about Max,' Laura would say, 'is that if he ever loses his marbles no one will notice.' At heart he was essentially a big kid, and right now, as he took control of her trolley and steered it through the crowd, occasionally shouting 'Coming through,' Izzy knew that if Laura had been here, she would have been rolling her eyes at his antics.

Big kid or not, she couldn't deny how relieved she was to be in Max's safe hands, even if he was now standing on the back of the speeding trolley like a latter-day Ben Hur and she was having to run to keep up with him. And though it was against all the rules laid down by the book she had been trying to read on the plane – *One Hundred Ways To Be A Thoroughly Modern Woman* – was it really such a sin to want to hand over responsibility and let somebody else take the strain?

'How was your flight?' Max asked, when they were standing outside in the bright sunshine and were loading her luggage into the back of an open-topped Jeep.

'Fine,' she said, 'although I came close to shoving a horrible child through the emergency exit at thirty-five thousand feet. Otherwise I don't have a minute's delay or a case of drunken air rage to report.'

'How very disappointing. Okay, then, that's the bags in, climb aboard and we'll be off. There's a bottle of Coke in the glove compartment if you're in need of a cold drink. Help yourself.'

She fished out the bottle, which was wrapped in a special thermal casing, and drank from it gratefully. 'As usual, Max, you've thought of everything. You're a life-saver.'

'*No problemo.* Now in the words of my sweet old

grandmother, Bette Davis, fasten your seat-belt, it's going to be a bumpy ride. These Jeeps are all very well, but the suspension's hard enough to rattle your eyes out of their sockets.'

Izzy had never been to Corfu before and she took in the journey with interest. After skirting the edge of Corfu Town, Max picked up the coastal road, and before long the landscape changed from urban scruff to rural charm.

'Breathtaking, isn't it?' he shouted, above the noise of the engine and the wind that was slapping their faces and sending Izzy's hair flying. Ahead was a glassy sea of translucent blue and a carpeted headland of lush green that went right down to the edge of a stretch of bleached white sand. It surpassed all Izzy's expectations. As though sensing her delight, Max remained silent and concentrated on the road, which twisted and turned through the spectacular scenery.

It seemed madness now that only a few days ago Izzy had nearly decided not to come. She had paid her mother a visit, to see if she would be all right without Izzy for the summer. It had been a weekend of pure, nerve-jangling hell: forty-eight hours of being cooped up with Prudence Jordan, a woman who had graduated with honours in How To Be A Repressive, Bitter Old Woman. Most of their time together had been spent in the small square sitting room at the back of the bungalow in which Izzy had grown up. The room was heavily sprigged with flowery décor – the sagging sofa and armchairs, the curtains, the lampshades, the wallpaper, the carpet, everything, had been given the floral treatment – and presiding over this horticultural nightmare was an army of china statues, lined up along the two low windows that looked out on to the garden, with their nasty unblinking, all-seeing eyes. They seemed to watch Izzy as she and her mother sanded down their teeth on stale

Battenberg cake and drank tea that could have creosoted garden sheds.

A fidgety woman who could never be still, lest she was taken for an idle good-for-nothing, Prudence would switch from pressing cup after cup of the throat-stripping tea on Izzy to ignoring her and knitting furiously. She clashed the old metal needles together, the taut, cheap wool squeaking and setting Izzy's teeth and nerves further on edge. Prudence was a compulsive knitter and had been for nearly ten years. It had started when the local church had launched a campaign calling for volunteers to make six-inch squares to be sewn into blankets and sent to Rwanda. Her mother had thrown herself into the mission with determined zeal but hadn't known when to stop. A decade on, and even though the plight of that part of Africa was no longer as desperate as it had been, she was still at it. Somewhere there was probably an enormous stockpile of patchwork blankets waiting to be unpicked and recycled into useful balls of wool.

'And while you're off enjoying yourself with your fancy high-and-mighty friends, leaving me alone,' her mother had flung across the room, 'where will you be if I need your help?'

'Where I've always been, squashed under your thumb,' was the honest answer, but Izzy said mildly, 'We've been through this before. I've given you the number for the villa, and Auntie Trixie only lives four miles away. She'd be—'

'Your auntie Patricia's a fool.'

It was always a case of 'your' auntie Patricia, never 'my' sister Trixie.

'Auntie Trixie isn't a fool, Mum.'

'Well, you would say that. You're two of a kind, aren't you?'

It was a well-aimed blow. Seven years ago Auntie Trixie had brought shame to the family by divorcing her womanising, beer-bellied husband; more recently Izzy had brought the family name into further disrepute by living in sin with a man, then being careless enough to let him slip away before she had got a ring on her finger.

'If you had picked more wisely at the outset, you wouldn't be in the mess you are,' her mother had consoled her last autumn, as Izzy got through each day convincing herself that tomorrow would be better, that tomorrow she would put Alan behind her. But it hadn't been that easy. She had thrown too much of herself into their relationship. They had just celebrated three years of being together when he had sprung on her that he felt they should take responsibility for their feelings and explore where they were going wrong.

Wrong?

That was the first she had heard of it going anywhere other than straight ahead, turn right, turn left, then up the aisle to the altar.

Though perhaps those weekends he had spent in Blackpool visiting his ailing great-aunt in the old people's home, the sudden change in clothes and aftershave, the frequent mood swings and need for personal space should have set the alarm bells of suspicion ringing. In truth, they had been chiming faintly, but she had told herself to ride it out, to see it through. It was a concept she had been taught from an early age. But she had failed the test so many times. All she had learnt from it was that she was destined to fail because she always made the wrong choice.

'Isobel Jordan,' her mother would say, her hands on her aproned hips, 'I see you've still not finished that embroidery. Do you want to know why? It's because you picked the most difficult one, didn't you? You always think you know best, but you don't . . . So you're giving up on the recorder lessons? Well, that doesn't surprise me. I said you'd be too lazy to practise . . . You always did pick the biggest sweet in the shop then find it tasted of nothing.'

The most frequent piece of advice was: 'You know what your problem is, young lady? You don't have the conviction to see anything through. You're a butterfly brain, just like your auntie Patricia.'

Now, with well-practised constraint, Izzy said, 'I'm sure if there was a real problem you wouldn't let your differences with your sister get in the way of her helping you, should the need arise. Which I doubt very much it will. You look extremely well to me.' She marvelled at her courage and self-control. There had even been a hint of assertiveness to her voice.

In response her mother gave her a flinty look, and slipped seamlessly into another line of attack. 'Have you been seeing that counsellor again?' She uttered the word *counsellor* with weighty disapproval. Prudence had never forgiven Izzy for airing her dirty washing in public.

Counselling had been Alan's idea. According to him, it had been the means by which they would explore and face the negative feelings that were destroying their relationship.

It turned out that it was an easy way for him to tell her he was leaving her for somebody else, that her own behaviour had driven him to it; a typical bit of playacting on his part. She supposed that he had thought the counsellor would protect him when Izzy learned the truth. That the non-threatening environment of her office, with its marshmallow pink walls, its comfortable chairs, the carefully positioned box of tissues, the thoughtful cups of coffee and the counsellor's earnest, reassuring voice, would keep the peace.

He could not have misjudged it more.

Once the truth was out, Izzy had leapt up, grabbed her untouched cup of coffee and thrown its cold contents at him. Then she had passed the therapist the tissues, told her to mop up the mess and to stick her non-threatening environment up her Freudian slip. 'How's that for naming that emotion?' she had added, flinging open the door to make her getaway, 'and guess what, I think I've just released the feeling and now I'm going to move beyond it!'

'No, I'm not seeing her again,' Izzy replied evenly, proud that she was still on top of this conversation. Then, she reached forward to put her cup on the coffee table, and somehow dropped her cake plate to the floor, scattering pink and yellow crumbs over the carpet.

So much for being a grown woman of thirty-one! She was instantly a fumbling, nervous six-year-old, waiting for the inevitable reprimand and wishing she could hide at the bottom of the garden with her father. With a sad, faraway look in his eye he had spent his time feeding leaves and small branches into a charred metal bin with a funny little chimney. His hair and clothes had always smelt of smoke, and Izzy could never pass a bonfire without being reminded of her father and the wall of silence that had surrounded him.

'Still as clumsy as ever, then,' her mother tutted. 'I suppose you want me to fetch you a clean plate from the kitchen, do you?' She made the journey to the kitchen sound like a two-month trek across the freezing wastelands of Siberia.

That night, Izzy had slept in her old bedroom. The mattress of her childhood bed, lumpy and unyielding, smelling of mothballs, had ensured a nostalgically restless night. As had the memories invoked by that poky room, with its flaking paintwork, swirly patterned carpet, tiny knee-hole dressing table and teak-effect shelves, which held an assortment of old board games and incomplete jigsaws, which only saw the light of day at Christmas.

Lying in bed, trying to sleep, she had felt the familiar sensation of being trapped inside an airtight plastic box.

She always felt like this when she came home. A few hours into any visit with all the secrets and memories stored in the ageing wallpaper and carpets, and the walls of the gloomy bungalow began to move in on her. As a child she had promised herself she would remember how many times she had hidden in this room, under this bed, wanting to escape the charged atmosphere but she hadn't been able to keep a tally: the occasions had been too numerous.

Any time spent with Prudence left her feeling drained, and this time she had been consumed with guilt that she had even considered a holiday.

Emotional blackmail was a relatively new trick of her mother's. It had surfaced last year, on the day they had buried her father, and a month before Alan had left her.

'I suppose one good thing will come out of his death,' her mother had said, as she had nodded to Izzy to pass round the corned-beef sandwiches to the mourners who had gathered awkwardly in the sitting room. 'It will bring Isobel and me closer together. She's all I have now.'

Her father had spent the last six weeks of his life in his dressing-gown, a blue and green tartan affair that had seemed to get the better of him, outgrowing his frail body, making him look small and redundant, diminished. He had had a stroke, had lost the power of speech and the use of his right arm and leg, and had spent most of his time staring out of the window, through the army of unblinking statues, at his beloved garden. Until Prudence had it covered with crazy paving. How unnecessarily cruel that had seemed to Izzy. She had visited as often as she could, reduced to tears each time she saw how fast her father was declining, flinching at her mother's no-nonsense rough handling of him, seeing the glimmer of light go out of his eyes, not that it had ever been very bright. He died on a Friday afternoon, his life trickling away quietly as Izzy set off on the long drive to see him, and his wife knitted another taut square while watching Richard Whiteley and Carol Vorderman on *Countdown*.

His death caused barely a dent in her mother's daily routine. She had her hands full anyway, what with the new postman to whip into shape and a young milkman who still hadn't learnt to close the gate quietly at six in the morning. If Prudence missed her husband at all, it was because she had no one on whom to take out her frustration.

Which was why Izzy was getting the full treatment.

Laura had shaken Izzy out of her guilt. 'She's a wicked old woman for trying to manipulate you like that,' she had said on the phone. Knowing Izzy as well as she did, she had called to make sure that the visit to Prudence had passed without incident. 'And what if she did snuff it while you were here with us enjoying yourself? So what? We'd get you back in time for the funeral. What more could she want?'

Izzy hadn't known Max and Laura for long, but it felt as though they knew her better than anybody else did. They had met when Izzy had moved up to Cheshire to start her new job and she had been renting a tiny cottage in the village where Max and Laura lived. She had been reversing into a small space in the high street, a manoeuvre she normally avoided at all costs – bonnet first or find a larger space, was her rule – but she had been in a hurry and there was nowhere else. Come on, she told herself, an articulated lorry could get in there. A thud, followed by a light tinkle of glass, told her, however, that she had failed. As she stepped out of the car to inspect the damage, her heart sank. Of all the cars she could have rubbed bumpers with, she had picked the shiniest of black Porsches. Damn! This would be expensive. She was just writing a note of apology for the car's owner when a voice said, 'Oh, dear, what a terrible shame. Will it be very difficult to replace the parts for your lovely old car?' The smiling man with his silvery-white hair didn't seem bothered by his smashed head-lamp, or the dent in the moulded bumper. He placed his shopping on the passenger seat, bent down to inspect the ruined chrome-work on Izzy's Triumph Herald, then said, 'You look a bit shaken, are you okay?'

'I'm so sorry. This could only happen to me. I knew I shouldn't have tried to park here.'

They exchanged addresses and phone numbers, and the following evening she had called on him with the necessary insurance details and a bottle of wine to add weight to her apology. His wife had answered the door of their fabulously large house and insisted she stay for a drink with them – 'Max said a beautiful girl had bumped into him in the high street,' she had laughed, leading the way through to the kitchen where the smell of cooking reminded Izzy that she had passed on lunch that day. 'I thought he was exaggerating his good fortune as usual. But it seems I was wrong.'

Meeting Max and Laura had been Izzy's good fortune, though, for since that chance encounter she had made two very good friends.

She was a great believer in chance, though she had to admit it didn't always work in her favour.

Chapter Three

Laura had set the table for lunch at the shaded end of the veranda, where the low, sloping eaves of the villa provided the most protection from the fierce midday sun. While Max poured the wine and Laura drizzled locally produced olive oil over a large pottery bowl of salad leaves and diced cucumber, Izzy took a moment to catch her breath. She and Laura hadn't stopped talking and laughing since Max had parked the Jeep an hour ago at the front of the villa and brought her inside.

Laura had given her an immediate guided tour, seeking approval, rather than fawning admiration. 'Stunning' was the word that kept tripping off Izzy's tongue, as she was shown each beautifully decorated and furnished room. The walls had either been washed with fresh white paint or a more subtle tone of buttermilk; dazzling watercolours of seascapes added splashes of vibrant colour. The floors were all of cool, polished marble or white tiles and in places were covered with antique rugs that were attractively worn and faded and helped to give the villa a lived-in look.

The sitting room, the largest and most spectacular of all the rooms, faced the sea, and its row of french windows opened directly on to the veranda, which ran the full length of the house. This was edged with a low, colonnaded wall that was painted white and lined with earthenware pots filled with shocking pink pelargoniums and pretty marguerites. It was here, in the shade, that they were having lunch and the mood round the table was as bright and informal as the setting.

'So what's it to be, Izzy?' asked Max, taking a hunk of bread from the basket in front of him and mopping up the pool of golden olive oil on his plate. 'An adventurous boat trip into Kassiópi with Captain Max or a swim and a gossip with Laura?'

'Hands off,' Laura intervened, before Izzy had a chance to reply. 'Izzy's mine for the rest of the afternoon.'

Max topped up Izzy's glass. 'Looks as though you're in for a tongue-wagging session.'

'I won't be fit for anything if I carry on drinking at this rate.'

'Oh, baloney! Alcohol intake doesn't count when you're on holiday, didn't you know that?'

'Is that true of calories?' asked Laura, giving Max's hand a playful slap as he reached for another piece of bread.

'Yes, my sweet,' he laughed. 'Nothing's ever the same when you're away from home. The value system changes completely.'

'Ah, so that's why so many people have a fling when they're on holiday,' joked Izzy.

'Well, not that I'm speaking from personal experience,' said Max, 'but you're probably right. It's like getting done for speeding in a foreign country – it doesn't mean anything because without any points on your licence it doesn't matter. Why? Thinking of giving it a whirl?'

'Heavens, no!'

'Perhaps you should,' said Laura.

Izzy looked at her, shocked. Was this really the woman who, only a few days ago, had agreed with her over coffee that she ought to give men a miss for a while? 'If I'm not mistaken, that's a slightly different tune from the one you've been whistling of late.'

'You're right, but maybe it's time to take stock and see what's out there.'

'But a holiday romance. It would be so shallow. So meaningless. So—'

'And potentially so much fun,' cut in Laura.

Since she had started reading that book on the plane Modern Woman seemed to have taken up residence inside Izzy's head. *Don't listen to her*, she warned. *In your current state you need an emotional entanglement like a fish needs a hook in its mouth.*

'It would be rather reckless, wouldn't it?' said Izzy, trying to be sensible but already tempted by a picture of herself wandering along the beach with a handsome man beneath a moonlit sky.

'But having fun doesn't have to be reckless,' persisted Laura. 'If you understood at the start what the outcome would be, that you would both know and accept that you'd be waving goodbye at the end of the holiday, where would be the harm?'

'Is it really possible to do that?' asked Izzy doubtfully, knowing that she was an all-or-nothing girl.

'There's only one way to find out,' smiled Laura. 'Give it a try.'

That afternoon when Max retreated to his den to watch Henri Le Conte in the over-thirty-fives doubles, Laura and Izzy changed into their swimsuits and took the path down to the beach. Tied to a post at the end of a wooden jetty that belonged to Villa Petros, two boats bobbed in the water; one was small and modest, the other a much more expensive affair.

'The little one is ours and the gin palace is owned by our neighbour,' explained Laura, catching Izzy's eye. 'He leaves it here because the water is too rough by his place and it would get smashed to pieces on the rocks. Fancy swimming out to the raft?'

They left their towels on the rocks and slipped into the cool, clear water. The raft wasn't far and they were soon climbing up the metal rungs and lying stretched out on their fronts on the sun-warmed decking. Though it was securely anchored, there was still a pleasing sense of motion and, with her eyes shut, Izzy felt as though she was drifting aimlessly. 'Is every day going to be as perfect as this?' she murmured, resting her head in the crook of her arm.

'I told you you'd like it. And, trust me, it just gets better and better.'

'You live a charmed life, you know that, don't you?'

Laura turned on to her side. 'I'd hate anyone to think that I don't know exactly how lucky I am.'

Concerned that she may have inadvertently upset her friend, Izzy opened her eyes. 'I'm sorry, I wasn't implying you took it for granted, I only meant—'

'It's okay. I know what you were getting at. But I'm all too aware that Max's little empire could come crashing down at any time, taking everything with it. Including us. If that happens, then so be it. We'd have to adapt and get on with it. Meanwhile, I'm quite happy to live by the creed that he's worked jolly hard for what he's got and I don't see any reason why he shouldn't make the most of it while he can.'

'A sound enough creed in anyone's book.'

They lay in silence, listening to the water lapping at the sides of the raft, and Izzy thought of her own rather more modest life at home. As a teacher in a small prep school her prospects were never going to reach the stratosphere of Max and Laura's gold-edged lifestyle. On the whole she had always enjoyed teaching, but she was conscious that recently what had appealed most to her about her job were the long holidays. That could mean only one thing: a change was due. She had been at the school for too long. She was growing stale. Also she disliked, no, hated, the new head, a woman who had been brought in to wield the axe. At the end of term, last Friday, there had been so many redundancies made that Izzy was sure it was only a matter of time before she herself was dismissed. Art teachers were hardly a high priority. If cuts were to be made, it was a generally held view that any old fool could teach the little dears to cut and paste.

She frowned guiltily. She shouldn't be here lazing in the sun on a raft, she should be at home scanning the *Times Educational Supplement* for a new job. But, hey, let the head make her redundant first.

It might even be for the best, given that her parting shot at the end of term had been that in the autumn the remaining members of staff were to dress in power suits. Power suits! What would she, an art teacher, do in a crisp two-piece? She didn't have anything in her wardrobe that remotely resembled one. Her clothes, at best, could be described as 'individual', or maybe 'eccentric', but 'cheap' was closer to the truth. The racks and rails of her local branch of Help the Aged were her favourite stamping ground for last season's fashion statements. Not that she was a complete fashion slouch – she knew a good label when she saw one and wasn't slow in handing over an extra pound for quality, especially if she needed something for a special occasion. But a power suit?

Other than school, little else was going on in Izzy's life, and had she been in danger of missing this, her mother had been only too quick to point it out to her. 'I had hoped to be a grandmother by now,' she had muttered on the phone, when Izzy was officially a single woman again. 'With your inability to maintain a steady relationship there's no chance of that ever happening, I suppose.'

'I'm sorry to have denied you that pleasure,' Izzy had said.

'There's no need to take that tone with me, young lady.

A couple of grandchildren, is that really so much to ask for?'

In the circumstances, yes, it was.

Izzy had wanted children, but Alan had refused to entertain the idea. Just as he had refused to talk about marriage. 'We're okay as we are,' he would say. 'Why go changing things?'

Izzy sat up and looked towards the shore where a selection of villas nestled into the hillside. 'Tell me about your neighbours,' she said. 'You and Max have often mentioned Theo, the man who sold you the villa, especially what a sex-god he thinks he is, but what about the others? What are they like?'

Laura sat up too and pointed to the furthest villa along the bay to the left. 'That's owned by an elderly French couple who have been coming here for over twenty years. They live in Paris and tend to keep themselves to themselves. And to the right is a villa with yellow shutters. Do you see it? It's just peeping through the trees.'

Izzy squinted in the glare of the bright sun. 'Yes.'

'That's owned by an Englishwoman, but nobody ever sees her. She used to come here for holidays with her husband, and when he died five years ago she moved in permanently.'

'So why doesn't anyone see her?'

Laura shrugged. 'Don't know. Everyone just accepts that she's a recluse and lets her get on with it. Now, do you see the tatty little pink house?'

Again Izzy squinted her eyes. 'Yes.'

'That's owned by another Brit. But he's let it go to rack and ruin and struggles to rent it to tourists. Apparently it's a mess inside and out. Moving up the hillside, there's a tiny little villa that's owned by a German businessman. According to the local gossip, he's not coming this summer, so it will probably be rented too.'

'Aren't there any locals who live here?'

'A few, but not many. Behind the German villa is where Dimitri and Marietta live. They own one of the jewellery shops in Kassiópi and spend their summers here, running the shop.'

'And where do they spend their winters?'

'In Athens, like Theo.'

'So which is his place?'

Laura pointed to the right of Villa Petros, to the tip of the lush green headland. 'That's his. It's lovely, isn't it? Quite the best house in Áyios Nikólaos. It used to be an olive press but he's done a wonderful job of extending and renovating it. It's a bit of a hobby for him.'

Izzy gazed up at the attractive mellow stone villa. 'What does he do when he's not renovating old houses – and flirting with you?'

Laura smiled. 'You've been listening to Max too much.'

Izzy smiled too. 'He may have mentioned Theo's interest in you.'

'It's just a game he plays. It's nothing serious. No, what he's really into is property. And lots of it. He owns half of Athens, if you believe a fraction of the scurrilous stories Angelos shares with Max.'

'And who's Angelos?'

'He and his wife practically run Áyios Nikólaos. Without them we'd be sunk. They take care of our villa, as well as Theo's and several others. Angelos does all the gardening and maintenance work, and Sophia does the cleaning. Look, that's their house, to the left of ours and further up the hill. You'll meet them soon. They're nice, very friendly.'

Izzy stretched her arms over her head and yawned. She had been up since five and was beginning to feel tired. 'And what about tomorrow, anything in mind for us to do?'

'We've got nothing planned. That's the beauty of coming here. It's total relaxation. What's more, I don't even have to cook tonight. Max is going to impress you with his barbecue skills. It'll just be the four of us.'

'Four?'

'Don't worry, it's only Theo joining us for the evening. Come on, I need to get out of the sun. Give me a head start and I'll race you back to the beach.'

Chapter Four

With a beer in his hand, Max was more than happy to be left to his own devices to deal with the intricate operation of lighting the barbecue. He waved Laura away with a stand-aside-and-leave-this-to-me expression and told her to go and relax.

Only too pleased to escape the rising cloud of smoke, she picked up her Campari and soda and went over to the group of wicker chairs, positioned to give them the best view of the setting sun when they settled there after their meal.

She leaned back into one and wondered how the evening would go. She was mildly surprised that Theo wasn't here already. Her initial concern over him sweeping Izzy off her feet had done a surprising U-turn. She had a good feeling about the effect his company would have on Izzy. She didn't know of a single woman who wouldn't relish being flattered by an attractive man. The reverse was also true, of course. Men found the flirtatious attention of a beautiful woman an irresistible draw. The difference between the two was that men were inclined to take the passing attention of a woman seriously – Wow, I always knew I was a catch! – while women treated it as they would a fragrant waft of freesias: lovely, but not lasting.

Which was as close as one could get to describing Theo. He was lovely, all right, but any intimate relationship with him would almost certainly be short and sweet.

Throughout last summer when she and Max had

occasionally stayed with Theo while the finishing touches were being put to Villa Petros, Laura had seen him in action with a number of women he brought with him from Athens. She had asked him once if he ever grew tired of the rapid turnaround in his love life.

'You are implying that I lead a shallow existence, Laura, is that it? Well, do not worry yourself on my account, I am quite happy as I am.'

She didn't doubt that he was happy, she just wondered if he could be happier.

Max had agreed with her, saying that he was a curious man. 'When he's having a drink on his own with me he's quite different,' he said, during one of their many conversations about Theo, 'but put a woman in front of him and it's as if a switch flicks – he goes into super-charged charmer mode.'

Hearing a change in the strength of the waves on the rocks below, Laura turned her gaze out to sea. One of the many Minoan ferries that passed this way between Brindisi and the port at Corfu Town was gliding across the horizon. Its smooth passage made her wonder just how smooth Theo would be this evening. What kind of a performance would he put on for Izzy's benefit?

And how would Izzy react?

Laura had deliberately not told her anything of the conversation she had had with Theo that morning. If she did, Izzy would automatically be on her guard, which would create an atmosphere of hostility between them. That would be a great shame.

No. It was much better that Izzy worked Theo out for herself, in her own time and in her own way, and decided just how seriously to take him. If she had any sense she would treat him in exactly the same way Laura did. Besides, Laura didn't want anything to spoil Izzy's holiday. After the tough year she had had, what with Alan, her father dying, and her dreadful mother to contend with, a relaxing summer was the least she deserved.

The sound of footsteps on the stony path below the terrace told her that Theo was about to make his entrance. 'Act one, scene one,' she muttered to herself, getting up from her chair and going to meet him.

On seeing him she burst out laughing: he was carrying a bottle in each hand and between his teeth there were two long-stemmed roses. She took the wine from him and led him to where Max was opening another beer.

'Oh, Theo,' gushed Max, 'red roses! How sweet! Really, you shouldn't have.'

'Ignore him,' said Laura. 'It's the fumes from the barbecue coals, they go straight to his head. One of those roses for me?'

'But of course, my darling Laura. Though only if I am permitted a kiss in exchange.' He leaned into her, was about to kiss her mouth when she neatly twisted her head and he had to make do with her cheek.

'She's getting too quick for you, Theo,' laughed Max. 'Now what can I get you to drink? Beer, wine, oúzo, gin and . . . Ah, Izzy, there you are.'

Both Laura and Theo turned to see Izzy coming towards them. She was dressed in a black camisole top with a calf-length flowing skirt, also in black, and on her feet she wore a pair of espadrilles. Even though she had spent scarcely any time in the sun that day, she was already exhibiting a tan. With her shoulder-length dark brown hair pulled back into a loose plait, she looked all of twenty-five. Laura would have liked to study Theo's face closely to see what his initial reaction was, but the telephone rang inside the villa.

'Can you get that, love?' Max said. 'I've just put the kebabs on. If it's for me,' he shouted after her, 'and it seems urgent, tell them I'll call back later.'

'It looks as if we shall just have to introduce ourselves,'

said Theo. 'Theo Vlamakis, friend to Max and Laura Sinclair, and hopefully soon to become your friend.' He offered Izzy the rose. 'To wish you a relaxing holiday here in Áyios Nikólaos. May today be the start of a happy love affair.'

Izzy took the rose from him, 'A love affair?' she repeated, thinking that he was George Clooney to a T. He had the same short dark hair, flecked with grey, and the same thick eyebrows above a pair of magnetic black eyes. Dressed in cream linen trousers with a pale peach short-sleeved shirt that showed a finely worked gold chain at his throat, there was no mistaking the aura of natural glamour and appeal about him.

'Yes, a love affair with Corfu and its beguiling people, of course,' he said. 'Now it is your turn. You have to introduce yourself.'

Self-conscious, but charmed by his words and manner, Izzy held out her hand and said, 'Izzy Jordan, friend to Max and Laura Sinclair, and I've a confession to make. I've heard a lot about you already.'

He gave a ceremonious little tilt of his head, took her hand and raised it to his lips. 'I am very pleased to meet you, Izzy Jordan. Though it seems you have the advantage. I know hardly anything about you. Is it very bad what Laura has confided in you about me? Does she make me sound like the empty-headed buffoon?'

Izzy laughed and withdrew her hand. Goodness, he was smooth. 'She speaks very highly of you, as a friend and a neighbour.'

'That's good. That means we step out in the right direction, you and me.'

'Theo, if you could lay off the Ionian charm for a couple of seconds, perhaps you'd be kind enough to get Izzy a drink.'

Dutifully leading her over to the table of drinks, Theo said, 'That Max, he has such a sharp tongue on him. Like so many English men, he is jealous of his Greek counterpart. We Greek men, we cannot understand how the English ever reproduce, especially the ones with the stiff-upper-lip public-school background. You know, Izzy, a night of passion for Max is sharing a beer with his highly esteemed Fergie.'

'What? The Duchess of York?' said Izzy, trying hard not to laugh.

'No,' grinned Theo, 'your great man of the people, Sir Alex Ferguson.'

'Theo, if you don't give it a rest, you'll feel the sharp end of one of these kebab sticks! Now, get the girl a drink.'

It wasn't until Max was serving the fruits of his labours and insisting that Theo and Izzy sit down that Laura reappeared. 'Who was that on the phone?' he asked.

'Francesca.'

Max stopped what he was doing. 'Nothing wrong, is there? She's not changed her mind about coming?'

Laura smiled. 'Poor old Daddy missing his beloved daughter, is he? Don't worry, she's still coming. She just wanted a chat.'

'Ah, mother-and-daughter stuff, was it?'

'Yes. Big bust-up with the boyfriend.'

Max tipped the last of the swordfish kebabs on to the large plate of seafood in the middle of the table and said, 'Good. He was an idiot. Didn't have an original thought in his head. He thought he was so cool and radical when all the time he was a jumped-up little jerk.'

'Aha, there speaks the father who thinks there is not a young man alive good enough for his daughter,' said Theo. 'Poor old Max, you would much rather be the one to choose a husband for her.'

Izzy knew quite a bit about the now ex-boyfriend. She had met him just once, but it had been enough to understand why Max was so glad to know that he had seen the last of him. He had been one of those slow-witted eco-warrior types with nose and eyebrow rings and dreadlocks crawling down his back. He had been a vegetarian as well, and Izzy recalled a beanburger that Laura had made specially for him, which he had prodded at rudely and said he couldn't eat because he could smell garlic in it. He was a far cry from what she knew was Max's idea of a perfect boyfriend for Francesca: he had to be motivated and smart, and if he could possibly manage it, straight out of the Tim Henman mould of clean-cut good looks and behaviour.

'Hah, baloney, to you, Theo!' Max retaliated. 'Just wait until you have children of your own before you start casting aspersions on my partiality.' Then, turning to Laura, 'She's okay, though, isn't she?'

'Relax, she's fine, currently denouncing all men as bastards. By the way, she asked if she could bring a friend with her when she comes over.'

'Anyone we know?'

'Sally Bartholomew.'

'What, *the* Sally? Man-eating Sally? A girl who can lasso a man to the ground with her own stockings. You said no, didn't you?'

Ignoring his question, Laura reached for the wine-cooler. 'Now then, who needs a refill? Darling, you're not going to wear those oven gloves all evening, are you?'

Max took them off and tossed them on to the table, then sat next to his wife. 'Go on, then, tell me the worst. How long is she staying?'

While Laura filled Max in on the details, Izzy offered Theo the plate of barbecued seafood.

'No, please,' he said, taking the dish from her, 'you are the guest here, I will serve you.'

'But you're a guest too.'

'No. I am just plain old Theo from next door.'

Izzy smiled. 'That sounds suspiciously like a man fishing for a compliment.'

He narrowed his dark eyes and looked puzzled. 'I am sorry. Fishing? What is the allusion here? I do not understand. Your English must be too refined for me.'

'Don't listen to a word, Izzy,' said Max, leaning across the table, helping himself to a jumbo-sized prawn and ripping it apart. 'Theo's English is as good as yours and mine, if not better. He was educated in England at one of those fancy public schools he was just condemning, and my guess is he learned very young to put people at a disadvantage with his linguistic ability. Usually pretty young girls. So be warned.'

Theo passed the plate he was holding to Laura. 'Is your husband going to be as bad-tempered for the rest of the evening just because a nymphet is coming to stay?'

'Lord, will you listen to him?' roared Max. But there was no anger to his voice. Giving Izzy a smile, he said, 'You see what you've let yourself in for this summer?'

'Ah, poor Izzy,' said Theo, turning to her and holding out a perfectly peeled prawn for her to take. 'I don't think you will stay sane here for long. Promise me, if you get tired of these crazy people you will come to me for a place of sanctuary. Villa Anna is so tranquil. I think it would suit you better. Eh? What do you say?'

Izzy took the proffered prawn. 'Thank you, but who's to say that I'm not as crazy as Max and Laura?'

By the time they had finished their meal and were sitting in the wicker chairs with a tray of liqueur bottles to choose from, the sun was setting, casting a coppery glow over the wide open sky, and across the darkening water, where the swelling outline of Albania could still be seen, lights were twinkling like stars. It was a beautiful sight and for a few minutes they all sat quietly enjoying it.

Laura was thinking how restrained Theo was being.

33

Compared to how she had seen him in the past, with women far less attractive than Izzy, he was playing it very cool. She hadn't seen him once attempt to touch her, nor had he commented on her appearance. For an Englishman this would have been par for the course, but for a Greek with a sex-god reputation to live up to it was unheard-of. Was Theo smarter than she had given him credit for? Perhaps so. Instead of smothering Izzy in ready-made flattery he had chatted to her so far about life in England, the school where she taught, and how she had been unfortunate enough to meet her and Max. He had laughed at her description of bumping into Max's Porsche. 'It serves him right for having such an ostentatious car,' he had said.

'That's rich coming from you,' retorted Max. 'What about the pimp-mobile you have here on the island? BMWs are as rare as hen's teeth in these parts, never mind the Z3.'

'You see how easy it is to rile poor old Max?' Theo had said to Izzy. 'Always he is coming from the defensive point of view.'

The sun had now slipped below the horizon, and Max asked Theo about his friend, who was arriving the following day. 'You never mentioned before that you knew Mark St James.'

'I am sure there are lots of people you know that you have not told me about.'

'But this is different. Mark St James is an author. Quite a well-known one at that. One of my favourites.'

Theo drained his glass of Metaxá and shrugged. 'You are entitled to your hero-worship, but to me he is just a friend. No more, no less.'

'Is he the one whose books have been on the telly back home?' asked Izzy. 'The writer they describe as *Cracker* meets *Silence of the Lambs*?'

'Yes that's him,' said Max. 'Those adaptations of his

34

books make a welcome change from all those bonnet dramas. Have you read any of his stuff?'

'No. I'm not sure they're quite my cup of tea.'

'You should give them a try,' urged Max. 'The psychology is brilliant. You really feel that he knows the mind of a criminal. It's rather disturbing, but you almost sympathise with the killer by the end of one of his books.'

'It is his forte,' said Theo, leaning forward to settle his empty glass on the low table. 'He studied criminal psychology at university. He knows his subject inside out.'

'How did you meet him?' asked Izzy.

'Ah, the perceptive Izzy. I see that the unlikely match of two such men intrigues you. But it is true, opposites really do attract. We met at college, and hit it off straight away. Mark thought I was a poncy fascist, and I thought he was an arrogant, foul-mouthed, narrow-minded bore.'

Izzy smiled. 'So what changed your opinion of each other?'

For a second Theo looked serious and stared into the darkening sky. 'He saved my life,' he said quietly. Then, 'But that's a story I will leave for Mark to tell you. Now, it is time for me to do some work. I have many phone calls to make. *Kaliníhta*, one and all.' He got to his feet, followed swiftly by the rest of them. He rested his hands on Laura's shoulders and kissed her cheeks. 'As ever, my darling, you were the perfect hostess.' He shook hands with Max, then turned to Izzy. 'Now that we are practically old friends, am I permitted to kiss you goodnight?'

He gave her a look and a smile that might easily have talked a girl into falling in love with him.

Chapter Five

Theo considered himself a lucky man. Just as Churchill and Napoleon had functioned on little sleep, so did he. He had worked until two in the morning, had risen at six fully refreshed, and by half past seven had been for a swim, showered, dressed and walked up the dusty potholed lane to see Nicos and his wife, who ran the local supermarket. He had returned a short while later with his breakfast: a melon and a *kataífi*, a finely shredded pastry bulging with almonds and soaked in honey. He was eating this now while sitting on the flower-filled terrace overlooking the sea. The scent of the roses enhanced the delicious sweetness of the cake.

His sweet tooth, according to his grandmother, was his only weakness, but then she had always seen him through such blinkered eyes, could never accept that he might be fallible. All over Greece there were women just like her, responsible for giving Greek children, and especially boys, the reputation of being the most indulged children in the world. Certainly Anna Vlamakis had seen to it that her only grandchild was the most pampered and fêted.

'You are spoiling that boy beyond redemption,' his parents would complain. But Anna ignored their pleas for restraint and took delight in presenting him to her friends and neighbours as a handsome prodigy who could do no wrong. From an early age he had developed a talent for talking to adults without feeling in awe of them, or being self-conscious in their presence. It made him a precocious star turn whenever Anna showed him off. As she frequently did.

After each visit he made to his grandmother in Corfu, his exasperated parents would say that he had returned to Athens with a head bigger than his shoulders and neck could support. It was as well that she had not lived any closer in those early days of his childhood, or she would have been the ruin of him. Though, of course, there might be some, including his old friend Mark, who would say that she had done exactly that.

His father had worked for the diplomatic service, and when he was posted to the Greek embassy in London, both his parents must have breathed a sigh of relief. At last, distance would ensure that Anna Vlamakis' influence was kept to a minimum. But their relief was short-lived: his father's duties increased rapidly, which meant that his mother was also busy, helping him host dinners and parties for visiting dignitaries. The inevitable happened: they agreed that he should spend the long holidays from school with his grandmother in Corfu.

Theo had loved Anna's old town-house in Kérkyra with its faded Venetian façade, pretty courtyard, and ever-changing view of the harbour and old fort. He especially enjoyed going out with her. After her customary afternoon siesta, she would take him through the dark maze of narrow streets – some so narrow he could stretch out his arms and touch both walls – to her favourite *zaharoplastía*, a sweet-shop that sold mouth-watering cakes, and biscuits decorated with sesame seeds, coconut, apricots or chocolate. While Anna chatted with the owner, Theo would be left to make their choice, and when the cardboard boxes had been filled and tied with a ribbon they would go on to visit her friends for tea. Like Anna, these ladies had also outlived their husbands and were wealthy enough to have few worries in the world. Over pastries and liqueurs, they would share with him *risqué* stories of their many lovers, during and after their marriages, smiling at each other and watching his face to see if he was shocked by their scandalous revelations. But nothing they said ever shocked him: he was too fascinated by the world of love and sensual desire they spoke of with such wistful longing.

On other days Anna would take him to the Esplanade where they would watch a cricket match while sitting in the cool shade of one of the elegant Listón bars. Often they were joined by Thomas Zika, a local businessman and lifelong admirer of his grandmother. He spoke in hushed tones, and wore a suit and tie even on the hottest of days. He was an amazing linguist and encouraged Theo to be the same, talking to him in English one minute, Italian the next.

But the days Theo enjoyed most were those he spent in the elegant high-ceilinged drawing rooms of Anna's widowed friends. It was from those ladies that he had learned the importance of passion. His grandmother said that no one had ever lived until they had experienced what she called a Grand Passion. When he was of an age to understand things better, he had asked Anna why she had never accepted one of Thomas Zika's many proposals. 'Ah, Theo,' she had said, sipping her dry martini, which she had taught him to mix, 'it is true that Thomas loves me, and it is also true that I am very fond of him. But I do not love him. I would rather keep matters as they are. He is a close friend, perhaps the closest I have ever had, and I would not want to risk losing that by marrying him.'

'So you think it is always better to travel through life not taking any risks?'

'No. That is not what I am saying. My marriage to your grandfather was the risk I took and it was my moment of Grand Passion. I have no desire to replace or even add to the memory of what I have already experienced and keep treasured in my heart.'

'But you could have something different with Thomas.'

Smiling she had said, 'Perhaps if he were more persistent I might reconsider. But he seems to have resigned himself quite happily to what we have.'

'Maybe he is frightened to press you any harder, that one more proposal will turn you against him.'

'What a lot of thought you have given to this, Theo. But I'm afraid you will have to accept that Thomas and I have reached an impasse and are both happy to live with it.'

With such an upbringing, it was no surprise that Theo tended to surround himself with women. He felt most at ease when in their company. With the exception of a few close friends and one or two business associates, he seldom trusted men.

He attributed this wariness to his time at school in England. He had hated the boarding-school just outside London to which his parents had sent him, and it was many years before he truly forgave them for forcing him into the barbarism of the English public-school system. After the life he had lived so far, it had come as a profound culture shock. He was in no way effeminate, but the regime he was expected to follow at school, with its tough macho image, appalled him. Naturally he suffered a degree of bullying for being a foreigner, but he fought back by beating his tormentors on and off the playing-fields. He pursued the goals and accolades they coveted, and with such vigour and success that in the end they accepted him into their world. After all, it was better to have the enemy in your own pocket than in someone else's.

It was during his adolescence that he lost his virginity. He was seventeen and was spending nearly all of his free time with the wife of the new classics master. He was dull man in his late thirties, with a pretty wife ten years his junior. Living in a small cottage within the school grounds, she was bored and lonely. To give her something to do, her husband had unwisely suggested that she help Theo perfect his English. Which she did, and a lot more besides.

She had been the only person he had missed when he left a year later. He had thought of returning to Athens, either to go to university there or to embark upon his national service, but with his parents still in London, he gave in to their wishes and stayed on in England. They wanted him to study in London, but he refused the university place he was offered there and went to Durham instead.

In Durham he experienced true bone-numbing coldness for the first time in his life. The freezing North Sea wind that came across the flat terrain cut through the layers of clothing with which he tried to protect himself as he cycled across town for a lecture. The rain was worse, icy cold, horizontal, and wetter than anything he had ever known; it slashed at his face, leaving him breathless and barely able to see the road in front of him. It was on such a raw, freezing cold day that he had met Mark.

He had heard of Mark St James already – his reputation, as they say, went well before him. He was a political activist intent on saving his generation, if not the world, from the evils of capitalism. His presence was advertised throughout college in the form of the posters he put up wherever he could, vilifying the leaders of the free world's major industrial nations, proclaiming them to be no better than the devil's disciples. When he wasn't organising a protest march or a silent sit-in, he was braving the elements selling copies of whatever radical paper he was currently supporting.

It was 1976 when punk rock was bursting on to the scene and, with his hair spiked and dyed an aggressive

peroxide blond, his skinny legs covered in black PVC
bondage trousers, decorated with zips and chains, the rest
of him blanketed in an oversized, hand-knitted sweater
that would not have looked out of place in a dog basket,
the infamous Mark St James was a distinctive sight as he
stood in the market-place in front of the church, ignored
by the busy Saturday morning shoppers.

Theo had watched him through the steamed-up window of the café where he was having a late breakfast of
coffee and doughnuts, and had admired his fellow
student for his dedication to the cause. He was about to
order a second mug of coffee when he noticed that it was
raining again. Shivering at the thought of yet more icy
rain, he suddenly felt compelled to go and offer this
foolish young man a hot drink.

'Fuck off!' was the snarled response.

'Considering I am the first person to offer you anything
other than a look of disparagement, don't you think you
are being just a little hasty?'

An expression of hostile disdain flickered across the
gaunt face, which appeared underfed and pinched with
cold. The sneering blue-eyed gaze then trailed over
Theo's clothes – cashmere coat and scarf, Italian leather
gloves, black woollen trousers and shiny burgundy-
coloured loafers.

'You're that flash Greek, aren't you?' His voice was
low and husky, as though he was recovering from a bout
of laryngitis.

Theo knew all too well that this was how he was
labelled in some quarters, but hearing it uttered with such
menacing contempt made him wince. 'I am only offering
you a drink, not an opportunity to enslave you with my
misguided political views.'

The look thawed and with a curl of lips that were
chapped and bruised with cold, he said, 'Yeah, okay

41

then. Who knows? I might be able to show a poncy fascist where he's going wrong.'

For the next fifteen minutes Theo was attacked for everything he had or hadn't done: global capitalism, world poverty, institutional power that was corrupt and killing those who weren't already starving to death, and ultimately for being too stupid to understand the manifesto that this angry young nihilist claimed would save the world from itself. And as if that wasn't enough, he was held personally responsible for the plight of the crumbling Acropolis in Athens. 'You realise, don't you,' Mark said, leaning forward in his chair and pointing a surprisingly clean and slender finger at Theo's face, 'it's the shit from all your cars that's the problem? The Acropolis is two thousand four hundred years old, it's survived God knows how many invasions, and you're wrecking it with your stinking pollution. So figure this one out, pretty boy, what the hell are you going to do to stop it?'

'Goodness, after such a display of sweet reason you mean I get a turn to speak? Well, I believe, and without my intervention, that help is at hand. UNESCO is sponsoring a rescue fund.'

'Yeah, but will it be enough?'

'Is anything we do enough?'

'Better something than nothing.'

'Which is why I offered you a cup of coffee. But now I must be on my way. I have an essay to write. It was good talking to you. Even if you are an arrogant, foul-mouthed, narrow-minded bore. Goodbye. Oh, and you should do something about that sore throat. Standing around in the cold will not do it any good. Trust me on that, if nothing else.'

They didn't see one another again until the following week when Theo was enjoying a late breakfast once more and watching Mark trying to sell his ideology to uninterested passers-by. This time, though, it was Mark who made the approach. He caught sight of Theo through the café window and marched straight over, comically restricted by his ridiculous trousers. He threw open the door, letting in a tornado of cold air, and sat uninvited in the chair opposite Theo. 'I object to being described as a narrow-minded bore,' he said angrily, causing several middle-aged women at a nearby table to raise their eyebrows and clutch at their handbags.

'But arrogant and foul-mouthed still stands, eh?'

'At least I'm not screwing every woman in Durham.'

'So who is?'

'You are, you bourgeois, time-wasting little—'

'Oh, please, spare me another come-the-revolution tirade. Now I hate to correct you, but your information is not all it could be. There are still a few women who I have yet to get into bed. Coffee? Or would you prefer hot chocolate? I see your throat is no better.'

'I'll have tea. Ordinary tea – none of that bloody fancy stuff. And if it's any of your sodding business I haven't got a sore throat. This is my normal speaking voice.'

'Then perhaps you would be kind enough to lower it so as not to disturb or intimidate the good ladies here.' He turned his head and gave them his most charming smile, the one he had used while visiting his grandmother's widowed friends.

When Theo had told Izzy last night that it was true about opposites attracting, he could not have described his friendship with Mark any better. There always had been, and always would be, a conflict of egos between them. They were two very strong characters, but because they were so different in nature, they amused and continually confounded each other. It was a real mystery to Theo, in these early days of their friendship, as to why an essentially shy, reserved person, who only wanted to

43

be left alone, forced himself into a position of antagonism that made him such an obvious focus of attention.

Though they openly despised each other on those two initial encounters, they also secretly admired each other. Theo couldn't help but be impressed by Mark's convictions, and though it was a long time before he ever admitted it, Mark was envious of Theo's track record with girls.

'I can't believe they fall for that smooth-bugger routine,' he said one evening, many months later, when they were sitting cross-legged on the floor of his room and eating a curry he had just cooked in the kitchen he shared with twelve other students.

'An air of sophistication is what they like,' Theo had answered, casting a critical eye over Mark's untidy room. The walls were papered with posters of the Sex Pistols, Che Guevara and the Jam; the single bed was covered with unwashed clothes; a small bookcase was filled to capacity with psychology textbooks, and the desk was hidden beneath a tide of files and papers. 'Of course, the money helps,' he added, 'that and my astonishingly good looks.'

'And you think *I'm* an arrogant bastard!'

'Ah, but my arrogance is not based on immature angst and confused anger, as yours is. Mine comes from confidence.'

Now Theo poured himself some more orange juice from the iced jug on the table and stared at the lovely view. Just as yesterday, the sea was as smooth as glass and a hazy early-morning mist hung languidly over the horizon. It was unusually calm, this narrow strait of water between Corfu and Albania. Normally it was a wind-surfer's paradise, especially in the afternoon when the breeze really whipped up. Sometimes the water became dangerously rough and the tourists who innocently hired boats in the morning, expecting a pleasant day of cove-hopping, got rather more than they had bargained for. One saw them all the time, low-powered motor boats struggling against strong waves, the men pretending they had it all under control, and the women slipping on their life-jackets and worrying whether they would see home again.

He shifted his gaze to look along the hillside towards Villa Petros. There was no sign of movement on the terrace or the veranda, and he guessed that its occupants were still asleep. He pictured Max and Laura lying together, Max with one arm placed protectively around his wife's pale, freckled shoulders, and Laura, her auburn hair fanned slightly across the pillow. They were a couple made for each other, perfectly in tune with the other's needs, and still perfectly in love after so many years.

A twinge of envy crept up on him. Not ugly, covetous envy for another man's wife, but a gentle twisting yearning that one day somebody would love him with the constancy with which Laura must always have loved Max.

He pushed the thought away.

It was futile to think along those lines. He could never expect somebody to love him with the intensity he craved, not when it seemed unlikely that he would be capable of offering the same in return. His track record, of which Mark had once been envious, proved that he simply wasn't cut out for long-term monogamous commitment. And almost certainly it was too late for him to change the habit of a lifetime.

His thoughts turned to Izzy. It had been pure idle amusement on his part to tease Laura that he could help her friend to enjoy her holiday, and it had touched him to see her concern. He would never do anything to upset or annoy Laura. Though that first glimpse of Izzy last night had made him wonder: there was no denying that he had felt the irresistible pull an attractive woman always exerted on him. It was the freshness of her face that had appealed. There was no artifice to her. No elaborate hairstyle. No ostentatious jewellery. No makeup. He couldn't even recall if she was wearing any perfume. But she had moved with a beguiling grace that made her unconsciously lovely. She was without pretension, and from her sombre grey eyes, which were both gentle and enquiring, he had guessed that a lot was going on inside her head, and not all of it happy.

She was very different from the women he usually felt attracted to. In fact, she was the complete opposite.

Just as he and Mark had once been. And still were, in many respects: resisting polarities, but with a very real synergy between them, was what Mark said of them.

He leaned back in his seat, stretched his arms over his head, and smiled at the coincidence. 'Well, well, well,' he said aloud. 'We shall just have to wait and see what the Fates have in store for us.'

Mark didn't like coincidences. As far as he was concerned he had experienced too many of them just recently, and none had been good.

But the woman in the seat beside him was not of the same opinion. She was rather drunk and seemed to think that because he was bound for the same holiday destination as she and her husband, some high priestess of fate was at work.

He put her at somewhere in her mid-fifties, and decided she was undergoing a serious identity crisis, kidding herself that she was still in her twenties. She was wearing a pair of Christian Dior sunglasses, a tight cream lace dress, and with a head of scuzzy showbiz blonde hair, she was a real middle-aged designer dolly-babe. She was brittle thin, too, and he had the feeling that if he accidentally knocked her he'd set off an avalanche of body parts. Her lipstick had partially rubbed off and she was left with an outline of lip-liner: it gave her a clown-like drawn-on smile.

Between her and her husband – a man of zero conversational skills but a fine comb-over: you could almost count the strands clinging to his pate – they had bought enough booze from the drinks trolley to ensure that Messrs Gordon and Johnnie Walker would be rubbing their hands with delight.

'You know what, darlin', I was told I'd have an important encounter with a fair-haired man today,' she had said, once they were pushing through the thick bank of clouds that were raining on a miserably wet Manchester below, 'but she didn't mention about him having such a sexy voice. You got a cold?'

'Sorry?' he had said, knowing that he would be. He was sorrier still that he had decided to fly from Manchester instead of Newcastle. Why the hell had he agreed to be a guest speaker for that dinner Waterstone's had put on? If he had said no, as he normally did, he wouldn't have changed his flight arrangements at the last minute and be sitting here next to this wretched woman.

With an irritating jingle-jangle of silver bangles on her skinny wrist, she leaned into him. 'My tarot companion said I'd meet a man who fits your description exactly. Tall, fair-haired and wearing jeans. It's you.'

It could also have been any number of other men on board the plane, but he kept this piece of information to himself, discretion invariably being the better part of valour.

'I hate flying,' she went on, undeterred by his silence, 'so last night I gave my tarot reader a quick tinkle. Just to put my mind at rest. If it's my turn to go, I told her, I want some warning. Like enough to book a later flight! But you're going to bring me luck. You're going to change my life.'

She believed it too. Every last gibbering word of

pound-a-minute make-believe. But then she would, wouldn't she? She was probably barking mad. Had to be.

His thoughts were interrupted again as she decided, since he was going to be playing such an important part in her life, that it was time they were properly introduced. Unscrewing the metal cap of one of the miniature bottles she had stashed in her vanity case, she told him her name was Liberty-Raquel Fitzgerald. After raising the bottle of crème-de-menthe to her lips and draining half in one well-practised swig, she added, 'This is my husband, Bob. He doesn't say much. Say hello, Bob.' Silent Bob obviously knew the score and did as he was told. He then got back to his book; a book Mark recognised only too well.

With nothing else for it, he knew that if he was going to get any peace he would have to lose himself in the in-flight movie: a soft-focus costume drama. He was just reaching for his headphones when she told him where she and Silent Bob would be staying.

His brain, which had thus far been lying dormant with boredom, did a double-take. 'Where did you say?'

'Áyios Nikólaos,' she repeated. Then, seeing what she mistook for well-I-never astonishment on his face, but which was actually horror, she said, 'No! Don't tell me, darlin', that's where you're staying! Whereabouts?'

He told her, not so much to provide her with the information but to clarify exactly where she would be in relation to him. Was it possible that there was more than one Áyios Nikólaos? No, he couldn't be that lucky.

The exchanging of geographical details confirmed what he foolishly thought were his worst fears, but then she said, 'We're there for most of the summer. Bob's looking to invest in property on the island. Isn't that right, Bob?' A nod indicated that she was correct. 'How about you? How long are you on holiday for?'

'It's a flexible arrangement,' he said evasively. 'When

I've had enough I'll be going home.' At this rate, some time tomorrow.

She rattled her jewellery at him again and pressed a long red nail into the flesh of his forearm. 'But you know that you won't be leaving before you've fulfilled your obligation to me, don't you?'

His dumb expression made her go on.

She pressed the nails further into his skin. 'You know, to change my life. It's written in the stars. It's going to happen. I just know it is. I've got a really good feeling about you.'

He wished he could say the same of her.

Chapter Six

The view from Izzy's bedroom window was enchanting, and with nobody else up on the first morning of her holiday, she was taking advantage of being able to absorb the magical beauty without interruption.

Despite the threat of mosquitoes, she had slept the night with only the shutters across her window, and the gauzy white muslin drapes had billowed gently as a cooling breeze had filled the room. She had fallen asleep to the rhythmic sound of the sea lapping at the shore below and had woken to the same. Now, as she sat on the small balcony that faced the sea, she could hear the muted clang of a church bell, and a second-shift cockerel crowing. Coming from the nearby eucalyptus trees was the motorised tone of chirruping cicadas.

It was such a heavenly morning she wished she had the talent to capture its essence. She glanced down at the sketchpad on her lap and looked at what she had achieved so far. Even to her self-critical eye, it didn't look too bad. She waggled her paintbrush in the jar of water on the table at her side, dabbed it into her tray of watercolours and resumed work again on the hazy lilac sky that was washed with a soft, pearly opalescence.

When Max and Laura had invited Izzy to spend the summer with them, her first thought had been to rush out and treat herself to a new set of paints and sketchpads. From then on she had been counting the days until the holiday, imagining the sheer bliss of being surrounded by so much beauty and having time to try to capture it on paper. It was perhaps an exaggeration, but it felt as though she was being given the chance to let her creativity have some fun. Normally constrained by the nature of her job, it was being given a moment of freedom in which to indulge itself.

At times, an art teacher's job was the most frustrating on earth. Or maybe it was just her. Perhaps the nurturing of creative young minds through rolling out Plasticine and making coil pots wasn't what she was cut out to do. Occasionally the children she taught were responsive to what she was trying to share with them, but too often they saw the lessons as an excuse to let off steam after the rigidity of too much formal teaching too early in their lives. Now and then a child responded to what she was trying to show them, but invariably she spent a large proportion of the lessons preventing paint fights, or washing glue off expensive school uniform. There were days when she fantasised that she could line up the worst of the troublemakers and fire a hose of red paint at them. This was after she had smothered them in glue and feathers. And also after she had locked them in the art cupboard overnight with nothing to eat but pasta tubes and sugar paper.

It didn't take an Ofsted inspector to tell her she was in the wrong job. She knew that she wasn't a particularly good teacher – not in the modern sense: her crowd-control technique was not all that it might be, and these days that seemed to be what mattered. But she had a genuine love of her subject and wished that she could instil just a fraction of it into her pupils. Oh, to have a budding Van Gogh in the class who, with just a few dabs of a brush, could portray the depths of a man's soul. Or a child who could draw with the rhythmic, spiritual intensity of William Blake. Surely it had to happen one day. The great artists of tomorrow had to go to school, didn't they? So why couldn't just one pass through her hands?

Because, as her mother had frequently told her, she was always in the wrong place at the wrong time doing the wrong thing. It would be just her luck that a future Picasso attended one of the neighbouring schools while she got lumbered with a fraud like Damien Hurst or that woman with the disgusting bed.

It had definitely been a case of being in the wrong place at the wrong time when she had met Alan.

She had moved up to Cheshire in the summer, and by the end of her first term in her new school she was suffering daily headaches and had found herself squinting late at night in bed as she tried to read. She became worried that something was seriously wrong with her. A tumour, for instance. A tumour that, if she played her cards right, would only be the size of a pea and would merely cause her to go blind. More likely it would be the size of a tangerine, pressing on a crucial bit of her brain, waiting to kill her when she was least expecting it. Ingrid Boardman, head of maths at school and the full-time wearer of bifocals – the person who had loaned her *One Hundred Ways To Be A Thoroughly Modern Woman* – had suggested that before she started writing out a will, Izzy might consider getting her eyes tested. She gave Izzy the address of her own optician and the next day she made an appointment. But when she turned up for her appointment and gave her name to the young receptionist she was informed that there was no record of a Miss Jordan booked in for that afternoon. 'Are you sure you've got the right day?' the cheeky youngster asked her. 'Today is Saturday.'

Annoyed that her ability to make an appointment was being queried, she said, 'Of course I'm certain. And I also know that tomorrow is Sunday.'

Giving Izzy a surly teenage pout, the girl got up from

her swivel chair. 'I'll go and see what Mr Leigh says about this,' she said, and with such menace Izzy half expected Mr Leigh, whoever he was, to come and box her ears. While she waited, she tried on a selection of spectacle frames. It was extraordinary how many different styles there were to choose from. Just for a laugh she put on a pair of thick-rimmed Jarvis Cocker frames. She looked hideous: a cross between Nana Mouskouri and Michael Caine. She gave the mirror a dead-pan expression and mouthed in her best Cockney, 'Not a lot of people know I'm a transvestite.'

'I think you'll find they're a touch heavy for a face with features as delicate as yours,' said a voice from behind her.

She spun round. It was the dreaded Mr Leigh. Except he didn't look so very dreadful. His hair was dark and springy, and like the rest of him – eyes quickly surveying her, hands slipping a pen into his breast pocket, mouth breaking into a wide smile and body bouncing energetically across the carpet as he came towards her – it gave the impression of only just being under control. He was a lot younger than she had expected – only a little older than herself, in fact. She snatched off the ugly frames, embarrassed, and fumbled to get them back on to the rack. He came over, took them from her, and slipped them easily on to the appropriate hooks. He wasn't very tall, but what he lacked in height he made up for with his shoulders: they were massively broad. He had rugby prop forward written all over him, and if he hadn't been dressed in a white jacket she might have thought his profession was hanging around seedy nightclubs pitching drunken undesirables on to the streets. She decided, there and then, that she would go quietly.

'My receptionist says there seems to be some kind of mix-up,' he said, smoothly interrupting her flustered thoughts. 'According to the diary you don't have an appointment, but you're in luck, I've a free slot so I could fit you in now.'

'Oh, well, if you're sure it's no trouble,' she said.

After the receptionist had taken the necessary details from her, she was shown through to a room where the lights were romantically dimmed. 'What made you think you needed to have your eyes tested?' he asked, indicating for her to sit in a raised black chair.

She told him about the squinting and the headaches. 'What work do you do?'

'I'm a teacher.'

'Under a lot of stress, are you?'

'Not really.'

'Stress,' he said. 'It's a real killer. Marriage, divorce, bereavement, moving house, they're the big four that wreak havoc on the body. Especially the eyes. Have you experienced any of these things in the last few months?'

'I've moved house and changed my job,' she admitted. She wondered whether it was worth mentioning her mother too. Perhaps not.

'Moved house *and* changed your job,' he repeated, shaking his head and whistling through his teeth, not unlike a garage mechanic diagnosing a terminally sick car. 'Well, Miss Jordan, let's take a look, shall we?' He reached into a drawer, pulled out a strange-looking piece of equipment, then lunged into her face and pressed it against her right eye. 'Don't look into the light,' he said too late. He smelt of aftershave and Polo mints and she wondered if the latter was to cover up the smell of tobacco. I could never go out with anyone who smoked, she found herself thinking. But his hands don't smell of cigarettes, she pointed out, and he is quite good-looking. In fact, he's rather nice. The old Abba song, '*Look into his angel eyes and you'll be hypnotised,*' popped into her mind.

When he finished, he pronounced her to be in possession of near-perfect vision. 'You've got nothing to worry about other than slightly lazy eye muscles.' He explained some eye exercises to do twice a day that would help, then asked if she would have a drink with him that night.

'Oh, um isn't that rather unethical?' she asked, taken aback by his directness.

He grinned mischievously. 'Only if you tell anyone.'

It was when he had shown her to the door and she was crossing the road to call in at the chemist, before going back to her car, that she had noticed another optician's further along the row of shops. With an awful sinking feeling she knew that this was where she should have been for the last hour. Skulking guiltily past the shop window, she contented herself with the thought that had she gone there she wouldn't now be considering what to wear for her date that evening.

It's Fate, she told herself, with cheery smugness.

But it was a long time before she realised the extent of her foolishness. Before that happened, Alan had thoroughly charmed her, he had fully absorbed her into his life, had made her his own. And she had loved it. There had been walks in the country, picnics by the river, trips to the theatre and thrilling white knuckle rides at a theme park. There had been candle-lit dinners, roses, chocolates and the best champagne. There had even been a surprise weekend in the Cotswolds where he had told her he loved her and asked her to move in with him. As lavish and as clichéd as it all was, it was impossible to resist. Having only recently moved to the area and not knowing anybody beyond the school gates of her new job – this was before she had met Max and Laura – a relationship with somebody as self-assured and fun-seeking as Alan was just what she thought she needed. She was only too willing to fall in love with a man who treated her with such a flourish of generosity, even if at times it felt as though he was being a little possessive. But given the circumstances, what girl wouldn't have been blinded by the amount of false glitter being showered upon her?

With hindsight she could see that one of the attractions Alan held for her was that she had hoped to gain some of his confidence from him, as if his energy and strength of character would magically rub off on her. In the end, when everything went wrong, all it did was chip away at her self-esteem. But that was later, much later, when he must have realised that she wanted more from him than he was able to give.

Commitment.

That was when he must have decided it was time to move on. For him the fun was over. Commitment meant being serious. Commitment meant acting like a grown-up, and that was something Alan wasn't very good at. He liked playing the part of charming, boyish rogue. Seemingly he could only do that by having a relationship with a girlfriend who was merely passing through rather than a wife who was here to stay.

Mark saw Theo before his friend caught sight of him. Flash git, he thought, seeing how much he stood out from the crowd of stockily built taxi-drivers, the older men fingering their worry-beads, the younger ones smoking and chatting up the holiday reps. He pushed his trolley towards Theo. 'Hasn't anyone told you that men over forty shouldn't wear their trousers so tight?' he said.

Theo's face broke into a wide grin. He removed his sunglasses and embraced Mark in the ebullient, rousing hug Greek men find so acceptable, but which would have the majority of Englishmen running in the opposite direction.

Mark pushed him away. 'Get off, you exhibitionist. You only do that to annoy me.'

'Yes, but it gives me such pleasure to know that I'm

embarrassing you.' Then, looking at the lone bag on Mark's trolley and the clothes he was wearing – faded jeans with an old T-shirt, which even Mark had to admit had seen better days – he said, 'Is that all the luggage you have brought with you?'

'I've come here to write, Theo. Bear that in mind, won't you? Now, can we hurry up and get the hell out of here? There's somebody I don't want to see again for as long as I—'

But he was interrupted by a loud voice he had hoped never to hear again. It was that awful dolly-babe woman yoo-hooing across the crowded arrivals hall with Silent Bob pushing a trolley of Louis Vuitton cases. She came over to him.

'Gawd, it's a real bun-fight round that conveyor belt, isn't it?' she said. 'And you were so quick getting away from the carousel I thought we wouldn't have the chance to arrange a little get-together.' Then, peering at Theo over the top of her sunglasses and giving him a more than passing look of interest, she said, 'Is he your taxi-driver?'

Mark opened his mouth to put her right, but Theo was ahead of him. With a respectful click of his heels, he stepped forward and said, 'I am Theodore Vlamakis. I am not just ordinary driver to *Meester* Saint James. I am his personal chauffeur. *Meester* Saint James very important man.'

She stared at Mark with renewed interest. She was clearly impressed. But Mark was furious. 'Thank you, *Theodore*,' he said, with heavy emphasis. 'Perhaps we could get going now.'

'And your friends?'

'My what?' hissed Mark.

Theo grinned like a simpleton. 'Could we not give them a lift?'

'He speaks very good English, doesn't he?'

'Better than is good for him at times,' answered Mark

coolly. 'But he's forgetting the size of my car. Sadly it isn't big enough for all of us. Not with so much luggage. Isn't that right, *Theodore*?' He gave Theo a warning look that dared him to contradict what he had just said.

Theo bowed neatly from the waist. 'As usual, *Meester* Saint James, you are right and I am wrong. Come, give me your luggage and I will keep my big stupid mouth shut while you say a nice bye-bye to your friends.'

'What the hell did you think you were doing back there?' demanded Mark when they were driving away from the airport.

'I'm sorry, but I could not help myself. Your face. Ah, it was the picture. Now tell me all about her.'

'I'd rather not. She's an experience I'd prefer to put behind me.' Nevertheless, he told Theo about the crazy conversation he had been subjected to throughout his flight.

'And her name, can it really be Dolly-Babe? That is a new one on me.'

'No, I'm afraid that's what I've christened her. Her real name is even more unlikely. It's Liberty-Raquel.'

Theo laughed. 'You mentioned that she and her husband are staying near us in Áyios Nikólaos? Did she tell you the name of their villa?'

'Yeah, Villa Mimosa. Mean anything to you?'

Theo laughed again. He pressed his foot on the accelerator and shot past a taxi, a dark blue Mercedes that was already moving at warp speed. Mark shuddered. He had forgotten, as he always did when they were apart for any length of time, how fast Theo drove. And how very Greek he really was.

Chapter Seven

At Laura's suggestion, she and Izzy were walking into Kassiópi for lunch. Max had stayed behind, claiming that Greg Rusedski needed his support for his big match that afternoon. 'You go without me,' he had said, 'you'll have much more fun on your own. You could bring me back a newspaper if there's anything decent left to read.'

The dusty little track they were following ran steeply through a large olive grove. At the foot of the trees, and wound around their trunks, were bundles of black netting which, as Laura had just explained, would be stretched out later in the year when it was time to harvest the olives. Though they were in the shade of the trees, the scorching heat of the midday sun forced them to walk at a comfortably unhurried pace. Also, the island was known for its tortoises, which roamed at will, and Laura was hoping they would catch sight of one in the clumps of parched grass. 'I nearly trod on one last year,' she said. 'It was so small it must have been a baby.'

Izzy pulled a face and took extra care where she put her feet.

The path soon levelled and they strolled along a wider, much clearer stretch of ground, where the air was fragrant with the smell of wild garlic and thyme. Laura pointed towards a tumbledown shed. 'Look,' she said, 'there's Zac.'

Zac was a large, scrawny dog of no discernible breed, with a ragged coat the colour of caramel. A short length of rope tied him to a wooden post and at their approach he jumped up, pushed his nose through the chain-link fence and wagged his tail, which was decorated with an assortment of dried leaves and twigs. To Izzy's surprise, Laura pulled a bone-shaped biscuit out of her bag and slipped it through the fence. Zac's tail went into over-drive and he devoured the biscuit in seconds. His nose came back through the fence and he wagged his tail hopefully. Then he barked loudly.

The noise summoned an elderly woman from a small stone building that, until now, Izzy hadn't noticed. She looked as ancient and gnarled as the surrounding olive trees and Izzy would have loved the opportunity to sketch her. The flesh beneath her jaw hung in two wobbling hanks at either side of her throat, her hair, iron-grey and wiry, was held down by a severe black headscarf, and the shabby dress she was wearing, which was partially covered by a floral overall, was also black; dark wrinkled tights and a pair of laced canvas shoes protruded beneath. In her large bony hands she held a broom. She gave Zac a sharp poke with it, instantly silencing him. She looked very fierce but when she turned to the cause of the commotion she gave Laura and Izzy a smile that was friendly and hospitable. Her parted lips displayed a gummy mouth, with a single badly stained tooth.

'How do you know the dog's name?' Izzy asked, after Laura had exchanged a few faltering words of Greek with the woman and they were on their way again.

'From Theo, of course. He knows everyone round here. You mustn't think he restricts his charm to pretty girls. The old women get the same treatment. He's very fair with his attentions.'

They walked on in silence, until Izzy ventured. 'He is rather nice, though, isn't he, in spite of all that charm?' She had been dying to bring up Theo in their conversation that morning, but hadn't dared for fear of making Laura think that she might be interested in him. In fact, she wasn't quite sure what to make of him. His attractiveness, much heralded by Laura, was everything she had been led to expect, but what lay beneath the glamorous image? Take away the stylish clothes, the trappings of his affluent lifestyle and the affectations he must have spent years cultivating, the boyish vanity and gregarious charm, and what would you be left with? What was he really like when he wasn't intent on making an impression on those around him?

In answer to her question, Laura said, 'Oh, he's nice, all right. Fatally so, I should think. Now, here's another friend I want to introduce you to. Max and I have christened him Neddy.'

Disappointed, Izzy acquainted herself with a tired old donkey. He was a sad, spindly-legged creature with a leathery, sagging body that clung to a frame of jutting bones. Like Zac, he, too, was going nowhere and was securely tied. 'The locals don't take very good care of their animals, do they?' Izzy said, as Laura delved into her bag again and this time brought out a carrot.

'It's a different culture,' Laura responded, patting Neddy's dusty coat. 'They can't afford to be sentimental over animals like we are at home. Here they're kept for one purpose and one purpose only. To work.'

'And when they're too old to work?'

'An all-too-short retirement awaits them. Which is what Neddy's enjoying. Aren't you, old boy?' She flicked away the flies that were buzzing round the sores near his rheumy eyes and gave him another carrot.

They carried on walking, and as the olive trees receded, houses appeared and the path joined a narrow lane of tarmac that twisted and turned its way down the hill into Kassiópi. Cats lay dozing in the sun on the side of the road, and in the shade of an open doorway, two elderly women sat gossiping on kitchen chairs, their stockinged and slippered feet resting on an upturned plastic crate. In the house next door, a baby lay sleeping contentedly in a pram while its mother watered the flowers in the terracotta pots on the spotless doorstep.

Izzy had expected Kassiópi to be busy and was surprised to find the streets deserted and quietly slumbering in the heat. 'Where is everybody?' she asked, when Laura suggested they make their way down to the harbour.

'Frying on the beach. That's why I like coming here at this time of the day. There are no jostling crowds of holidaymakers. Now, before I forget, just let me nip in here and get Max his paper.' Leaving Laura to hunt through the revolving racks of British, German and Italian newspapers, Izzy explored the rails of fake designer T-shirts and leather belts.

'He'll just have to make do with the *Express*,' Laura said, when she rejoined Izzy. She showed her what was headline news back home. 'Mother of Two Absconds with Schoolboy Lover.'

'Good Lord, whatever possessed the silly woman?' said Izzy.

Laura laughed. 'Not everyone is as cautious as you, Izzy.'

'Obviously. But she must be mad to do it – the press will crucify her. They'll turn her into a latter-day Lucrezia Borgia.'

'If she isn't one already. Come on, let's head for a drink and a bite to eat.'

The taverna Laura chose overlooked the picturesque horseshoe-shaped harbour where, in the sleepy afternoon peace, brightly coloured boats of varying shapes and sizes bobbed at anchor. A young waiter took their order and, within no time at all, they were relaxing in their chairs beneath a yellow and white striped awning with two plates of kalamári in front of them and a carafe of red wine to share.

'So, apart from thinking that Theo was rather nice,' said Laura, passing Izzy her napkin, 'what else did you conclude from last night?'

Izzy smiled to herself. So, what she had said about Theo back in the olive grove hadn't gone unnoticed by Laura. 'That it must be the easiest thing in the world to fall in love with him,' she said, 'or at least to think that you loved him. It would probably only ever be infatuation.'

'That's a very cynical view to take. Is it based on the belief that you think he's incapable of anything more?'

'I guess so.'

'Well, you've got to agree that makes him ideal material for a holiday romance.'

'Absolutely. But if you're thinking of him and me, forget it.'

'Why?'

'Because I'm not his type.'

'Says who?'

'Oh, come off it, Laura. You know perfectly well that the type of woman Theo would be attracted to would be a stunning beauty. She'd be tall, blonde, acquiescent, and mind-blowingly good in bed.'

'And who's been telling you that you're not mind-blowingly good in bed?'

Izzy lowered her eyes.

Laura frowned. 'Do I detect more of Alan's handi-work? Don't tell me, he took the trouble to tell you you were no good.'

Picturing the scene in that pink room and the therapist asking them to comment on their sex life, Izzy felt her insides melt. It had been so cruel of him. So humiliating. She knew she should be over all this nonsense by now, but it was still there niggling away at her, taunting her at the slightest provocation.

'It's like being with a child,' Alan had said, leaning

forward in his chair, eager to share with someone the details of their most intimate moments. 'She does everything I ask, but it doesn't work.'

'Doesn't work?' the woman had repeated. 'In what way?'

There was a silence while Alan just stared at Izzy. She found this more unnerving than any of the hurtful accusations he had thrown at her. It had been too reminiscent of those chilly, silent pauses that had punctuated her relationship with her mother. From an early age Izzy had learned that conversation, no matter how trivial or how stilted, defused a tricky situation. It meant, though, that she had a worrying tendency to blurt out the first thing that came into her head. She did it then, with Alan staring at her.

'Can I help it that I'm not as experienced as he'd prefer?' she had murmured, mortified that he could do this to her, horrified at the extent of his betrayal.

She had played right into his hands and, giving her a pitying look, he had returned his attention to the therapist. 'She doesn't turn me on, that's the nuts and bolts of it. And you can see why, can't you? You can see why it would be such a lacklustre performance.'

'Perhaps you should be telling Izzy this, and not me,' the woman had said. Her gaze and neutral tone never faltered.

'Yes, Alan,' she had agreed, her own voice spiralling dangerously out of control. 'If it was always so bad, why did you keep up the pretence? Why did you bother? And more importantly,' her voice wobbled, 'if I didn't turn you on, how did you ever manage to get an . . . well, to go through with it?'

'You see what I mean?' he had said to the other woman, a triumphant smile snaking across his face. 'She can't even bring herself to say the word erection. Is it so bad to want a woman in bed with me and not an embarrassed child? Look, she's flinching.'

The hour-long session had finished on that appalling note and they had driven home in silence. They went to bed that night each intent on proving the other wrong. It was a disaster. A ghastly humiliating disaster. She ended up in tears and Alan, victorious, declared her useless. 'You need help, Izzy,' he had said, coming out of the bathroom without a stitch on.

She had turned away from the sight of his naked body and wondered if he was right. The truth was, she wasn't very experienced. A brief encounter here, a regrettable dalliance there, had done nothing to alter her opinion that sex seemed guaranteed to undermine a girl's confidence. In the complex world of everybody's birthright to complete satisfaction, how did she rate? Was she doing it right? How did her technique compare with that of Alan's previous lovers? He often spoke of his past relationships, referring to them as stepping-stones. 'And they've led me to you, Izzy,' he had said, the first time they had slept together.

Nervously she had followed his lead and allowed him to strip away her clothes and as he dropped them on the floor, her instinct, even in such a moment, was to tidy them into a neatly folded pile – jeans at the bottom, sweater on top, socks tucked into shoes. Or had it been a need to distract him? Or a distraction for herself?

He must have sensed her awkwardness for he said, 'Relax Izzy, you're quite safe with me.'

'Sexually repressed' was what he had called her three years on in that silly pink room. Funny that it had taken him so long to reach that conclusion. Funny, too, that it had never bothered him until he felt the desire to leave her for somebody else.

'Well?' prompted Laura, when Izzy still hadn't

responded. 'Did he claim that you were neither use nor ornament in bed?'

'Actually, he was more explicit than that,' Izzy said, forcing herself to be honest. 'He said I was sexually repressed. Also that I was boring.'

Laura burst out laughing. But soon stopped. 'Oh, Izzy, don't look so hurt, I wasn't laughing at you. Please don't think that. It's Alan I'm laughing at. When men start throwing accusations about like that, you can bet your bottom dollar that it's their own inadequacies they're running from. Did you never stop to think that maybe he was a bit lacking in that department? That by blaming you he was hiding from his own problems? All that counselling stuff he put you through was just a ruse in which he hoped to bury the truth with his horrible lies and twisted accusations.'

'Do you really think so?'

Laura's face hardened. 'Yes I do. What's more, and I promised myself I'd never say this, but Max and I never liked him, and the sooner you get over him the better. You need to prove to yourself that he was wrong. And wrong with a capital W. If I were a doctor, you know what I'd prescribe you?'

'Don't tell me, an intensive course of holiday romance.'

Laura smiled. 'Got it in one. What you need is a relationship that has perfectly defined boundaries. When your holiday comes to an end, you walk away with your pride and dignity fully intact. And because love was never asked to join in, there's no danger of you getting hurt. For the first time in your life you could be in control of something. Who knows? You might prove to yourself that you're not such a disaster in bed as Alan has made you think you are.' She pointed to the front page of the *Express*, and added, 'That's probably what that woman is doing. I bet she's led a really boring existence, been dictated to all her marriage and has now finally done something about it. Her life will never be the same again. When the moment of passion has died she'll sell her story to the highest bidder and make herself some money. She'll be a celebrity. Hats off to her, I say.'

'But what about the boy?'

'He'll sell his story too, if he's got any sense. Let's not delude ourselves that he's a poor shy little lad who doesn't know what he's doing. Odds on, he's up for it just as much as she is.'

'And what effect will it have on him when he's older? How will he view women?'

'Time will tell. But for now, let's worry about your neurosis, shall we?'

'Which in particular? Alan? Or my mother?'

'Oh, Lord, I'd need another carafe of wine to find the enthusiasm or strength to dissect your mother. No, I've a better idea. Let's discuss you and Theo. What would you do if he did take a liking to you? How would you react?'

'With distrust, I suppose.'

'And what if he was able to allay your suspicions, what then?'

Izzy lowered her knife and fork. 'I'm not sure he, or any other man, would be able to do that.'

A determined note came into Laura's voice. 'Look, we both know that Alan was a creep of the highest order, but you've got to get it into your head that not all men are as cruel as him. You'll have to let one of them slip under the wire at some time in the not-too-distant future.'

'I know, I know, but you're speaking from the comfort zone of your own marriage to Max, which is bound to make you hold men in higher regard than I ever could.'

'I haven't always been married to Max. There was a time before him, a time when I was hurt just as badly as you.'

This was news to Izzy. Because Max and Laura were

so happy and well suited, she had never thought of them with other partners. 'Really? You've never mentioned it before.'

'It's not something I like to remind myself of.'

'Why, because it still hurts?'

'No,' Laura said emphatically. 'Because I was so stupid, and on two counts. Stupid to believe a word he ever uttered, and stupid enough to let him cause me a single moment of pain. But if there's one thing I've learned from the experience, it's that Max proved to me that not all men are such pigs. It's only the occasional rotten apple that gives the rest of the barrel a bad name.'

'And you're determined that I should learn that lesson as well?'

'Is that so very bad of me?'

'It would explain why I feel that you're literally throwing Theo at me.'

Laura smiled. 'Go on, hand on heart, tell me you wouldn't be tempted if he made a play for you. *Well*, wouldn't you?'

'Laura, I can honestly say, with my hand on my heart, that I'm not going to answer any more of your daft questions. Another glass of wine?'

Chapter Eight

Theo was on the phone, and with the likelihood of the call going on for some time yet – judging from the expression on his face and the rapidity of his words – Mark decided to leave him to it. It always amused Mark that when Theo was speaking in his native tongue he could never work out whether an enthusiastic exchange was taking place or a heated argument: the tone was always the same, hugely expressive and bordering on volatile.

He went through to the kitchen; a large rectangular room with rough uneven walls of stone that, in places, were more than twenty inches deep. There were no fitted cupboards, just two enormous wooden dressers that held a variety of brightly coloured crockery and glassware. At the furthest end there was a small walk-in pantry where the shelves were neatly packed with everyday requirements, including at least a dozen different varieties of olive oil. In front of one of the dressers, and in the middle of the room, was a chunky oblong table with six wooden chairs around it; they varied in size and design, and Mark guessed they were handmade. Beneath a small window that looked out on to a vegetable plot and a glimpse of the sea, there was a white ceramic sink; it was modern but masquerading discreetly as old. Next to this, and taking up most of the available wall space, was a massive American fridge. Mark opened its shiny blue door and helped himself to a glass of water. He added ice to it and strolled through the rest of the house, out on to the terrace. He paused for a few minutes in the dazzling sunshine to slip on his sunglasses, the heat coming at him as a hammer-blow, before going down the stone steps to the area of garden that overlooked the swimming-pool.

Villa Anna was not at all what he had expected. Having stayed with Theo many times in Athens, he had made the assumption that his friend's recently acquired and renovated country retreat would be a replica of the many soulless apartments Theo had lived in over the years. But he should have known better than to presume anything of Theo. A friendship that had spanned more than two decades should have prepared him for the unexpected. Villa Anna wasn't even a toned-down version of the chic minimal furnishings and discordant sculptures with which Theo normally surrounded himself: instead it was a comfortable home with leanings towards tasteful modesty rather than expensive artifice. The cluttered shelves of books that lined the irregular, sloping stone walls, the simply framed sketches, the family photographs, the blend of faded rugs and muted fabrics, and the antique furniture – some of which Mark recognised as having once belonged to Anna Vlamakis – gave an air of permanency to the house. It's a home, had been Mark's first thought when Theo had unlocked the front door and brought him inside, less than half an hour ago.

So, was this where his friend was finally putting down some roots?

If it was, Mark could understand it. His own memories of previous trips to Corfu, together with the little he had seen so far of Áyios Nikólaos, was enough to make him see that Theo had found himself an ideal bolthole for when he tired of the madness of Athens.

Wanting to explore further, Mark followed a winding gravel path bordered on either side by bushes of scarlet oleander and large urns of broad-leafed ferns. It took him to a small clearing that was almost at the very tip of the headland. To his right was the bay of Áyios Nikólaos with its narrow stretch of beach, gently sloping hillside of cypress trees and clusters of villas, and to his left, a verdant coastline that led, he supposed, to the nearest village. Theo had given him a brief run-down on the local geographical landmarks during the drive from the airport, but until he saw it for himself it would mean nothing.

Back home he, too, lived near the sea: the North Sea. Admittedly the water wasn't as clear, or anywhere near as warm, but in its own way the view he lived with was just as spectacular as this. He had lived in Robin Hood's Bay for the last six years, in a three-storey Georgian house he had bought on the proceeds from his first book. It had originally been built for a sea captain in the mid-eighteenth century and had a great sense of history. Over the years it had been well documented by countless local historians. Living in a historic landmark was a pain at times, but he wasn't alone in that: practically everyone in the tightly packed village suffered from the same affliction. Perched on the cliff edge with its maze of little streets and the jumble of cottages with their distinctive pan-tiled roofs and an identity that was firmly anchored in fishing and smuggling, Robin Hood's Bay was a real tourist pull. People came from all over to *ooh* and *aah* at its quaintness, especially in the summer. In the winter months, when few people had the urge to cope with the cold rain and gusting winds that came in off the sea, the village became a different place altogether. It was that time of year that Mark liked best. A grim bleakness descended on the landscape and gave him the sense of brooding isolation that inspired his writing and which had become his trademark. When Theo had made his first visit in the depths of one of the coldest winters Mark

71

had known, he had shaken his head and said, 'So, this is where you intend to hide for the rest of your life, is it?'

'Who said anything about hiding?'

'You have another word for it?'

There had been an element of truth in what Theo had said. After a long period in his life when everything he had touched had seemingly gone wrong, he had felt the need to disappear, to submerge himself in another world. But for all Theo's initial cynicism, he had soon come to realise why Mark had chosen to live where he had. 'It is a place of paradox,' he said, when he made his second visit in the height of summer and saw the carefree crowds of holidaymakers sunning themselves in the harbour with their ice-creams, heard the laughter of children playing in the rock pools, watched the fishing-boats coming in after a day at sea, and strolled through the expanse of purple-flowering heather that covered the moors only a few miles away, 'but I can see that this quaint little village suits you well. It reflects perfectly the dark and dour side to you, and the quirky mercurial bit you keep for those who know you best. But it is good, I see an improvement in you already. You are not so uptight.'

Theo had been right, as he so often was. Robin Hood's Bay suited him well: it felt comfortably secure and made few demands of him. That was how he wanted to live. Quietly. Unobtrusively. Doing what he enjoyed most, which was writing, and with nothing of his past to cast a shadow over his new life.

And that was what he had achieved, until February of this year when his latest novel, *Silent Footsteps*, was published. Within a week of the book hitting the shelves, he had received the first of the letters. To begin with he had ignored them, treating the typewritten notes as nothing more than the weird work of a crank. But then a familiar pattern emerged, and he began to feel spooked. The crank, whoever he was, was carrying out a copycat version of the killer's actions in *Silent Footsteps*. The story-line had revolved around a stalker who had written repeatedly to his victims telling them that he was their friend, that he was looking out for them. He always started the message in the same way: 'Remember, you're never alone. I am your friend.' It was classic stalker mentality: the stalker's need to feel involved in his victim's life, to become the focus of that person's every waking thought. But it wasn't just the wording of the letters that concerned Mark, it was the postmark on each envelope that caused him the most anxiety: the crank was replicating the sequence of postmarks that Mark had written into his book. The order in which the letters arrived was identical to the pattern in *Silent Footsteps*: Winchester first, followed by Salisbury, Lincoln, Norwich, Chester, Liverpool, Guildford, Durham, and finally Hereford. They were all cities that had cathedrals of notable interest, but while there hadn't been any particular reason why Mark had used this in his novel – it had simply been one of those lucky ideas plucked from the ether, which seemed to work well in the plot he was pursuing – the man, or woman for that matter, who was behind the letters Mark had so far received must have chosen the places with a very specific purpose in mind: to put the wind up him. It made him think, What if this person is serious? What if he's *deadly* serious?

Determined not to overreact, he had thrown the letters away, consigning the unspoken threat they contained to the rubbish bin where it belonged.

Fleetingly he had considered going to the police, but even in a quiet backwater such as Robin Hood's Bay there were more tangible crimes to deal with than the letters of a saddo who had nothing better to do with his time. No actual threat was being made, so it would be understandable if the police put it low on their list of priorities to follow up. Besides which, if he had taken the matter to them, within hours the local rag would have got hold of it, followed no doubt by a keen-eyed freelancer for one of the nationals. And how would that look? Sure, his publishers might like the thought of all the free publicity, but for Mark it would just be an excuse for his past to be dredged up once more. It would also play straight into the hands of the stalker. When he saw for himself, in black and white, the success he was having in rattling his victim, the stalker's insecure ego would get a terrific boost. Self-aggrandisement, big-time!

Though he wasn't being stalked as intensely as the characters in his novel – there had been no phone calls and no visible presence as such – Mark understood the very real sense of torment to which an innocent victim was subjected. The invasion of one's privacy means nothing until you experience at first hand what it feels like to read a letter written by somebody who has made it their business to watch and follow you.

Then, six weeks ago, the letters stopped, Hereford being the last point of contact. Anyone else might have breathed a sigh of relief and thought that the stalker had got bored with the game. But Mark was far from relieved. More than anyone, he knew the plot of *Silent Footsteps* and felt that the absence of the stalker's presence in his life was more threatening than when it had been there, and for the simple fact that in his novel, like a lull before a storm, a silence always came before the victim's death.

So the big joke was, if life was going to imitate art fully, Mark was going to meet his death before he was good and ready for it.

Soft footsteps on the gravel path behind him had him spinning round on his heel. 'Goddamnit, Theo! What the hell are you doing creeping up on me like that?'

That evening Theo cooked them supper. 'I'm told by my

neighbours Max and Laura that my cooking is something to be admired,' he said. 'Your verdict, please.'

Mark chewed on a tender piece of lamb that was appetisingly pink and flavoured with oregano and lemon juice. 'Not bad,' he said, 'not bad at all.'

'Praise indeed from the maestro who introduced me to Pot Noodles and taught me to cook Spam curries on a Baby Belling. Ah, the spicy shite days, how I miss them. Can I get you anything else to drink?'

'No, this is fine.'

'More ice?'

'Theo, everything is fine. Stop fussing. You're worse than a Jewish mother.'

Theo poured some more wine for himself and thought that everything was far from fine. Mark was not the picture of health he had been when they had last met. He had lost weight and was distinctly on edge. But, then, who could blame him? Theo was glad now that he had been so insistent that his friend should spend the summer with him. Last month when Mark had told him about the crazy business with the letters he had been sent, he had said at once, 'Trust your instinct, Mark. If you think you are in any danger, come and stay with me.' He had been shocked to think that Mark had been on the receiving end of such a sinister campaign of fear, but more shocked that his old friend had not confided in him sooner. 'Even if you don't think you're in danger, I think you should still get away. It would do you good.' He had known that because Mark didn't try to refute this advice, he was genuinely concerned for his own welfare. Which, in years gone by, he hadn't always been too interested in.

Throughout his twenties and early thirties Mark had put himself through the very worst kind of hell. Addiction had nearly killed him. It had cost him his marriage, his home, countless jobs, most of his friends, very nearly his family but, worst of all, every last scrap of his self-esteem. He had sunk so low he had seemed an impossible case, deliberately isolating himself from anyone who had ever been close to him, including Theo. In desperation Mark's family had turned to him for help. 'You're the only one he has ever listened to,' Mark's mother had said. 'We've tried to help him, really we have, but he simply won't accept that a rehabilitation centre would do him any good. He says he's beyond help. He says . . . he says he wants to die. Oh, please, Theo, please help us.'

Theo had known for a long time that Mark was in trouble. Back in Durham he had often witnessed Mark drunk and seen how alcohol darkened his mood, how it revealed the savage anger in him, as well as the unimaginable self-hate. He had tried on several occasions to step in and make Mark see what he was doing to himself, but without success. Helpless, he had had to stand back and watch his friend's gradual decline as he turned ever more to alcohol and drugs. Though it had been painful to admit, he had known that if his friend was ever going to get better he was going to have to reach rock bottom.

After the conversation with Mark's mother, Theo flew over and tracked him down. He was living, if one could call it that, in a squalid, cockroach-infested bed-sit. The room was poorly lit, the single window obliterated by a piece of dirty cloth hanging from a broken rail. The walls were grubby and peeling, the carpetless floor littered with filthy clothes, the sink piled high with unwashed crockery. It was a stifling hellhole, the air fetid with the stench of sweat, alcohol and despair. And sitting hunched on a damp, uncovered mattress against a wall was Mark. Except it wasn't Mark. It wasn't the vigorous strong-minded, volatile man Theo had known from college, a man whose sharp humour and clarity of thought could cut through the most persuasive argument. To his horror, he was looking at the remnants of a dying man. He had known real anger in that moment as he had held out a hand to Mark and helped him to his feet. Anger that, somewhere beyond those walls, people were making money from Mark's misery.

The rancid smell of that awful room had lingered in Theo's nostrils as he had driven Mark the length of the country and admitted him to the clinic his parents had found for him.

'How did you manage it?' they asked Theo. 'How did you make him get in the car with you?'

'I didn't need to do anything,' he told them. 'It was as if he was waiting for me.'

That was the picture Theo had of Mark for many years to come. The ashamed acceptance in his painfully thin body, the unshaven face fixed on Theo with eyes hollow and dark, pleading, reproachful, as though saying, 'What took you so long? I could have died.'

The pain of that encounter eight years ago had never left Theo. He imagined that it must haunt Mark too. And though Mark had made a full recovery, he would probably be the first to say that, if the circumstances were right, it might happen all over again. 'I have to remind myself that once an alcoholic, always an alcoholic,' he had said when he came out of the clinic. Out of deference to his friend's ability to turn his life round, and knowing that it would only be by the most extraordinary effort of will that Mark would be able to stay clean, Theo had been fanatical about not having alcohol in his apartment when Mark came to stay. He even hid packets of paracetamol and aspirin where he thought no one would dream of looking. 'Go easy, pal,' Mark had told him one day when he had caught him turning the apartment upside down because he had a headache and couldn't find any aspirin. 'Temptation is there every day, with or without your hindrance. It's me who can't handle the booze and pills, not you. It's also bloody insulting. Stop treating me like a criminal. Have you tried the fridge? That's where Kim used to try to hide things from me. An empty egg box was a favourite of hers.'

It still felt insensitive to drink in front of Mark, but in spite of that, Theo made himself do it so that his friend would never think he doubted that he had the strength of character to say no to temptation.

Their meal was finished now, and turning their chairs round, they faced the sea and the darkening sky. Theo looked at Mark's pale face. 'You won't be spending the entire summer working, will you?' he asked.

Without turning his head, Mark said, 'Probably. Why?'

'No reason.'

'Oh, come on, Theo. You've always been lousy at subtlety. What are you really saying?'

'Okay. I think this business with the stalker has affected you more than you are letting on. I think that when I surprised you in the garden and nearly made you jump out of your skin, for a split second, you were more than just alarmed.'

Chapter Nine

'How about we invite Theo to join us?' asked Max. He had just proposed that they take the boat out for the morning to go cove-hopping, then stop for lunch at one of his favourite tavernas in Áyios Stéfanos.

'You're forgetting, he's got company,' said Laura, looking up from *Captain Corelli's Mandolin* and noting that, as usual, her husband was incapable of sitting still for longer than ten minutes without searching for something to occupy him. He had already swept the veranda and terrace and watered the plants, despite paying Sophia and Angelos to do it for them; he was now repositioning the umbrella above her sun-lounger so that she was safely in the shade. She tilted her wide-brimmed hat back on her head, looked at him over the top of her sunglasses and added, 'I don't think we should bother him, do you? Not today. We don't want to make a nuisance of ourselves.'

'Who said anything about bothering anyone?' Max said indignantly. 'I don't call it making a nuisance of ourselves by being friendly. Naturally I was including Theo's friend in the invitation.'

Laura exchanged a smile with Izzy, who was stretched out in the sun a few feet away, tanning nicely. 'Of course you were, darling.'

'Okay, okay,' he said, 'so I'm as transparent as polished glass. And what if I am curious to meet the man behind so many good books?'

Laura laughed. She closed *Captain Corelli*, slipped the

paperback on to the floor, and held out her arms to Max. 'My husband, the star-struck little boy, wants to rub shoulders with his hero. How sweet.'

He leaned down to her and gave her a kiss. 'I thought perhaps you could go and see if they'd like to come,' he said, when he emerged from nuzzling her breasts.

She pushed him away with a playful shove and rearranged her swimsuit. 'Why me? Why not you?'

'It'll be more of a temptation coming from you. You know how Theo panders to your every whim.'

'But this isn't *my* whim,' she teased, 'it's *yours*. Try asking Izzy to help you out. I'm sure Theo would be just as persuaded by her. If not more.'

Izzy raised her head. 'Oh, no, you don't,' she said. 'Don't go including me in this.'

'I think it's a brilliant idea,' said Laura, warming to the suggestion and seeing it as a way to push Izzy in Theo's direction. 'How could he say no to you, especially if you go just as you are in that very-nearly bikini?'

Izzy flushed. She had known she would regret buying such a skimpy little thing. It had been one of those impulse buys that was supposed to boost her confidence, confirm her independence. You see, she was telling her mother, this is what I can wear when you're not around. Except it wasn't really working: her mother's disapproving influence was only a stone's throw away. Self-conscious, she sat up, pulled on her sun-top, and wondered if she would ever shake off the nagging voice that followed her wherever she went.

In the end Laura put Max out of his misery and agreed to go and see Theo. She tied a sarong around her waist and set off. When she reached Villa Anna she found him sitting on the terrace reading a newspaper while eating his breakfast.

'An unexpected pleasure,' he said, rising to his feet and bending his head to kiss her cheek beneath her hat. He hadn't shaved yet and his stubbly chin grazed her skin. It was not an unpleasant sensation. His shirt was unbuttoned and flapped loosely at his sides in the breeze. 'Please, sit down. I am having a late breakfast. Would you care to keep me company. A drink? Or maybe something to eat?'

'No, thanks. I'm here on an errand.'

'Oh?'

'I'm sorry, but it's Max. He's dying to meet your friend and has sent me here to invite you both to join us on a little boat trip down to Áyios Stéfanos.'

He gave her a shrewd look. 'And why did Max not come here himself?'

Laura smiled.

'Aha, the cunning Max. He is a man with so much guile. So you are the bait, are you? What a dangerous game he plays.'

'Dangerous?'

He bit into the cake on the plate in front of him. 'Yes,' he said, when he had finished chewing. 'Am I not the hungry shark who might be tempted to snap up the bait in one delicious mouthful?'

'Now, Theo, you really must stop fantasising like this.'

He licked his fingers provocatively. 'Sadly, it is all I am allowed.'

'Well, I wish you'd transfer your affections to a more worthwhile recipient.'

'So tell me, how is the lovely Izzy? Did I play the situation well the other night during dinner? Is she madly in love with me already?'

His quickness of thought – not to say his arrogance – surprised even Laura. 'You really are the most dreadful man. Of course she isn't in love with you. What on earth makes you think she'd fall for a shallow flirt like you?'

He made a pretence of considering her question before answering it. 'Mm . . . could it be because I am a devastatingly handsome devil? Charming too. Not to say witty.'

'And let's not forget how self-effacing you are.'

'I was coming to that.' He poured himself a glass of orange juice. 'Are you sure you won't join me?'

'No, thanks. So what did you think of Izzy?'

A slow smile spread over his face. 'She is the perfect *ingénue*. She is as innocent as a child and as sweet and as delicate as a rose.'

Laura groaned. 'Good heavens, what a lot of ghastly sentimental twaddle you do come up with.'

'Twaddle?'

'It means rubbish. Nonsense.'

'Aha. You want me to describe her in the manner of a typical Englishman, is that it? Okay. So be it. I think she would be an excellent shag.'

'*Theo!*'

He feigned a look of innocence. 'What now? Am I too blunt for you?'

'Is there no middle ground with you?'

He shook his head. 'I prefer extremes. But if you want I'll be honest with you . . . but only this once. I thought she was very nice. So nice, that I promise that I will do my best not to encourage her to fall in love with me.'

'How very thoughtful of you.'

'I think so too.'

'But what if *you* fall in love with *her*?'

He dabbed at the sticky crumbs on his plate, then licked his finger. 'Ah, now, that would be a fine state of affairs, would it not? It would be an interesting conundrum for me to resolve.'

'And novel, I would imagine.'

'Oh, highly original.' He pushed the plate away from him, got to his feet, and walked over to a rosebush. He snapped the stem of a delicate white bloom, breathed in its scent, then handed it to Laura.

She, too, drew in its fragrance. 'Have you never really been in love, Theo?' she said, after he had sat down again.

He faced her, his head slightly tilted. 'No, I don't believe I have.'

'Not ever?'

He paused. 'Perhaps once or twice I have come close.'

'But you never felt like pursuing it?'

He shrugged. 'I have a low boredom threshold.'

'Or maybe a fear of commitment.' Her words, like the scent of the rose, hung between them.

Removing his sunglasses, he looked at her closely. 'Why is it, Laura, that again and again I let you start these conversations with me?'

'Because . . .' she hesitated '. . . because deep down you love talking about yourself.'

He laughed. 'Ah, Laura, you know me so well. Now then, about Max and his desire to meet his hero. Let me go and find Mark and see what he has to say. I have to warn you, though, he is not very sociable just at the moment. My instinct tells me that you might have to make do with only my company for the day.'

Theo's instinct was right, that and the fact that he knew his friend implicitly.

'Oh, well,' said Max, when Theo and Laura broke the news to him, 'another time perhaps.'

'I'm sorry to disappoint you,' said Theo, 'but Mark sends his apologies. He is keen to spend the day working. The creative soul is a single-minded and determined taskmaster.'

But Mark's reason to stay behind had less to do with the driven artistic soul that Theo was now describing, and everything to do with fear: he was terrified of boats and water, and Theo had known all along that no invitation, however sweetly put, would have encouraged Mark to spend the day afloat.

Fear, though not actually voiced as such, had figured largely in their conversation last night about the letters Mark had received back in England. Theo had not been taken in by Mark's attempt to make light of it, or his denial that he was on edge. 'I'm tired, that's all,' he had said, 'in need of a holiday, so please, give me a break, will you, and cut the patronising pep talk? You're making me out to be some kind of convalescing invalid.' He had taken the same tone just a moment ago when Theo had asked if he minded him joining Max and Laura for the day: 'Of course I don't. I've got plenty of work to occupy me here. I'd rather have the peace and quiet.'

'Very well, I shall leave you to your writing. You will find plenty to eat in the—'

'Yes, I know where to look for food if I'm hungry. Just stop worrying about me.'

Helping Max to launch the boat, Theo untied the rope from the post on the jetty, and stepped lightly into the back of the small craft. He had offered the use of his own boat, but Max had laughed, telling him that it would do him good to rough it in theirs for a change. 'You English,' Theo had joked, 'you are so hung up on the concept that size does not matter!'

There was only one seat left for him and it was next to Izzy. 'Do you mind if I sit here with you?' he asked.

She smiled and shifted along the bench to make room for him. As he sat down he noticed the looks that passed between Max and Laura. Ah, so they were watching his every move, were they? They were playing a little game with him. He smiled to himself. Well, he could either go along with their expectations or he could play the game his own way.

*

84

Alone on the terrace in the shade of the vine-covered pergola that stretched from one end of Theo's house to the other, Mark was reading through the notes he had made late last night, long after Theo had gone to bed. He was underlining those he thought worthy of being added to the manuscript of his latest book, and crossing out with a single neat stroke anything he thought superfluous. The notebook was nearly full, yet there wasn't one page of messy scribble within its pristine pages. It always amazed people that he was so orderly. They tended to regard his unimaginative dress code – faded jeans, T-shirt and CAT boots – as an indication of how he ran his life, that it would be as casual and thoughtlessly thrown together. In the chaotic mind-blown days of his addiction, this had certainly been the case, but not now. Now he was obsessively organised. His home was ruthlessly cleansed of all irrelevant clutter; his days were planned meticulously; his every hour was accounted for. 'A tidy mind is a happy mind' was a stupid maxim, but as trite as it was, it was a theory that held sufficient water for him to believe it. In the early days of his recovery he had been comforted by the petty rituals he had contrived for himself, using them to ground his mental state in the real world and not the hell he had inhabited previously. Now they were a matter of routine.

The desire to be so regulated and orderly was a side-effect of his brief spell in the clinic that had helped him to overcome his addiction, which had encompassed a variety of substances, but predominantly cocaine and alcohol. Hand in hand, they had been his partners in crime, partners that had taken him to the brink, convincing him, with each deadly, deceitful step they took him towards his downfall, that they were the only friends he needed, that they, and they alone, would give him the confidence and sense of worth he lacked.

By his mid-twenties he had been drinking with a

determined vengeance that had nothing to do with social drinking. It was warfare. A war against himself. It wasn't the taste he craved, it was the obliterating effect he needed: the desire to drink was as strong as the need to eat, if not stronger. Seeking refuge in sleep – and a sleep in which he wasn't jerked awake by nightmares – he would fill himself with beer and whisky chasers until he collapsed on the bed and slept comatose for at least half the night.

Drugs came later, when desperation kicked in.

It was several months after he had married Kim, something he should never have done. He had done it primarily to annoy his parents, but also he believed that by marrying Kim he would be cutting himself off from his past, that he would be free of the destructive demons that had always plagued him. For a time it had worked and he and Kim were okay together. Not exactly happy and trouble-free with fairy-tale roses growing up the trellis of blissful matrimony – that would have been impossible in his state of severe alcohol dependency – but it had been a period of remission. Until, out of the blue, the old demons showed up. He had thought Kim was having an affair, but instead of confronting her, he put more energy into his drinking until eventually, knowing he couldn't go on as he was, he turned to cocaine: it would slow him down and take the pressure off, he thought. But it didn't. In no time at all, he was addicted, not so much to the drug but to the person he became when he was high. Without that buzz, he was nothing. A nobody. He got to the point where he couldn't get out of bed or go to the local shop for a loaf of bread unless his confidence had been fuelled by a line or two. What little sense of value he had soon went, as did his money. Without a moment's hesitation he would spend a week's wages in a single evening. Nothing mattered to him any more.

A year later he was uttering the immortal words, 'Hi, I'm Mark and I'm an addict.'

His first few days in the clinic had been a nightmare. He had truly believed he was going to die. His whole body had cried out for his faithful old buddies who never let him down, who boosted his self-esteem and gave him the strength he depended on to get through another day. The first day he had cursed and raged that he had ever set eyes on the traitor who had pretended he was a friend and brought him here. In his wild confusion he blamed Theo for everything wrong in his life. On his second day he tried to escape, never once thinking that his behaviour was that of a desperate madman. It had seemed so reasonable to him: he was being denied the two things that made his life worth living, so why wouldn't he make a run for it?

But escape wasn't on offer at the clinic. When the worst agony of the shakes and sweats of detox had passed he was given a timetable of what to do and firmly encouraged to stick to it. The hope was that it would keep his mind off the inner voice that told him all he needed was one small drink to ease him through the next hour. There was a never-ending regime of therapy to get through: group therapy of share and tell; individual therapy; even family therapy towards the end of his stay. He had never been so bloody busy. There was also time for private contemplation. This was always a low point for him. He never wanted to be alone with the person he hated so much – at least, not when he wasn't coked-up or drunk and there was nothing to hide behind. That was another thing about the clinic he hadn't been able to cope with initially: there was nowhere for him to hide, no quiet corners to lose himself in; the whole place was designed and run so that all was laid bare.

For some people the road to recovery starts within days of being admitted, but for Mark it was three weeks before he began to open up. The trigger had come from, of all things, the music that was played in the evenings. It was the only form of entertainment provided: no television, radio, papers, or magazines were available. The selection of music was not what he normally listened to – his taste had always been for satisfyingly aggressive rock – but here he was forced to listen to music his parents had tried to make him appreciate. And during this one evening at the clinic, when he had been eating his supper along with all the other inmates, his attention had been drawn away from the conversation he had been having with a guy who had been addicted to sex since the age of fifteen and he had listened with near mesmerised attentiveness to Mozart's Requiem. As though hearing it for the first time, he felt himself floating out of his body, soaring on the powerful, swelling notes, experiencing the heartbreaking magic of such an uplifting and glorious piece of choral work. He had started to shiver, as though an icy cold wind had ripped through the room, and then a searing heat had exploded deep within his chest. Then his head was in his hands and his hands were wet with tears. He was sobbing, his shoulders were shaking, his chest heaving. There was a voice, not his, surely not his, saying that he was sorry. Sorry that he was so screwed up. Sorry, too, that he had screwed up so many others. People gathered round him. They held him. They cried with him. Then they took him away and he slept. Really slept.

The following morning, the man everyone called Bones – because his surname was McCoy – was assigned to talk to him. They sat in a room that had been stripped down to nothing more than two chairs and a desk, a floor of moss green carpet tiles, four walls of magnolia woodchip and a window. There was nothing to distract him – again, nothing to hide behind: no comfortable armchairs, no potted plants or soothing colour schemes designed to draw out deeply rooted fears. Slumped in his chair, his legs extended, crossed at the ankles, his hands hanging at either side of him, Mark had viewed the man before him. He was very small, not much more than five feet tall, with short, stumpy legs. He wore a cardigan with sleeves that were too long for his arms, and straight away Mark could see that his manner was annoyingly slow and thoughtful. But to an addict, who was used to his head buzzing at full tilt, everyone else always appeared to be moving at half speed. It was difficult to take him seriously, though – he looked like he would be more at home washing his car or trimming the hedge than working in a rehab clinic playing hardball with sex addicts and junkies.

First he asked Mark what had particularly moved him about the music he had heard the night before.

'It was the beauty of it,' he said simply, affecting an air of indifference and raising a foot to his knee to pick at a shoelace. 'It detached me from reality. Or what I see as reality.'

'Sounds like your average kind of trip. What exactly did it separate you from?' Silence.

Bones stared at him, waiting patiently for an answer. In the absence of one, he got up and opened the window. He sat down again. 'Do I need to repeat the question, or rephrase it, perhaps?' His tone was bland.

But, like a tiny pull on a thread, it somehow tugged an answer out of him. 'From the . . . the death of a friend.'

It had taken real gut-wrenching courage to utter those words. Okay, he hadn't been able to look Bones in the eye but, if nothing else, his efforts should have been rewarded with at least a round of applause. But all he had got was: 'You mean the painful memory of that friend's death?'

'What else?'

Bones surveyed him thoughtfully. 'Mark, you've been

here for three weeks now, and to my knowledge, this is the first time you've mentioned this. Why's that?'

'Why the hell do you think?'

'It's not what *I* think that's at stake.'

They had two-stepped like that for some time, and with each exchange, Mark gained a vicarious thrill in knowing he could outwit this inferior little man, who every now and then did nothing more constructive than dip his hand into his desk drawer and pull out a sweet.

His parents had tried this same trick on him when he was thirteen, taking him to see several child psychologists in the hope that he would walk away reborn. They had even tried hypnosis, but that had just been more of a challenge for him as he had forced his brain to keep alert, not to let it be fooled by the smooth tone of the doctor. But nothing had worked: he had always been too smart to let anyone know what he was really thinking.

But Mark was about to discover that Bones didn't always play by the book. Gentle and ponderous he could be, but as the weeks went by, Mark came to realise that he had seriously underestimated the man. When it was necessary Bones had no compunction in pulling the rug from under Mark, then watching him crack open his head on the hard floor of his arrogance.

'Now, Mark,' he said, on that first meeting after thirty minutes of prevaricating, 'I know that this whole scenario of ink blots and potty-training theories offends your intellect. After all, you're a former student of criminal psychology, what possible help could I offer a fine man like you? Who in their right mind would want to share their innermost feelings with an insignificant person such as me? But think on this while you're devoting yourself to blagging your way through this session. If you're so clever, what are you doing here?' He held up his hand. 'No, that was a rhetorical question. For now, I am doing all the talking. And I'll tell you what you're doing here, Mark. You're here because you're not in your right mind. In fact, you're in dire need of a clear-thinking outsider to give you a true perspective of yourself. And guess what, I'm just the man for the job. But don't worry that you'll become too dependent on me, I won't allow that to happen. The needy love–hate relationship you fear might develop between us if you open up to me will not take root. Believe me, I am too good at psychoanalysis for that to happen.'

'I'm bowled over by your modest claims.'

'And I by your scarcely controlled rage and dislike of me. But that's enough of the flattery. Let's get this straight, you're an alcoholic and a substance user, and it's down to me to help you get your head clean. The fact that you're here at all means that, deep down, you knew your number was up. And here's an interesting point I want you to consider, and consider well. An intellectual understanding of addiction isn't enough. You need to have an emotional response to it. So tell me about this friend who died and for whom you're still mourning. Or was it a girl? A girlfriend, perhaps?'

Another silence.

'Take your time. There's no hurry.'

But still Mark couldn't speak. And then, unbelievably, this extraordinary little man had the gall to stare straight at him and start whistling Joe Cocker's 'Let The Healing Begin'.

He didn't know how it happened, just as he couldn't explain the icy-cold feeling he had experienced the night before followed by the explosion of white heat in his body, but a tiny key slowly turned inside him and Mark heard himself say, 'His name was Niall and . . . and he drowned.'

Hearing the noise of a small engine, Mark raised his gaze from his notebook and looked down into the bay.

Beneath a cloudless sky, where the turquoise water glinted in the glare of the sun, a motor-boat was cutting smoothly through the waves. Even at this distance he could hear its occupants laughing and joking. It made him wonder how Theo was getting on.

Chapter Ten

Izzy stood poised, every muscle taut, her toes clinging to the smooth rock, her arms in front of her, her eyes focused on the crystal clear water below. Modern Woman was threatening to push her in if she didn't get a move on, but her mother was alerting her to the dangers that lurked beneath the surface of the water. *Reckless! Wantonly reckless! This is just how people end up with their backs broken.*

It was her own fault, of course. She shouldn't have been so silly as to follow the crowd. Just because everyone else had thought it a good idea to drop anchor and spend time diving off the rocks, there had been no need for her to join in. She could have swum happily to the shore and left them to it. But oh, no, she'd had to pretend she wasn't frightened and could go along with them.

'It's quite safe, Izzy,' encouraged Max. 'There aren't any hidden rocks where you are.'

'He's right,' agreed Laura. 'It's so deep none of us have ever reached the bottom.'

'Perhaps if I jumped with you, it would help.' It was Theo, and somehow he had sneaked up behind her without her noticing. But, far from reassuring her, his presence only added to her trepidation. The sight of him with water trickling from his hair, down his neck and shoulders to his chest had her heart shifting to her mouth.

'I know I'm being silly,' Izzy said nervously, 'but I've –

I've always been frightened of diving or jumping into the unknown.'

No! How could she have said that? It was a classic blurt-out-and-repent-at-leisure comment. An open invitation for him to take advantage of her.

Which he did.

'Then take my hand and I will show you what fun it can be.' And before she had a chance to protest he had grasped her hand, counted, '*Éna, dhío, tría*', and taken her with him. She screamed, but remembered just in time to close her mouth. And her eyes. She hit the water feet first, then sank into the cold and the dark, bubbles escaping from her mouth. A helpless, tumbling Alice came into her mind. As well as the thought that at least she had changed out of her skimpy little bikini and worn something that would hopefully stay on. At last she floated up to the surface. Theo was waiting for her. 'Now, was that so very scary?'

She pushed her hair out of her face and blinked salt water from her eyes. She managed a shaky laugh. 'I survived.'

He smiled. 'Another go?'

'Um . . .'

'The answer you are looking for is yes, Izzy. Come, now I will teach you to dive properly. Jumping is for babies.'

Max and Laura had swum to the shore and Izzy could feel them watching her with Theo. 'The trick is to balance the weight and to lean forward,' he said, showing her the correct position to adopt. Shyly, she copied the line of his body, but he turned to her and gently lowered her arms. 'There, that's better. You don't want them too high. Now, this is how you use your hands to cut through the water. You see? Like this.'

After a few hesitant dives her nerves subsided and she began to get the hang of it. By her sixth attempt he proclaimed her a fast learner. 'Congratulations, you are as good as Laura.'

'Is that good?' she asked, swimming alongside him.

'It is very good.'

She turned on to her back and floated, letting the hot sun warm her face. She felt euphoric. She had overcome one of those niggling phobias she had had ever since she was a small child and the sense of achievement was fantastic. She closed her eyes and continued floating happily, smiling to herself, cherishing the feeling.

'You have a lovely body,' Theo remarked, after a few minutes' silence, 'and beautiful legs to go with it.'

Self-conscious, she flipped on to her front.

He laughed. 'Englishwomen are not used to compliments, are they? Anyone would think I had just insulted you.'

'You're probably right.'

'What? You think I insulted you?'

'No. I mean, we're not used to such open flattery.'

'Did your boyfriend not tell you what I have just said?'

'Um . . . not exactly. Not in so many words.'

'Which words did he choose?'

'I can't really remember.'

'Ah, well, if they had been the right words they would have been memorable. Did he hurt you very badly?'

She blushed and swam away from him. She wasn't used to discussing her problems with a man. Not even with Max who, through Laura, knew most of the details of her pathetic relationship with Alan. And now, apparently, so did Theo. 'How much of my hapless love-life has Laura discussed with you?' she asked, as he swam parallel to her.

'Hardly anything. Just that there was a boyfriend who was very cruel to you.'

'He wasn't that bad.'

95

'So why do you let his cruelty linger on? Surely he is past history. He is gone. It is time for you to be happy.'

'I am happy.'

'Are you? You don't always look it.'

His directness made her defensive, and equally candid. 'Well, I'm *sorry* I look so miserable, but when you've given every little bit of yourself to a person and then they smash you apart, it's hard not to keep playing the same game of putting yourself back together. It becomes a habit.'

'Did you really love him so much?'

'Fool that I was, yes, I did. Or perhaps I only thought I did.'

'But that could be hindsight distorting the memory. Let us conclude that you did love him. Did you plan to marry?'

'I was keener than he was. As daft as it sounds, I saw us having children and growing old together. I suppose that must sound very dull to a man like you.'

He frowned. 'Why do you say that?'

'You don't give the impression of being the type to be interested in settling down.'

'Ah, you believe, just as Laura does, that I want to spend the rest of my life playing the field. That I am destined to spend an eternity chasing pretty young girls even when I am wrinkled and white-haired and hobbling round on a stick. Is that the future you predict for me?'

For a moment he looked quite cross, his thick brows drawn together, his eyes narrowed. At a loss to know what to say to placate him, and feeling that she ought to, she said, 'I'm sorry, I didn't . . .' but her words trailed away as in one fluid movement he swam up to her, placed a hand behind her neck and kissed her on the mouth.

The kiss, so sudden, so unexpected, was over almost before she had realised what he was doing, and when he pulled away, he smiled and said, 'Perhaps I just haven't been lucky enough to meet the right woman to settle down with.'

Izzy stared at him, stunned. Where had that come from?

Though it wasn't yet high season, the waterfront at Áyios Stéfanos was busy with boats searching for a mooring spot at the rows of wooden jetties. Max waited patiently for a large tourist-filled caïque to manoeuvre itself into position before he, too, found a suitable space alongside a stylish yacht with a Norwegian flag. He cut the engine and the boat drifted gently into place. Theo helped him secure it, and when all was done they strolled along the jetty to Galini's.

Max had had the foresight to book a table in advance, and it was just as well: the taverna, with its ringside view of the pretty sheltered harbour and all its comings and goings, was almost full. But, then, Áyios Stéfanos was always popular: it was one of the most visited beauty spots along this part of the coast, and despite the number of tourists who came to the small fishing village, it had lost little of its original charm. Theo had considered buying a property here for himself, but in the end he had decided that he preferred the quiet of Áyios Nikólaos with its less obvious congregation of tourists. It always amused him that even on holiday the British needed to be with likeminded folk. Just as they required tea made in a proper pot – none of this bag-in-a-cup nonsense – they needed a safety-net of their own culture around them. Right across the island one could see the invading colonies massing accordingly: the lively youngsters in the south of the island down at Kávos with its sun, sea, sex and cheap package deals; the Kensington-on-Sea crowd in Áyios Stéfanos, with its air of sophistication and quality, and further north, the middle ground of Kassiópi, where the mix of nationalities and type was greatest. But what annoyed Theo most about the British on holiday was their lack of integration. Some visitors came to the island year after year, but never made an effort to get to know the people who lived here or learn to speak Greek. Not even *kaliméra*, or *kalispéra*. Why be so insular? It was beyond him.

They were shown to their table and Max immediately ordered some drinks. The waiter listened politely as he tried to get his tongue round the words and phrases Theo had been teaching him, but only when he stumbled over the word for ice and looked to Theo for help did he come to his aid. '*Págho*,' he said, with a smile.

'Another five minutes and I'd have got it,' laughed Max, when the waiter left them alone.

'Another five minutes and it would have melted,' teased Laura. She opened her menu. 'I don't know about the rest of you but I'm starving. And as for you, Izzy, you must be exhausted after all that expert diving tuition.' She shot Theo a sly sidelong glance.

He gave her a knowing look in return, then immersed himself in his menu. So, she had seen him kiss Izzy, had she? He had wondered at the time if she had noticed. But, as predictable as his actions might have seemed to Laura, it had come as something of a surprise to him. An irrational impulse had seized him and he wished for the life of him that he could explain it.

The waiter returned with their drinks. After they had been handed round, Theo raised his oúzo and ice to his lips and glanced across the table to where Izzy was talking to Max. He knew from the many affairs he'd had, that she really wasn't his type. She was too quiet, too serious, too unsure of herself. Too sexually unaware. And yet . . . and yet there was something about her, something that intrigued him. But what was it? He looked at her hard, studying her face for the answer. It was a face, he decided, that would stay young for many

98

years; a face that would probably grow more beautiful as she aged, and aged gracefully. But there was more to it than that. There was something irresistibly cautious in her expression and he sensed that she was a long way from trusting him. Or trusting any man, for that matter. Was that the attraction, then? Was it, he wondered, with disturbing cynicism, that he saw her as the archetypal vulnerable young girl who needed her broken heart mending? Was it just the machismo challenge?

Aware that a worrying amount of introspection was creeping into his thoughts, he tossed back the remains of his oúzo and turned to Laura on his right to lighten his mood.

'So, Laura,' he said in a low voice, 'what did you think of my little display? Was it just as you would have wanted?'

'Are you referring to the diving lessons? Or what went on afterwards?' Her tone was playful.

'I think you know very well what I am referring to.'

'You played your part beautifully. But, a word of warning, you're not to hurt her. You go only as far as she's prepared to go.'

'Of course. I remember the promise I made this morning, no hearts to be broken. Mine included.'

'What's that about a broken heart?' asked Max, his conversation with Izzy having come to an end.

Theo was saved from lying by the sound of a commotion coming from the jetty nearest to the taverna. They all strained to see what was going on. Somebody, an English woman, was shouting, her furious words skimming across the water faster and more threatening than any tidal wave. 'You stupid, *stupid* man! Gawd help us, couldn't you see us coming?'

Theo smiled. It was Mark's friend, Dolly-Babe.

One of the waiters went to investigate and, no doubt,

99

to ingratiate himself with a potential customer. Anywhere else in the world the woman would have been shooed away as an undesirable punter, but here in Greece business was business.

'What a hoot of a woman,' said Laura, 'and just look what she's wearing. That dress must have been sprayed on.'

She looked much the same as when Theo had met her at the airport and he watched her struggle to climb out of the boat, her legs pinned together at the knees by the impossible tightness of her dress. The young waiter extended his hand and she took it without a word of thanks. Her husband – baggy shorts, florid shirt, white socks, shoes and peaked cap – was left to manage as best he could. Eventually they approached the taverna and the waiter, spying a free table, guided them towards it.

'Oh, no, that won't do at all,' Dolly-Babe said. 'I need to be in the shade. The sun does terrible things to your skin. How about that one over there?' She pointed to a table a few yards away from where Theo and his friends were sitting and which was in full shade. 'Lovely,' she said, settling herself into the chair. 'A crème-de-menthe for me – and, Bob, what'll you have?'

'A large beer.'

The waiter looked apologetic. He was very young, and Theo guessed that his English probably wasn't up to full speed yet. 'Sorry, no crème-de-menthe,' he said.

'What? No crème-de-menthe?'

'You like oúzo? Oúzo very good.'

Dolly-Babe looked positively scandalised, as if she had just been offered a glass of meths. 'No, I don't like oúzo.'

'Retsína?'

She added another expression of disgust to her face. 'Gin. I'll have a gin and tonic, but go easy on the ice. Got that? Oh, and make it a double. A generous double.' She used her hands to indicate that it was a large glass she wanted.

The waiter nodded obligingly, as though he was too stupid to notice her patronising manner, but Theo knew that, despite the young man's faultless courtesy, he would be sorely tempted to spit in her drink before he served it to her.

She took out a lipstick and a small mirror from her handbag and touched up her makeup. She was just messing with her hair when she raised her eyes and caught sight of Theo. She stopped what she was doing. 'Bob!' she hissed across the table. '*Bob!* Look! Isn't that the driver, you know, the driver of that man who sat next to me on the plane? No, there, behind you. I know they all look the same, but I'm sure I'm right. Coo-ee!' A flutter of red nails waved in Theo's direction.

'Good gracious,' said Max, who also had been watching what was going on, 'she's waving at you, Theo. Do you know her? Someone from your past?'

Theo waved back politely, and out of the corner of his mouth, said, 'Max, please, do I look the type to have a past that would include her? Ah, she's coming over. I will explain later, but for now, will you do me the kindness of following my lead?'

'Hello there. What a coincidence meeting you here.'

Theo got to his feet. He bowed and held out his hand. 'All goes well with you on your holiday?'

She laughed loudly. 'Well, it was until some fool Italian geezer drove into our boat. Still, no real damage done. But take it from me, if there had been there'd be hell to pay for.' She raised her sunglasses and cast a curious eye over Theo's companions. 'More people you work for?' she asked.

'Yes. Today Theo Vlamakis *ees* captain of their ship. I bring them here for lunch.'

A stifled snigger from Laura went unnoticed by Dolly-Babe.

'Perhaps I introduce everyone to you? Yes? *Thees ees Meester* Sinclair and *hees* wife, and *thees ees Mees Issy* Jordan.'

'Hi,' she said to everyone. 'I'm Liberty-Raquel Fitzgerald, and over there is my Bob. Where are you all staying?'

'Áyios Nikólaos,' said Max, 'and you?'

'Snap. We're there too. Arrived yesterday. In fact, we were on the same plane that Mr Vlama-vlam-whatsisname here was meeting.'

'Whereabouts in Áyios Nikólaos are you staying?' asked Laura. She seemed to have got the sniggering under control now and sounded all politeness.

'Villa Mimosa. Apparently it's very near Mr St James's place.' She turned back to Theo. 'Mr St James not with you today?'

Theo made another self-deprecating little bow. 'Sadly, no.'

She looked disappointed.

'You have me pass on a message, maybe?'

She hesitated, and Theo could see that she was debating with herself whether or not a foreigner could really be trusted. 'No, that's all right,' she said at length. 'I'll call on him in person. That's probably the best thing to do. But perhaps you could help me. Exactly which villa is it he's staying in? Is it that big posh one right on the end?'

There seemed no point in lying to her, she would find out easily enough anyway, so Theo reluctantly told her that it was indeed the big posh house that Mr St James was staying in.

'I thought it might be,' she said. 'Well, then, I'd best be getting back to my Bob or he'll think I've abandoned him.' She suddenly looked at Izzy. 'You want to be careful sitting in the sun like that, you'll end up with wrinkles. See this complexion,' she used a red nail as a pointer, 'as good as the day I was born with it. And how have I kept it that way? Sunscreen and lots of shade. That's how. Oh, it looks like Sunny-Jim Spiros has pulled his finger out and found us some drinks at last. See you.'

As soon as she was out of earshot, everyone fell on Theo for an explanation.

'Who on earth is she? And why does she think you work for your friend Mark?' asked Laura.

Theo explained about Mark being trapped on the plane with her and her husband and the nicknames he had given them, and his own response at the airport. 'It was a joke on my part. She gave me such a look I could not help myself.'

'What kind of look?' asked Izzy.

'Like this.' He ran his eye over her body, leaving nobody in any doubt what he meant. It was a look that could have peeled a banana. Izzy blushed and lowered her eyes.

'That's a bit rich coming from you, Theo,' said Max. 'Isn't that what you do to every pretty girl who passes your way?'

'But that is different. Greek men are expected to behave like that. Besides, it is second nature to us.'

'Is it, indeed?'

'Ah, but, Laura, it was also her manner. She made the assumption that so many of you Brits make, that because I was Greek I was good for little more than driving a taxi. Believe me, there is nothing that annoys a Greek more than to have his country rubbished, or his humble and generous nature mistaken for stupidity.'

'And you think that's what she was doing?'

'Yes,' said Theo fiercely. 'I was Zorba the Greek to her. A rustic peasant. A parody to be laughed at.'

'But Zorba was a noble and wise man,' Izzy said softly, 'a little excessive, maybe, but not a bad stereotype.'

Hearing Izzy's gentle words and the contrast they made with his own, Theo suddenly realised how petulant he sounded. He raised his hands, his palms facing his friends. '*Lipáme*,' he apologised, with a light laugh, 'please forgive me. In my desire to defend my nation I got a little carried away. I was, as you say, very much on my low horse.'

Nobody was brave enough to correct his English, and the conversation moved on to what they were going to eat. Having already made her choice, Izzy peered discreetly at Theo over the top of her menu. What a surprising man he is, she thought, and not just because he dishes out kisses so freely. Beneath all that light-hearted flirty banter, there was quite a different person. There was a man with strong views, who was quite prepared to reveal foolish ignorance and prejudice in others.

He might not like to believe it, she reflected, disappearing again behind her menu, but he wasn't so dissimilar from the fictional character of Alexis Zorba. Neither man was afraid to confront his desires, and to do so quite openly. Especially their love of women.

She suspected that there was a lot more to Theo Vlamakis than at first met the eye.

Chapter Eleven

By the time they had finished their lunch and paid their bill it was late afternoon. It was still very hot with a perfectly clear sky, but the wind had risen, and the sea was much rougher than when they had set off.

'I hope you're a good sailor,' Max said to Izzy, as they left behind them the calm water of the picturesque harbour and embraced the first of the choppy waves. The boat reared up out of the water then dropped with a suddenness that jolted Izzy almost out of her seat. She placed her hands firmly either side of her and gripped the bench. It was just as well she did: the next wave was bigger than the first and made even Laura give a scream of alarm.

'You'd better hold on tight,' Max shouted over his shoulder, his words only just audible as the wind gusted and whipped them out of his mouth. Spray was coming into the boat, and stung as it struck Izzy's cheek. It was like *The Cruel Sea* but without the duffel coats and cocoa! She wondered if there were any life-jackets on board. She wasn't a bad swimmer and thought she could probably make it to the shore, but what if . . . what if the boat capsized and they were all stuck under it? Or supposing she banged her head and knocked herself unconscious? What then? She gripped the bench harder still, willing her panicky thoughts away.

'There's no need to worry,' said Theo, sitting once again at her side, 'Max knows what he is doing. It is only dangerous if one tries to go too fast.' Then, with a wink, he said, 'His boat may be smaller than mine, but his engine is powerful enough to get us home safely.' He put a protective arm round her shoulders and invited her to lean into him. It was not an invitation she had any intention of turning down. Right then she would have happily accepted reassurance from a peckish Hannibal Lecter.

They weren't the only ones struggling against the elements. In front of them was a boat Izzy recognised, whose departure from the waterfront at Áyios Stéfanos they had watched with amusement. Its departing grace had matched that of its earlier arrival. But this had been after its occupants had joined them for a post-lunch coffee and glass of Metaxá and they had been treated to a brief run-down on the lives of Bob and Dolly-Babe Fitzgerald. Dolly-Babe had done most of the talking but occasionally her husband squeezed a word in. He was here on business, doing a recce of several new resorts that were being built in the south of the island. 'No good looking round here,' he had said. 'Too expensive. Though if I could get a foot in the door, I wouldn't say no. Strikes me this place is in dire need of a massive overhaul.'

'I think you will find *thees* area *ees* protected from any further development,' Theo had said, still maintaining the charade of ignorant taxi-driver and piling on the exaggerated accent.

'What? You mean there's a restriction on any new building work? You sure about that?'

Izzy had wondered how Theo would react to having his word doubted. But with perfect composure, he said, 'It *ees* an area of *houtstanding* beauty. The government *weeshes* it to remain so.'

After this Bob went back to being Silent Bob and Dolly-Babe took up the conversation, telling them how she had met Bob – her diamond in the rough, as she called him. She had been a croupier on a cruise ship and it had been love at first sight with this self-made man who had cracked his first million at the age of twenty-eight from owning a caravan park. Nothing to do with money, then? Izzy had wanted to ask. 'He was my destiny,' Dolly-Babe had said, giving Bob a dig in the ribs with one of her sharp little elbows, 'it was in the cards. And I don't mean the Black Jack cards!' Her raucous laughter had had heads turning their way.

They had gained on the Fitzgerald boat now and Izzy could see Bob at the helm. His wife, pale-faced and shrieking, was telling him in no uncertain terms to slow down. She was also holding on desperately to the remains of her windswept hair-do. When she realised they weren't alone on the high seas, a look of relief passed over her face. Max slowed his speed and came in alongside. 'Ahoy, there,' he said jovially, 'everything all right?'

Bob's response was restricted to an I-can't-see-what-all-the-fuss-is-about expression, but Dolly-Babe's wide-eyed look of near-hysteria told a different story.

'If the engine isn't up to it, it's best to take it slowly,' Max advised. 'It gets even rougher round the next headland.'

'You see?' shouted Dolly-Babe at her husband, who was wearing the look of a man who didn't appreciate the helpful tip he was being given by somebody in a bigger boat than his. His weary face reminded Izzy of her father's expression in the car whenever her mother had instructed him on how best to overtake. 'I told you not to go so fast,' continued Dolly-Babe. 'I knew I was right and you were wrong.' She turned back to Max, as if to say something else, but the combination of a strong swell of water beneath their boats and an increase of pressure from Bob's hand on the throttle had her toppling backwards. She landed with an undignified bump on her skinny bottom and lost one of her high-heeled slip-on shoes. 'Bleeding hell, Bob!' she yelled, just managing to steady herself. 'What the sweet Fanny Adams do you think you're doing? I could have gone overboard.'

Something in Silent Bob's eyes suggested this thought had occurred to him. And not just once.

'Well, so long as you're okay,' Max said. He let out the throttle, turned the boat sharply away, sending up an arc of white spray, and went on ahead. Izzy noticed, though, that he was thoughtful enough not to leave too great a gap between the two boats.

'He is all heart, is he not?' said Theo, in her ear and above the noise of the engine.

'Who, Max?'

'Yes. He is so kind-hearted he would not dream of leaving them to the mercy of the sharks. You are beginning to look very pale. Are you going to be sick?'

They were beyond the headland that Max had warned Silent Bob about and the increase in the pitch and roll of the boat was causing Izzy's stomach to reconsider lunch. 'I hope not,' she said, closing her eyes and mentally crossing her fingers.

From the terrace of Villa Anna, and with the benefit of a pair of binoculars he had found in Theo's study, Mark saw two boats approaching. As they drew nearer he was able to make out Theo and his friends in the leading boat – Theo had his arm around a dark-haired girl, no surprises there – and in the other . . . was that dreadful couple from the plane.

He kept the powerful glasses fixed on the two boats, swinging them from one to the other. He checked out Theo's friends: a man with silver hair was doing all the hard work, probably Max Sinclair, and an attractive woman, his wife presumably, was sitting beside him smoothing back her auburn hair as the wind kept blowing it into her face. And behind them was the girl with Theo. She looked a lot younger than everyone else, in her mid-twenties, perhaps, and of them all seemed to be enjoying herself least. Perhaps she wasn't appreciating the attentions of the pram-chaser sitting next to her, thought Mark wryly.

He watched the two boats battle their way into the shallow, more sheltered water of the bay, until at last they slowed their engines and dropped anchor. The silver-haired man was out first, followed swiftly by Theo who went to assist Silent Bob. They must all be mad, thought Mark, as he watched them chatting on the jetty. From the safety of the terrace, where he had spent most of the day working, he had seen the rapid change in the sea conditions as a strong wind had sprung up, and had wondered how much it would affect Theo and his friends' homeward journey.

He went and sat in one of the chairs by the pool, which was in full sun. He stripped off his shirt and decided that he had finished work for the day. He was pleased with the amount he had got done. He had fully expected, given the dramatic upheaval in his routine, not to get anything of any worth written. Normally when he was working, he had to stick to a strict code of conduct; so ritualistic it was absurd. The first draft of a manuscript was always hand-written in blue ink – real ink from a fountain pen, never a biro. He used W.H. Smith A4 Jotter Pads, with a ruled left-hand margin, though he never wrote close up to it, he always had to leave a further half-inch space clear. There was no reason why he did this, he just had to do it. He put his written pages into black lever-arch files, never any other colour, and any notes he added to the pages once they'd reached the file had to be written in pencil, never pen. It went without saying that he had his collection of lucky pens and pencils. And sure, the next step was lunacy, when he'd be claiming he couldn't work unless he was wearing his lucky boxers. He also had to have music playing in the background, especially when he was doing the final draft on his PC. For his last book he had listened constantly to Bruce Springsteen. He didn't always hear the music, but he heard its absence keenly. It was a cheap brain-washing trick that never failed to fool his subconscious into getting down to work.

Here, though, sitting in Theo's garden with only the cicadas for musical accompaniment, he had been a ritual down, and had had to crank up his brain as best he could. It would be a nice irony if, when he returned home, he was only able to write with the sound of a hundred-piece cicada orchestra playing for him. Fortunately he had already made a good start on the first draft of his latest novel – *Flashback Again* – so at least he had a shove of momentum behind him before he had started this morning.

Flashback Again was his sixth novel, and was proving to be his most ambitious. There were times when he woke in the middle of the night convinced that the plot was unfeasible, convinced, too, that his run of luck was on the verge of ending. As irritating as these disturbed nights were, they were nothing compared to those he had once lived with. During his days as an alcoholic, he had been tormented with nightmares of the most ferocious realism. Nightmares that began with the same hypnotic feel to them but climaxed with a brutal and horrifying dénouement that had him staggering to the nearest sink or loo. He rarely had anything in his stomach, other than alcohol, and he would vomit so violently that he coughed up blood. Unable to get back to sleep he often got dressed and prowled the streets, looking for something to obliterate the fear.

Writing had been Theo's idea. He had put it to Mark when he had insisted that his friend stay with him in Athens after he was discharged from the clinic. They had been sitting in a taverna in Pláka, the old quarter that lay at the foot of the Acropolis, where quiet winding streets and balconies of fragrant jasmine made it an oasis of calm in a crazy city. Athens was robust, disorderly, a place of haphazard growth, where classical old and insolent new rubbed shoulders to create a stupendous disharmony.

'We need to think seriously about what you are going to do next,' Theo had said.

The statement, as true as it was, panicked Mark. In his fragile, vulnerable state, the here and now was all he could cope with. Anything more freaked him out. But he had known that Theo was right: he had to have a plan. He was all too aware of the danger in not having any structure to his days. Previously drugs and alcohol had filled the void in his life; now he had to find something new. If he didn't, he might falter and screw up again.

'I think you should invest your past in your future,' Theo had continued.

'Any suggestions?'

'Yes. Write a book.'

'Just like that?'

'Why not? Despite the number of brain cells you must have destroyed, you are still highly intelligent and more than capable of writing a novel. You have plenty going on inside that head of yours to write at least half a dozen books.'

'It takes more than intelligence. It takes creativity, discipline, and a hell of a lot of determination.'

'You have all of those things, Mark. Think back to our college days when you wrote for those student magazines. Your stuff was far superior to anything else they carried. Think also of the discipline and determination you needed to keep up with the onerous task of feeding your addiction over the years. But that is all behind you. Now it is time for you to divert that energy and allow yourself to reach your full capacity.'

Of course, Theo had only been voicing what had been in Mark's mind ever since he could remember. What big-headed student hadn't imagined that he would produce a life-affirming work of fiction that would set the world alight with its magnificent prose and original line of thought? But it was only now as an adult, now that his head was clear for the first time, that he allowed himself to pursue what had previously been little more than pie in the sky.

Theo had been right on the button when he had said that Mark's past was the key to his future. With his wealth of first-hand experience of fear, writing a psychological thriller had seemed the most natural step for him to take. Fear, after all, begets fear. And who better to play to the dark side of the imagination than somebody who had been there since he was a child?

He wrote his first book in less than nine months while he remained in Athens with Theo. Once or twice, in the early days of his recovery, when Theo needed to travel overseas Mark went with him. 'Believe me, it is not that I don't trust you,' Theo had said, during a flight to Sydney where he was currently negotiating a deal to snap up some prime water-front properties in the harbour, 'It is more a case of keeping an eye on my investment.'

'Theo, you're an obscenely rich, upper-class Greek suburbanite. What the hell kind of investment do you see in me?'

'Ah, but one never knows how things will turn out. Maybe one day you will be the wealthy author and I the penniless Greek peasant. I would then call in my debt.'

'You're forgetting, we're quits. I saved your rotten life and now you've saved mine. The debt's already settled, and seeing as my life is infinitely more valuable than yours, I reckon you owe me.'

The 'debt' had been a long-standing joke between the pair, though its origins were not the least bit funny. In Durham, about a month after they had first met, Mark had been walking aimlessly about the town late one night, as he often did if he couldn't sleep. He had walked along the towpath, down by the river, then headed for the cathedral. There was nobody about, probably because it was so damned cold: a bitter, bone-blasting wind was slicing straight through him, stinging his eyes, making them water. It had rained earlier, and the streets were wet and shining in the soft light cast from the lamps. He stood for a moment to admire the chunky no-nonsense Norman architecture of the cathedral, and to shelter from the worst of the wind. He was just cursing the lack of buttons on his second-hand greatcoat and blowing on his hands to warm them when he heard a scuffling sound, followed by a cry. He retraced his steps to where he thought the noise was coming from and peered into the shadowy gloom of a litter-strewn alleyway. There he saw two lads kicking the hell out of some poor bloke on the ground. The sickening thud of boot on bone galvanised him, as did the sight of the victim's expensive shoes and clothes.

'Hey, you two,' he yelled, 'anybody can work over a ponce like that. How about a real fight?' He shrugged off his coat, threw it on top of a pile of overflowing bin-bags and cardboard boxes, and walked towards them. He must have looked a menacing sight – viciously dyed hair, Doc Martens and a snarl that would have threatened the hardiest mugger. 'Come on, then,' he challenged, 'one at a time, or both together, it makes no odds to me.' He raised his fists and they came at him. He had never approved of the expensive school his parents had sent him to, but now he was grateful for it, especially for the choice of sports on offer, which had included boxing. The first thug received a broken nose for his trouble and ran off. The second, however, was more determined and pulled a wide, jagged-edged knife on Mark. He dodged out of the way to begin with, as the blade flashed and swooped within inches of his face, but then he tripped, lost his balance and fell against the wall. It was a mistake his assailant leaped on, and in one swift movement the cold steel was thrust deep into his side, and was left there as the mugger hightailed it into the darkness. Reeling with pain, and disbelief that this was happening to him – it was a bloody high price to pay for a night of insomnia in anyone's book! – he held his breath, drew out the knife and watched his blood flow through the grubby whiteness of his T-shirt and down his jeans. Clutching his side, he went over to the motionless figure lying on the ground in a filthy puddle. 'You'd better not be dead after all the trouble I've just gone to,' he muttered. But for all his bravado, he flinched at the bloodied mess that had been Theo's face. Pretty boy no more. He bent down to feel for a pulse and nearly lost consciousness at the pain that ripped through him. He pressed his fingers to Theo's neck, located a faint ticking, then, like the thieves before him, rifled through his pockets, knowing that if anyone would have what he needed it would be this flash git. He found what he was looking for and, pushing the clean, neatly folded handkerchief against his side, he got to his feet. He retrieved his coat from the pile of rubbish, covered Theo with it, then made his way to where he knew there was a phone box. He called for an ambulance and staggered back to the alleyway, shivering with cold and shock.

The ambulance soon arrived and Theo, still showing no real sign of life, was put on a stretcher. It was only when Mark dropped the blood-soaked handkerchief from his side, that the extent of his own injury was realised.

He was hailed as a hero by Theo and his family, as well as by the college authorities. Even his own parents, unused to lavishing praise on their youngest son, applauded his bravery.

But he still felt like the same old loser he had always been.

Chapter Twelve

Theo had said his goodbyes and was now climbing the steep path up to Villa Anna, but even when he had put a sizeable distance between him and the jetty, he could still make out Dolly-Babe's jarring voice. She was talking about him as though he couldn't hear or, more probably, as though he was an imbecile who couldn't understand her.

'You'd think he'd make more of an effort, wouldn't you?' she was saying. 'He's a bit too casual for my liking. If I was employing him I'd expect him to wear trousers for work, not shorts. And, if you'll take a tip from me, it doesn't do to be too familiar with the hired help. The next thing you'll know, he'll be taking you for a ride. I suppose he will pass on my message to Mr St James. You never can be sure with his type. Charming, but totally unreliable.'

Theo laughed to himself and was still smiling when he came upon Mark lazing comfortably in a chair beside the pool. His eyes were closed and he looked unusually relaxed and at ease, stripped off to the waist and with his arms raised behind his head. Theo could see the line of the scar that remained from the wound Mark had received on the night he had saved a relative stranger's life. It had laid down the foundations of their friendship and bonded it for ever. They were told by the medical staff at the hospital that they were probably both lucky to be alive. Theo's skull had been fractured, his nose broken and Mark had very nearly had his spleen ruptured. It was while they were lying in adjacent beds the following morning that Theo had thanked Mark for coming to his aid. Through his bruised, swollen lips he had said, 'It is not everyone who would have been brave enough to do what you did. I am very grateful.'

'I didn't feel as if I had any choice,' had been the terse response.

'You could have pretended not to hear and walked away.'

'I'm not that kind of guy. My only regret is that it wasn't a more worthwhile life I'd saved. What the hell were you doing out so late anyway? Some sensible woman denied you access to her bed, did she?'

'I had been to a party.'

'And hadn't got lucky? Hah! Serves you right.'

The exchange was brought to an end with the arrival of Theo's parents. Sweeping into the ward, and seeing the state of him, his mother had burst into a paroxysm of tears. 'It looks worse than it really is,' he said, in an attempt to placate her, his voice raised above her noisy sobbing. Everyone in the ward was watching them, their curiosity aroused by the uninhibited cacophony of a language they couldn't understand. In an effort to calm the situation, Theo indicated Mark and told his parents that if it hadn't been for him he wouldn't be there. 'You must thank him,' he said. 'He was very brave.' Sadly, his words only fuelled his mother's hysteria, but his father glanced across to the other bed and took in the dyed hair. He went over and introduced himself, holding out a cautious hand and regarding the young man, who made such a curious contrast to his son. 'I am very pleased to meet you. You were injured also in the attack?'

'One of them had a knife. It was my own fault, I should have moved quicker.'

Theo's father looked shocked. 'We owe you so much. If there is ever anything we can do to help you, you must allow us to do so. Have you and Theo been friends for long?'

Theo had heard the trace of politely disguised disbelief in his father's voice – surely his son didn't mix with this type of person?

'No,' had been Mark's blunt reply. 'I just happened to be passing.'

If he had expected his remark to end the conversation, it didn't. Instantly his status in Theo's parents' eyes went up: he, a passing stranger, had saved the life of their only son.

'And your parents, are they here too?'

The same blunt reply. 'No.'

Taking a moment off from her weeping, Theo's mother said, 'But they are coming later to see you?'

'They don't know anything about this. And they don't need to know. I'll be out of here at the first opportunity.'

'But what will you do?' Theo had asked. 'Who will take care of you?'

Mark gave him a withering stare as if to say, 'You might be a soft mummy's boy, but some of us can cope on our own. I'll manage, just as I always have.'

When a nurse joined them and insisted that her patients needed to rest, Theo motioned to his father to come back to his side. He spoke in Greek so that Mark wouldn't understand what he was saying and, hoping that Mark wouldn't be too furious with him, he asked his father to see if he could get in touch with Mark's parents.

Later that evening, Mr and Mrs St James arrived, white with worry. But it soon became clear that their concern for their son was as great as his disregard for them. Growing up in a culture that valued families, especially mothers who were loved and revered, Theo was horrified to see how rude and cruel Mark was to his.

'Come to see if I've died yet?' he said, as they stood

looking down at him. 'Well, sorry to disappoint you, but I'm going to be around for a while yet.'

Theo could see from their faces that they were not unused to such brutal comments. He wondered what had gone on in their family to make Mark vent such hatred towards them.

'You're looking very serious,' Mark said, lowering his arms and squinting into the sun as he looked up at Theo. 'Though from what I saw of you in the boat, it looked as if your charm was having no great effect. Perhaps that's why you look so miserable.'

Theo spotted the binoculars beneath Mark's seat, and smiled. 'As you well know, what you see on the surface is not always the true picture.'

'Oh, come off it, Theo, you're losing it. And, besides, she's way too young for you. There's nothing dignified about an ageing pram-chaser.'

Theo raised an eyebrow. 'And, there speaks the man with a string of successful relationships behind him.'

'Yeah, well, relationships aren't my thing. But at least I gave marriage a go, as brief as it was, which is more than can be said of you. Do you want a drink? I was just going in for one.' Up on his feet, he added, 'Oh, and by the way, somebody phoned while you were out. I left his message on your desk in your study. He said you were to ring him soon as you could.'

Minutes later, when they had poured themselves a drink and Theo had dealt with the phone call, they went back outside into the sunshine by the pool. Theo said, 'She is not so very young, you know.'

'Who?'

'The girl in the boat.'

'And does this girl in the boat, who is *not so very young*, have a name?'

'Izzy. Izzy Jordan. She is staying with my neighbours, the Sinclairs.'

'And?'

Theo leaned back in his chair. 'I cannot put my finger on it, but there is something about her that is quite appealing.'

With a wry laugh, Mark said, 'You mean she's a woman?'

'There is that.'

'And with a click of your fingers you assume you can have her, don't you? God, you make me sick. You don't change, do you?'

'Aha, the green-eyed monster makes his appearance once more.'

'Oh, shut up! Of course I'm not jealous. Just deeply cynical.'

'You never have been able to stomach my success with—'

'Please, Theo, not that old number. If I wanted to spend all my time chasing a cracking pair of legs, then I would do exactly that. What's more, I'd make a better job of it than you!'

Theo grinned. 'So you noticed her legs, did you?'

'I was speaking generally,' snapped Mark.

'Well, my old friend,' he taunted, 'all I will say is that if she is too young for me, she is too young for you also.'

'Look, I told you, I wasn't talking specifically. It was a stupid chauvinistic turn of phrase. And, anyway, didn't you just say she was older than she looks?'

Theo conceded the point to Mark, sipped his drink and listened to the waves crashing on the rocks below. It always amused him when they argued like this. It was a familiar routine they went through, an enjoyable game they had played since they were students: Mark, full of cynical, vitriolic disapproval, and he full of his own self-importance, as they battled it out each trying to prove the other wrong. In the old days there had been no surer way to fire Mark up. 'Oh, I nearly forgot to tell you,' he said brightly, 'I have good news, and I have bad. Which do you want first?'

'Go on, then, give me the bad. You know how I like to punish myself.'

'Your ladyfriend, Dolly-Babe, she is determined to meet you again. She is talking of inviting you to have a cosy drink with her and Silent Bob. She wants Max and Laura and Izzy to go as well, and is planning to call round and make her invitation in person.'

Mark's face darkened. 'Well, she can forget it. I shan't be going. I trust you did the decent thing and made a suitable excuse for me.'

Theo shifted in his seat.

'Theo? You did, didn't you?'

'I could not easily turn down an invitation on your behalf. You have to remember, she still thinks I am no more than the hired help for the wealthy visitors to the island.' He explained how he had pretended to be employed by Max and Laura for the day, and also how Dolly-Babe must have decided at the last minute that he was trustworthy enough to pass on a message. 'She thinks this is your villa and that I am your live-in chauffeur.'

'You idiot. What are you going to do when she finds out the truth?'

He shrugged. 'What do I care what she says or thinks any more than she cares for what I think or do?'

'So if that was the bad news, cheer me up with the good.'

'Ah, the good news is that you will see less of me than you thought. That phone call was a summons for me to return to Athens the day after tomorrow. Yes, I thought that would cheer you. You will have the place to yourself. It will be a pleasant and peaceful holiday for you.'

'You're forgetting, I'm not here on holiday, I'm here to work.'

*

'Well, what have you got to say for yourself?'

Max had taken himself off for a late-afternoon siesta, leaving Laura and Izzy alone on the veranda, which meant that Laura was now giving Izzy a thorough grilling on the events of the day. 'I saw him kiss you,' she said, 'so don't try and make out that nothing happened.'

'It wasn't much of a kiss, it was only—'

'Not much of a kiss! This is Theo we're discussing. How many times in your life have you been kissed by a man as heart-stoppingly gorgeous as him?'

Izzy blushed. 'I was going to say it was so quick that it was over before I had a chance to think about it.'

Laura gave her a cunning smile. 'But you've had plenty of time since. Time in the boat as well when he had his arm around you.'

'Sorry to disappoint you, but I felt too sick in the boat to think of anything other than getting my feet back on *terra firma*. Is it always as bad as that? Because if so, count me out on any other expeditions that involve water.'

'It was particularly rough this afternoon. We're probably in for a run of similar days. But back to you and Theo.'

'Oh, Laura, don't be absurd. I'm sure he did it out of force of habit. Or, more likely, he did it to see how I would react.'

'From where I was sitting, I thought you were very cool about it.'

'What did you expect me to do? Slap his face? It was only a kiss.' As nonchalant as she forced herself to sound, Izzy knew that was the last thing she felt when she thought of Theo. She had known him no longer than a blink of an eye, but it was long enough to know that he made her feel nervous.

It was nervousness born of the fear that he might be capable of making her do something she would regret.

Chapter Thirteen

Early the next morning, without disturbing Max and Laura, Izzy crept out of the villa and went for a walk along the beach. The air was fresh and clean, and the sea sparkled as though someone had been up all night polishing it. There was nobody else about as the bleached white stones crunched noisily beneath her feet and she felt guilty to be disturbing the serenity of the day. *There you go again, Isobel Jordan, ruining it for everyone else! Can't you ever be quiet?*

She paused to admire the stunning view where, across the soft blue of the water, a layer of mist entwined itself around the Albanian hills. Slipping her bag of sketching things off her shoulder, she sat down, rummaged for her pencil and paper, and cast her eyes for something to sketch. She settled on the half-way point in the bay, to her right, focusing on one particular spot, where a small formation of circular rocks jutted out like chunky discs from a toy construction kit.

Minutes later, and unhappy with her drawing, she put it aside and lay back on the stones, which were already warm from the sun. She closed her eyes and thought how lucky she was to be here. It was so kind of Max and Laura to invite her to spend the summer with them. But, then, that was Max and Laura all over, generous and big-hearted, eager for those around them to enjoy life as much as they did. She had been touched by this spirit of generosity right from the outset of getting to know them. 'It was lucky I was parked in your way,' Max had joked.

'You've got to be very careful who you tangle bumpers with these days. There are some strange people about.'

'Yes, darling,' Laura had said, 'you for one! Would you like to stay for supper, Izzy? It's only a lamb hotpot, nothing special.' The invitation had taken her by surprise. She had caused goodness knows how many hundreds of pounds' worth of damage to a man's car and here was his wife offering her a meal. She accepted the invitation and stayed until nearly midnight, not realising how the time was flying by as they laughed and chatted. As he helped Izzy into her coat when she insisted that she really had to go, Max had said to Laura, 'Why don't you invite Izzy to go along to that pseudo-intellectual-artsy-fartsy group you've recently joined?'

Laura had laughed. 'It might not be Izzy's idea of a fun evening. To be honest, I'm not sure that it's mine. I've only been to three sessions, but it seems to be an excuse for a lot of legitimised snobbery in the name of appreciating art.'

But that was how Izzy's friendship with Laura had really taken off. They had become allies as they sat at the back of the class in the draughty village hall, trying not to laugh at the pretentious lecturer as he pranced about the creaking wooden floor with his bow-tie, *pince-nez* and hand-embroidered waistcoats. 'Brian Sewell meets Lionel Blair,' Izzy had whispered to Laura, two minutes into the first class. Luckily the lecturer was so caught up in the sound of his own pedantic voice that he didn't hear them sniggering. However, from then on one or two other members of the group went out of their way to give them looks of open hostility. 'Oh dear, I'll be getting you a terribly bad name,' Izzy had said in the car on the way home, later that evening.

'No worse than it already is,' Laura had said. 'Don't forget the crazy man I'm married to.'

With her head resting on the stones, Izzy was alerted to

the sound of footsteps. She sat up and saw Theo approaching. He was dressed for a swim, which meant that, other than a towel slung loosely around his shoulders, he was wearing only a pair of swimming shorts. Seeing her, he raised his hand and made his way along the sunlit beach.

'Hello, Izzy,' he said, drawing level and sitting beside her, 'you're up very early.'

'So are you.'

'Ah, with me, it is habit. And you? What is your excuse?'

'It seems a shame to waste a single moment here. It's so lovely. I'm beginning to wonder if I'll be able to leave when it's time to go back to England.'

'But that is such a long way off. There is no need for you to think of that now. Allow yourself to enjoy what you have today, don't spoil it with tomorrow's anxieties. You have been drawing, eh?' He reached a hand over her legs to the discarded sketchpad. He studied it for a few seconds then raised his eyes to the rocky outcrop she had drawn. 'This is very good. Do you draw people as well?'

'I do, but not very well. I can't do noses. It doesn't matter who they are, they all end up with the same nose.'

'Anyone's in particular?'

She laughed. 'A Medici hawk-nose, so don't ever ask me to do your portrait.'

He laughed too and held her gaze. 'Would you have dinner with me tonight?'

When she didn't say anything, he passed her the sketchpad. 'My question has surprised you?'

'Um . . . What about your guest?'

'You want him to join us?'

She could see that he was teasing her. 'I meant, won't it be rude leaving him on his own?'

'He is a good friend. He will not mind. Or maybe you

are prevaricating. Perhaps you do not want to have dinner with me. Is it possible that you don't trust me?'

Yes, he was definitely teasing her. But as his dark eyes bored into hers, she found herself wondering whom she trusted less. Him with his smooth, worldly charm, or herself with her pitiful inexperience.

As if sensing her thoughts, he said, 'I will behave very well with you, Izzy. I will be the perfect gentleman. You will be quite safe.'

Now, where had she heard that before?

Then suddenly it wasn't Theo sitting next to her, but Alan. Alan making the same claim – *You're quite safe with me.*

Instantly any notion of saying yes to Theo was blown away. A tornado of anger ripped through her, Theo was after only one thing, and once he'd got it, he would be on his way, laughing quietly to himself with not a thought for her feelings.

What a monumental fool she had so very nearly made of herself.

And how much easier could she have made it for him?

Well, this was one notch on the bedpost that he wouldn't be carving.

To the sound of Modern Woman cheering in approval, Izzy slid her things into her bag and stood up. 'You're right,' she said, looking down at him, 'I don't trust you. But don't take it personally. Enjoy your swim.' To her ears, there was no bitterness in her words, just a reassuring ring of finality. And triumph. This was an important victory for her self-esteem.

Puzzled, Theo watched Izzy stride away. Was it something he had said?

Over breakfast at Villa Anna, he put the same question to Mark. 'Clearly I said something to offend her, but I cannot think what it was.'

Mark laughed. 'I told you yesterday. It's time to face up to it – you're losing it, mate.'

Banging his cup of coffee down on the table, and spilling some, Theo said, 'Mark, please, I am being serious.'

'Hey, easy there, Casanova. So why does it bother you so much that she turned you down? Is it really such a strange phenomenon for you?'

'I know what you're thinking, that it's merely vanity, but it is more than that, I promise you. I am concerned that I may have upset her.'

'And that bothers you?'

'You seem surprised.'

'Well, put it this way. We could sit here until this evening putting together a list of all the women you must have upset at some time or other in a life given over to the thrill of the chase. Admittedly your game-plan never included deliberately hurting them, but think how used they must have felt when you moved on to the next conquest.'

'Oh, but you're wrong. They used me as much as I used them.'

'Maybe some of them did, but I bet the majority thought they would mean something more to you than a casual affair. As deluded as they were, I guarantee that they all thought they would be the one to change you.'

'To tie me down?'

Mark shook his head. 'No. To make you fall in love with them.'

'But you know as well as I do, nobody can make another person fall in love with them.'

'But isn't that what you've always tried to do? Isn't that why you continually pursue one woman after another? You want them to love you. Just as I pursued drugs and alcohol with such conviction, so you have used women. I don't think it's labouring the point when I say you're probably addicted to the attention women give you.'

Even if Theo had got an answer for Mark's outrageous statement, which he hadn't, he was let off the hook by the appearance of Angelos, who had come to clean the pool and tend the garden.

Another time.

Chapter Fourteen

Until now Max had been listening to Laura and Izzy's conversation with only half an ear, but something in their tone diverted his attention from his breakfast-time reading of the latest exploits of the old-enough-to-know-better woman and her schoolboy lover. The story, though no longer front-page news, was maintaining a good head of steam. Apparently they were still on the run, their whereabouts a mystery, but they were popping up everywhere: there had been sightings of them in Taunton, Hull, Dublin and the Algarve.

'But why, Izzy? Why did you say no to him?'

Lowering his paper and glancing at his wife's face, Max thought he detected more than just mild disbelief in her expression. 'Well, if anyone's interested in my opinion,' he said, 'as fond as I am of Theo, I think it serves the cocky devil right. It's about time somebody gave him a metaphorical knee in the groin. Well done, Izzy. Good for you.'

'You're only saying that because you're jealous,' said Laura, giving him a look he couldn't quite fathom.

'Jealous, my little honey-pie?' he responded, trying to share a conspiratorial wink with Izzy, but failing miserably. Her eyes were on Laura. 'Of what precisely?'

'Like most men, you're envious of one of your number who has a flair for—' She stopped short, as if thinking better of what she had been going to say.

'What flair would that be?' asked Izzy, her face like thunder. 'Would it by any chance have something to do with him thinking he has the ability to lead the stupidest of fools straight to his bed? And is that what you want for me? A one-night stand that leaves me feeling used and abused? Well, is it?'

'Of course not,' Laura said defensively, 'but you're deliberately and wildly distorting the situation.'

Max didn't consider himself the most observant or sensitive of men, but even he sensed the air of tension around the breakfast table. He had never seen Izzy look cross before. He had seen her miserable and upset, but never angry. Especially not towards Laura. Back at home when Laura and Francesca were having one of their occasional spats, he would leave them to it, retreating to the sanctuary of the office, but here escape wasn't going to be so easy. He folded his paper carefully, put it on the ground beside his chair and said, 'I know I'm a dull old fellow when it comes to finer feelings and sub-plots, but has something been going on of which I've been kept in ignorance? Or are you both having a bad bout of PMT?'

When Laura didn't respond, even after he had thrown in the patronising query about PMT – he had thought it might unite the women and consequently defuse the moment – his suspicions were aroused. There was more going on here than he had imagined. 'Laura, you haven't gone behind Izzy's back and tried to fix her up with Theo, have you? Not Theo. Not him of all men.'

Both Max and Izzy waited for Laura to deny the accusation.

But Laura didn't.

Which was proof enough to confirm her guilt.

'It's not as bad as you're making out,' she said. Her words were directed at Max but her eyes were on Izzy. 'Oh, come on, Izzy, we discussed it. We agreed it might be good for you. Just a bit of fun.'

'No, Laura, you took the line that it would be good for me. And had I known that you and Theo were already in cahoots planning my seduction I would never have listened to a word you had to say about him.'

'I thought it would give you a lift – you know, give you back some of your self-esteem.'

'Oh, well, that makes perfect sense. I see it all now. There I'd be, thinking how wonderful it was that Theo was paying me so much attention and I'd have you to thank for my self-esteem being so high it was in need of oxygen.' Her voice was tight with cynicism.

To his dismay, Max knew it was down to him to bring about a truce. He did it almost every day at work, bringing headstrong and opposing views to meet half-way to find a compromise, but caught between the woman he loved, who had obviously meddled too far, and a close friend who was giving out more distress signals than a sinking ship, he knew which of the two options he'd rather deal with. Emotions were best left to experts. 'I'm sure you meant well, Laura,' he said tactfully, 'but I really do think you should apologise to Izzy.'

All three sat in silence for some moments. Until, at last, Laura offered Izzy a hesitant, conciliatory smile. 'I'm sorry,' she said, 'truly I am. You know I wouldn't do anything to hurt you. Am I forgiven?'

Max turned to Izzy, willing her to accept the olive branch. And to add a note of reviving humour to the mood round the table, he said, 'Come on, Izzy, I know Laura was way off the mark with what she did, but let's face it, only a fool would take a man like Theo seriously.' As soon as the words were out, he realised it was the worst thing he could have said. He received a kick under the table from Laura and a look from Izzy of mingled fury and pain. Appalled at his clumsiness, he wished now that he'd not got involved.

Izzy could see his discomfort and knew that all she had to do to make everything right was swallow her pride and laugh the matter off. But she couldn't. She was too choked with anger – which was made all the worse by knowing that she had been in danger of taking Theo seriously. Of *wanting* to take him seriously.

Not trusting herself to speak, she stood up and left Laura and Max to finish breakfast on their own.

'Should I go after her and apologise?' she heard Max say, as she headed for the beach.

'No,' said Laura. 'Between us, I think we've both said and done enough. Let's give her space to cool off.'

By the time Izzy had stomped part-way down the steep hillside in the baking sun and had lingered awhile to take in the fragrant scent of pine on the air, her fury had begun to subside. She suspected that in such beautiful surroundings it would be difficult for anyone to maintain a bad mood for long. It was probably what made the Corfiots as warm and gregarious as they were. Life was too good to harbour a grudge for more than a couple of minutes. She pressed on down the path and along the beach, towards the rocky outcrop she had tried earlier to draw. She knew that, as a guest in somebody else's house, she was behaving atrociously. She also knew that she was far more angry with herself than she was with Max and Laura.

Only a fool would take a man like Theo seriously.

'Well, there's no bigger fool than Izzy Jordan,' she muttered. She threw herself on the hot white stones and sighed. Then did a double-take.

She wasn't alone. A man was sitting on one of the rocks a few yards from her. She had seen him here before, had noticed him from her balcony when she had been painting the bay. He was sideways on to her, and though she couldn't make out all of his face, she could see that his attention was held by a fishing-boat rising and falling on the swell of the incoming tide. He was very still, and had an absorbed, faraway look. He didn't look relaxed, though: his lean, rangy frame was taut, his back and shoulders slightly rounded, as if he were ready for flight, should the need arise. Suddenly she longed to have her sketchpad to hand. He had an interesting face, what she could see of it, with a side profile that was pale, angular, and caught in a frown of concentration. She could only see his left eye, but she liked the way it was narrowed against the sun, and the starburst of lines that creased his skin. He was clean-shaven, with fair hair long enough to be messed up by the warm sea breeze. Every now and then he pushed it out of his face with long fingers. The sleeves of his T-shirt, one slightly ripped under the armpit, flapped loosely in the wind and accentuated the thinness of his arms. Unlike Theo, he didn't look like a man who gave much thought to his appearance. She wondered who he was and which villa he was staying at. Was it possible that he was Theo's writer friend, Mark St James? He was about the right age.

Drawing her knees up to her chest and clasping her arms around them, she closed her eyes and concentrated her thoughts so that by the time she returned to the villa she would be able to commit him to paper.

Watching the men on the boat finish hauling in their bundles of yellow nets, metal weights banging on the side of the boat, shaking heads indicating their disappointment at catching only a couple of slippery grey squid, Mark was reminded of similar scenes he had witnessed back in Robin Hood's Bay when, at the end of the day, the fishermen brought home empty lobster pots.

As the boat puttered away, he turned his head towards the shore. He recognised Izzy instantly, and while her eyes were shut he took the opportunity to see what it was about her that had Theo so intrigued. Based on what he knew about Theo's taste in women, his conclusion was vague. It had to be her naturalness, he surmised, after he had taken in the slender figure dressed in khaki shorts and vest top; the long evenly tanned legs drawn up so that she was resting her chin on them, and the loose, dark-brown shoulder-length hair that was being tossed in the wind. She was what he called a low-maintenance girl and he found himself thinking that there was a comfortable haphazardness about her that he strongly approved of. And, with growing certainty, he decided that this was what appealed to Theo. He was captured by her lack of sophistication. She would make a change from the glamorous, hard-faced beauties he usually went in for.

He continued to watch her, struck by the odd pose she had adopted, and for such a length of time. With her eyes squeezed shut, it was as if she was concentrating hard on something. Maybe she was meditating.

He had been encouraged to have a go at meditation when he was in rehab, which he hadn't found easy, given that he had spent a lifetime running away from what went on in his disorderly brain – sitting in silence and trying to be at peace with a person who had scared the hell out of him ever since he could remember was not something to which he'd taken. Bones had suggested that perhaps he should forget whose head he was trying to get inside, and after whistling Carole King's 'You've Got A Friend', while unwrapping a Murraymint, the sly old devil had said, 'Think of somebody you admire. A friend, perhaps. A friend who has had a great influence on you.'

In other words, think of the man who cared enough to bring you here.

Irritating as the suggestion was, it had worked. By focusing on Theo and the reasons why they were friends, he had found himself dwelling less on the negative facets of his own life and more on the positive. It was a lesson in counting one's blessings.

Back in Durham, lying alongside Theo in the hospital after his parents had made their unexpected, futile visit, he had turned on Theo with a savagery that even now he was ashamed to recall. 'I suppose that was your bloody doing, was it? Had a word with somebody, did you? Flashed some cash to pull some strings?'

'But why would you not wish for your parents to know that you needed their help?' Theo had asked.

'Listen, pal, I don't need my parents' help. Got that? In fact, it's the last bloody thing I need. And I certainly don't need your interference. So butt out of my life or I'll finish off what those fools couldn't manage last night.'

Luckily for him, Theo had paid no attention to anything he said and when they were discharged from hospital Theo enlisted Mr and Mrs Vlamakis' help to take care of him. While Mark had no qualms in telling his own parents to shove off, he was not so rude as to treat Theo's parents in the same offhand manner. He realised quickly that he had no choice but to give in to their offers of help. They took one look at the room he was living in and whisked him away to stay in some five-star luxury accommodation: a recently restored town-house, which they had bought for Theo at the start of term. Only when Mr Vlamakis was convinced that his son and heir was going to survive his ordeal did he return to London, leaving his wife to fuss over her charges. And fuss she did.

'You might just as well give in gracefully,' Theo told him one evening, when his mother was in the kitchen preparing yet another meal of gigantic proportions to build up their strength. 'My mother will not rest until she has you fully recovered.'

It was during those weeks that Mark had grown grudgingly to like Theo. If nothing else, he had to admire him for his tenacity. It didn't matter how rude Mark was, Theo simply flung aside his insults with a single-minded determination that was unshakeable.

'Why are you doing this for me?' Mark asked him one

night, when Theo's mother was on the phone to her husband giving him the latest update on Theo's progress – to their great relief, the cuts and bruises to his handsome face were relatively superficial and there would be no long-term scarring: the skull fracture was healing and prompt surgery had also ensured that his nose would eventually be as good as new.

'Because in spite of everything you do and say I find myself liking you.'

'Well, you shouldn't.'

'Why not?'

'I'll bring you bad luck.'

Theo had laughed. 'So far history has proved you wrong. Have you forgotten already that you saved my life? It was the greatest of luck for me that you were passing that night.'

From that day on, Theo swore that if ever Mark needed his help, it would be there for the asking. It was one of his typically over-the-top gestures but, all the same, it was a promise he more than lived up to. And although in theory he and Theo had cancelled the debt between them, Mark still felt that Theo was in credit. Anyone would have done what Mark had done, that cold wintry night in Durham, but not everybody would have had sufficient faith or patience to stand by Mark during the worst of his addiction days, then support him on the long, painful road to recovery.

Once again he turned his gaze back to the girl on the stones, and the thought occurred to him that if Theo was serious about this Izzy – and Mark had every reason to believe that he was, judging from his mood at breakfast – then maybe he could help. A few choice words from him and perhaps she would view Theo more favourably. He smiled to himself, thinking of the irony that he, of all people, should consider himself qualified to further Theo's love-life.

He was still mulling over this thought when he realised that the girl was on her feet and walking along the beach towards the path that would take her up the hillside. Well, if he had hoped to put a good word in on his friend's behalf, he had just lost his opportunity.

Chapter Fifteen

The following week slipped by in a languid haze of quiet inertia and as the month of July progressed, bringing the height of the holiday season ever nearer, there was an increase in visitors to the island. In Kassiópi, the shops and bars, the tavernas and apartments were steadily filling, adding an extra width to the smiles on the faces of their owners. Inland, the temperature continued to soar, but the wind that blew in across the water brought a refreshing coolness to Áyios Nikólaos. And this morning, as Izzy lay in bed watching the muslin drapes billowing gently at the open french windows, she thought she had seldom felt so happy or relaxed.

Even the ridiculous scene that had taken place last week with Max and Laura caused her only an occasional pang of guilt. When she had returned to the villa after calming down on the beach, she had found Laura on her own and apologised straight away. 'I'm sorry,' she had said. 'I behaved worse than a stroppy teenager. Forgive me, please?'

'I'm sorry too,' Laura had said. 'I shouldn't have been acting so deviously. Max has all but put me over his knee and smacked my bottom.'

'And don't think I wouldn't try it,' he had called from his den, where he was reading a roll of faxes that had come in that morning. Then he had poked his head out through the open window and said, 'I'm sorry too, Izzy, for shooting my big mouth off without first engaging my heat-fried brain.'

'Oh, stop being so nice the pair of you,' she had said, 'you're making me feel a hundred times worse, I'm shrivelling up with embarrassment.'

'Don't do that, there's little enough of you as it is. Now stop pestering me, I've got work to do, an honest crust to earn. Talking of which, we're out of bread. Any chance of you two making yourselves useful by going shopping?'

'Yes, O Master,' Laura had laughed, 'and when we get back shall we throw ourselves at your feet and worship you?'

'Now you're talking. By the way, ask Nicos if he's got any of that decent olive oil he keeps under the counter. Tell him he's not to palm us off with that overpriced stuff he sells to the tourists.'

'Anything else, O Bossy One?'

'Yes, you can take some travellers' cheques and change them. We're running low on cash.'

'He's missing work, bless him,' Laura had muttered to Izzy, with a smile, when Max had disappeared from view, 'feeling the need to assert himself.'

On the way up the hill to the supermarket, Izzy had tried to explain to Laura why she had been so cross. 'It wasn't you I was angry with, it was me,' she had said, as they plodded breathlessly in the dry heat. 'I realised that I was stupidly following the same old route I've been down before. Needy old Izzy, so desperate for a bit of affection she was gullible enough to be flattered by a good-looking man and not care about the consequences. Honestly I could kick myself for my naïvety.'

'You don't think you're being too hard on yourself?' Laura said. 'After all, he was only inviting you to have dinner with him.'

'Oh, come on, men like Theo expect something in return, it's an unspoken agreement. They think they're on a promise.'

'Not necessarily. And anyway, it's down to you

whether or not you go along with such an unspoken agreement.'

'But don't you see? That's the whole problem. I'd be taken in by him, wouldn't I? A few nice words, a kiss or two, and heaven only knows what I'd be getting myself into.'

'Well, let's forget about Theo and all his kind. We've got to decide what we're going to do with our time before the hordes arrive. I recommend a week of doing nothing because, believe me, when Francesca and Sally arrive along with Max's parents, it'll be a non-stop whirl of activity.'

The weather was so hot over the following days that they had given in to lethargy and lazed around the villa and the beach. Their only exercise, other than swimming, was their evening walk into Kassiópi where they had supper in the harbour. Sometimes they were too lazy to do even that and one of them would draw the short straw and drive. They didn't see anything of Theo. According to a message relayed by Sophia and Angelos, he had flown back to Athens on business leaving his house-guest to work in peace. 'You don't suppose we ought to see if he'd appreciate an evening's worth of company?' Max had asked hopefully. He was still anxious to meet the elusive Mark St James. 'It seems rude not to check on him, just to see if he's okay.'

But Laura had been firm. 'Sophia and Angelos are there every other day,' she said. 'If there was a problem they'd be on to it.'

'You don't think he would—'

Laura had sat on his lap, silenced him with a kiss, and told him to wait until Theo returned. 'If you're good I might invite them both for dinner when your parents and the girls are here. I'll even flirt outrageously with Theo to ensure he brings his friend with him. How does that sound?'

Max had kissed her back. 'Not too outrageously, I hope.'

Yawning now, and stretching her arms above her head, Izzy decided it was time to get up. Everyone was arriving today and she had promised to help Laura with some of the last-minute arrangements.

She found her friend in the kitchen, pouring olive oil over a large piece of meat. 'Lamb with rosemary and garlic,' she said, when she saw Izzy. 'I know it's a disgusting sight at this time of the day, but I thought I'd get it prepared now before it gets so hot that I won't feel like doing it. Just pass me that salt mill, will you?'

They worked together steadily for the next couple of hours. While Laura concentrated on the evening meal, Izzy got on with making a selection of scones and cakes.

'I know it's madness,' said Laura, as Izzy weighed out flour and sugar, 'but wherever they are in the world, Max's parents have to stop what they're doing and have afternoon tea. It's quite an obsession with them. Though I'm probably the nuttier one for pandering to them. After today I shan't go on spoiling them – they'll be on local cakes and pastries.'

Izzy had met Corky and Olivia Sinclair several times before and knew that they were a wonderful couple who enjoyed life to the full. Max joked that whenever they came to stay an air-raid warning had to be sounded so that anyone with a weak disposition could head for the hills.

'As you know, for a pair of septuagenarians they're extremely boisterous,' Laura said now, as she stood at the sink washing her hands. 'They'll be far more trouble than Francesca and Sally, and that's saying something.'

In the preceding days, there had been much talk of Nympho Sally, as Max called Francesca's friend, and Izzy had been told why he was so terrified of her. At a Christmas party last year, she hadn't realised that he was

Francesca's father and had come on to him like a pouting, hip-wiggling Marilyn Monroe, dangling a piece of mistletoe in front of his nose and making a pass at him. Even when she had found out who he was, she hadn't seemed bothered. 'She wasn't the slightest bit embarrassed,' Max said.

'Unlike my poor innocent husband,' laughed Laura.

'And the worst of it was she wasn't drunk.'

'Weren't you a tiny bit flattered?'

'No, Izzy, I wasn't. Terrified, more like. So I'd appreciate it if you both promise not to leave me alone with her.'

'Oh, go on with you,' Laura teased, 'you're flattering yourself. She's got all those handsome waiters in Kassiópi to amuse her. You won't get a look in.'

'Thank God for that.'

'And let's not forget Theo,' Izzy had added. 'Sounds like she's bound to make a play for him. Perfect sugar-daddy material.'

Max had laughed heartily. 'A match made in heaven. Oh, thank you, Izzy, you've quite cheered me.'

But Laura had pulled a face at them. 'I think the pair of you are being quite unfair to Theo. He's nowhere near as bad as you're making him sound. I bet you any money you like that there's more to him than meets the eye.'

And now, as Izzy took the tray of scones out of the oven and slipped them on to a wire rack, she recalled that she, too, had thought the same when they were having lunch in Áyios Stéfanos. Well, maybe there were hidden depths to Theo, but one thing she was sure of: if there were any depths to explore it wouldn't be her who would risk getting the emotional bends from trying to fathom him out.

Max was the spitting image of his father, and seeing them together always amused Laura; it gave her a clear view of what her husband would be like in years to come. There were the obvious similarities between them: they were the same height, the same width – which naturally they disputed, each claiming the other had the larger paunch – and had the same hair colouring, with Max's nearly as white as his father's. But beyond that there was the same thoughtfulness for others, as well as a shared artless and self-deprecating humour, and neither was afraid to shoot straight from the hip. Corky was doing so now.

They were sitting outside in the shade on the terrace having tea, Francesca and Sally having gone down to the beach to make a start on their tans. 'You look as if you've gained some more weight,' Corky was saying to Max. 'Those shorts look a tad tight to me.' He was gloating with delight, having just boasted for the last ten minutes that he had lost half a stone. He gave his not-obviously depleted waistline a pat. 'You've been living too much of the high life,' he continued. 'It'll be your downfall, mark my words.'

'In your dreams, Dad,' said Max, while discreetly sucking in his stomach. 'Snake-hips Max is what Laura calls me, these days. Isn't that right, cupcake?'

She smiled back at him. 'Among other things, darling. More to eat, anyone?' She offered the last of the chocolate sponge cake Izzy had made that morning, there being nothing else left on the table: Corky and Olivia had all but licked the plates clean – goodness knows where they put it all. Or where they got their energy. They had only been here for a few hours but they had already devoured a hearty lunch, gone for a walk, unpacked their cases and stored them neatly under their beds. Laura felt drained of what little energy she had started out with. It was worse than having a houseful of teenagers. 'How about you, Olivia? Another slice of cake?'

She shook her head. 'I'd love another cup of tea, though. Any more in the pot?' Olivia could drink tea for

England. There was nobody to touch her. She had even brought with her a supply of Twinings English Breakfast.

Izzy rose from the table. 'It won't be worth drinking now, I'll make you some fresh.'

'Oh, thanks, Izzy. Now what about you, Corky? Have you got room for another slice?'

Max's father looked longingly at the cake.

'Best to keep it all tidy,' he said. 'You can't keep food lying about in this heat.'

By the time Izzy had returned with a fresh pot of tea, every last crumb had gone and Corky and Olivia wanted to know the itinerary for the days ahead.

'I thought we could go over to the other side of the island tomorrow and show you Paleokastrítsa,' Laura said, thinking of the long climb up the hill to the monastery, hoping it might tire them out and make them want to have a day off to recover. The suggestion had Corky reaching for his guidebook. 'Here we are,' he said, flicking to the appropriate page. '"Paleokastrítsa,"' he read aloud, '"sixteen miles from Corfu Town and the island's most celebrated beauty spot."' He turned the book round and held it aloft so that everyone could see where they would be going. He pointed out the monastery perched high on the hill.

'Looks to me like a first-rate HT2 expedition,' Olivia said knowledgeably.

'Yes,' agreed Corky. 'Probably NS, as well.'

In response to Izzy's questioning look, Max explained. 'Hats, Trainers and two litres of water. It's how they grade their days out. They do this every holiday they go on.'

'And what's NS? No Smoking?'

'No,' laughed Corky. 'No Shorts. I bet the monastery will only let us chaps in if we're wearing regulation long trousers.'

'In that case, don't forget NC,' added Olivia.

'No Cameras?' suggested Izzy.

'Nice try,' said Corky, 'but it's No Cleavage.'

A sudden peal of laughter had them peering down into the bay towards the raft where Francesca and Sally were both sunbathing topless. Olivia smiled. 'The girls will have to cover up if they're going to come with us. Any more tea in that pot?'

Having offered again to make some more tea, Izzy stood at the kitchen window looking out at Max's parents on the veranda. They were older than her mother, yet seemed a generation younger. Not a word of complaint had passed their lips since they had arrived; not one fault had they found with their flight, their fellow passengers, the heat, or the peculiar Corfiot plumbing that necessitated separate arrangements for toilet paper. 'How quaint,' had been Olivia's remark when this had been explained to her. In comparison, Prudence Jordan would have been snorting her disapproval all the way back to the airport for the next flight home. What a difference there was between her mother and them. Taking life at face value, they threw themselves into it with enthusiasm, determined to enjoy themselves. Her poor mother was incapable of doing the same: she had never allowed herself the pleasure of being happy. And was that, perhaps, what Izzy would end up doing? Was she, like her mother, destined to be a lonely old woman because she was too frightened to let go and have a little fun? Was that why she had turned down Theo's dinner invitation? Scared that she might have been caught out enjoying herself?

No. That was nonsense. She had said no because she had seen straight through his wily charm. For once she had been sensible.

But wasn't sensible another word for boring?

She took the freshly made tea outside and saw that, down in the bay, Francesca and Sally were on their feet preparing to dive off the raft. Their happy shrieks as they jostled each other made her smile and think of the day she had learned to dive with Theo.

Further along the bay somebody else was watching Francesca and Sally. He had seen them earlier on the plane, then later at the carousel when they had been waiting for their luggage.

'How old do you reckon?' Nick Patterson said, over his shoulder to his brother.

Reluctantly, Harry looked up from the book he had started reading during the flight, Lawrence Durrell's *Prospero's Cell*. 'What're you on about now?'

Nick pointed down the hillside, towards the beach. 'I asked how old you thought they were.'

Harry pushed his glasses up on to his nose, and after a few seconds, said, 'Same as us, probably. Maybe a bit older. It's hard to tell at this distance. You know I'm no expert.'

'Older isn't good. Older is seriously bad news. The chicks don't go for younger. Well, not at this age they don't.'

Calling them chicks wouldn't help either, thought Harry. 'Then give it up as a bad job before you waste any more time on them.'

'No way. If we're going to be stuck here playing Happy bloody Families while Mum and Dad go through a traveller's pack version of their mid-life crisis routine, then I might just as well have something to do.'

Harry returned his attention to his book. He didn't want to think about his parents. And certainly not his father. As a young child he had longed to have a father who was normal, in the sense of having a regular job sitting behind a desk bossing others about and coming home late to eat his supper while watching the television and occasionally complaining that his sons played their music too loud. Instead, he had been lumbered with a pseudo-Bohemian who had been going through an extended state of middle-aged neurosis since, well ... probably since the age of five. Not a day went by when his father wasn't consumed with some personal or professional disaster. Nobody else was allowed to have problems of their own as he veered from one drama to the next: of losing his hair, what there was of it; of suspecting he had some unmentionable disease of the prostate; of living in fear that he was being talked about, countered by an even greater fear that he wasn't being talked about.

He worked in the film industry, and when he told people this, he made it sound as though he and Steven Spielberg were best mates and constantly on the phone to each other. He had done it to Nick and Harry's friends, years ago, trying to impress them with his stories of whom he had recently rubbed shoulders with – a euphemism for standing in the queue in the canteen and watching Michael Parkinson help himself to a plate of steak and kidney pudding. But that was in the days of his career with the BBC, before he had suffered the ignominy of being made redundant. Now he worked for an independent film company that put together small-budget documentaries. His last project had recently gone out on Channel Four and was yet another example of his late-night shock-and-titillate explorations of the human mind and body. As Nick often said, 'Oh, man, it's okay to be obsessed with sex when you're in your prime, but it's sick to see your ageing hippie father parading his hang-ups on telly.'

Their mother rarely watched his programmes but, then, she was seldom at home – there was always some committee or cause she felt compelled to support. When the first episode of *Sexual Rites of Passage* had been due to go out last month, his father had approached her and asked her if she would watch it because he would appreciate her opinion. She had glared at him and said, 'You really want my honest view on why, yet again, you're pedalling pornography, Adrian? Well, in my opinion, you need help. The sooner the better. Was there anything else?'

Between them, Harry's parents took up far too much space in his life. He was still cross with them, and himself, that he had agreed to come on this holiday. With the end of his third year at college drawing to a close, he and his friends had decided to go backpacking in Turkey – it was to have been their last fling before finals next year. His father had put paid to that by whingeing on at him that this would probably be their last family holiday and Harry had stupidly given in.

'Fancy a swim?' asked Nick.

Knowing that he wouldn't get any peace unless he did, he said, 'Oh, go on, then.'

Francesca and Sally might have given the impression that they hadn't noticed Nick and Harry at the airport but, like any girls their age, their testosterone antennae had been picking up signals loud and clear. They weren't entirely impressed with what was coming their way on the beach, but were prepared to reserve judgement for now.

'How old do you reckon?' asked Sally, swimming over to Francesca.

'Too young for you.'

'I could make an exception.'

'Oh, yes? Which one of them has caught your eye?'

'The tall dark-haired one with glasses. He looks as if butter wouldn't melt.'

Francesca laughed. 'Yeah, and you'd like to be the one to prove otherwise. So you're leaving me the small funky one, are you?'

'Well, the Jamiroquai look is more your bag, isn't it? And the hair of the dog might make you feel better.'

'He looks nothing like Carl. Carl never wore his hair in pigtails.'

'Oh, who cares? It's a generic look. Shall we stick around to find out what they're like?'

'Nah, there's plenty of time for that. For now let's play hard to get. On the count of three we make for the shore and sashay our way back up to the villa.'

Chapter Sixteen

Theo returned to Áyios Nikólaos late that evening. Mercifully, there had been no delay to the short flight from Athens, and the drive along the winding coast road from the airport had been a clear run. He felt tired but elated as he approached the rutted track that led to his villa. He had got exactly what he had wanted from his week in Athens, and had outwitted two of his arch business rivals. There was nothing to beat the thrill of a chase that culminated in a successfully clinched deal. He knew that the day when he no longer experienced the same level of excitement would be the day he retired gracefully. But that was a long way off. For now, his hunger was as keen as ever. As was his golden touch. A Midas touch that Mark used to say would be his undoing. But Mark didn't know the half of his success. Few people did. He kept the extent of his wealth between himself and the handful of lawyers and accountants he had known for many years and whom he trusted implicitly. Mark didn't know – any more than the financial pundits in Athens who liked to keep abreast of his affairs – about the portfolio of stocks and shares he had steadily accrued, or the many companies he controlled.

But for all Mark liked to criticise him – 'You're a flash show-off with more money than sense' – Theo was a modest man. While it was true that he had always appreciated the good things money could provide, he now favoured a simpler approach to life, which was why he had made his first real home here in Áyios Nikólaos. Much as he enjoyed Athens, with all its thrusting energy, it gave him no real sense of belonging. It was clear to him that Athens was where he worked, and Corfu was where he lived, where he could be himself.

After he had showered and changed, he found Mark in the kitchen cooking supper.

'Don't go getting the wrong idea about this,' Mark said, as he slipped a cheese and herb omelette on to a plate and passed it to Theo, 'I'm only playing at doting housewife just this once. Wine?'

They ate outside. The evening was very still, with only the faintest of breezes to rustle the leaves on the nearby eucalyptus trees and stir up the scent of basil from one of the pots on the terrace. Though it was dark, it was still warm and the balmy night sky flickered with bats as they swooped and circled overhead. Attracted by the candles on the table, a broad-winged moth was risking its short life by fluttering around the flames, and below them in the bay an incoming tide quietly washed the arc of stones. This is undeniably my home, thought Theo, with contentment, as he stared out at the inky water and the moon streaking its shimmering silvery light across the surface.

'You have had a good week?' he asked Mark, breaking the comfortable silence between them. 'The writing went well?'

'Not bad. How about you? Made yourself another bag of gold?'

'Several,' he said noncommittally, keeping to himself that he would sell on the decrepit office block he had just acquired for a handsome profit after he had had it restored and refurbished into luxurious apartments. 'And were you left alone,' he asked Mark, 'or did the determined Dolly-Babe pay a call as she threatened?'

'Thankfully I've seen no one, other than Angelos and Sophia, and Nicos up at the shop. It's been very quiet. Just how I like it. Though I did have a call from my publisher or, more accurately, the fool of a new publicist who's been appointed to take care of me.'

Theo tried to keep the smile from his face. He knew of old what a lousy self-promoter Mark was, and how he despised anyone else's attempts to do it for him. 'And what did that poor lamb to the slaughter want of you?'

'Oh, the usual, a bit more of my soul.'

'Any bit in particular?'

'Yes, the part I'd rather keep to myself.'

'Ah, I see it all. They want you to agree to be interviewed, is that it?' Theo still had the video tape of one of Mark's rare TV appearances in which he had presented the inexperienced interviewer with, possibly, her worst moment. She had innocently asked him if he ever thought he would get married again, only to have flung back at her, 'That's none of your goddamn business!'

Mark nodded. 'Yeah, it's a familiar tale – sell the personal story to sell the book. Sod the product, let's hit 'em with brand definition. And while they're doing that they'll turn me into some kind of bloody media tart.'

'What did you tell them?'

'What do you think?'

'I should imagine that the line was sizzling with your hot-tempered response.'

Running his fingers through his hair, then leaning forward to flick them at the moth, Mark took a moment to think about what Theo had just said. His response had, indeed, been hot-tempered, and had resulted in a stunned silence from the girl. She hadn't known what to say in the face of his adamant refusal to be swept along with her plans for hyping his book.

'You've had such an interesting and colourful life,' she

had twittered. 'It would be a fabulous hook on which to hang the publicity campaign.'

An interesting and colourful life.

Hell on wheels!

Was the whole nightmare experience that he had lived through, and been lucky to survive, to be labelled as nothing more than an *interesting and colourful* episode?

Well, they could all go to hell. Goddamnit, the books had sold well in the past without him having to prostitute himself, which meant there was no good reason why he should have to start doing so now.

It was at times like this that he regretted ever writing under the name Mark St James. With hindsight he should have used a pseudonym and kept his anonymity, but in the early days of his recovery he had needed to reaffirm who he really was. It had been a mistake. He had realised that as soon as his private life suddenly became public property. With the overnight success of his first book, which went straight into the bestseller lists – in the UK, the States and Germany – and was then televised, press interviews had been expected of him. Once it was known that he had been an alcoholic and substance abuser, journalists only wanted to know how many bottles of vodka he had got through a day, or how much his cocaine habit had cost him. That it had very nearly cost him his life was of no real significance to them. He was a story in himself. He was a ready-made package of saleable interest.

When he had finished his third novel he stopped playing ball. He gave them the finger and retreated behind a wall of silence. No more interviews. No more days-of-hell-and-road-to-recovery stories. He had had enough. Disappointed, his publishers had had to find a new way to promote him. Working off the slipstream of his previous bestsellers, they came up with the Enigmatic

Reclusive Mark St James, an angle, cloying as it was, that had worked just fine.

Until now, when some slip of a girl had proposed to resurrect the old approach. 'I've been going through the press cuttings from way back,' she'd said, 'and it strikes me that you never once told anyone why you'd been an alcoholic. And I'm wondering if this isn't a line we could follow now. What do you think?'

Struggling to control his anger, he had said, 'I think you're wasting your time as well as mine. The answer's no. Goodbye.'

For all that, she had hit on a point that many before her had missed. Or perhaps they had deliberately over-looked it. The reason behind another person's misery is usually so uninteresting that it's invariably pushed aside. People only want to know about the seedy details of an addict's decline into the underworld, to know just how low someone could fall, smug in the knowledge that it could never be them. Addiction is always somebody else's problem, somebody else's destructive weakness. There are those who slip into it without realising and others, like him, who throw themselves in head first, wanting to drown in the bittersweet nirvana it offers.

Seeing that Theo was watching him and waiting for him to speak, he said, 'I probably wasn't as polite as I should have been, but I needed to make her understand that I have no intention of doing any more interviews. Besides, you know as well as I do, you live and die by the stuff you're reported to have said.'

Pouring more wine into his glass, Theo said, 'Please, Mark, this is me you are talking to. You do not have to justify yourself with simple old Theo. I know better than anyone that you see yourself as an artist and not a performing dog. Perish the thought that anyone would ever confuse the two with you.'

'Bastard! Now you're just trying to make me sound pretentious.'

Theo smiled. 'And with so little effort.'

'Can I help it that I don't have anything of great worth to say? If I thought I had some deep emotional philosophy to pass on to mankind, then I'd be the first to pontificate.'

'But that's just the point. You do have something worthwhile to say. Your books are full of dire warnings of man's failings.'

'Now who's sounding pretentious?'

The next day, and with Albania lost behind early-morning cloud, Theo went for a swim in the sea. Floating on his back he glanced up the hillside and saw Laura staring down at him. He waved and gestured for her to join him. Within minutes she was on the beach and easing herself into the cool, refreshing water.

'We got your message from Angelos,' she said, swimming out to him. 'How was Athens?'

'Hotter than the devil's breath, though slightly more fragrant. But only just. I hear from Mark, who has been my ears and eyes in my absence, that you have guests. Does that mean you and Max are too busy to join me for dinner tonight?'

She groaned. 'By this afternoon I'll be fit for bed and little else.'

He raised an eyebrow. 'Really, Laura, you must stop putting such outrageous thoughts into my head.'

She splashed water at him. 'I meant that I'll be too tired for anything other than sleep. We've got Max's parents here, along with Francesca and her friend Sally.'

'Aha, yes, I recall now. Sally is the girl Max was so keen to see again. Is she behaving herself?'

'More or less. Two lads arrived on the same plane as they did yesterday – they're staying in the house over there.' She pointed in the direction of the faded pink villa further along the bay. 'I think she and Francesca are waiting to see what they have to offer. If anything.'

There was a pause, but not an insignificant one.

'And how is Izzy?'

'She's very well.'

They swam out towards the raft and climbed up on to it. Keeping his voice as neutral as he could, as he stared up at the soft blue sky, Theo said, 'Tell me, Laura, has Izzy spoken to you about me?'

Squeezing the water out of her hair, Laura said, 'Why? Should she have?'

He kept his face turned upwards. 'I think that just before I went away I might have inadvertently upset her. Did she mention it to you? Only I would hate to be responsible for annoying the sweet girl.'

There was another pause while Laura thought what to say. She had already run into trouble with Izzy over discussing her with Theo and she was reluctant to upset her friend again, but seeing the amount of effort that Theo was putting into his apparently casual interest in Izzy's welfare, she decided it wouldn't do any harm for him to be told the truth. Perhaps he was being serious for once.

'So what you are saying,' he said, when she had finished, 'is that I reminded her of this dreadful Alan?'

'That's about the height of it. You must have come on too strong with her. But why the concern, Theo? This can't be the first time you've upset a member of the opposite sex. Or is it just that you can't cope with being turned down?'

Laura's words were uncomfortably similar to those that Mark had uttered a short while ago and Theo didn't like the sound of them. Why was it that everyone made such unjust assumptions about him? Would it shock them to know that he, too, had feelings? That he could

155

genuinely feel something for a woman? Mark had accused him of using women to fill a void, which Theo had wanted to refute vigorously at the time, but last week when he was lying in bed with one of his more regular companions – a woman he knew to be actively seeking a ring for her finger – he had pondered on Mark's theory and had not liked the conclusion he had reached.

Without answering Laura's question, he touched her shoulder lightly and said, 'Come, despite the early hour of the day, you are already turning pink in the sun. It's time to swim back to the beach and return you safely to Max.'

When they reached the shore, Laura said, 'We're all off to Paleokastrítsa for the day, but why don't you join us for a drink tonight? Bring your friend, Mark, if he'll come. You know how anxious Max is to meet him.'

'Thank you, that would be nice. *Ti óra?*'

Laura smiled, took a moment to think, and counted on her fingers. '*Enyá i óra.*'

'Bravo! Nine o'clock it is, then. Have fun today in Paleokastrítsa. Take care in the sun, though – it is going to be very hot, I fear.'

Chapter Seventeen

Theo was right. The day was proving to be one of the hottest of the summer so far, and Paleokastrítsa had been awarded a rating of HT4 – Hats, Trainers and four litres of water. 'A cracking-the-flagstones scorcher of a day,' Corky had called it, as the sun blazed down on them. However, while Laura was finding that the heat was getting to her, Max's parents were showing no sign of tiring. They had led the way in hiring a boat to explore the small coves and grottoes; they had swum in water the colour of pure turquoise; they had skipped like mountain goats up the steep path to the monastery; they had rattled off several rolls of film and bought a dozen or so postcards. And now, as Laura lay dozing on the crowded beach in the shade of an umbrella, they were off with Max inspecting the local shops. She turned to Izzy and said, 'You see what I mean about Corky and Olivia? They're exhausting, aren't they?'

'I think they're wonderful.'

'Oh, they're wonderful, all right, and I love them to pieces. It's just that I wish I had half their energy. They make me feel so inadequate when they're around. All I feel good for is a long, long sleep. I should have done what the girls opted to do – stayed at home and relaxed.'

Izzy laughed. 'I'm not sure that relaxing was entirely what Francesca and Sally had on their minds.' Sitting on her balcony first thing that morning, she had heard them in the room next to hers discussing their plans for the day. It seemed to involve an awful lot of hard work, namely being as visible as they could manage, yet maintaining an air of distant allure. Izzy hadn't yet seen the two young men whose presence in the bay warranted such meticulous scheming, but Olivia had mentioned them yesterday afternoon when the girls had come up to the house after their swim and declared them both to be of above-average appearance. 'Aren't they the two good-looking boys who were on the plane with us?' she had asked her granddaughter, as the girls stood staring down on to the beach. 'It might be nice for you to get to know one another.' Francesca's casual, 'Mm . . . were they on the plane with us? I don't recall,' had amused Izzy and she had been tempted to tiptoe across the veranda and take a peek at them.

A yawn from Laura prompted her to say, 'What you need is an early night.'

'Chance would be a fine thing,' said Laura. 'Just as well Theo and Mark are joining us this evening. At least Max's parents won't be able to get the cards out and keep us up into the wee small hours.'

'They're not into bridge, are they?' asked Izzy, with a sinking heart. It was one of those games that terrified her. Alan and his parents had played it. They would sit around the little felt-topped card table and stare at one another in deadly combative silence, which in turn made her uptight and nervous and caused her mind to wander from her cards. It had to be the most boring pastime ever invented.

'Bridge? Good Lord, no,' said Laura. 'Canasta's their game. I'll warn you now, though, they like nothing more than a convert, and once they've roped you in you'll never be the same again. They'll fill you up with wine and thrash you senseless. You won't see your bed before three in the morning. Some of the worst hangovers Max and I have ever had have been inflicted on us by his own parents at one of their curry-and-Canasta evenings.'

Izzy thought it sounded a lot more fun than bridge. She closed her eyes and sank into a happy state of pre-sleep contentment. She listened to what was going on around her on the crowded beach: the crying of a small fractious child; the bickering of a couple with a strong Brummy accent, each blaming the other for having forgotten to pack the camera; the insistent voice of a German, who was reading aloud from his newspaper; and the flirtatious laughter of a group of young Italian girls, who were as stunningly pretty as they were vain.

Having spent so much time in the quiet seclusion of Áyios Nikólaos, the brash commercialism of Paleo-kastrítsa had come as something of a culture shock. Despite the warnings in the guidebooks that the area was one of the island's top tourist attractions, nothing had prepared Izzy for the sight that had met them after they had driven through the twisting, rural landscape and arrived to find hundreds of people spilling out of rows of coaches and all dashing for the sun-loungers and fringed umbrellas on the beach. For all that, though, the resort was breathtakingly beautiful, with its unbelievably clear water and dramatic cliffs, and Izzy was glad she had tagged along for the day. Thinking that Max and Laura might prefer to spend a day alone with his parents, she had mentioned to them last night that she would stay behind, but they would have none of it. 'For heaven's sake, stop being so considerate,' Laura had said.

'Quite right,' Max had agreed. 'You're not an optional extra, Izzy, you're here on holiday with us, so you can jolly well pull your weight when it comes to joining in with the fun. There'll be no slacking from anybody.'

It was a funny phrase to use – *optional extra* – but it came close to how, as a child, Izzy had sometimes seen herself. Though a more precise analogy was that she had viewed herself as one of those free gifts in the cereal packet: something that nobody needed.

She couldn't be the first person who had grown up knowing that her birth had not been a much longed-for event. There had certainly been no planning for hers, no sense of joyful anticipation. But how could there have been, when her mother had been through the process once before, pinning all her happiness and expectations on a tiny boy who had died within days of his arrival in the world?

Without him knowing it, that child's whole life had been mapped out for him in his mother's mind. He would have been perfect in every way; the gifted son every parent would have wanted. Clever. Handsome. Kind. Loving. Musical. Artistic. Nothing would have been beyond his capabilities. He would have excelled at school, college, and in his career. And it would have been no ordinary career. He would have been dynamic. A key player. A man to be admired.

Izzy knew all this because her mother had raised her on a daily diet of everything her dead brother would have been. No one else would listen. No one cared enough. Izzy had taken it upon herself to be her mother's audience and had listened attentively, as if her life depended on it.

It was an unworthy thought, but she believed that John Richard Jordan had been fortunate not to survive. He had got off lightly. How could he have hoped ever to live up to his mother's expectations?

No expectations had been laid down for Izzy when, five years later, she had been born. From an early age she heard her mother arguing with her father, blaming him for whatever trouble Izzy had caused that day, blaming him for her very existence.

One of her earliest memories was of feeling sorry for her father. How awful it must be for him, she had thought, watching his sad face as he sat reading a book. From then on she had tried hard to please her mother, always to keep on her good side. Because if she could do that, she told herself, her father wouldn't be blamed and he might smile at her. With steadfast determination she learned where it was safe to tread, and where the landmines of her mother's black moods were hidden. She learned the importance of being invisible and when to hide from her mother when she was in the throes of one of her terrifying rages, which came from nowhere but always had to run its course.

It was such a strain and it made her an uneasy child, never comfortable with herself – or with anyone else, for that matter. She was quick to make mistakes and quicker still to be flustered over the slightest things. She was accident-prone too, which only added to her mother's frustration. She tried to be careful – to pick up her feet, to watch where she was going, to hold the glass properly, not to bang the door shut – but it rarely worked and a stinging hand would catch her on the back of her head, making her eyes feel loose and her ears ring. Often she would go to school with vivid bruises on her arms and legs and had to pretend to anyone who asked that she had tripped and fallen over in the garden.

She had assumed, in the way that children do with their trusting, unquestioning acceptance, that whatever went on at home was normal, that all children had to dodge blows. Didn't all mothers scream at their daughters that they hated them, that they wished they were dead? It never occurred to her that it could be different. Not until it was too late, when shame kept her mouth shut, preventing any words of disloyalty slipping out

She had never forgotten the day she broke one of her mother's statues. Or its consequences. She was helping to clear away the breakfast things when she accidentally knocked a tight-lipped lady in a rose-pink crinoline dress off the draining-board where, along with her silent partners, she was waiting to be dusted. Only five years old, Izzy knew she was in trouble. She had stared down at her feet, at the pieces of china on the grey-tiled floor, then slowly, holding her breath, she had found the courage to raise her eyes to her mother's face. For the longest of moments their eyes had met and held. Then hands reached out to her, and the room began to move, the walls bending like those weird mirrors at the funfair.

She was being shaken.

Up and down, backwards and forwards, her head snapping painfully on her neck.

Then she was spinning, round and round.

Everything was moving.

The kitchen clock whizzed by.

Followed by the cooker.

Then the big cupboard where they kept their coats and shoes, the carpet-sweeper with the little swirly brushes that stuck out at the front and back.

She saw the table she had been helping to clear: the plates; the bowls; the packet of cornflakes; the metal teapot, and the little milk jug. But it was all moving so fast, their shapes and colours blurred in a whirlpool of surreal confusion, just like in *The Wizard of Oz*.

Faster and faster the room went.

She felt hot.

Clammy.

Dizzy.

And frightened that she was going to be sick.

Her legs felt loose as they dangled beneath her. One of her slippers flew off. Her teeth were clattering inside her head. Her ribs were hurting, something was crushing them. She wanted to scream but she could hardly breathe. She closed her eyes, wanting it to stop. Then suddenly there was a crash and a thud that hurt more than anything else had. But at last it had stopped. The room was still.

When she opened her eyes nothing made sense. Everything was a mess. Her mother was on her knees, surrounded by upturned chairs, bits of broken china and glass. She was crying. Her father was there. And he was shouting. She had never heard him shout before. It scared her more than all the blood that was coming from her head. Frightened, she began to cry. 'I'm sorry,' she sobbed, when she felt her father's arms around her, 'I didn't mean to do it.'

Chapter Eighteen

It was a poor excuse he had given, and not for one moment did Mark think Theo had been taken in by his claim that he needed to work that evening. Besides, his friend understood well enough that a neighbourly drinks get-together was never going to be high on his list of hot options. So, having passed up the opportunity to spend an evening dodging a zealous hostess with an overflowing drinks tray, he was going for a quiet walk around Kassiópi to explore the harbour.

He set off shortly after Theo had left for next door. The day he had arrived, Theo had shown Mark a footpath situated just yards from the end of his oleander-lined drive. It went through the nearby olive grove and, according to his friend, was a handy short-cut into Kassiópi. He followed the stony, uneven path for a while then remembered with annoyance that Theo had said it was advisable to take a torch when using this route late at night. It was light now, but give it a couple of hours and it would probably be pitch black. Well, he could either risk it or come back the long way via the road, though even then he would have the last hundred yards of ankle-turning potholed track to negotiate in the darkness. Despite his misgivings he pressed on, the parched grass swishing at the bottoms of his jeans, the low branches of the olive trees nearly catching his head, and the cool evening air rich with the scent of wild garlic and thyme.

The rock-studded path rose steeply, deceptively so,

until finally it flattened out and he came to a clearing. He paused to catch his breath, and cursed himself for his lack of fitness. Then he heard something move behind him. He stiffened. He turned slowly. Nothing. He let out his breath, swallowed the lump of fear that had lodged in his throat, then pushed a hand through his hair. Just as he had convinced himself he had imagined it, he caught a faint rustle of something – *someone* – moving in the dried tangle of undergrowth. A rush of adrenaline surged through his bloodstream and he clenched his fists.

Then he saw it.

Relief made him laugh out loud. 'Jeez, a bloody tortoise!' He went over to take a closer look. 'Well, I was pretty sure this wasn't bandit country,' he said, bending down to inspect the scaly expressionless face. Beady eyes peered back at him, then the long neck, face and curved stumpy legs withdrew into the safety of the shell. 'Don't blame you, mate,' said Mark, straightening up. 'I know the feeling.'

He had only been walking a short while when a dog leaped up against a fence and barked at him. Once again the suddenness made him start. Not only am I the most unfit man who ever lived, he thought angrily, I'm probably the most neurotic. His annoyance stayed with him as he walked on. How long was it going to take him to lose this irrational fear and realise that he was quite safe? There was no way that the nutter who had been sending him those letters back in England could be stalking him here. Nobody, other than his agent, publishers and family knew he was here.

Rule number one, he told himself firmly, going over familiar ground, don't let it get to you. It's what goes on inside your head that causes all the damage. It's what all stalkers set out to do. They want their victim to become as obsessed with them as they are with you.

But it didn't matter how many times he repeated this

calming mantra to himself, or reminded himself that he had written an entire novel based on the theory of what goes on in a stalker's mind, he couldn't shake off the anger that this unknown man – and, yes, he was sure it was a man – had the power to invade his life in the way he had. That even here, thousands of miles from home, his pernicious presence could still get to Mark.

Back in England Mark had got used to looking over his shoulder: it had become part of his routine. It had turned a walk up the hill to the post office into a bizarre parody of Cold War espionage. Locking his door, he would glance right, then left, walk a little distance, then stop to retie a shoelace, or maybe pause in front of the gift shop to take a furtive look around him. But it was always the same; the only person acting strangely was himself. Paranoid was not a word he wanted to start using about his behaviour – it reminded him of his cokehead days – but it was there waiting in the wings of his mind.

By the time he reached Kassiópi, he had calmed down and was looking forward to sitting in a bar with a cup of coffee and watching the world go by. It was busier than he had expected, and as he walked along the main street, lost in the crowd of suntanned tourists looking for somewhere to eat, he took pleasure from knowing that he was just another anonymous face in the crowd. He chose what appeared to be the busiest bar and a table close to the road, which gave him the best vantage-point to see everything that was going on.

Across the road was a small square, occupied mostly by the village elders. Sitting on green wrought-iron seats, chatting and smoking, their lives seemed untouched by the noisy, incongruous mix of people around them. No doubt they had seen it all before: the young British men with their cropped hair, earrings and tattoos; the Scandi-navian contingent marked out by their startlingly blond hair, long legs and enormous feet in Ellesse flip-flops; and the girls, of whatever nationality, wearing more makeup than clothing. It was probably a safe bet to say that nothing surprised these local folk any more.

A waiter took Mark's order and brought it to him with smooth efficiency. To his shame, and even after such a long-standing friendship with Theo, '*Éna kafé parakaló*,' was just about the extent of Mark's Greek. At college he had secretly envied Theo's effortless ability to switch between English, German, Italian and Greek. Not that he had ever said as much. In those days he could never have openly admitted that Theo, or anyone else, was better at something than him. But age and experience had mellowed him and now he had no trouble in giving Theo the credit he deserved. But, then, he had always known that Theo was a far better man than he was or ever could be. He had hinted as much to Bones, during one of their spilling-the-guts-of-his-deepest-and-innermost-feelings sessions. 'And is that something you wish you could be?' had been Bones's measured response.

'What are you getting at now?'

'I was asking if it was important to you to feel that you were Theo's equal. Or, indeed, anybody's equal. Because you don't, do you, Mark? Beneath the outward show of swaggering arrogance and conceit that has taken everybody clse in, you know that it's all a lie. You're convinced that you're nobody's equal. Am I right?'

'Equality is something we have to strive for.'

'Is it? How strange. I thought we were put on this earth with nothing but our circumstances dividing us from others. So what is it about Theo that makes you think he's more special than you are? I recall only a few weeks ago, when he brought you here, you were claiming he was nothing short of . . .' he lowered his eyes to the notes he had made in his file '. . . ah, yes. "An effing devil in cashmere" is what you called him. My, how quickly your opinion has changed.'

Bones's pathetic attempt at irony had provoked a smile from Mark. But not an answer. Which was a mistake. Up until then, and in the manner of a predatory cat chasing a frightened mouse, Bones had been playing with him. Now, in the silence that had fallen between them, he went in for the kill.

'So, tell me more about the boating accident,' he said. 'Yesterday you told me about your friend dying, but now I want you to go further. When you knew your friend was drowning and you couldn't reach him, what did you feel?'

'I was a twelve-year-old boy. What the hell do you think I felt?'

'I don't know, Mark, I wasn't there.'

'Then use your imagination.'

'Mark, listen to me, you will only discover your true worth when you are brave enough to let someone help you confront the repressed memories of that tragic day.'

'They're not repressed. They're there all the time. Every day. Every night.'

'I'm sure they are, but you're not facing them. You're just cramming the lid down on them, keeping them at bay. And how much more strength will it take, do you think, to keep that lid down?'

But Bones was asking too much of him. In response, his body betrayed him: his skin crawled, and then his scalp pricked painfully. And, though the room was cool – Bones always insisted on having the window open – he felt sickeningly hot. His nerves were raw. He clenched his fists, knowing that if he didn't, the trembling would kick in. Then came the final betrayal. The reassuring voice that told him a drink would help him through it. A comforting glass of whisky. Or vodka. Or anything. The whispering grew louder. And louder still until it was a roaring, insistent demand inside his head. *Get me a drink!*

He tried to think of what Bones had told him to do when this happened: to think of his own strength overcoming the power of the fear that made him want to drink. 'Always remember,' Bones had said, 'it's not the drink you have to resist, but the giving in to the fear of the past.'

Bones must have known what was going on in his mind, for he said, 'Come and stand at the window with me, Mark. There's something I want to show you.'

Surprised by his own obedience, he struggled to his feet. He knew it was a diverting technique, but he was beyond caring. He leaned against the window-ledge for support, briefly closed his eyes, and breathed in the fresh morning air, taking great gulps of it as though trying to cheat his body with a fix of oxygen rather than alcohol. Beside him Bones rattled on about the amazing view, about the prettiness of the steeple on the nearby church and how it had been saved in the early eighties from toppling over. 'Nobody believed it could be saved,' he said, going back to his desk. 'Everyone said it would have to be pulled down, but there it is, as beautiful, as perfect as the day it was built. Just goes to show, doesn't it?'

Thumping his fists on the window-ledge, Mark shouted, 'Enough! I get the analogy.'

'Good. So let's recap. Niall was your best friend and you were on holiday together.'

He sighed, knowing there was no escape. If he was ever going to be truly exorcised and free of the constant shadow-boxing with the memory of Niall's death, he would have to put himself through this. Very slowly, still fighting the need in his body for a drink, he took up the story. He and Niall had been on a school camping holiday. They should have been joining in with a table-tennis tournament with another school party also staying at the outward-bound centre, but neither had fancied it. At Mark's suggestion they sneaked down to the small marina with something more exciting in mind. It was usually Mark's idea that they do something they weren't supposed to do, which had repeatedly brought his parents into conflict with Niall's. Mr and Mrs Percival didn't approve of Mark: they claimed he was a bad influence on their only son, leading him astray and encouraging him to do things he wouldn't otherwise have dreamed of doing. But the disapproval went deeper than that: not to put too fine a point on it, the St James family was loaded, and Niall's was not. It didn't help either that Mr Percival worked for Mark's father. At that age, the two boys could see no problem with this, but Niall's parents saw the disparity in their lifestyles as divisive and a blatant reminder of everything they couldn't offer their son.

But this supposed disparity between Mark and Niall was the last thing on their minds that day as they knelt on the wooden pontoon untying one of the dinghies. They were both foolish enough to think that, after three lessons, they could handle a boat, especially one as small as this.

Slipping away unseen, they congratulated themselves on their smartness. The wind was strong and it wasn't long before they had skittered out to sea, far away from the sailing centre. What they didn't know was that they were heading straight towards a squall, a brief localised storm. The first they knew about it was a mass of low-lying clouds, black and threatening, rolling towards them. Then the rain started, heavy drops that splattered against their faces. They began to wonder if they had been so smart after all. But as quickly as the clouds had appeared, they passed over and the sky brightened. Their earlier mood of cocksure confidence returned. Had they known better, they would have realised that worse was to come. The rain fell again harder this time, the wind gathered and the temperature dropped. Huge waves buffeted the boat and they tried to remember what the sailing instructor had taught them. But it was no use: fear had blotted out everything they had been told. The rain was coming down so hard that Mark couldn't even see the shore. Everything was an endless roll of turbulent, impenetrable grey. The sea was grey and the sky was leaden. The sail was straining in the fierce wind and there didn't seem to be anything they could do to control the dinghy. Pulling on the rudder or sail did nothing. They were helpless, at the mercy of the sea and weather.

It was then that Mark began to get a sense of the danger they were in. With no lifejackets on board, what would happen if they capsized? And just as he had thought this, the sky lit up with a flash of lightning. It made them both jump and, hanging on to each other, panic set in. With growing horror, they watched mountainous waves grow and swell. Tossed from one to the next, they were powerless. But when the final violent gust of wind hit they never saw it coming. The boat went over and, knowing that Niall wasn't as strong a swimmer as he was, Mark had screamed, 'Hold on to me,' as the billowing sea swallowed them up.

But the strength of the water pushed them clean away from the boat, and when eventually Mark surfaced there was no sign of Niall.

He dived back under the water, kicking his legs, pulling at the ice-cold water with his arms. But still he couldn't see his friend. Out of breath, he rose to the surface again, filled his lungs with air and dived once more. Again and again, he dived, surfaced and dived, desperate to reach Niall in time. The salt water was stinging his eyes, his chest was aching as though it would burst and his fingers were numb with cold.

Suddenly he saw Niall. He was trapped under the hull of the boat. He swam over and pulled frantically at his arms to free him. But even as he was doing this, he knew it was too late. Hooking a hand under his chin, he dragged him to the surface and tried to hold him against the overturned boat. Choking for breath, he screamed at Niall to wake up. He tried to give him mouth-to-mouth, but it was no good, he couldn't hold him still for long enough. With tears running down his cheeks he knew that Niall was dead. And knew, too, that it was his fault. He prayed then that the waves would take him and that he, too, would die.

But he didn't die. His sense of self-preservation wouldn't allow it to happen, and with the worst of the storm now over he managed to extend the centreboard on the boat and right it. Just as he was clambering in, a lifeboat alerted by the local coastguard came speeding into view. He was wrapped in a blanket and told he had had a lucky escape.

'Well done, Mark,' Bones had said, when he had finished. 'That was good. Very good. Now, in tomorrow's session we'll explore why you've persisted in acting out this old conflict. And if there's time, we'll look at why you're still behaving like an angry teenager masquerading as an intellectualising adult opposing anyone in authority, or those you think lucky enough to have their lives neatly sewn up. We might even touch base with your parents. The hinterland of bad parenting is always a rich vein to tap into. My spies tell me that *chilli con carne* is on the menu for lunch. Do you think I ought to risk it? Or should I steer clear?'

That was the extraordinary thing about being in a rehab clinic: one minute you could be dissecting the carnage of your most intimate experiences, and the next you could be mulling over something as mundane as what to have for lunch.

Wanting to order another cup of coffee, Mark looked about him to catch the eye of a passing waiter. The bar was busier than when he had arrived. Darkness had brought with it dazzling Vegas-style neon lights advertising Woodpecker Cider, Heineken, Becks and Amstel beer. And to complement the bright lights, the music had been turned up – Will Smith was getting jiggy with it and doing another of his rap-meets-Stevie-Wonder numbers on a large-screen TV hung from the ceiling in a corner of the bar – and a vibrant party atmosphere was in the air.

He decided to move on. His coffee already paid for, he left a tip on the table, stepped into the road and strolled down towards the harbour. Not that it was much of a stroll: the streets were packed and he had to run the gauntlet of numerous knick-knack stalls. There was something for everyone, or so they claimed. You could have your portrait done, buy yourself some cheap silver jewellery, have your name written on a grain of rice – for some strange reason – have your hair braided or a temporary tattoo applied. He was certainly spoiled for choice! And if none of that appealed, he could always go for the Albanian woman selling cheap, unromantic polyester roses and those silly light-up wristbands.

Beneath a sky of midnight blue, the still water in the harbour was ablaze with the reflection of coloured lights from all the bars, shops and restaurants around the quay. It was just as busy down here as at the top of the town, but seeing that one of the benches at the harbour's edge was free, Mark headed over to it. He had just settled himself, pulled out his notebook and pen from his shirt pocket, when he heard a voice from behind him.

'Hello there. Mind if we join you?'

It was Dolly-Babe with Silent Bob in tow.

Oh, joy! Now, why the hell hadn't he done the sensible thing and gone along with Theo's plans for the evening? It served him right for lying, he supposed.

Theo had gone for the honest option when he had arrived at Villa Petros. He hadn't thought it fair to keep fobbing his friends off with lame excuses about Mark's work so he told them the truth.

'I'm sorry,' he said, when Laura had offered him a chair on the veranda and Max had poured him a glass of wine, 'but not only is Mark a very private man, he used to be an alcoholic. The invitation to spend the evening with a reprobate boozer like you, Max, is not good for him.'

'Oh, Theo,' said Laura, 'why didn't you say something sooner?'

'Because I am a man of discretion. Mark's affairs are his own.'

'Now you come to mention it,' said Max, 'I recall something about him in the papers. Can't think why I hadn't thought of it before. If my memory serves me right, he went through a hell of a time of it, didn't he?'

Theo nodded. 'He did.' And then, more cheerfully, 'Now where are you hiding your parents Max? And what about Francesca and the nymphomaniac Sally, are they not here?'

'The girls have gone into Kassiópi. And Mum and Dad are doing sterling stuff in the kitchen with Izzy; they're stacking the dishwasher and tidying up.'

'Aha, you have been cracking the whip over them, have you?'

'Let's just say that they have an abundance of energy, and Laura thought it a good idea to put it to use. And it looks as if they've done their chores for the day – here they come. Let me introduce you.'

Rising to his feet, Theo shook hands first with Olivia then Corky. 'What a beautiful mother you have Max,' Theo said.

Max smiled. 'Now you can understand why I had to marry someone equally beautiful.'

Laura went to him and gave him a kiss. 'You old smoothie, you.'

Seeing Izzy standing on the edge of the group and sensing her awkwardness, Theo moved towards her. 'One big happy family, eh? You have parents like these?'

'Um . . . no. My father died last year. What about you?'

'I'm fortunate to have both my parents still alive. I'm sorry about your father. Were you very close?' As soon as the question was out, Theo regretted it. He saw her eyes fill and her lips tauten until they were white. She looked intensely unhappy. He mentally kicked himself. What was it with him, that he always managed to say the wrong thing? He had come here this evening determined to make amends for upsetting her on the beach that day, and now look what he had done. 'Come,' he said brightly, 'while Max is busy schmoozing his wife, let me get you a drink. You must be thirsty after all that work in the kitchen.'

'No, really,' she said, resisting his hand as it touched her elbow to steer her across the terrace, 'I don't need one.' Her voice was as stiff as the look she gave him.

He let go of her, realising that his spontaneous gesture had been to her a gross act of intrusion. 'I'm sorry,' he said, perplexed, and racking his brains for some way to put her at ease. In the end all he could think of was to repeat his apology, and quickly, before she moved away from him. 'Izzy, please, I am sorry. Will you give me a chance?'

'What for?'

Even he was surprised by what he had just said. Used to thinking fast on his feet, he now found himself completely deficient. Automatically he reached out to her arm again, thinking his touch would instil in her a sense of reassurance. Just in time, he stopped himself. More physical contact and she might slap his face. 'I'm not really sure myself,' he said at last. 'All I know is that I would like the opportunity to apologise to you properly.

The last time we spoke I upset you, and tonight I have done it again. Please, won't you—' But he was interrupted as Max joined them.

'Now, stop pestering poor Izzy, Theo. You're needed over here. My parents are keen to learn some Greek and we've appointed you their teacher.'

He allowed himself to be dragged back to the rest of the group, and as he set about entertaining them by imitating their inaccurate pronunciation, he watched Izzy's face grow steadily more sombre. He had a strong urge to leap from his chair and go to her. More than anything he wanted to see her face light up with a smile.

Chapter Nineteen

Izzy was never going to be able to get back to sleep. She had tossed and turned for most of the night and when eventually she had dozed off, it had been only for a couple of hours.

She kicked off the sheet, which had twisted itself into a wrinkled second skin around her, and went and stood outside on the balcony. The sky was pearly-pink, fresh and beautiful, glowing in the dawn light. Still and subdued, the smooth surface of the sea glistened serenely, scarcely a trace of a wave breaking against the shore.

Images of smashed china, of her mother crying, of her father cradling her in his arms had kept her awake. She had thought she was over her father, but after yesterday she realised that all she had been doing since his death was to keep on adding yet more layers of pretence to cover the cracks in their relationship. She understood now that the tears she had shed for him since the day he had died were nothing compared to the unshed tears of confused sadness and regret that she must have been storing up since she was a child.

She had been cross with herself yesterday for reliving that morning in the kitchen when her mother had lost control. Cross, because it had provoked too many other memories, too many other disturbing incidents. She had never blamed her mother for what she had done. Her mother had been ill with depression, her self-control precariously balanced as she struggled through each day as fraught and uptight as those little squares she knitted later in life.

After that terrible day her mother was admitted to a psychiatric hospital and arrangements were made for Izzy to go into a children's home. To this day, Izzy never knew why she had been put in the home – it was not a subject that was ever discussed in front of her. Why hadn't her father taken care of her? Or her aunt?

Her memories of the place were mostly a kaleidoscope of hazy but evocative sensations, of smells and sounds – but there were other more vivid flashes of recollection.

It had been just before Christmas that she had been taken there. She knew it was Christmas, because on a table at one end of the echoey dormitory she had slept in there had been a small silver tree draped in red tinsel and wonky decorations speckled with glitter that the other children had made. The floor had been shiny clean and smelt of polish and disinfectant, but the clanking bed with its austere metal frame and peeling white paint had seemed dirty. The sheets had been like paper, hard and starched; the woollen blanket, rough and scratchy, and the pillow had smelt of vomit. Above the bed there was a flickering light and a window criss-crossed with metal bars.

Mealtimes were noisy and chaotic. The food wasn't what she was used to. One day she had been forced to eat a bowl of rice pudding sprinkled with brown sugar. That night she was sick, and pushed into a freezing cold bath. When she had been lifted out, shivering and frightened, somebody had dressed her, changed the plaster on her head, and taken her back to bed where the sheets had been changed. Impatient hands had tucked her in, jolted the mattress with quick-tempered movements. She was given a stern warning that she wasn't to be sick again. With the smell of unfamiliar soap in her nostrils, and pinned down by the taut bedclothes, she had cried herself quietly to sleep, terrified of causing any more trouble and thinking – *knowing* – that this was her punishment for having broken one of her mother's precious statues.

Her greatest fear was that if she wasn't good she might stay for ever in this prison. And it was a prison, she knew that, for why else were there bars at the windows? She missed her own small bedroom, where she could hide under the ancient wooden bed that had once belonged to her father, and which was so high she had to climb up on to it. It was there, hidden in the dark and by the light of a torch, that she would draw her pictures, slipping them beneath the rug if she heard the sound of her mother's sharp, impatient footsteps approaching.

Her father visited her at the home.

As she was so young, and had no grasp of time, she never knew when he would arrive. She would sit waiting anxiously for him in one of the playrooms, watching the other children dig around in the large toy boxes. She would close her eyes and imagine that when she opened them he would be there, that he had come to take her home.

The people in charge tried to make her join in, but she wouldn't. The other children frightened her: they were all bigger, noisier too. They seemed quite happy to be there. The only toy she played with was a box of Fuzzy-felt. While she waited for her father to come, she would sit at a table near a window – just to make sure she didn't miss him, or that he didn't miss her – and watch the snow fall while putting together brightly coloured scenes of make-believe happiness: a house with a red door, a tree with green apples, a yellow sun, a mummy with curly brown hair, a daddy with long legs and a black triangle for a hat, and a little girl with a pet dog at her feet. Except there wasn't a dog in the faded and stained box, it had got lost, so she had made do with a pig. It was from another box of shapes and she knew it looked silly, its fat pink body dwarfing the rest of the picture, but she had wanted it to be as complete in her mind as she could make it.

She hated it when her father had to leave. It seemed that he had only just arrived when he was getting his coat back on, patting her shoulder and saying goodbye. She would watch him from the window as he walked away, his collar pulled up, his head hunched into his shoulders. Sometimes he waved, sometimes he didn't. When he didn't wave, she would carefully, and very slowly, dismantle the Fuzzy-felt picture, and return the pieces to its box.

She had no idea how long she was there, but she was sure it was weeks rather than days because the artificial Christmas tree disappeared. When she went home nobody spoke about what had happened. Her mother seemed different. Quieter. Slower. More watchful. Which made her even more scary.

As time went by, Izzy began to wonder if the home had been a frightening dream. But one look in the mirror told her that she hadn't imagined it. Reflected back at her were the familiar silvery grey eyes – poor man's blue, as her mother called them – and a vivid scar on her right temple that hadn't been there before. Something else new about her was that she couldn't bear to have her face immersed in water – it brought back that petrifying night when she had been sick and plunged into the bath of icy-cold water.

The following Christmas, when Auntie Trixie had been staying with them Izzy had heard her say, 'Well, thank goodness Isobel was so young when she went into that dreadful home, she doesn't remember it.' The crashing silence that had filled the room had convinced Izzy that she had not dreamed her time away from her parents. It also reaffirmed what she had pieced together from snatches of grown-up conversation: that it was a subject best not mentioned. And though her mother's mood swings were less marked, Izzy lived in dread of doing anything that might upset her, and which would result in a return to that prison. She moved around the bungalow as though on eggshells, trying to make herself less obtrusive.

Exhausted with the strain, she soon became a bundle of nerves, jumping if her mother spoke her name too sharply, flinching if a hand moved too fast. She searched constantly for ways to help, to make everything right.

Yet nothing she did helped. She was destined to cause trouble, to be in the wrong place at the wrong time.

But it was all such a long time ago. It shouldn't still affect her. But it did, of course. She wouldn't be human if when the threads of her childhood tweaked she didn't feel it. She realised now, with guilty confusion, that she felt angry with her father – that he had never protected her from her mother, and angrier still that he had left her in that home.

This newly identified emotion wrapped itself around her heart and squeezed painfully.

For once, Mark was up before Theo. He made himself a pot of coffee and took it out on to the terrace, with his A4 notepad and fountain pen. His intention was to work, but as he sat at the wooden table where he had found Theo last night when he got back from Kassiópi, he suspected this would not be the case. For one thing, it was too quiet – he was up so early that not even the cicadas had got going yet – and the second reason was that he was annoyed with Theo for making a fool of himself.

'I've upset her again,' he had said forlornly last night, as Mark had sat down with him, noting the empty bottle of Metaxá and the unusually miserable expression on his friend's face. 'What is wrong with me, eh? And please, do not suggest that I'm losing it. Do that, and I will happily smash this bottle over your big ugly head.'

Having arrived back from Kassiópi, expecting to share his tale of having bumped into Dolly-Babe and Silent Bob, Mark had been unprepared for this impromptu late-night heart-to-heart. It wasn't often that Theo got drunk.

'Izzy?' he had asked.

'Well, of course it's Izzy,' snapped Theo. 'Who else would it be?'

'So what did you say this time?'

'I put my foot straight into it.' He groaned, holding his head. 'No deeper could I have gone.'

'Oh, come on, it can't be that bad.' Mark's tone was slightly impatient. Since he had kicked the bottle into touch he had a limited supply of patience for anyone else's alcohol-induced ramblings. Was this really the man who ran a mini empire and had an intellect sharp enough to slice bread?

Theo raised his head and looked at him petulantly. 'You think I am play-acting, eh? You think I am behaving in the manner of a spoilt child who can't get his way, is that it?'

Mark looked at him thoughtfully, seeing two very different men. There was Theo the sharp, practical businessman, and Theo the sentimental and hopelessly romantic philosopher. It was probably a fair summing up of your typical Greek man. 'You've always been a spoilt child, Theo,' he said, 'so I'm not going to refute that. But what I think you're experiencing, and for the first time, is what the rest of us mere mortals have to endure more regularly. The phenomenon of rejection. Welcome to the club. I wish I could say that membership was exclusive, but I'm afraid it isn't. So tell me where it went wrong.'

'*Ti hálya!* I blundered in where angels—'

'Keep to English, Theo, and just get to the point.'

He did.

'But that's a mistake anyone could have made,' said Mark, once again feeling that his friend was turning the episode into an over-the-top Greek tragedy. It still puzzled him why and how this girl had got under Theo's skin in the way that she had. 'How were you to know that she hasn't got over her father's death? My advice is not to take it personally. The next time you see her, just apologise as discreetly and courteously as you can.'

'That is easier said than done. The look she gave me, it could have yammered a nail into a wall.'

Mark had laughed. 'I think you mean *hammered*. I also think you've drunk too much. I guarantee that in the morning you'll see I'm right.'

He gave up on the idea of working. He wasn't in the mood. He finished his cup of coffee and decided to go for a walk, as he frequently did at this time of the day when he could be sure of having the beach to himself.

But today he found he didn't have that luxury. Perched on the rock where he often sat was the cause of Theo's problems. He stopped short, was about to retrace his steps and slip away unseen when she turned and looked straight at him. He could see she had been crying. That she still was.

Few men know what to do when confronted with tears, and Mark was no exception. He would also be the first to agree that listening isn't instinctive to men. Without another thought, he pretended he hadn't seen her and started walking in the direction he had just come. He didn't need this. There was no reason for him to get involved in somebody else's emotional problems. But gradually he slowed down and thought of Theo. What if Theo had turned his back on him all those years ago? What if he hadn't searched for him until he had found him in that hell-hole of a squat? And what if Bones hadn't been patient enough, or thick-skinned enough, to ignore the abuse Mark had flung at him?

But this was different. He was a stranger to this girl. How could he possibly help her?

But a stranger could sometimes be of more use than one's friends or family. A stranger could offer an objective view, a detached analysis of the problem.

And if that wasn't straight from Bones's gob, he didn't know what was.

He came to a standstill. Okay, he told himself. I'll do it this once. I'll interfere, just this once. For the first time in my life I'll be Mark the Comforter. He was relieved when he approached her to find that she had stopped crying. He noticed, though, that it was now her turn to pretend she hadn't seen him, and even when he was standing no more than a few feet from her, she still kept her head resolutely turned away. He felt oddly cheated. Here he was, prepared to do his bit, and she was trying to ignore him. So much for Mark the Bloody Comforter. But he had come this far, he was damned if he was going to let her get off without offering her some glib piece of reassuring advice. The least she could do was play along and stop him from feeling such a prize idiot.

He cleared his throat to speak, but couldn't think of one sensible thing to say. He might earn his living by the pen and be known for writing realistic dialogue, but in this situation it was clear he was no spontaneous soother. And as she continued to ignore him, he despaired of ever finding the right words.

And the longer the silence continued between them, the worse it became. He was well and truly caught between a rock and a hard place – creep away once more and look a fool, or brazen it out and look as big a fool. Then, luckily for him, the matter was taken out of his hands.

'I'm sorry, I'm taking your place, aren't I?' Her voice was soft, lower than he had expected.

'Sorry? Place?'

She swung her legs round and hopped down until she

was level with him. 'I've seen you sitting here most days. It's where you like to come first thing in the morning when nobody's about, isn't it? I'll leave you to it.'

Her words had been rushed, and her grey gaze slid over him, elusive as quicksilver. He detected within her a nervous energy that wasn't dissimilar from what he was feeling. 'No, don't do that. Well, not unless you have to,' he said.

Their roles reversed again and now it was she who hesitated. 'I . . . I ought to be getting back.'

'To the Sinclairs'?'

She gave him a puzzled look. 'You know them?'

'I know *of* them,' he said. It was as good a way as any to break the ice. 'I also know that your name is Izzy. I'm staying next door with Theo.'

'Oh, so you *are* who I thought you were.'

'And who might that be? Anyone I know?'

Her lips curved into a shy smile. 'The phantom Mark St James. Max was beginning to think that Theo was only pretending to know you.'

'Well, now you'll be able to put him right.' He inclined his head towards the rocks. 'Won't you stay a little longer? I'd hate to feel I'd chivvied you away.'

'But then you won't have your opportunity to sit here and enjoy the view.'

'We could compromise, enjoy the view together. Then I wouldn't feel guilty thinking that I'd cut short your enjoyment.' He could see that his suggestion had surprised her. For that matter, he had surprised himself.

'Okay,' she agreed. 'So long as you're sure.'

Thinking that he would tell Theo not to mess with this girl, that she was far too sweet to be spoiled by him, he helped her back up on to the rock where she had been sitting. 'At least this way we both get to ease our consciences,' he said, when they were settled. Staring out over the stretch of water, they watched a ferry slide along the imperceptible line of the horizon. As its progress continued, a swell of water travelled across the narrow strait, until it finally broke into a series of noisy, crashing waves on the shore, churning up the sand, shifting the stones and pebbles. When the ship had passed, the water reverted to its former steady calm; a gently rippling swathe of silk. And for two people who had never met before, they sat in a curiously companionable silence, taking in the pale, golden sunlight and a translucent sky that hadn't yet fully woken to its mantle of dazzling blue.

Only minutes before, Izzy had been cursing the appearance of somebody else on the beach, but now she was glad of the distraction he had brought with him, grateful that his presence alone had magically stemmed her tears: tears she had allowed to get the better of her.

Her earlier attempt at drifting off to sleep again had been futile, just as she had known it would be, so she had dressed and come down here. It had seemed the perfect place to lose her maudlin thoughts but, sadly, it had only added to them. The beauty and serenity of the secluded cove were supposed to have cleared her mind and coaxed her into a peaceful state of all's-right-with-the-world, and to a degree it had worked, yet at the same time the perfection had caught her off guard. In the end, she had given in to her feelings: a good cry was what she needed, she told herself, as the tears gathered momentum and made her feel much worse. And if it hadn't been for the man sitting next to her, she would probably still be bawling her eyes out. She felt she ought to thank him for rescuing her from herself, but she suspected it would embarrass him. She had witnessed all too plainly the expression on his face just before he had turned and walked away. But what else could he have done? She had been taken aback, though, when he had reappeared by her side. She wondered now what had changed his mind.

Had it simply been his determination to have his fix of early-morning solitary space?

She winced at her unfortunate choice of words. Last night, and after Theo had left, Max had filled her in on part of the conversation she had missed while she had been in the kitchen with Corky and Olivia, and the reason why Theo's friend had turned down their invitation to join them for a drink. She didn't know anything about alcoholism or drugs, and couldn't imagine what it must be like to live each day so thoroughly out of control. Or what might drive a person into such a hopeless situation. She thought of the day she had seen him here sitting on these very rocks, and how she had thought he had an interesting face, not knowing that, at some stage in his life, he must have been unutterably wretched.

Taking a sideways glance at him, she decided that her original description still held good. Not quite what you'd call handsome, but definitely interesting. Close up, the angular lines of his face were a little more pronounced, his nose a touch longer and straighter, and his mouth firmer. But what she hadn't been able to appreciate before was the colour of his eyes. They were a brilliant blue, which surprised her: for some reason she had expected brown. She was also surprised by the depth of sensitivity she saw within them. Recalling the charcoal sketch she had done of him from memory, and which was in her sketchpad in the bag at her feet, she realised she might have drawn him quite differently had she caught a glimpse of those eyes: they would have softened the harsh, dramatic features she had given him.

They had been silent for some minutes now and, worried that he might feel she was being rude and ignoring him again, she asked the first question that came into her head. 'I bet you get asked this all the time, but is it very lonely being a writer?'

187

'Not really. You have to take into account that when I'm working I'm surrounded by some of the weirdest, most absorbing people in the world. Take it from me, psychopaths are anything but dull.'

His voice was low and husky, nearly as compelling as his eyes. 'What a strange life you must lead.'

'Yeah, I know, I should get out more. But I enjoy what I do. It gives me the ideal excuse not to join in with the rest of the world. I can be an official observer without ever having to participate. So what do you do for a living?'

'I'm a teacher.'

'Ooh, now that's what I call a scary job. What do you teach?'

'Apart from idiots?'

He turned and beamed his extraordinary blue gaze on her. 'Do I detect a schoolmarm with attitude?'

'A frustrated art teacher, actually.'

'Is there any other kind?'

'Mm . . . I think you're right. It would be a reassuring thought if art teachers the world over were as frustrated as I was. I'd feel normal then.'

'Normal is boring. Have no truck with it. So when you grow up, what will you do?'

'What do you mean when I grow up?'

He smiled and caused her again to reconsider the anatomy of his face. The lifting of the corners of his mouth softened all those angles and lines.

'Easy there, girl, I was paying you a compliment. Isn't it every woman's wish to be thought younger than she really is?'

'Not if it puts her at a disadvantage.'

He pushed a hand through his fine collar-length blond hair, which was fairer at the tips than at the roots; she suspected he didn't visit the hairdresser too often. 'Bad experience with ageism?' he said.

'Regularly. Only last month I answered the door to a man collecting for some charity or other and he asked if my mother was at home.'

'What did you do? Bludgeon him to death for his cheek?'

'No, I put an extra fifty pence in his tin. He was collecting for the blind.'

He laughed. 'So, given that you're all grown-up, what would you rather be doing instead of teaching? Painting for a living, perhaps?'

She shook her head. 'A nice dream, but not a viable one, I'm afraid. The truth is, I'm not good enough.'

'Says who?'

'Um . . . says me.'

'And you'd know, would you? You're objective enough with your own creative endeavours, are you?' His low, gravelly voice sounded sharp, almost querulous. 'I'm sorry,' he said, and in a more gentle tone, 'I got carried away then. It just seemed as though you were being unnecessarily hard on yourself and, believe me, I know how that feels.'

Glancing up at his face and catching another glimpse of his eyes, she sensed that he meant what he was saying. It made her think how very different he was from his friend, Theo. And thinking now of Theo, she realised that she had been excessively hard on him last night. He hadn't deserved the treatment she had given him. It wasn't his fault that the words he had uttered about her father had cut her to the quick – *Were you very close?* How was he to know that closeness was the very thing she had never experienced with her father, that as a child it had been what she had craved above all else. Most daughters go through a period of idolising their fathers, but given the inflammatory atmosphere in which Izzy had grown up, she had needed hers as an ally. But he had never been there for her. He had turned a blind eye to what was going on. Until now, she had never wanted to think badly of him, but that was what her earlier outburst of tears had been about. The raw injustice of it all had finally pressed down on her, shocking her with its revelatory intensity. It was the sudden realisation that, after all these years, she had been harbouring a desperate need to tell him what she really thought of him. She wondered if the violent anger she had felt for Alan in that counsellor's room when she had thrown her cold coffee at him had had nothing to do with his stupid infidelity, but had been her latent desire to hurt her father, to let him know what it felt like to be so completely betrayed.

And, in a very small way, she had done the same thing to Theo last night. She decided to be bold and ask Mark if he would pass on her apologies to Theo. 'Would you do me a favour?' she asked.

'Depends what it is. If it involves gun running, I'm not your man.'

She smiled. 'No, this is quite legal. It's just that I've been very rude to Theo and, well, I think he deserves an apology. Do you think you could tell him that I'm sorry for being so short with him?'

He took a moment to consider her words, then said, 'You know, apologies are always best delivered in person. Why don't you come back to the villa now and tell him yourself?'

She hesitated. 'It's still quite early. Will he be awake?'

'Let's go and find out, shall we?'

Chapter Twenty

All the way up to Villa Anna Izzy tried to work out how best to apologise to Theo. Too much of an apology and he would probably take it as a come-on, and he was in no need of encouragement. But too little and it would appear insincere. She wondered, too, why she had let herself be persuaded into this out-of-character act of spontaneity, and by someone she had only just met.

But all thoughts of what she would say were pushed aside when Mark opened a small wooden gate, and led her through a garden that was a sumptuous paradise of colour and scent. They found Theo floating on his back in the pool. His eyes were closed, and his body was a picture of relaxed pleasure. It was also naked.

'Theo,' Mark said, 'you might want to put something on, I've brought someone to see you.'

It was clear, from the expression on Theo's face as he opened his eyes and saw Izzy staring down at him, that he was shocked. Without a word, he swam to the shallow end where Mark was waiting for him with a towelling robe that had been hanging on the back of a chair. Izzy was surprised by his manner. She would have expected him to brazen it out, which would have been more in keeping with his behaviour to date. Was he genuinely embarrassed? Or was he just being a gentleman and saving her blushes? Either way, she found it rather endearing.

'I met Izzy down on the beach,' said Mark. 'We got

chatting and I invited her to join us for breakfast. That all right with you?'

This was news to Izzy. She thought she was here to apologise and then go home. She didn't hear Theo's muttered answer but Mark simply laughed and said, 'I'll go and throw some breakfast together, leave you two to chat.'

'Perhaps this wasn't such a good idea,' Izzy said, when they were alone and she watched Theo tighten the belt on his robe. 'I shouldn't have accepted Mark's invitation.'

Theo's unshaven face, which until now had been clouded with what she had taken to be annoyance, suddenly cleared with one of his familiar smiles, his usual equanimity shining through. 'I'm glad that you did. I'm just sorry that you have found me in such a state of disrepair. I'm ashamed to admit it, but I have a hangover. A little too much Metaxá last night.' He raised a hand and touched his head lightly. 'Which was why you found me in the pool as you did. In my weakened state, the sea did not appeal. Please, sit down. Or perhaps you would like a look round. My garden is very beautiful at this time of day. The scent from the roses is quite magnificent.'

'Thank you, I'd like that.'

He slipped on a pair of smooth leather sandals and led the way. They followed a gravel path, lined at either side with stone urns containing luxuriant ferns and the occasional lemon and kumquat tree, until they came to a lower level that was a pretty oasis of green and cream. 'This is one of my favourite areas,' he said. Behind them was a towering Scots pine and the ground they stood on was soft and cushiony, where needles had dropped from the tree. The still morning air was heavy with the scent of pine, but a headier, more exotic and luscious fragrance came from the creamy blooms of a curved bed of exquisite roses. 'It may seem a little grand, but I call this my rose garden,' he said, fingering a petal that looked as perfect as it smelt. 'Some of these are very old – they came from my grandmother's garden. I would hate to lose a single one of them. It would be a great loss. Angelos is under strict orders to take good care of them. Especially when I'm not here.'

'How touchingly sentimental that sounds,' Izzy said.

For a couple of seconds he didn't say anything. Then: 'You think me incapable of sentiment, Izzy? You think I am not able to feel real emotion?' His tone was accusing, and the vehemence behind his words baffled her.

When she didn't answer, he turned away from her and said, 'Well, no matter. You would not be the first to jump to such a conclusion.'

He seemed so strangely introverted that she decided it was time to get her apology over and done with before she caused any more antagonism between them. 'Before I offend you further,' she said, 'I've got something I'd like to say.'

He returned his gaze to her, and stared at her keenly, his head slightly tilted. His attentiveness made it all the more difficult for her to get the words out.

'Um . . . I was very rude to you last night,' she pressed on, 'and . . . and I just wanted you to know that it wasn't anything to do with you. It was me. I was in a terrible mood and I took it out on you. I'm sorry. I just wanted you to know that.'

He came towards her, visibly lightened by what she had said. The gap between them suddenly seemed dangerously small and the atmosphere dangerously intoxicating with the potent fragrance of the flowers as the sunlight filtered through the trees.

'We have only known one another for a short time,' he said, 'but it seems to me that on several occasions I have annoyed and offended you. So I, too, would like to say that I am sorry. I think also that you have an opinion of me that, if I am honest, is one I have stupidly encouraged.

But I would very much like to be given the opportunity to change that perception, if it isn't too late. What do you say? Do you think we could be friends?'

She smiled.

He took another step towards her. 'Is that a yes?'

'Um . . . a cautious yes.'

He reached for her hand, lifted it to his lips and kissed it, while all the time keeping his dark eyes on hers. 'There,' he said, lowering her hand and flashing a smile, 'that was not so bad, was it?'

Despite the presence of Modern Woman tapping her foot and warning that if she wasn't careful she'd be right back where she'd started, Izzy agreed that it wasn't.

Chapter Twenty-One

Laura poured bottled water into the kettle and plugged it in. She put the empty plastic container in the bin and made a mental note to check how much they had left. What with her mother's insatiable desire for tea, they were getting through an inordinate amount of water. Last year she had made the mistake of using water straight from the tap, and while it was perfectly safe to do so, the brackish aftertaste was far from appetising or refreshing.

The tea made, she took it outside and was about to settle down with her book, which she still hadn't finished, when she heard footsteps behind her.

It was Francesca, looking as slothful and bleary-eyed as she herself felt. She dipped her head and kissed Laura's cheek. 'Morning, Mum.'

'It's a little early for you, isn't it? Couldn't you sleep?'

'Sally's snoring like an volcano.'

'Oh dear. Not a lot we can do about that. Do you want a cup of tea? I've just made a pot.'

'Nah, I'll make some coffee in a moment, when I've got myself together.' She yawned and stretched out on the sun-lounger beside Laura, her slim, lithe body already dressed for action in a fluorescent pink bikini. Since it was her first real opportunity to talk to her daughter on her own since she had arrived, Laura broached the subject of the recently departed boyfriend. She wanted to be sure that Francesca's apparent easy-come-easy-go attitude wasn't just a brave front. Regrets were seldom of any use and, as Max would be the first to say, the boy simply wasn't worth the trouble.

'Glad you came?' she asked. 'The change doing you good?'

Francesca turned her head. There were smudgy signs of eye makeup that hadn't been cleaned off from last night, and with her henna-dyed hair still loosely plaited and sticking out at either side of her ears, she reminded Laura of Pippy Longstocking from the books she used to read to her when she was little. 'Are we venturing into heart-to-heart territory?' Francesca asked.

'Only if you want to go there.'

'Cool it, Mum, you should know me better than that. For once I agree with Dad. Carl was a pillock and I'm not going to lose any sleep over him. Anyway, it looks as if Sally and I have got something better to interest us right here.'

'Some local colour?'

'No, home-grown is safer. Less risk of being misunderstood. We got chatting to them last night in Kassiópi.'

When she embarked upon these conversations Laura knew she was treading a difficult path: she wanted her daughter to confide in her, but at the same time she didn't want to acknowledge just how much of an adult Francesca was. She said, 'Would I be right in thinking it's the two lads from the pink villa?'

'You're remarkably well informed. Or has Dad been spying on me?'

Laura laughed. 'Are their parents with them?' She was wondering if she dared invite them for a drink so that she and Max could carry out a thorough inspection of the boys. After all, they had Sally's welfare to consider: while she was staying with them she was their responsibility whether she liked it or not.

'Yes,' confirmed Francesca, with an exaggerated roll of her eyes. 'So no worries about a shagathon taking place.'

'A shagathon,' repeated a voice from behind them. 'What a delightful expression. In our day we called it an orgy.'

It was Olivia. She patted the top of her granddaughter's head affectionately and pulled up a chair. 'Is that fresh tea?'

'Yes, it is. Francesca, would you fetch your grandmother a cup, please?'

In the brief space of time that they were alone, Laura said, 'You could at least pretend to be shocked.'

'But why?'

'I bet you wouldn't have let Max get away with anything half so outrageous. A shagathon indeed!'

Olivia smiled. 'But that's what's so good about the age we live in. Grandparents are allowed to behave as disgracefully as their grandchildren. It's the middle years when we're expected to conform. Take it from me, Corky and I have much more fun, these days.'

Laura groaned. 'I knew it would happen sooner or later – *Grans Behaving Badly*!'

Francesca returned with a cup for Corky, and the foresight to bring a few extras. 'For everyone else when they surface,' she said, plonking them on the table. 'I'm off for a swim. See you later.'

The first thing Harry saw when he pushed back the shutters, was a blurred outline of blue, white and green. He slipped on his glasses, and the blue became sky and sea, the white, sand, and the green, the verdant hillside. He stepped outside and leaned against the wrought-iron rail that separated his cramped bedroom terrace from the more spacious terrace below, where they congregated as a family for indigestible meals of combat and tension. He pushed his hands through his sleep-tousled hair and took in the splendour of the morning. It was then that he saw somebody swimming.

Squinting, he saw that it was Francesca, the more attractive of the two girls they had got talking to last night. And, naturally, because she was the most attractive, Nick had stepped in straight away and staked out the boundaries. They had been sitting in one of the bars in Kassiópi; he had been watching *Saving Private Ryan* on a large screen above the bar while his brother had been eyeing up the potential. The two girls had seen them the minute they had walked in but, in the way all girls did, they had pretended not to see them. 'Hold tight,' Nick had said, out of the corner of his mouth. 'Chick alert. I'll give them a few minutes to settle in, then I'll make a move on them. You can have the tall one. Mine's the one with the sticky-out plaits. Cute or what?'

'What if you're not her type?' Harry had said.

Nick had given him a look of mocking disbelief. 'Drink up, and I'll get us another round in.'

He had watched Nick saunter over to the bar and wondered why girls were always drawn to his brother. Even when he had been at junior school he could pull a crowd of them around him. But whatever cheesy line he had given these two, it had had the desired effect: they had followed him back to the table and introduced themselves. The tall one was called Sally, and the one his brother had labelled as cute was Francesca. It turned out that they were the same age as his brother, a few months short of twenty. Being older by two years he had felt alienated from them as a group, and had found his attention wandering from the conversation, letting it settle on Tom Hanks and his platoon. As a consequence they had probably written him off as boring. Well, so be it. What did it matter?

But as he watched Francesca diving from the raft opposite her parents' villa, he realised that it did matter. Just for once, he wanted people to think that he was as interesting as his brother.

With a rueful shake of his head, he went back into his room. What would be the point? Faced with the choice between him – Mr Dullsville – and his brother – Mr Hip-Hop-Goin'-With-The-Groove – who seemed to possess all the magnetic pull of a crushed-velvet Austin Powers, he wouldn't get a look in.

Smirking quietly to himself, Mark was impressed at the show Theo was putting on for Izzy's benefit. It was a top performance of carefully measured moves that he obviously thought would put her at ease. It had been Mark's intention to leave Theo and Izzy to eat their breakfast alone, but Theo had sought him out in the kitchen and said, 'Please, you must stay with me. I sense that she will be more relaxed with you acting as a chaperon.'

Watching the almost reverential manner in which he was treating her, Mark wondered if he had misjudged Theo. Wasn't it bound to happen, that sooner or later he would find a woman who would mean more to him than a potential bedroom tumble? And who was he to doubt his friend's ability to love? His past was hardly a glowing account of starry-eyed romance. Perhaps he had allowed his history of disastrous relationships to colour his opinion of what Theo might be capable of feeling for Izzy.

Or was he jealous?

The treachery of this thought appalled him. Was it possible that he was jealous that his friend might find happiness – while he might not?

It was such a disagreeable thought that he quickly manoeuvred it to the back of his mind, to the storehouse of conundrums he had yet to unravel. A writer's mind was packed with useful and not so useful fragments of information. He had a mental picture of his brain as an old-fashioned ironmonger's shop, its walls covered in shelves overflowing with bits and bobs. Trouble was, when he wanted to find anything in a hurry, he needed an ancient, efficient employee who could lay his hands instantly on exactly what Mark was looking for. Which was why he had to write things down: if he didn't he might never retrieve the irreplaceable flashes of inspiration that slipped in and out of his mind.

He had been on the verge of doing exactly this last night when he had been in the harbour. He had thought of something, which, at the time, had seemed earth-shatteringly important. But with the appearance of Dolly-Babe and Silent Bob, it had wriggled away. He hated losing ideas. It was like being robbed of something precious, and the perpetrators of this heinous crime had joined him on the bench.

'Did you get my message?' Dolly-Babe had asked.

He had decided to play dumb. 'Message?'

She tutted, giving him the benefit of alcohol-tainted breath. She leaned in close to him, so close he could see his bored face reflected back in her sunglasses – didn't she ever take them off? It was dark, for pity's sake. 'You know, you wanna watch that chauffeur of yours,' she said. 'I asked him to tell you that I wanted to invite you over to our villa for a drink.'

'It must have slipped his memory.'

Another tut.

'I was going to invite your neighbours as well, the Sinclairs. But I never got round to it. Bob's been rushed off his size nines. He's been dashing all over the island. Isn't that right, Bob?'

But Bob wasn't listening. He was talking quietly to somebody on his mobile phone.

'He's very busy,' she said, lowering her voice. 'Lots of irons in the fire. He's found some land for sale that he says is just the job.' And then, 'This is no coincidence, you know. Us seeing you this evening.'

'Really?'

She smiled. 'I gave Ria, my tarot reader, a call this morning, just to see what was in store for me. For Bob too.' She lowered her voice again. 'He's got some important decisions to make over the coming weeks and I want to be sure he knows what he's doing. Anyway, I asked her about the tall, fair-haired man who was going to bring me luck, and . . .' She paused, obviously building up the tension to an enthralling dénouement.

'And?' he filled in for her, providing the necessary drumroll.

'And she said we'd meet again. *Soon.*'

'How extraordinary.'

'There's no denying the psychic forces that surround us, is there?' she said. 'You feel it too, don't you?'

'Did she see anything else on your horizon?' he asked, curious to hear what further madness she could be convinced of.

'Well, the Eight of Cups showed up.'

His clueless expression invited her to expand. 'It's a card that promises new and bigger social horizons,' she said helpfully. 'New faces. New places. New experiences. New everything, in fact.'

It sounded a fair description of just about anybody's annual holiday. It was time for him to make his escape. 'It's been great seeing you again,' he lied, 'but I ought to be getting back.'

'We're off now as well. Where are you parked? Just here in the harbour?'

'No, I'm on foot.' Too late he realised his mistake. A lift home was eagerly pressed upon him, as was a firm invitation for him to drop in at Villa Mimosa. 'Don't be a stranger, call in for a chat any time,' she said, as they pulled up outside Theo's villa. 'It must be very dull being here all on your lonesome.'

Thanking them for the lift and watching their hire car disappear down the drive, he began to change his opinion of Dolly-Babe. Behind the glossy make-up, the too young designer frocks, the sunglasses and the ridiculous belief that some Mystic Meg at the other end of a telephone line had the answers to what lay ahead for her, there was a sad and lonely woman. A woman who, while her husband was playing the big wheeler-dealer, probably drank more than was good for her. It made him wonder what she was running away from.

They had long since finished breakfast – fresh figs, toast with local honey and a pot of coffee – and had moved into the shaded area of the terrace, which was covered by a pergola of twisted vine. Theo was explaining to Izzy how the fruit above their heads, green and tiny now, would grow into fat red grapes that would be harvested in the autumn and made into wine. She was looking at Theo with what Mark could only describe as a private half-smile, as though she had just thought of something that amused her. He was intrigued to know what it was.

'Don't you believe a word of it, Izzy,' he said, as he heard Theo trying to convince her that he would be taking off his socks and shoes to help Angelos tread the grapes. 'Can you imagine him risking his expensive hand-made clothes with such dirty work?'

'Ha! And do you see so much as a callus on my friend's hands?' asked Theo. 'He is no more a sweaty son of the soil than I am. Ever since I have known him, he has tried to make himself out to be a friend of the people, a working-class hero, but it is nothing more than an act with him. Don't let him fool you, Izzy.'

'I think if I have any sense at all I won't let either of you fool me,' Izzy said, with a laugh. 'Are you always like this?'

'Like what?' asked Theo.

'So rude and horrible to each other.'

'This is us being nice to each other,' said Mark. 'You

should be around when we're going at it hammer and tong.'

'And who usually gets the upper hand?'

'You think that I, Theo Vlamakis, would let a fraud like Mark get the better of me? Tsk, tsk, Izzy, you disappointment me. I never lose at verbal fisticuffs.'

'The hell you don't! I let you win occasionally just so you don't lose heart.'

'But I allow you to think that you have let me win so that your poor little ego can give itself a pat on its back.'

'Oh, you poor sick bastard, how did you ever climb to the top of the food chain?'

Theo turned to Izzy with a triumphant smile. 'There! You see how easily I have won the argument? When Mark resorts to profanity, it is because he knows he is losing the debate. He is a hopeless case, but one I take pity on. More coffee?'

'No, thank you. I really ought to be going.' She glanced at her watch. 'Goodness! Just look at the time. Laura will be wondering where I am.' She picked up her bag, slipped it over her shoulder and got to her feet. 'I had no idea I'd been here so long. I hope I haven't kept you from anything important.'

'Not at all,' urged Theo. 'But calm yourself, there's no need to hurry. It is but a short walk to next door.'

They saw her to the wooden gate that led to the path which would take her back to Villa Petros. 'And thank you again for breakfast,' she said, as she turned to leave them, 'I really enjoyed it. You've both cheered me up.'

'You will come again, perhaps? When you are in need of more cheering up?'

She didn't answer Theo's question, but gave him a flicker of a smile. Then she waved goodbye and hurried away.

Watching her go, Theo sighed. 'You know, Mark, I was very cross with you earlier for bringing Izzy here when I was in no state to be seen, but it seems that once again I am in your debt. How did you persuade her to come?'

Mark shrugged. 'She mentioned that she felt bad about last night and asked if I would pass on an apology to you. I simply said that apologies were best made in person.'

'As easy as that?'

Mark slapped him on the back. 'Yeah, old mate, as easy as that.'

Chapter Twenty-Two

A week later when Theo asked Izzy to have dinner with him, the response at Villa Petros was mixed.

Laura just smiled knowingly behind *Captain Corelli*, which she still hadn't finished, and Max slipped into old-fashioned parental mode, warning Izzy not to take any nonsense from Theo. 'Don't give him so much as a hint of encouragement,' he muttered darkly, leaning against the balustrade on the terrace and watching Theo make his way back down the path towards his own villa.

Francesca nudged Sally. 'Good to see somebody else getting the treatment that's usually reserved for me.'

'I don't see why Izzy shouldn't encourage him,' said Olivia. 'He's a perfect dear, utterly adorable.'

'Oh, good Lord,' said Corky, glancing in Max's direction, 'I knew that late-night Greek lesson would be a mistake. That fellow's unleashed something dangerous in your mother.'

'Well, if Izzy changes her mind, I'll be more than happy to fill in for her,' said Sally. 'Two minutes' notice would be all I'd need to get this body buffed up ready for him.'

'More like an entire afternoon,' sniggered Francesca.

Sally dealt her a nifty swipe with the magazine she was reading. 'Two minutes and I'd be irresistible to him. I'd have him panting at my feet.'

'Yeah, but he'd still be two decades older than you,' laughed Francesca. She raised herself from her sun-lounger. 'Come on, let's go for a swim and see if those Patterson boys are out and about.'

Izzy watched the two girls gather together their towels, flip-flops, sunglasses and bottles of Ambre Solaire, then picked up Sally's well-thumbed copy of *Cosmopolitan*, opened it at random and hid behind it, not wanting to catch anybody's eye, especially not Laura's. Too much had already been said on the subject of her having dinner with Theo and she really didn't want the fuss to continue. She felt a little as though she had been tricked into accepting his invitation. He had made it in front of everyone and she had known that she would have looked rude and churlish if she had said no. Although, curiously enough, she hadn't wanted to say no.

Since last week when she had made her peace with Theo he had behaved with impeccable restraint towards her. Not that they had seen much of him. Like Max, he had been busy with work – much to Laura's disappointment Max had even flown home for three days of important meetings. But when she had seen Theo, it had been down on the beach, before anyone else was up and while she had been sketching the bay. He would come and sit next to her after his early-morning swim. Yesterday Mark had joined them too, though he hadn't swum.

'Don't you like swimming?' she had asked him.

'I could ask the same of you,' he had said.

'It's too early for me. Too cold. I need the sea to have warmed up before I venture in.'

'Then that's the excuse I shall use as well. May I see?'

She passed him her sketchpad and watched his face for his reaction.

'I thought you said you weren't any good at this game?'

She looked critically at the charcoal drawing, a view of the headland showing Theo's villa peeping through the cypress trees. 'It's one of my better attempts.'

'So what are the bad ones like?' He began flicking

through the pages, but Izzy remembered that the pad contained the drawing she had done of him some weeks earlier and snatched it out of his hands.

'That bad, eh? Well, I suppose we all underestimate our talents.'

'Even you?'

He raised an eyebrow. 'Implying that I don't seem the type to be insecure?'

'You seem very confident to me.'

'It's all a front. I'm as riven as the next artistic soul.' She laughed.

'Why do I get the feeling you're not taking me seriously?'

'Perhaps I should read one of your books. Maybe then I'd be able to judge you better. Reading between the lines, I might get to see the real you.'

He feigned a look of hurt pride and put a clenched fist to his heart. 'You mean you haven't read one of my novels? I'm deeply wounded.' Then, dropping the act, he said, 'So if you don't like my kind of fiction, what do you read?'

'All sorts,' she said evasively. She let a handful of sand slip through her fingers, strongly suspecting that he would frown upon her choice of reading matter which usually contained romance and a happy ending.

'And specifically?' he pressed. 'What was the last book you read?'

'Don't let him bully you, Izzy.' Theo had emerged from the water. 'He is too used to mixing with literary snobs to appreciate that some people read for pleasure and escape rather than to be lectured.'

'That's simply not true, Theo, as well you know. I've never been able to abide that affected attitude. Pejorative conceit is what I've always fought against. Perhaps you should let Izzy speak for herself.'

They both looked at her, each waiting for her to take their side.

'Um . . . I think I'd rather leave you both to it,' she said, feeling that she couldn't answer one without offending the other. She put her things into her bag and stood up.

'You see what you've done, Mark?' Theo exclaimed. 'With your intimidating arrogance you have scared her away.'

'Hey, she was fine until you poked your nose in.'

'Stop it, you two.' She had laughed. 'I have enough of bickering children during term-time. When I'm on holiday I expect a break from it.'

They had been quick to apologise, and Theo said, 'Come and have breakfast with us and we'll prove to you that we can behave quite civilly.'

'And if we misbehave you can scold us again,' smiled Mark. 'You do it so beautifully.'

'Another time perhaps,' she had said. 'It's my turn this morning to go up to Nicos and fetch the rolls and croissants for everybody.'

That had been yesterday, and this morning Theo had appeared with a present for her. It was a book. 'It's from both of us and is by way of an apology for behaving like two naughty schoolboys yesterday. You mentioned to Mark that you were interested in reading one of his books and he wondered if you would enjoy this one. It is his first, and possibly his least bloodthirsty, but by no means the least unnerving. Please, borrow it for as long as you wish.'

She had read the blurb on the jacket and, under everyone's gaze, had opened the book and read the printed dedication: 'To Theo, because he was stupid enough to care.' Underneath was written, in a large loose hand, 'Don't worry, I'm not going soft on you – Mark.'

Intrigued, she had asked, 'What did you care so much about?'

He had closed the book in her hands, flashed her one of his brilliant smiles, and said, 'Have dinner with me tonight and I'll tell you.'

Confident now that everybody was going to leave her alone, she put down Sally's magazine and reached for the book Theo had brought for her. Its title – *Culling The Good* – didn't give the impression that she was in for a light-hearted romp. She looked at the photograph of Mark on the inside back flap: it showed him leaning against a wall in a darkened archway, his arms folded across his chest. He was wearing a leather jacket and an air of open hostility. The photographer must have spent an age getting the light and shadows just right, ensuring that they fell across his cheekbones to accentuate their sharpness as well as hollow out his eyes and emphasise the slight twist to his mouth. His hair was shorter than it was now, savagely so, and gave him a chilling insolence that was as disagreeable as it was threatening. He looked quite terrifying, the kind of man anyone with any sense would cross the road to avoid late at night. "The new prince of darkness," was one of the quotes on the back of the book, and certainly the man in the picture gave the appearance of more than living up to that description. Yet it was difficult to equate the man she had met, who made her smile with his unexpected humour, with the bleak person portrayed here. She turned to the author's biographical notes, to see if she could learn more about him, but there was only the year in which he had been born and the wide-ranging number of jobs he had had a go at: she could quite easily see him as a cub reporter, but not as a milkman. Nor could she visualise him working in a funeral parlour. Perhaps it was *de rigueur* to have an off-the-wall CV if you were going to be a successful author.

*

Exactly on time, Theo brought his car to a halt outside Villa Petros. He had been ready for over half an hour, but Mark had insisted that he play it cool. 'Early just won't do at all,' he had said.

'And you would know, would you?' Theo had thrown at him, while fiddling with his keys and checking his shirt collar in the mirror.

'Okay, I might not have your experience, but I know for sure that women don't like to be surprised when they're getting ready. Hurry her through those last few moments and the evening could be a disaster. She'll spend the first thirty minutes worrying that her makeup isn't right, or cursing you for making her forget those essential pieces of jewellery.'

'Izzy doesn't wear makeup.'

'She might tonight. She might feel she has to impress you.'

Now, as Theo pressed the doorbell, he hoped that Mark was wrong, that Izzy didn't feel the need to impress him. The last thing he wanted was for her to have spoiled her natural charm by covering herself in what she didn't need. She was perfect just as she was. He thought of the night when he had first met her and hoped that he was in for a repeat performance.

Max opened the door to him and led him through to the sitting room. Straight away Theo sensed that the relationship between them had shifted from its customary friendliness.

'So, where are you taking Izzy?' asked Max. He spoke stiffly, with all the authority of a Victorian father. He might just as well have been standing with his back to the fireplace, his hands clasped behind him, ready to take a horsewhip to Theo. It was tempting to taunt him and he was on the verge of doing so when he heard voices. Francesca and Sally came in from the terrace through one of the open french windows.

'Hi, Theo,' said Francesca. She threw herself on to one of the sofas and kicked off her fluorescent orange flip-flops. 'All ready for your hot date with Izzy?'

He smiled. 'I was under the impression I was merely having dinner with her. It has now turned into a hot date, has it? What fun. I look forward to the evening with greater anticipation.' Out of the corner of his eye he saw Sally draping her slinky body along the length of the sofa to his right. She was doing her best to attract his attention, running a hand through her long hair and sighing exaggeratedly. Amused, he turned to Max and suggested they go outside.

'How is it going with your young house guest?' he asked, when they were beyond eavesdropping distance. He hoped the question might help to restore the equilibrium of their friendship.

'She's behaving herself quite well, really. She's been as good as gold, apart from that little display in there just now.'

'Well, to put your mind at rest, she is wasting her time with me.'

Max looked at him closely. 'It's not you and Sally I'm worried about.'

'Oh?'

'Come off it, Theo. Don't play the innocent with me. This thing you seem to have going with Izzy, you won't . . . well, you won't do anything to upset her, will you? I'm very fond of her and I'd hate to see her . . .' He cleared his throat and tried again. 'I'd hate to see her used in any way.'

Levelling his gaze on Max's concerned face, Theo said, 'Two questions, Max. What "thing" is it you assume that I have going with Izzy, and why would I want to upset her?'

'You know jolly well what I mean. You have a certain attitude when it comes to women.'

Theo shook his head. 'No, Max. You have decided for me that I have a certain attitude towards women. You have leaped to a conclusion regarding my private life and refuse to see me in any other light. But I will give you this promise: I have no more intention of hurting Izzy than you did when you first got to know Laura.'

'But that was different. It was love that I felt for Laura, it wasn't any of this fly-by-night—'

'And there you go again, leaping to conclusions. Now, then, if I am not mistaken, I hear the object of your desire approaching.'

Both men rose to their feet, and at once Theo saw that his wish had been granted. Flanked by Laura and Olivia, the object of his own desire looked as charming as she had the first night they had met.

Chapter Twenty-Three

Shirley Maclaine singing, 'If My Friends Could See Me Now' from the film *Sweet Charity* kept going through Izzy's mind as Theo, smiling and relaxed, decked out sexily in a loose-fitting linen suit, sunglasses and a litre or two of intoxicating aftershave, drove at an alarming speed through the sluggish early evening traffic. As he zigzagged his BMW through the slower-moving cars that threatened to slow his progress he struck Izzy as a man who had been born to drive flashy sports cars.

With the invigorating cool air rushing at her face as they drove along narrow winding roads that took them high into the hills, she was glad that she had elected to wear her hair in a plait – she had known that two minutes in an open-topped car with her hair loose would have been asking for trouble.

Throughout the day Francesca and Sally had been full of useful fashion tips and advice for her evening out with Theo. Francesca had been keen to lend her some outlandish clothes from her wardrobe as well as give her a head of stumpy little bumps threaded with bits of rag, while Sally had advocated the I've-just-tumbled-out-of-bed-but-for-you-I'm-willing-to-get-back-in look. 'Forget Francesca's funky look. Wanton allure is what you want to go for,' she had urged. 'Take it from me, it works every time.'

So would hanging out her tongue and pasting a Bonk Me Now label to it, Izzy had thought. She turned down Sally's offer to let her plunder the bewildering depths of her makeup bag, shooed the girls away and got ready alone, determined not to associate herself with purses made from sows' ears.

Just as Izzy was wondering if there were any more heart-stopping hairpin bends to negotiate, they arrived at the restaurant. It was tucked into the hillside and a craggy-faced man called Spiros greeted them. He looked much older than Theo, but amazingly they were the same age. 'We were in the army together for our national service,' Theo explained. 'That was where Spiros learned to cook so badly.'

'Yes – and, as a military chauffeur, it was where Theo learned to drive so fast,' laughed Spiros. He led them through the air-conditioned interior of the restaurant and outside to a covered area that gave them a perfect view of the slope of the hill they had just climbed, and which stretched away into the lush green valley. The light was already fading and pretty lanterns glowed on the white-clothed tables. Only a few tables were empty, but Spiros guided them to one that was reserved.

No sooner had they taken their seats and Spiros had left them than a short, overweight woman, hot and flushed, appeared. Theo immediately got to his feet and embraced her. After much kissing and a voluble exchange of words, he turned to Izzy and introduced her: 'Izzy, this is Marika, Spiros' wife. She doesn't speak any English, but if you are very nice to her she will cook you the best meal of your life.'

Izzy held out her hand and smiled. '*Kalispéra*,' she said, adding hesitantly '*ti kanete?*'

The other woman's face lit up with approval, but her quick-fired response was way beyond the simple words and phrases Izzy had picked up so far, and she looked to Theo for help. Smiling, he said, 'Marika says she is very well and compliments you on your accent.' Another lively and incomprehensible blast of banter from Marika followed, involving a lot of head-shaking and even a wagging finger. When they were alone, Izzy asked him what else Marika had said – 'She sounded very cross with you.'

He laughed. 'She was saying how beautiful you were, and that you were probably far too good for me.'

Izzy blushed, reached for her menu and studied it hard.

Theo smiled to himself. It hadn't been exactly what Marika had said, but he had seen it as a perfect opportunity to pay Izzy a compliment without frightening her off. Marika had in fact told him that this was yet another attractive woman he had brought to their restaurant and when was he going to make a return visit with the same one?

It amused him that Izzy still took fright every time he said anything nice about her. No matter how sincere he tried to make his words sound, they never penetrated the barrier of embarrassed awkwardness she hid behind. He had mentioned it to Mark. 'It doesn't matter how serious I try to be, she clearly thinks I am falsely flattering her. The guard, it goes straight up.'

'She's intelligent and English, Theo. *Ergo*, she has a natural suspicion of foreign men such as you, who make it their business to trade flattery for sex.'

'I don't recall my being a foreigner presenting itself as a problem when we were students.'

'The girls then were young and foolishly taken in by your supposed Continental good looks and money. You were one of the swankiest students in college, infamous for your extravagant parties. Of course they fell for you. You were a good catch – you were the Aristotle Onassis of Old Durham Town.'

'So how am I to gain her trust?'

'Perhaps you never will. Maybe you should just give in to the fact that she doesn't fancy you.'

Thinking of what Mark had said, and glancing at

Izzy's pensive face, Theo felt even more determined to convince her – and everybody else – that he was serious about her. He wasn't used to being denied what he wanted but, to his surprise, the experience was not without its appeal. It would make the moment when it came – and he was certain it would – that much more pleasurable. Denial, he was coming to know, was good for sharpening one's sexual appetite.

Once Spiros had taken their order, brought them their wine and then their starter, they both relaxed into the evening. It was Izzy who asked the first question. 'I've kept my part of the bargain and agreed to have dinner with you. Now you must keep yours.'

'And what would that be?'

'You said you'd tell me the significance of Mark's dedication to you in *Culling The Good*.'

'Ah, I see. Well, before I solve the mystery for you, tell me, have you started reading it, and if so, what do you think of it?'

'I haven't been able to put it down,' she said, truthfully. All that day she had been gripped by its dark, menacing pace. 'I can see that I'm going to have to view Mark in a whole new light.'

He laughed. 'You think, then, that he is more interesting after reading a few chapters of his book?'

She caught his mocking tone. 'Not quite, but it does leave me wondering what else he's got going on inside that head of his.'

'You would not be the first.'

This time Theo's words were weighted with a seriousness that made Izzy's curiosity get the better of her. 'The first night I met you, you said that Mark had saved your life. What happened to you?'

He helped himself to another piece of bread from the basket between them, wiped it across his plate of fried aubergine salad, and said, 'It was when we were students. Late one night, on my way home after a party, I was attacked by a couple of young gentlemen who were eager to part me from my wallet. It was lucky for me that Mark is such a hooligan and is able to fight so well.' Finishing what was in his mouth, he added, 'According to the doctors, I was fortunate that Mark was passing at the time. If it had not been for him—' He stopped abruptly.

'Go on,' she said softly. She sensed that for once Theo was in earnest.

But if he had been, it was short-lived. His face lit up with a sexy grin and he said, 'If it had not been for Mark I would not be here tonight enjoying myself with you.'

Annoyed, she fiddled with her wine-glass, twisting its stem between her fingers. 'I wish you wouldn't do that.'

'I should very much like for your every wish to be my command, but what is it exactly that I must stop doing?'

'You always . . . oh, I don't know, but everything turns into a joke with you.'

'Why should that be a problem?'

'It means I never know where I stand with you.'

'You would rather I was more sombre?'

'Yes, if it meant I didn't think you were laughing at me.'

In an instant the smile was gone from his face. He reached across the table, took her wine-glass from her, then held her hand. 'Is that what you think I have been doing? Is that why you refuse to let your guard down with me?'

She tried to slip away her hand, but he grasped it firmly.

'Izzy, please, I want you to know that I would never laugh at you. I'm not playing some silly game. It is important to me that you understand that.'

Izzy wished the conversation hadn't taken this particular turn, and suddenly felt tense, wary of where Theo might think he could lead her. But then she chided herself for overreacting. She forced herself to relax, to listen to the plinkety-plink of the bouzoúki music coming from inside the restaurant. 'Did you ever see the film *Shirley Valentine*?' She asked at last, hoping that she had hit upon a way to make Theo understand why she was so cautious of him.

Without releasing her hand, he nodded. 'Yes, of course I have. And I think, much as it will amuse you, most Corfiot men aspire to be your esteemed Mr Tom Conti. But what is the point you are making?'

'Um ... Well, do you remember the part when she discovers that Tom Conti, with whom she has—'

'Yes,' he interrupted, 'the boat looked in danger of capsizing.'

'I wasn't thinking of that bit specifically. I was going to say, do you remember when she realises he's been using the same chat-up line for countless other female tourists?'

Letting go of Izzy's hand, Theo said, 'Ah, so you see me in the same role. You think that I try out the same old routine on any pretty girl who comes my way, is that it?'

She wanted to say, 'Swear that that isn't *exactly* what you do,' but said, 'Maybe you're a tiny bit more subtle.'

He frowned. 'Do you not find me just a little attractive, Izzy?'

'You have your moments,' almost tripped off her tongue, but she doused the confession with a sip of her wine.

Still frowning, he said, 'So how do I convince you that I have the potential to be totally different?'

'You could spend the rest of the evening by not trying to come on to me.'

'What? Not one compliment?'

She shook her head.

'Not one? "Your eyes are like the stars in the heavens—"'

'Definitely not!'

'How about a—'

'Nothing, Theo. You're to be completely straight with me. No silliness.'

'Am I allowed to touch you?'

She hesitated. It had been quite pleasant a few minutes ago when his strong square hand had held hers. 'No,' she said resolutely. There were to be no half measures.

'And what then? If I behave myself all evening, what will be my prize? A kiss maybe?'

With perfect timing, saving her from giving him an answer, Spiros came across the restaurant to take away their empty plates. He returned shortly with their main course, an extravagant seafood platter for them to share. Its crowning glory was a lobster, which Theo got to work on immediately, skilfully dissecting it and passing Izzy pieces of tender white meat. 'Now that I am too scared to open my mouth for fear of breaking our agreement,' he said, 'tell me about yourself. Where in England did you grow up and what kind of a child were you?'

'Well, I think it's fairly safe to say that I was a mistake. My mother didn't want me, and if she'd thought she could get away with it she would probably have lost me in the hospital where I was born. A large laundry basket would have done the trick.'

'Is that, as I have learned from Mark, a classic example of one of your famously ironic English jokes?'

'Actually, no. It's the truth.' To her surprise, she found herself telling him about the brother she had never known, whose tragically short life had eclipsed hers and had caused her mother's breakdown. She skirted briefly over her time in the children's home and the extent of what her mother had inflicted on her. She spoke with detached composure, as if it were someone else's story she was telling. Until now, she hadn't shared with anyone, not even Laura, the details of her childhood. It felt strange lifting the lid after so many years of silence. Part of her had always been afraid to admit what had gone on, as though she would be judged and found wanting in some way. That, maybe, it had been her fault.

'*Ti apésyo!*' Theo said, when she finished speaking.

'Sorry?'

'I said, that's terrible.'

'You're right. It was terrible that my mother's depression wasn't diagnosed sooner.'

'I meant it was awful for you.'

She gave a casual shrug, as if this had never occurred to her before. 'It's not a perfect world that we live in,' she said dismissively. 'All we can do is square our shoulders and put these things behind us.' It was sound advice, and she had tried hard to follow it all her life, but had never truly achieved it.

'So, having squared your shoulders in your typically English Dunkirk spirit, what kind of relationship do you have with your mother now?'

A picture of a vindictive Bette Davis serving up a dish of dead rats in *Whatever Happened to Baby Jane?* came into Izzy's mind. 'Um . . . a difficult one.'

Pouring more wine into their glasses, Theo looked at Izzy thoughtfully. Knowing he was heading into dangerous territory, he said, 'And your father, how did you get on with him?' He saw her hesitate, and waited for her to realign her composure.

'To be honest with you, I never really knew where I stood with him. I spent most of my childhood hoping desperately that he would notice me.'

Theo found it impossible to imagine that any father would not have wanted to hug a younger version of the woman he saw before him and tell her how special she was. 'He was distant with you?'

'I think he had to be. He was caught between my

mother and me. We were both terrified of upsetting or annoying her.'

'You paint a picture that is very black. Were there no good times?'

'Of course there were. I loved school and I was always—'

'But nothing happy in your home life?'

'I suppose to a Greek man this must sound rather strange.'

He nodded. 'Families are very important to us. Generations live together and all in a degree of domestic harmony.'

'No arguments at all?'

'Ah, well, disagreements come naturally to us, but we blow up over them and then we carry on as though nothing has happened. We are used to living in close quarters with those we love and who drive us to distraction. Take Angelos and Sophia, for instance. Under the one roof they have Angelos' mother living with them, a classic matriarchal figure who makes most of the important decisions for the family. They have two young daughters still at school, and they have Giorgios who is in his early twenties and who is quite happy to remain at home. It probably has not occurred to him that he could leave his parents and find a place of his own. He will stay there until he marries. He might even move his bride in with him. And yet it works. Despite the heated disagreements and differences of opinions, they get along famously.'

'Goodness! It sounds the perfect recipe for disaster. Could you live like that?'

'I would prefer not to. But if my parents had nowhere to live, I would gladly have them live with me.'

The thought of her mother moving into Izzy's neat little flat bringing with her the army of china statues made Izzy shudder.

'You are cold? Would you like my jacket to keep you warm?'

'No,' she laughed, 'I was picturing the nightmare scene of my mother moving in with me.'

'Would it be so very bad?'

'It would be awful. Just one weekend with her is enough to sap the most resilient spirit. Within a month I'd lose what little sanity and self-confidence I've scraped together since I left home.'

'She would criticise you?'

'Constantly. It would be one snide comment after another. I'm a terrible disappointment to her.'

'But I, too, am a disappointment to my mother.'

'You?'

'Why, yes. All the time I have to listen to my mother asking me when I am going to settle down with a nice girl. She desperately wants a grandchild. She feels aggrieved not to have gained the same status as her friends, that of doting grandmother.'

'What do you tell her?'

He looked as though he was holding back a smile. 'I tell her that I'm waiting for the right woman.' Then, 'Have you never tried standing up to your mother?'

Izzy snorted. 'You're joking!'

'Why not? Why not be honest with her? Tell her that she has done her best so far to ruin your life but you are not prepared to let her spoil the rest.'

'You make it sound the most natural thing in the world.'

'That's because it is.'

'You haven't met Prudence Jordan.'

'I admit that is a pleasure I have been denied, but one that I would be curious to experience.'

Contemplating the dangerously attractive face before her, Izzy thought that it was something she would pay good money to see as well. Just what effect would Theo

222

Vlamakis, with his dark-eyed charm and good looks, have on her mother? She pictured his broad-shouldered body restrained in her mother's flower-sprigged sitting room and heard Prudence say, 'Isobel tells me that you're *Greek*.' She would make it sound as if he was of an inferior race. Her mother considered foreigners a clumsy mistake on God's part, a bit of tinkering in his celestial workshop – *Just trying out an idea I had, Mrs Jordan, soon have it put right*. Knitting blankets for the overseas poor was all very well, but perish the thought she should have to entertain them for tea.

Across the valley, the setting sun had almost completed its descent, and as the light drained from the sky, their dessert arrived. Theo explained that it was a speciality of Marika's called *locamades* – a melt-in-the-mouth concoction of deep-fried batter covered in honey and dusted with cinnamon.

'You still haven't told me about the dedication in *Culling The Good*,' Izzy said, eyeing the dish with anticipation. 'Does it refer to something specific you did for Mark?'

'Aha, Izzy, you have all the makings of a fine detective. Nothing eludes you. But here, try one of these, they are delicious.' He held out his fork. She tried to take it from him, but he smiled and said, 'No innuendo intended, but open wide.' She did as he said. The warm sweetness melted in her mouth. Watching her lick her lips, he said, 'You should feel honoured. It is not for everyone that Marika makes this dish.'

When Marika herself had appeared at their table with the unasked-for dessert, he had known it was her way of giving her seal of approval to his dinner guest. She had only ever done it twice before. Would this be third time lucky? Realising he still hadn't answered Izzy's question, he speared another honeyed ball of sweetness on his fork, held it across the table for her, and said, 'Mark and I have a friendship that is unlike most others. Each of us has saved the other from an untimely death. And, no, I'm not exaggerating. Mark really did save my life that night back in Durham when I was a careless student with more money than sense. I made myself an easy target. I should have known better.'

'And Mark? How did you save his life?'

Theo hesitated. He knew better than anyone that his friend hated his past to be discussed. 'It is a very personal matter, and one that perhaps only Mark should share with you. But I will say this, what Mark did for me took an immense amount of courage and what I did for him needed no such thing, only patience. Not that he would agree with me. But that is so typical of the man – he likes to disagree with everything I say and do.'

'With anything in particular?'

'Ah, well, the list is long and varied, but perhaps my worst crime in his opinion is to be a fat capitalist pig.'

'And are you?'

'I like to think not. But who knows? Maybe I am. I enjoy what I do. I hope I don't sound arrogant if I say that I am proud of my success. I also have no shame in appreciating what money can do for a person. Used wisely it can be a powerful tool against a lot of unnecessary suffering in the world. But enough of me. What would your friends consider your worst crime to be?'

'Probably my inability to decide what I really want to do with the rest of my life.'

'A crime indeed, when you consider that you are only given the one. So what is wrong with your current existence that you feel you should be changing it?'

'I don't think I'm cut out for teaching.'

'You don't like children? You surprise me. I would have thought you would have been very good with them.

I see you as being one of the most patient and understanding people I have come across.' And, with a smile, he added quickly, 'That is said as a comment on your ability as I see it, a fact, not a reflection of my feelings for you. It was not a compliment.'

'As a matter of fact I really like children,' she said, letting his remark pass with a smile of her own. 'The problem lies in the school I work in and what's going on there. We've got a headmistress who's on a mission to cleanse the staffroom of faces she doesn't like.'

'Does she like yours?'

'I couldn't tell you. So far I've done my best to keep out of her way, but I wouldn't be at all surprised to get home at the end of the summer and find a redundancy notice on my doormat.'

'Can she do that?'

'She can do more or less whatever she wants. She's been brought in by the school governors to solve the problem of dwindling numbers and escalating costs by a process of reshaping. Which is a nasty word for getting rid of dedicated, hardworking teachers.'

He was surprised at the depth of bitterness in her voice. 'So, change is in the air?'

She sighed. 'I guess so. But what exactly? That's what I should be deciding while I'm here on holiday.'

'That day we all went to Áyios Stéfanos,' he said thoughtfully, 'you said you saw yourself growing old with Alan and having children. Is that what you really want to do with your life, marry the man of your dreams and have a family?'

She sat back in her chair, horrified at what he had just said. But it was horribly near the truth. Yet how could she admit, in this intimidating age of women having it all, that if the circumstances were right she would be quite happy to give up work and devote herself to full-time motherhood? And was it fair that she should be made to feel guilty for wanting that, as though she was harbouring some awful subversive secret? When had it become socially unacceptable to be a full-time mother? And just where had the concept of choice gone, now that women always had to be on top?

She stared at Theo in the soft light cast from the glowing lantern on the table, searching his face for signs of cynicism. But, try as she might, she could detect no mockery in him. The reverse seemed to be true: he was gazing at her with such a look of sincerity that it forced her to speak the truth. 'Perhaps that's partly what has upset me so much this past year. Mistakenly, I thought I was in a relationship that had a natural progression towards marriage and children, something I'd always thought I would be lucky enough to have, then suddenly—'

'Then suddenly all your dreams were snatched away from you?'

She nodded. 'You know, when I was young I believed that if I wished hard enough my dreams would come true.'

'And now you don't believe that?'

She laughed, but it didn't sound a happy laugh. 'Dreams are for children. So is wishing.'

'I disagree. I think that to live without a dream is what causes so much misery in this world. Dreams, hopes, aspirations, those are the things that make each day worth waking up for. Mark had all that taken away from him for a time and it was the worst hell anybody could live through. If you have a dream, Izzy, you should hang on to it, no matter how far-fetched you imagine it to be. Don't let anyone talk you out of it. Now, shall I order coffee, or would you prefer one later when I invite you in for a night-cap?'

'Assuming that I'll accept?'

'Assuming that you will reward me for having behaved

myself . . .' he glanced at his watch '. . . for nearly three whole hours.'

'Is that a record for you?'

He grinned. 'I think it is.'

Chapter Twenty-Four

It was eleven o'clock, and in one of the busy harbourside bars in Kassiópi, Francesca and Sally were just starting their evening. They had arranged to meet Nick and Harry, who were having dinner with their parents beforehand. Nick had described the evening as a command performance: 'It's Pa's fiftieth, so we've all got to be there in attendance lying through our back teeth convincing him fifty is the new forty. Some bloody hope!'

Having arrived early, the girls ordered two vodkas with Coke and sat back to take in the view of passers-by.

'How's that for an entry into the Biggest Bum in the Universe competition?' said Sally, indicating with her eyes a woman in tight white jeans, a low-cut top and shocking pink stilettos. 'What do you think she's going for, the Trailer Trash ensemble, or the Rover's Return look?'

'You're so cruel, Sally.'

'Not a malicious thought in my head, just speaking as I find. But take a look over there, I bet you could fry an egg on that back.'

Francesca winced at the sight of a pair of excruciatingly red shoulders branded by white strap marks where the top half of a bikini had been. 'Poor woman, she looks as though she should be in intensive care.'

'She looks completely gross, you mean.' Then noticing a man at a nearby table, Sally leaned in closer. 'Clock the guy behind you.'

Francesca twisted round to see who Sally was referring

to. He was fair-haired, casually dressed, almost scruffily so, but not bad-looking in a lean, hawkish, lived-in way. He was sitting low down in his seat, his head resting on the back of the chair, one of his legs crossed over the other, a hand picking absently at the laces of his CAT boot as he gazed across the water. She watched him take out a small notebook and pen from his shirt pocket and scribble something down. She thought he looked vaguely familiar. 'Maybe he's got one of those faces,' she said, turning back to Sally and lowering her voice, 'but I feel as if I've seen him before.'

'Yeah, I know what you mean. He's kinda fit, wouldn't you say?'

'Not bad, if you go for the type who looks old enough to be married with a brood of runny-nosed children.'

'So where are they? I see no wife. I see no snivelling kids. And I'll tell you what else I don't see, a wedding ring.'

'He could be divorced.'

'Or widowed.'

'Perhaps he's a serial wife murderer. He bumps them off for the life insurance.'

'Yeah, a wife murderer who goes off on holiday with the spoils once the body's been cremated and the evidence has gone up in smoke.'

'And he's here hoping to pick up his next victim, trawling the streets of Kassiópi for a beautiful woman with a desire to die young. Shall I introduce you?'

Their laughter caused several heads to turn, including, and much to Sally's delight, the fair-haired man's. 'It's official,' she said, when he had turned away. She scooped out the slice of lemon from her drink and sucked it. 'He's divine and I wish he was mine.'

'Sorry to be the bearer of bad news, but I've just recognised who he is. He's Theo's friend, the one who's staying with him. Anyway, I thought you liked Harry. Isn't that why we're here tonight?'

'Oh, come off it, Francesca. You know very well I'm out of the running there. He doesn't even know I exist. It's quite clear he's got the hots for you and you've got his number. And don't give me any of that wide-eyed stuff. No, there's nothing else for it, I'll just have to do the honourable thing and get Nick off your back for you.'

'Sounds like you've got it all worked out. Ever thought to check with me and see what I think about it?'

Sally grinned. 'Go on, tell me I've got it wrong.'

Unable to deny what Sally was suggesting, Francesca smiled too. 'But Harry's so shy. He'll never get it together to ask me out.'

'Well, we'll just have to give him a shove in the right direction, won't we?'

'And what'll you do with Nick?'

'Oh, I'll let him do what he's best at, I'll give him the opportunity to shoot his mouth off the whole time.'

'Two of a kind, then,' laughed Francesca. 'A match made in heaven.'

Sally flicked her discarded lemon across the table; it landed in Francesca's lap. 'In the absence of anything better I'm not too proud to sweep up the crumbs. It's a shame about Theo fancying Izzy, isn't it?' She sighed. 'Looks, age and money. I could have been a happy woman.'

'You're dreadful, you really are. What is it with you and older men?'

'I was a deprived child, no father figure in my life.'

'Depraved, maybe, but your father's great.'

'Okay, I'll admit it. It's the sex. Older men are miles better at it. They've all the experience that idiots like Nick haven't. There's none of that awful fumbling around, looking for where things go. They're also keen to impress, to prove they're still up for it. It's a great combination.'

Francesca smirked. 'And you thought my dad would be good in bed with you. You're one sick girl.'

Coming as near as she would ever be to embarrassment, Sally flushed faintly and recrossed her legs. 'How was I to know he was your father? We hadn't been introduced or anything.' And changing the subject, she said, 'You know what really gets me about Izzy is that she doesn't seem interested in Theo. Or do you suppose she's just playing it super-cool?'

'Haven't a clue. But whatever she's doing, it seems to be working. Mum says he's been really persistent. The harder she's made it for him, the more he's pursued her. Oh, and about time too. Here's Nick and Harry.'

'Top banana to you, girls!' Nick greeted them. He plonked himself in the chair next to Francesca. 'So, how's it going? Sorry we're late, but the aged ones have trouble feeding themselves these days. It takes for ever. I tell you, when they start dribbling, I'll be long gone.'

Harry took the seat beside Sally. 'Excuse my intolerant brother, won't you? I'm hoping that one day he'll meet with a terrible accident and we'll all be put out of our misery.'

'Hey, who released your comedy valve, mate? You should be grateful that we're in the company of women and years of good breeding forbids me from taking a swing at you. Now, who's drinking what?'

They ordered a round of drinks, followed shortly by another. The bar was really busy now, and the warm night air was filled with raised voices and the pounding of a heavy pop-Latin beat. Having developed a headache after her second vodka and Coke, Francesca found that she wasn't in the mood for Nick's constant stream of jokes and putdown lines aimed at his brother. She liked him well enough, but he was one of those guys who liked himself better than anybody else did, and had long since lost touch with where the on-off switch was for his mouth. Harry was his brother's antithesis: was clean-cut and dead straight while Nick went for the funky surf gear and pony-tail look, and could have done with a lesson in opening up. She could see that he felt awkward in this situation. He was probably one of those anti-social students who spent most of the term with his door shut, his nose in a book. He certainly didn't seem the type to be off his head at some club every night. That was more his brother's scene. It used to be hers too. Well, not the off-her-head bit, it was the music she and Sally had been into. It was how she had met Carl. But now with the demise of her relationship with Carl she had the feeling she had outgrown it. Across the table, Sally, the perpetual thrill-seeker, was telling Nick all about one of the clubs in Manchester that had been a regular night out for them.

'You must have heard of the Tiger Lounge,' Sally was saying. 'It's dead famous. I can't believe you've been to Manchester and not heard of it.'

'So what's so special about it? What kind of music do they do?'

'The best in all things kitsch. Sixties, seventies, eighties. They even do classic movie themes. The last time we were there it was nothing but Andy Williams and Shirley Bassey.'

Francesca remembered that night all too well. She and Sally had spent most of the day getting ready for it, dressing in mini-skirts, and false nails and eyelashes. Another friend had done their hair for them, whipping it into outrageous beehives that they sprayed green. It was that night when she realised she had reached the end of the road with Carl. She had caught him chatting to a redhead in a fluffy pink bra top, and overheard him asking for her phone number and when he could see her again. She hadn't stuck around to hear the answer.

'Kitsch is great once in a while,' Nick shouted, above the music that seemed even louder now, 'but you can't beat a good rock festival. Ever been to Glastonbury, Sal?'

'No. Don't fancy all the mud.'

'You should give it a go. But I'll tell you what I'm doing next year. I'm planning a trip to Goa; that's where the hardcore ravers go. A mate of mine's been. He said the tropical beach parties are out of this world. Only trouble is, the drug laws are so harsh that if you get caught with so much as a Tic-Tac in your pocket, you'll end up in prison for the rest of your life. Another drink, anyone? How about you, Frankie? You're not saying much – losing the power of speech, are you?'

'No, just the will to live. And please, don't call me Frankie.'

'Oo-er, and what medication have you missed today?'

'You okay?' asked Sally.

'I've got a headache.'

'That's a woman for you.'

'Give it a rest, Nick, and leave her alone. Would you like a glass of water?'

She looked gratefully across the table to Harry. 'Thanks,' she said, 'but I think I'll take some time out, go for a walk round the harbour. The music's too loud here.'

Making room for her to slip by, Harry rose uncertainly to his feet. Even more uncertainly, he said, 'Do you want some company?'

Avoiding Sally's eyes, she said, 'If you like.'

With the sound of Nick calling after them, 'Harry, behave yourself, don't go doing anything with Frankie that I'll regret,' they moved off.

'Do you want me to throttle him now or later?' Harry asked. 'It would be a pleasure either way.'

'When I'm feeling better I'll do it myself.'

They walked slowly round the harbour, dodging the swarms of scooters and the gangs of promenading Greek grandmothers with their pushchairs of sleeping children. 'There's a small bar further up the hill owned by a strange old woman in slippers,' Harry said. 'Would you like to sit there? It would at least be quiet.'

'What's strange about the old lady?'

'Well ... I hardly like to mention it, but she suffers from an excess of facial hair.'

'A full set?'

'No. Only a moustache. It's possible, though, that she's working on growing a beard.'

In spite of the thumping pain in her head, Francesca smiled. 'Well, lead on and let me see for myself.'

The bar was blissfully quiet, just as Harry had said it would be, and almost at once she began to feel better. It was in a slightly elevated position with no more than half a dozen tables overlooking the harbour. They were the only customers and Francesca felt a pang of pity for the owner, who must barely scrape a living from the place. She was as old and strange as Harry had described, and after she had shuffled along in her sheepskin slippers with their drinks – a cup of coffee for Francesca and bottle of Amstel for Harry, who was also the lucky recipient of a beaming smile – she shuffled back to her wooden chair in the doorway of the bar and resumed her lace-making.

'How often do you come here?' asked Francesca. 'I'm getting the impression she knows you.'

'I sometimes hang out here when Nick's in one of his party moods.'

'Which is quite often, I should think. Does he ever stop?'

'Nope. The dweeb's been hyperactive since the day he was born.'

'But you prefer a more leisurely pace?'

'Is that a polite way of asking if I'm always this boring?'

'Whoa, the boy has a raw spot.'

'Doesn't everyone?'

'Some more tender and exposed than others. And I'd like it known that I didn't accuse you of being boring, you did it all yourself. Which is a shame, really, because you're not.'

'Patronising me now?'

She ripped open a sachet of white sugar and tipped it into her coffee. 'What is it with you? Don't you recognise a compliment when you hear one? Or have you been in your brother's shadow too long?'

He pushed his glasses back up on to his nose. 'Something like that, yes.'

'Then maybe it's time you did something about it.'

'Any suggestions?'

'Well, yes, seeing as you've asked. When we've finished our drinks you can walk me home. That's if you don't think you've drawn the short straw.'

As he poured the beer into his glass, Harry couldn't believe his luck. He had been wondering for days how to steal a march over his brother and get this girl on her own, and now it had happened. 'No, no, of course I don't think that,' he said, suddenly realising that she might take his silence for indifference. 'But I thought you and Sally would be staying on with Nick for—'

'The last thing I'm in the mood for is a long session in a nightclub with your brother strutting his top-banana stuff. I vote we leave them to it.'

'You're sure, then?'

'A rule you need to learn, Harry,' she said, dipping her finger into the froth of his beer then licking it off, 'we girls don't like to be accused of not knowing our minds. Do you think you can grasp that?'

He stared at her as though she had just committed an erotic act. 'I'll try,' he murmured.

Erotic acts were on Mark's mind as he walked home with

the aid of a torch that, this time, he had remembered to bring with him. Though the moon was full, its silvery rays did not penetrate the dense foliage of the trees in the olive grove, and the stony path he was carefully negotiating was as black as his mood.

While sitting in the harbour in Kassiópi, he had been trying to get his head round the next chapter of his book, without success. It was the point in the story-line that invariably gave him the most difficulty. It concerned the protagonist's sex life, or rather the protagonist's prospective foray into some erotic action betwixt the sheets. If it weren't for his publisher's insistence that nearly all crime novels had to have a will-they-won't-they element of suspense, he wouldn't bother. 'But I'm writing psychological gore-fests not bloody bodice-rippers!' had been his response when his editor had first raised the question of whether or not he couldn't include some sexual chemistry between his characters. 'Just a touch,' his editor had reasoned bravely. 'It would engage the reader's interest further. It would also broaden the appeal of your novels.' It was back to that old number of him being a marketable commodity.

Stupidly he had let his principles fly out of the window and done what he had been asked to do. Which meant that because it had happened once it would go on happening. But it didn't get any easier. Theo said he was no good at it because (a) he was British – what did the British know about passion? – and (b) he lacked experience. Such a cheap sense of humour, that boy! Even relying on his imagination, which was as vivid as the next man's, if not more so, he still found that the sex scenes he wrote lacked emotion and spontaneity.

He had spent most of today trying to write this chapter but hadn't got anywhere with it. Not long after Theo had left to take Izzy out for dinner, he had decided to give himself a change of scene by going into Kassiópi for the evening, but that had proved as big a waste of time as the rest of the day had.

Maybe not entirely. People-watching could always be put to good use and he had been quietly amused by the group of youngsters sitting at a nearby table. The dynamics of any group of people never failed to interest him. It was always fascinating to see who was the leader and who were the followers, and in this instance, the smallest guy was the one with the biggest mouth and ego. Mark had recognised the two girls as part of the Sinclair contingent – he had seen them swimming out to the raft below their villa – and the lads were presumably the ones Izzy had said were staying with their parents in the pink villa next door to Dolly-Babe and Silent Bob's. It was funny how easily their little community had been put together. Here they all were, two thousand miles from home, but already they had restructured themselves into a microcosm of what they had come here to escape.

Climbing the first of the steady uphill slopes of the path, Mark wished that he, too, could escape. If he could find a way round that chapter, he would. But he knew there was no avoiding it: it had to be done, and soon, or it might make him freeze up. Writer's block was only ever a stone's throw away for any novelist, and he knew that the smallest problem could grow into a wall of self-doubt and neurosis. Then, with a wry smile, he thought, he should let Theo write it. After all, he was the one with all the experience.

That was the trouble with writing. It took up the vast majority of his time and made for a lousy social life. Most days he would get up early, work through till lunch, then make himself a sandwich. He would eat it standing at the sink planning his afternoon session, which inevitably struck through most of the evening, or he would go out for a walk along the coastal path to clear his head. If he was feeling generous to himself he might wander up the hill and have lunch at the village bookshop, where they had an extraordinary selection of second-hand books as well as a great café. On warm sunny days he ate outside on the terrace, fending off the gulls while eavesdropping on the tourists and gaining all sorts of fascinating insights into their lives.

Other than his writing and the writing group he led, he had no commitments to tie him to anyone or anything. Initially, that was exactly how he had wanted it. He hadn't wanted another person's life touching his. But once he had gained sufficient belief in himself that he was straight enough to consider a relationship little had come his way. It had seemed easier in the long run to cut his losses and absorb himself in his work. When he was on a roll there was nothing better, it gave him the ultimate high: the satisfying high that drugs and alcohol had never provided. What more mysterious and mind-altering process could there be than to sit down of a morning and, at the touch of his fingertips, lose himself in a world that at times was more real than the one in which he lived?

He turned to his right and stood at the end of Theo's drive. It was lit up every few yards by a series of mushroom-shaped lights. Outside the villa, he saw Theo's car. Surprised that his friend was back so soon, he hunted through his pockets for his key, then hesitated. Supposing Theo was back early because he and Izzy were on the verge of doing what the protagonist in his current book was supposed to be enjoying?

Theo wouldn't thank him for bursting in and ruining it. Do that and he'd never hear the last of it.

So, what should he do?

Go in and ruin everything for his friend, or wander down to the beach and wait for the lights to go out?

He favoured the last option. Edging his way quietly round the side of the house, he took the path down to the beach.

Chapter Twenty-Five

Theo knew that his garden made the perfect romantic setting, so he led Izzy to the edge of the terrace and put their glasses of Metaxá on the low wall, then watched her stare up at the stars that pricked the velvet night sky. He knew that the next few moments would be crucial. Turn on the charm now, and she would run. He had come so far this evening in gaining her trust and he didn't want to do anything to jeopardise that.

While driving back from the restaurant he had been trying to come to terms with exactly what he felt for Izzy. His conclusion had surprised him. Or had it?

Beside him on the terrace, Izzy said, 'I've had a wonderful evening, Theo. Thank you, it's been lovely.'

Any number of snappy one-liners came into his mind, but with iron-will restraint, he said, 'I'm delighted you enjoyed yourself. Do you think you would want to do it again sometime?'

She smiled cautiously. 'I might.'

'And has my behaviour met with your exacting standards?'

'Um . . . I think so.'

He moved in closer. 'Does that mean I get my prize?'

'Well, perhaps just a small one.'

'Not too small, I hope.'

Backing away from him, Izzy reached for her glass, took a sip of the smooth brandy and wondered why she was still keeping Theo at what she thought was a safe distance. Wasn't she being absurd? Why not go for it?

What was to stop her seizing the day and enjoying a sparkle of brightness in an otherwise lacklustre life? It was only a kiss he wanted.

So why did the idea make her feel so nervous?

She took another sip of her drink and forced herself to face the truth. She was nervous that he might be disappointed in her. Doubtless he would be a skilled kisser and would know a good kiss from a bad one.

But as convinced as she was that Theo was about to try to kiss her, he didn't. Instead, he stepped away from her and began to pace the terrace.

'What is it?' she asked.

He came and stood in front of her again. 'I'm sorry,' he said, 'it's just that you make me feel nervous.'

'Nervous? I make *you* nervous?'

'Yes, Izzy. I know this sounds crazy when we have known each other for so little time, and yet . . . and yet . . .' His words fizzled out and he resumed his pacing.

'And yet, what?' she asked. What was going on here? Was she missing something?

He came to a sudden stop, just in front of her. 'I think there is a very real danger that I am falling in love with you.'

She stared at him dumbfounded. 'You're kidding, right?'

He looked hurt. 'From the moment I first saw you, you have had an extraordinary effect on me. Not so much as a kiss has passed between us, but I know I feel so very strongly for you.'

'But you know nothing about me.'

'I have learned more than you think. When you talk, Izzy, I listen. And tonight you have spoken a lot about yourself.'

There was no refuting this. Perhaps it was all the wine she had drunk, but she had shared with Theo more about herself than she had with anybody else. To fill in the silence she said, 'We have kissed, actually.'

'We have?'

'Yes, that day when you taught me to dive.'

He shook his head. 'That was no kiss.'

'Your lips touched mine, if I remember rightly. Sorry to be pedantic, but by my definition that makes it a kiss.'

With one of his brilliant smiles, he said, 'By my definition that was merely a touching of lips, it was not a touching of souls. Now this is what I call a kiss.'

In what seemed like one deft movement, he stepped in close, drew her to him and kissed her. But that's not fair, she thought, I wasn't ready! She willed herself to relax, to enjoy the sensation of Theo's firm mouth familiarising itself with hers. But it was no good. She felt stiff and awkward in his arms, conscious of everything she was doing wrong, or might do wrong.

It was at this moment, down on the beach where he was still killing time, that Mark looked up the hillside. In the light cast from the villa, he had no problem in identifying Theo and Izzy on the terrace above him and what they were doing. Troubled, he pushed his hands into his trouser pockets. For some reason that wasn't clear to him, he was disappointed that Izzy hadn't held out longer on Theo. Why was everything so bloody easy for the man?

He kicked at a rock, feeling that strange sixth-sense thing he got when his writing wasn't going well. It was what he called a plot snag. It was a warning sensation that pestered him, kept him awake at night, kept him from thinking straight, giving him no peace until he hit on what the problem was and where the answer lay. Sometimes it was days before the solution came to him.

He bent down, picked up a large, heavy stone and hurled it into the calm sea. It made a satisfyingly loud splash. So loud that it caused a distraction for the happy lovers above him.

'Is that you, Mark?' came Theo's voice. 'What are you doing down there?'

'Enjoying a late-night stroll. Why? What the hell are you doing up there?' His words had slipped out before he could stop them.

'Izzy is here and I'm supposed to be making her some coffee. Why not join us?'

By the time he had reached the terrace there was no sign of either Izzy or Theo. He went inside. Through an open door at the far end of the sitting room he saw that Theo was on the phone in his study. With both elbows resting on the desk, he appeared to be engaged in one of his typically heated Greek conversations and looked far from happy at having his attention diverted.

Mark found Izzy in the kitchen making the coffee. 'I'll get the mugs,' he said, reaching for them from a shelf on one of the dressers. He set them down on the chunky wooden table behind them. 'Good meal?' he asked, searching the tall fridge for a carton of milk.

'Yes, it was excellent. But I ate far too much.'

'Where did he take you?'

'I've no idea. It was way off in the hills. The people who run the taverna are friends of his.'

'Spiros and Marika?'

'That's right. Have you been there too?'

'Once or twice. As a matter of interest what did you have for your dessert?'

She gave him a puzzled look. 'Um . . . something delicious with a name I can't quite remember. *Loc-, loca—*'

'*Locamades?*'

'Yes, that's it,' she said. 'Why do you ask?'

'No special reason. It looks like Theo's going to be a while on the phone, let's take our coffee outside.'

They sat at a small table where Mark lit several candles designed to keep mosquitoes at bay. 'I'll leave you to add your own milk and sugar,' he said. Leaning back in his chair, he hooked one leg over the other and fiddled with a fraying shoelace. He stared morosely into the darkness. It had been the worst kind of day for him: depressingly uncreative. In his uncommunicative state, he knew he wasn't good company, that he should have stayed down on the beach until Izzy had gone home. But, then, common sense had never been his strong suit.

As though reading his mind, Izzy said, 'So how was your evening?'

He shifted his gaze, settled it on her face. 'Disappointing. I went into Kassiópi hoping that a change of scene might improve my mood.'

'And it didn't?'

'No.' The finality in his voice sounded harsh and discordant. Realising how rude he was being, he added, 'Sorry, I've had a bad day, got nothing of any worth done.'

'Do you get many days like this?'

'It varies.' He told her about his struggle with his protagonist's miserable love-life. 'It's an on-going thing I have with each book I write. You'd think it would get easier, but it doesn't.'

'I've made a start on *Culling The Good*.'

'And your verdict?'

'I'd be a fool if I sat here and told you I wasn't enjoying it.'

'You'd be surprised how brutally candid people can be. I'm continually criticised for being too grim and bleak, too realistic. Not that it bothers me. In-your-face realism is what I'm aiming to achieve. I want to offend. It means I've hit home, touched a nerve. I'm not interested in the cosy crime world of purple rinses, thatched cottages and mass redemption. I like to think that my books have a

243

touch more gravitas and shock value in them than your average episode of *Scooby-Doo*.'

'Based on the little I've read so far of your book, I think that goes without saying. But perhaps you could answer this for me – it's something Max and I were discussing this afternoon. If all comedians are supposed to have a dark side, does it naturally follow that writers of your genre have a comedic side to them?'

In spite of his ill-humour, Mark smiled. 'Gee, you think?'

She smiled too. 'Perhaps I'll ask you again when you've had a better day. Do you suppose Theo is going to be much longer? I ought to be going, really.'

'I'll go and have a word with him, shall I?'

'Please. I don't have a key and I know that Max will be waiting up for me.'

'He will? Why? Doesn't he trust you?'

'It's not me he doesn't trust, it's Theo. Oh, perhaps I shouldn't have said that. You won't tell Theo, will you?'

'The lips are sealed. Hang on here a minute and I'll see what he's got to say.'

He returned shortly. 'Looks like Theo's going to be stuck for some time. He's asked me to do the honourable thing and walk you home or he'll get it in the neck from Max. That okay with you?'

'Mm . . . With the insight I now have of what goes on in your mind I'm not sure I want to go anywhere in the dark with you.'

He pulled out a small torch from his back pocket, switched it on, held it against his face, and let out a hollow, ghoulish laugh. 'You have nothing to fear, my dear. Take my hand and step into the madness of the world I inhabit.'

She laughed and allowed herself to be pulled across the garden towards the gate that led to the hillside path. 'Has anyone ever told you that you're quite mad?'

'That's really not the kind of thing you should say to a madman, especially if he's the one in charge of the torch.' He flicked it off and for a moment they were plunged into darkness.

When their eyes had adjusted, Izzy said, 'Look, over there.' She pointed through a gap in the cypress trees, down to the sea, where moonlight danced on the softly rippling surface and a man in a small fishing-boat with a lantern was casting his nets. 'Isn't that the most magical sight? See the way the light from his lantern is falling across the still water. It's almost phosphorescent. And those shadows, the way they glisten on the water.' She turned and faced him, her expression as eager and delighted as a child on Christmas morning. 'You're not looking,' she frowned.

'I was. I just got sidetracked by somebody getting over-excited with a perfect Kodak moment.'

She gave him a playful swipe on the arm. 'Like most men, you have no soul.'

'Oh, I sold that to the devil a long time ago.'

'Don't tell me, he returned it as faulty.'

'Why you little—' But he got no further as, laughing, she hared off into the darkness. He chased after her but she was lighter on her feet than he was and was soon nowhere to be seen. Then, suddenly, he heard a cry. Switching on the torch, he quickened his pace. When he found her, she was on the ground rubbing her ankle. He crouched beside her. 'You okay?'

'I think I've twisted it.'

'Can you wriggle your toes?'

She did as he said. 'Does that mean I haven't broken anything?' she asked, when all five toes seemed to be in working order.

'Sorry, haven't a clue.'

'Fat lot of use you are in an emergency.'

'Hey, easy there, time for a reality check. If I'm about

to carry you up the rest of this hill you'd better be nice to me. What do you fancy, fireman's lift or Heathcliff carrying Cathy in his arms across the moors?'

'Oh, definitely the Heathcliff mode of transport.'

'Now, how did I know you'd go for that option?'

They made slow going, and despite the pain in her ankle, Izzy started to laugh.

'No,' he said, stumbling over some loose stones and staggering, 'no laughing, it's not allowed. If you laugh, I swear I'll drop you and watch you bounce all the way down to the beach.'

'No, you won't, you're enjoying yourself too much playing at being a super-hero.'

'I am? Hell, why didn't you tell me before?'

'If I'm not allowed to laugh, can I sing?'

'Go ahead,' he puffed, his arms feeling like lead, 'whatever does it for you, Izzy Jordan.'

'Jack and Jill went up the hill to fetch a pail of water . . .'

He groaned. 'Beneath that pretty benign exterior, you enjoy living dangerously, don't you? How much further is it? Tell me there'll be oxygen when we reach the top.'

'We're on the final ascent now.'

He paused to catch his breath. 'Any chance of you radioing for assistance? I'm dying on my feet here.'

'Are you saying I'm overweight?'

'For a weakling like me, excessively so.'

They eventually made it to the top, and hearing their voices, Max and Corky, who were still up, came to investigate. Izzy introduced Mark and explained what had happened.

'I'm sorry I'm being such a nuisance,' she said after she had been helped to a sun-lounger and Max had despatched Corky to fetch an ice-pack from the freezer in the kitchen.

'Didn't I warn you no good would come of an evening out with Theo?' Max smiled.

'What bothers me most,' said Mark, kneeling on the ground to inspect Izzy's ankle, 'is that he trusted me to get Izzy home safely. I'll never hear the last of this.'

'It wasn't anybody's fault but my own. I shouldn't have been running away from you. Thanks for carrying me, it was very kind of you.'

He stood up. 'Stop right there. I'm no good with schmaltzy words of thanks. They bring me out in a nasty rash of embarrassment.'

'Can't suggest anything to help with a rash,' said Corky, appearing from behind, 'but this should help with the ankle.' He handed an ice-pack to Izzy along with a tea-towel. 'Thought that would do to strap it on with.' He also fished an elegant silver hip flask out of his trouser pocket. 'A snifter or two should help as well. What do you say?'

'I shouldn't really, I've already had plenty to drink.'

'Purely medicinal, my dear. Good for the shock.'

'What's good for what shock?'

Everybody turned to see Francesca coming across the terrace. She wasn't alone. Beside her was a tall, good-looking young man whom Izzy recognised as one of the Patterson boys.

'What on earth have you been up to, Izzy?' she asked, when she drew level and saw the ice-pack. 'A night out with Theo and you're an invalid.'

'I fell and did something painful to my ankle, and rather embarrassingly everyone's making too much fuss over me.'

'So where's Mum? Not like her to miss out on a good fussing session.'

'She's in bed,' said Max, 'as is your grandmother. So if you could keep your voice down to a dull roar we won't disturb them. Ahem, who's your friend?'

With an airy wave of her hand, Francesca introduced Harry. 'Everyone, this is Harry. And, Harry, this is my father. You can't miss him – he's the one sizing you up as a potential son-in-law. You're just the respectable sort of young man he'd choose for me. Do you fancy something to eat? I do. How about the rest of you?'

Chapter Twenty-Six

The next morning, Theo drove Izzy to the doctor's surgery in Kassiópi. After a thorough inspection, Dr Katerina Tsipa strapped up Izzy's impressively swollen ankle and declared it badly twisted. She prescribed some tablets to ease the swelling and complete rest. Her English was sufficient to get this across without too much difficulty, but Izzy was grateful that Theo was there to help her fill in the necessary forms and translate anything she didn't understand. Arrangements were made for a pair of crutches to be brought to the villa, which, when they arrived, gave Francesca and Sally hours of fun as they took it in turns to race up and down the veranda on them while shrieking at the top of their voices, 'Yo, ho, ho and a bottle of oúzo,' and 'Out of my way, Jim lad, or I'll be scraping the barnacles off your bum!'

For the following week, while Max and Laura took Corky and Olivia sightseeing, Izzy spent her days reading – she had finished *Culling The Good* and had moved on to *When Darkness Falls*, another of Mark's books. It was just as spine-tingling as *Culling The Good* but with an even higher body-count. The level of violence portrayed was far greater than she was used to reading, and the same was true of the language. She had never seen the F word so liberally employed and once or twice she found herself blushing at the extremes to which Mark had gone in expressing himself. The more she read, the harder it was for her to equate the author of these novels with the man she knew; the man who had carried her up the hill and displayed such a dry, ready wit. But there was no humour in what Mark wrote, only a grim portrayal of human nature at its worst. It struck her that he walked a fine line of creating stories that were essentially moralistic but without preaching.

When she needed a breather from all this carnage and drama, she caught up with news from home. If it could be classed as news.

It was definitely the silly season and the papers that Max brought back with him from his daily walk into Kassiópi were full of sensationalist trivia. In the absence of any newsworthy story, they were relying on the old standbys of royal cock-ups: the Duke of Edinburgh had, once again, insulted a minority group, and a lesser-known royal, one of those so far down the pecking order you could never remember their name, had apparently been caught speeding. But the one story that seemed set to run and run, and which had truly caught the public's imagination, was the tale of the mother of two and her schoolboy lover, who were still missing. 'At the rate they're going,' Laura had said, 'the boy will be old enough to marry her by the time anyone finds them.'

There were reports of the infamous pair – Christine and Mikey, the world and his wife were on first-name terms with them now – having been seen all over Europe. Most sightings had taken place in the Costas, though Ibiza was also mentioned, and a hotel in Reykjavik was claiming to have had the runaway lovers there for an overnight stay. 'They looked very much in love,' the manager was quoted as saying 'They were no trouble at all. Very quiet. Very clean. I do not know what the problem is. You British, you always have such a closed mind when it comes to sex.'

One of the papers had even set up a hotline. 'If you've seen this couple, phone this number,' the caption read, above a picture that made Christine look like a cross between Lily Savage and Myra Hindley. There was one of Mikey dressed in his school uniform, which had probably been taken when he was about eleven.

As soap operas went, it was up there with the best of them, riveting stuff.

When she wasn't reading, Izzy was playing cards with Max's parents. Just as Laura had predicted, they had seized upon the opportunity to teach her Canasta. The wine had flowed too, despite her protests that perhaps she shouldn't mix her tablets with alcohol.

'The odd drop won't make any difference,' Corky had said, filling her glass, 'It'll help you relax.'

'It'll also help her on her way to an almighty hangover,' Laura had said.

Her greatest frustration at being immobile was that she missed her early-morning sessions on the beach. Negotiating the steep hillside path was out of the question, her ankle just couldn't take any weight on it yet, and annoyingly she had to make do with tantalising glimpses of the bay from the small balcony off her bedroom or the terrace. To ease her frustration she spent the first couple of hours of each day painting and sketching. With so much free time on her hands, she could see that her technique was improving. So much so that Olivia had raved about some of her watercolours and bought a set from her to take home. Even Sally had picked one for herself.

During the day when everybody was out and the villa was quiet, she took the opportunity to write all the postcards she had been meaning to send ever since she had arrived. While she had been lax over keeping in touch with Ingrid and the other staff at school, her mother was up to date. Duty had forced Izzy to write a letter each week she had been away. And that was a proper letter, a full two-page inconsequential missive. A postcard just wouldn't do. In her mother's opinion they were far too informal. 'A lot of badly written sentences put together with little thought for grammar or punctuation,' she would say, if one slipped through her draught-proof letter-box. She also didn't want the postman reading her private mail.

And now, sitting in the shade on the veranda, everyone having gone off for the day in the boat, Izzy was trying to write once again to her mother. It was a tortuous, thankless endeavour.

'Dear Mother, how are you?' was all she had written so far.

It was a daft question. Prudence Jordan would, as ever, claim to be not long for this world. It was tempting to sidetrack her attention-seeking hypochondria by taking the radical approach: 'Hi Mum,' it would be great to write, 'I'm having a wonderful time here without you. The weather is as hot as the misguided handsome Greek man who professes to be falling in love with me.' But, of course, she never would. Any more than she would ever find the courage to stand up to Prudence as Theo had said she should.

That was as likely as her taking Theo seriously.

I think there is a very real danger that I am falling in love with you.

An extraordinary declaration that had been left hanging between them ever since that night. Due to Mark's appearance on the beach and the phone call Theo had had to take, there had been no time to pursue what Theo had meant by it. Nor had there been time to linger over that kiss. For which she was grateful. A humiliating post-mortem – 'Call that a kiss? *Ha!*' – was not what she needed.

The only time Izzy and Theo had been alone since then was when he had driven her to the doctor. His concern for her as he had helped her in and out of the car had made her laugh. Especially when he had insisted on carrying her into the surgery. 'No, Theo,' she had cried, 'put me down, and give me your arm.' But he wouldn't listen.

'It is all my fault that you have hurt yourself, so it is I who will carry you.'

'You make it sound like a punishment. You'll be falling on your sword next.'

When they left the surgery and were driving home, he had stopped the car in the shade of a tree just before they reached Max and Laura's driveway. 'Izzy,' he said, his face as earnest as she had ever seen it, 'I want you to know that what I said last night, it was not said flippantly. I meant every word.'

She had been worried, as she sat beside him, that he might try to kiss her again, and a tiny knot of panic formed in her stomach. A day-time kiss would really sort out the women from the girls. With no romantic moonlight to fill in the gaps and make up for any inadequacy on her part, she was well and truly on her own.

But the sudden blast of a horn from an approaching Jeep with an inflatable whale rearing up from the back seat resolved the problem for her. Parked in the narrowest stretch of the road, with no room for a car to overtake, Theo had had no alternative but to drive on.

Once Izzy was back at the villa, there was no chance for the two of them to be alone together. She could see from Theo's frown of frustration as everyone gathered around her to hear what the doctor had said that he knew he had lost his opportunity to have her to himself. She was torn between relief and feeling sorry for him. Though if she were completely honest, relief had the edge. She had just got used to having Theo as a friend when he had nudged their friendship to a level that made her feel uneasy with him again.

Before now, she hadn't stopped to think how important it was for her to feel she was in control. It was another reason why she was so wary of Theo. With his charming and persuasive manner he could take away any sense of control she thought she had, leaving her feeling irrationally frightened and defenceless. And it wasn't difficult to work out why this would be: as a child she had witnessed all too often the terrifying consequences of her mother's loss of control. She had seen, heard and felt things that had left an indelible impression on her young mind.

To lose control was bad.

To be in control was good.

It was as simple as that, and until now she hadn't realised how closely she had stuck to this subconscious rule. But looking back on her life, she could see that everything she had ever done had been carefully and calmly thought out and entirely of her own making. There had been no room for spontaneous outbursts.

And yet . . . and yet there had been the awful incident with Alan when she had lost her temper with him. More recently, there had been that embarrassing display of pique with Max and Laura over Theo.

So what did these slips of inner rage say about her? That, deep down, and if sufficiently provoked, she was as close to the edge as her mother had once been? Or did they mean, and please, God, let this be the answer, that she was capable of a lot more than she gave herself credit for? And, if so, where did that leave her with regard to Theo? Was it possible that, and with a bit more effort on her part, she could learn to let go when she was with him and enjoy a whole new sense of freedom?

When she thought of Theo in more rational moments, especially when he was being so nice to her, the way she was treating him didn't seem fair to him.

Since she had hurt her ankle – and between his many

business commitments, which had taken him into Corfu Town and once to Athens – Theo had been a frequent visitor to the villa, often bearing gifts of the sweet and sticky variety for them all.

Yesterday he had joined them for lunch and brought her *When Darkness Falls*.

'How's Mark?' Max had asked, when they were all seated around the table. Much to Max's disappointment, he hadn't accompanied Theo on any of his visits.

'Working hard. He scarcely speaks to me these days. He is writing all hours. He says he is on a roll. Is that the right phrase?'

'Sounds like it could be.'

Then, lowering his voice to a low whisper and resting a hand on Izzy's leg under the table, he had said, 'So, Izzy, am I on a roll with you?'

She had blushed so much that, at the other end of the table, Laura had raised her eyebrows and smiled. Sally had noticed too and winked. But Max, bless him, unaware of the situation, had asked Theo what was taking him into Corfu Town later that afternoon. 'It's such a scorching day, it'll be murder.'

'I know, but I have an appointment I must keep.'

'Doctor or dentist?' asked Francesca.

'Neither. With a lawyer.'

'Oh, another acquisition?' asked Max.

'Yes. A piece of land. The contract has to be signed today, or the owner will sell to somebody else. Somebody less desirable.'

'In my experience, the rival businessman is always the one who is less desirable,' said Corky. 'Is it much land?'

Theo shrugged. 'A fair amount.' Izzy got the impression that he was being modestly evasive.

'On the island?'

He smiled at Olivia. 'What is this we are playing? A game of Twenty Questions?'

'Come on, Theo,' laughed Max, 'you've got us curious now. What are you up to? A spot of property developing here on Corfu?'

'If you must know, I am up to precisely the opposite. I am buying some land to prevent an area of great beauty from being spoiled.'

'How altruistic of you,' sighed Sally. 'I just love a man who does something for the good of everybody else, don't you, Izzy?'

'An admirable quality indeed,' Izzy said, without meeting Sally's eye – or anybody else's for that matter. 'Are we allowed to know where the land is, Theo?'

To everybody's surprise, he said, 'It's right here in Áyios Nikólaos, the olive grove that leads down into Kassiópi. I discovered last week that the family who own it have been offered a substantial amount of money to sell up. The buyer wants to erect several blocks of apartments.'

'But that's awful,' said Izzy, horrified. 'It would destroy the magic of this whole area.'

'Which is why I am buying the land and putting a stop to any such plans.'

Later, when Theo had left them to drive down the coast for his meeting, taking Sally and Francesca with him so that they could go shopping, Laura had got Izzy on her own and asked her what Theo had said to make her blush so dramatically. 'I've never seen anyone look so red. Or so guilty,' she added.

Since the night she had gone out for dinner with Theo, Izzy had kept Laura informed of most of what went on between them, and as far as Laura was concerned, she was on to a winner. 'Go for it, Izzy. He's crazy about you. We can all see it. Even Max is coming round and admits that he was perhaps a little quick to judge Theo.'

'But I'm scared of him,' Izzy had confessed. 'I know it's silly, but I can't relax when I'm on my own with him.'

'That's because you haven't learned to trust him. Or, more accurately, because you haven't learned to trust yourself to trust again. You think that because you made one error of judgement, you'll keep on doing it. Just relax with him and you'll find that everything will slip into place. I guarantee it.'

But that, Izzy said to herself, resuming her letter to her mother, is not as easy as Laura thinks it is. There were far too many reasons why it would be simpler for her to keep well away from Theo.

And, besides, what would be the point?

Why get involved with a man who, in all probability, when her holiday ended, she would never see again?

Chapter Twenty-Seven

That evening, Laura sank into her chair on the terrace beside Izzy, who, as she so often was these days, was engrossed in her book. Exhausted – too tired even to admire the setting sun, she closed her eyes, grateful that Corky and Olivia had gone into Kassiópi with Francesca and Sally.

As kind, as thoughtful and as fun as they were, her in-laws were running her ragged. With most of the sights now ticked off on their extensive list of places to visit, Laura was almost out of ideas and energy to keep them amused.

Why couldn't they be lazier? A little more like her own parents.

Why this constant need to be so active?

And why on earth did she feel so dog-tired? Surely she should be used to the heat by now. Last night during supper Francesca had caught her with her eyelids drooping and had teased her that she was hitting the menopause. 'When all those hot flushes kick in we won't need to bother with a log fire in the winter,' she had laughed. 'We'll sit in front of you and warm our toes.'

Oh, the cruelty of youth.

Olivia had suggested a course of HRT, saying she wished she had been young enough to take advantage of it when she had gone through the change. 'My hot flushes were so awful, they were more like tropical rainstorms,' she had said. 'I had several fainting phases as well. Very unpleasant.' Maybe, with all that behind her, it was no wonder that Olivia was so full of beans.

She and Max had done their best to occupy his parents, taking them far and wide. They had been to Kanóni to see the much-photographed Mouse Island with its chapel tucked into the cypress trees. Another day they had been to the top of Corfu's highest mountain, Mount Pantokrator, all 2,972 feet of it. They had been lucky with the weather: the sky had been crystal clear, and they had been able to make out Paxos, and even a glimpse of mainland Greece. They had also been to Corfu Town and had covered what to Laura had felt like every square inch of it. They had taken in the new and old fortresses, the paper money museum, the leather and jewellery shops, of which there were hundreds, and all had had to be inspected before Max's mother decided what to treat herself to. Then they had sat in the cool, gloomy interior of the beautiful old church of St Spiridon, with its towering campanile and red onion dome, which they all decided bore an uncanny resemblance to a fireman's helmet. In true Anglican fascination, they had watched locals hurrying in during their lunch-break to light candles and plant ritualistic kisses on the tomb of their much-loved patron saint, their lips murmuring prayers of hope and exultation. They had finished the day by relaxing over a drink in the quiet, arcaded street of the Listón where Max and Corky had got involved in the drama of a local cricket team showing a guest side from England how the game should be played.

On another day they had taken the boat out and explored the coastline south of Kassiópi, spending an afternoon at Kalámi Bay where Corky was keen to see where Gerald Durrell had lived as a boy. Then they had moved on to Kouloúra where several minutes of *For Your Eyes Only* had been filmed. 'Not one of the best Bond movies, I'll grant you,' Corky had said, when they stopped off for lunch at a waterside taverna. His comment had inevitably led to a discussion as to which had been the best 007 extravaganza. Olivia claimed that Sean Connery was the only true Bond, though she was prepared to give Pierce Brosnan the benefit of the doubt. But Francesca claimed that the early movies had been nothing but a blatant display of misogyny. 'You should all be ashamed of yourselves,' she said, with disdain. 'Ian Fleming hated women – you can see it in the way they were portrayed in those early films, targets of sexual and physical abuse every time.' That shut them all up. There was nothing like a verbal knuckle-rapping from the younger generation to put the older one in its place.

The following day they had visited the Achillíon. Originally built as a hideaway palace of over-the-top kitsch for the Empress Elizabeth of Austria, a lonely, unhappy woman with a penchant for statues, it was now one of the island's most popular sights. Its more recent claim to fame – other than having been a casino for some years – was that, like Kouloúra, it, too, had been used as a setpiece in *For Your Eyes Only*. After several hours of admiring statues and taking photographs, Laura had assumed – had hoped – they were set for home, but Olivia had suddenly been consumed by an irresistible urge to venture into the nearby distillery where they had been roped into tasting and, unbelievably, buying several bottles of kumquat liqueur. It was terrible stuff, so sweet it had turned Laura's mouth inside out. She couldn't think what Olivia was going to do with it all, apart from contribute it to the Christmas tombola she and Corky organised every year for their local church.

Having rested for a short while, Laura now opened her eyes and said to Izzy, 'Whatever shall I do with Max's parents for the rest of their stay? The thought of yet another crowded beauty-spot fills me with dread. I wish it had been my ankle that had got twisted. It would have let me off the hook nicely.'

'You could tell them there's nothing else worth seeing,' Izzy said, lowering her book.

'But they've got their guidebooks to prove me wrong.'

'Then your only course of action is to tell them the truth. Honesty is always the best policy.'

'I quite agree with you, Izzy.'

They turned to see Max coming towards them with a bottle of wine and three glasses. 'Which is as good a cue as any to say that I'm not just your wine waiter for the evening, but the bearer of bad news.'

Laura took the glass he offered her. 'Oh, and what's that?'

'I've just been on the phone to Phil from the office. I have to go home sooner than I thought.'

'Trouble?'

He sat down in the chair next to Laura and smiled. 'Nothing a whiz kid like me can't handle. Do you mind very much?'

'Yes,' she pouted. 'Lots. When are you planning on going?'

'I thought I could leave with Mum and Dad on Friday, if I can get on the flight. A later one, if not.'

Unable to keep the disappointment out of her voice, Laura said, 'How long do you think you'll be away this time?'

'Difficult to say until I get a feel for what needs doing. It's a new client we'd be mad to lose out on. But at least you'll still have Izzy for company, not forgetting the girls. How about we have a lavish, all button-popping meal in Kassiópi the night before I go?'

'I suppose that might soften the blow.'

The next morning, while lying in bed next to Max, Laura had a change of heart. 'Let's not eat out on Thursday night,' she said, 'let's have a party instead. It'll be more fun.'

'But won't that make more work for you? You keep saying how tired you are.'

'Such concern for your poor ageing wife does you credit. But I'm being more cunning than you think. I'm relying on your parents to take over. You know how they love organising a party. This will keep them busy for the rest of their holiday.'

'You clever old thing, you.'

During breakfast, and just as Laura had predicted, Corky and Olivia seized on the idea.

'Why don't we make it a theme party?' suggested Olivia.

'Fancy dress, you mean?' asked Sally.

'Oh dear, does that sound very dull to you? In our day fancy-dress parties were all the rage.'

'No way, it sounds cool. How about we do the whole Greek myth scene?'

Across the table, Laura saw Max roll his eyes and knew what he was thinking – Sally licensed to thrill in nothing but a transparent sheen of gossamer.

A guest list was immediately drawn up. Francesca took charge of this. At the top she wrote Theo's name. Laura saw her give Izzy a sly look, which Izzy tried to ignore, but the colour of her cheeks gave her away. Laura smiled to herself and said, 'Do you think we could persuade Mark to come along as well?'

'We can but try,' said Francesca, adding his name, then Harry and Nick.

'You'd better include their parents,' Laura said. 'It's about time we met them.'

'Subtle, Mum,' said Francesca, twirling the pencil between her fingers, then tapping it against her teeth. 'I was wondering when you'd get round to checking them out.'

Since the night Izzy had hurt her ankle and Francesca had brought Harry home, the Patterson boys had put in more than the occasional appearance. Usually late at night. Much to Francesca's amusement, Max had taken a liking to Harry, referring to him as PM – Promising Material. 'He's clean, good-looking and polite. What more could I want for my daughter?' he teased her. 'And just think, he might even be the type to hold down a steady and well-paid job when the time comes.'

'You're so woefully predictable, Dad!' had been Francesca's response.

The guest list was extended to include Dimitri and Marietta, who ran the jewellery shop in Kassiópi; and Sophia and Angelos, plus Giorgios and his two younger sisters.

'You know who we can't miss off the list, don't you?' said Max.

Everybody looked at him.

'The Fitzgeralds.'

'You're right,' said Laura. 'It would be very rude to exclude them. Go on, Francesca, add their names. And we'll have to remember to tell Theo that his little game of pretending to be Mark's chauffeur will have to come to an end before then. I don't want Dolly-Babe being made to look a fool in front of everybody.'

'Oh, you're all heart, Mum.'

'Now then,' said Olivia, after she had fetched one of the many books she had brought with her – *Who's Who in Greek Mythology*. 'Who shall we dress up as?' She flicked through the pages until one caught her eye. 'Aha, anyone fancy being Medea?'

'What's she famous for?' asked Sally.

'Wasn't she the one who was into rejuvenation?' said Izzy, flexing her ankle experimentally – she had removed the strapping last night in bed to see if she could manage a day without its support. 'She chopped up an old ram, popped it into the cauldron of bubbling potion and out leaped a young lamb.'

'She was also a ruthless so-and-so,' added Corky. 'Keen to teach Jason a lesson for his infidelity, she murdered their children.'

'Hey, I like her style,' laughed Sally, 'a woman not to tangle with. Read on, Mrs S, and let's see who else you've got for us.'

Quietly relieved that everyone was now absorbed in preparing for the party, Laura slipped away to the far end of the terrace where she lay down on a sun-lounger. Happy in the knowledge that she no longer had to entertain the troops, she closed her eyes and, without meaning to, was soon dozing. She dreamed that, on his return to England, Max impressed his new client by dressing up as Hercules and wrestling his competitors to the floor.

Chapter Twenty-Eight

While everyone else was trying to decide which mytho-
logical character they wanted to be at the party, Francesca and Sally knocked up some invitations on Max's
computer and offered to deliver them.

Their first port of call was Nick and Harry. 'It makes
sense to start off at the furthest point and work our way
back,' said Francesca, as they took the path down to the
beach.

'It wouldn't have anything to do with being keen to see
Harry, would it?'

Francesca pretended she hadn't heard what Sally had
said, but it wasn't a million miles from the truth. Rarely
did she and Sally keep anything of a personal nature from
each other, but in this instance Francesca was keen to
preserve a degree of privacy. Not that there was much to
tell. Well, not by Sally's standards, anyway. But discussing Harry with anyone might taint what Francesca felt
for him. Though she wasn't entirely sure what it was. He
was so unlike any previous boyfriend she had had.
Maybe that was the appeal.

But what she did or did not feel for Harry was beside
the point. Three nights ago, without meaning to, she had
annoyed and upset him. They had been on their own,
Nick and Sally having gone to a bar for another all-night
session, and they were walking home through the olive
grove. It was nearly two o'clock in the morning and they
were following the small beams of light cast from their
torches. The path had seemed steeper and bumpier in the

dark and, in her high platform shoes, the going was even harder. It wasn't long before she missed her step, and because Harry was the kind of bloke he was, gentle and caring, his hand was immediately there to stop her going over. 'You don't need to let go,' she had said, feeling his hand loosen on her arm once she had regained her balance. It sounded as if she was teasing him, and she probably was, just a little, but she quite fancied the thought of him holding her hand. Without a word, he slipped his hand into hers and they continued on their way.

It had been a long time since she had felt like this – cherished, as though she mattered. It made her wonder what she had ever seen in a jerk like Carl – whose idea of a romantic moment was to lick his lips and say, 'How about it?' She cringed at the memory of him saying this the first time they had met, at a party. How could she have fallen for such a crass line? What on earth had been the attraction? Perhaps her parents had been right that the whole episode had been her need to rebel, to shock her father into believing that she was all grown-up. She realised now that, far from shocking him, she had only disappointed him.

She had been so deep in thought that she missed her footing again, and if it hadn't been for Harry she would have fallen flat on her face. He held on to her tightly, his fingers digging into her arm. 'You okay?' he asked.

'Thanks to you I am,' she said, her face raised to his. Aware of how close their bodies were, she waited to see what he would do.

The wait was worth while.

Every delicious, anticipatory second of it.

He removed his glasses, and very slowly brought his mouth down to hers. His timing was supreme: not too fast, not too slow, just perfect. And when he got down to it – when he got into his stride and held her to him – she realised she had never been kissed so beautifully.

'You've done this before, haven't you?' she said, when at last he let her go.

'Not like this I haven't.'

His honesty, and the sweet, tender way in which he was looking at her, squinting to focus on her face, made her smile. She reached up and pulled his head down to her again. But after the briefest of kisses, he gently pushed her from him.

'What's wrong?' she asked.

Suddenly he looked awkward. His glasses were in place again, as was his shy reserve. 'Nothing's wrong,' he mumbled, more to himself than to her. He wasn't even meeting her gaze now.

'Liar,' she retorted. 'Tell me what's wrong.' She sensed rejection only a short slippery step away and didn't like the idea. Not so soon after Carl.

'I'm sorry,' he said, still not looking at her, 'it's just . . . if we carry on I'm not sure I'd know how to stop myself from . . .'

This was the last thing she had expected him to say, and relief made her laugh. 'From what?' she asked, curious to see how he would answer.

'I think you know. I also think you're having a joke at my expense.' In the shadowy darkness, his face was tight with condemnation.

'Hey, there, Mr Sensitive, before you start accusing me of teasing you, how about you considering that the boot might be on the other foot? No girl likes being kissed – a kiss that would score highly in the history of your one hundred best snogs, and then have a repeat sample denied her.'

He nudged his glasses. 'Are you always this stroppy when a guy tries to act decently?'

'No!' she snapped. 'It's a first. I've never met a bloke who hasn't tried to grope me at the first opportunity.'

He frowned. 'So where does that leave me? Mr Bloody Boring again, I suppose. Someone you and Sally can have a good laugh at.'

She hesitated. 'Actually, it makes you a refreshing change. So quit blathering, and if it isn't too much of a turn-on for you, give me your hand so I can get home in one piece.'

'I'll do my best to contain myself,' he responded, his expression stern, which was at odds with his normally good-natured face.

They walked on in stony, nerve-jarring silence. At the gate to Villa Petros, he let go of her hand and was all set to leave without another word when she touched his arm lightly and said, 'I'm sorry that you thought I was laughing at you. I wasn't, really. It was relief. It was—'

But he wasn't interested in what she had to say. 'Goodnight, Francesca.' He turned and left her.

She let herself in and went to bed. But she couldn't sleep. All she could think of was turning the clock back to that moment in the olive grove when Harry had kissed her, and before she had blown it with him. Not for the first time in her life, her hot-headedness had got the better of her.

That had been three nights ago and she hadn't seen him since. And now, as she and Sally approached the pink villa that Harry and his family were renting, she wondered how he would react to seeing her again.

'It's a bit of a wreck, isn't it?' said Sally, as they pushed through the tangle of overgrown bushes and weeds that had invaded the path. Everything about the villa looked tired and worn out. The faded walls had long since lost their original vibrancy and the green paintwork on the shutters was peeling badly. Even the bougainvillaea clinging to one of the walls looked as if it had had enough.

Without catching a glimpse of Mr and Mrs Patterson, Francesca and Sally could hear them. It was obvious from the raised voices coming from inside the villa that an argument was in full swing. Nick had often referred to the warring tension between 'the aged ones' but Francesca hadn't taken him seriously. Now she knew he hadn't been exaggerating. 'Perhaps we ought not to bother them,' she said, thinking of Harry and how he would hate her to see his parents like this. 'Let's leave them till later.'

'What? And miss out on embarrassing them? No way.'

When they reached the terrace they saw Nick and Harry. They were dressed for the beach, in swimming shorts with a towel slung over a shoulder, snorkels and masks in hand. Despite the commotion still going on inside the villa, Nick was instantly all smiles. 'Welcome to the madhouse. As you can no doubt hear the lovebirds, Ma and Pa Patterson, are a bit preoccupied with each other at the moment so I shan't introduce you. We have to make allowances, love blinds them. We're off for a swim, want to join us?'

Sneaking a look at Harry, Francesca said, 'Later, maybe.' She handed over the invitation to Nick. 'Mum and Dad are giving a party and you're all invited.'

With Sally's help, she explained about the party and its theme. 'If you're stuck for ideas, we've got a brilliant book on Greek mythology we could lend you.'

'And, please, don't say you want to be Hercules, Nick,' said Sally. 'We've got them queuing up for him.'

But Nick dismissed Hercules out of hand. 'The man was a fool going along with all those tedious labours. I think I'll go as Cronus.'

'Who was he?' asked Francesca. Nick had never struck her as being the sharpest knife in the cutlery box and she was amazed that he knew anything about Greek mythology.

Throwing a look over his shoulder, towards the villa where the noise had at last died down, Nick said, 'At his mother's request, Cronus hacked off his dad's genitals with a sickle and tossed them into the sea. It was poor old Gaia's answer to the vasectomy.'

'They were a sick old bunch, weren't they?' laughed Sally.

'What will you be going as, Francesca?' Harry asked, and Francesca, who until now had been sure that he was doing his best to avoid eye-contact with her, met his gaze.

'I haven't decided yet,' she said, 'though I did wonder about Cassandra.'

He pushed up his glasses. 'Cassandra,' he repeated, keeping his eyes on her. 'The daughter of Hecuba and Priam whose fate it was never to be believed.'

She smiled. 'That's her. Good choice or not?'

His mouth twitched amiably. 'I'd have to reserve judgement.'

'You do that, then.'

'Sure you don't want to join us for a swim now?' he asked.

'I'd love to but we've got the rest of these invitations to deliver. See you later perhaps?'

'That would be nice.'

Once they had left the boys and were out of earshot, Sally said, 'A seriously weird family, wouldn't you say, all that arguing?'

'Explains why Nick's such a head-case, doesn't it?'

'So where does Harry fit in, then?'

Francesca laughed. 'He has to be adopted. Nobody as normal as he is could have been conceived by such genetically impaired parents.'

They headed for their next port of call, Villa Mimosa.

270

This was a large, buttermilk-coloured, two-storeyed house about a hundred yards higher up the hillside and just beyond a smaller villa that seemed uninhabited. In the baking midday sun, the steep climb left them both breathless. With the sound of cicadas chirruping noisily all around them, they paused to catch their breath and to take in the view below them. Down on the beach, Nick and Harry were swimming in the sparkling sea, their snorkels poking up through the choppy waves. Thinking of the brief exchange, just now, with Harry, Francesca was hopeful that another of his off-the-chart kisses might be on offer. She smiled at the prospect.

'Come on,' she said, turning round and climbing further up the path. 'We'll burn if we stand here much longer. Let's go and see if Dolly-Babe's in.'

They found her reclining on a sun-lounger in the shade of a large canvas parasol. She was wearing a white swimsuit that couldn't have been designed with swimming in mind – it was a dazzling sight of pearls and rhinestones. But Francesca was more struck by the two very upright boobs thrusting through the glitter – silicone-enhanced for sure. When Dolly-Babe saw the girls, she put down her glass and hurriedly tied a sarong around her tiny waist. 'Can I help you?' she asked, lowering her sunglasses and peering at them in a less-than-welcoming fashion.

Francesca explained who they were and handed over the invitation.

'Ooh,' said Dolly-Babe, her demeanour undergoing a dramatic change. 'A party! That's nice. Care to join me for a drink, girls?' She slipped on a pair of gold-trimmed Prada mules that had Sally's tongue hanging out with envy and tip-tapped inside the house, returning minutes later with an open bottle of chilled wine and two extra glasses. 'Now, then,' she said, when they had settled into their chairs and raised their glasses, 'what kind of a bash is it that your parents are throwing?'

Sally took up the reins of the conversation – it was now one party girl to another. But Dolly-Babe looked unsure when she learned that it was to be a fancy-dress do. 'I don't see my Bob going for that somehow,' she said doubtfully. 'It's as much as he can do to put on a shirt and tie to go out for dinner. He never likes any fuss.'

'It's nothing too over the top,' Francesca said. 'You don't have to make your costume too elaborate, just enough to hint at your character. For instance, if your husband wanted to come as Atlas, all he'd have to do was draw a map of the world on a balloon and stick it to his shoulder.'

The idea of her husband wearing nothing more complicated than a balloon attached to his shoulder seemed to allay Dolly-Babe's fears. 'But what about me? I know diddley-squat about Greek myths. What do you think I should go as?'

With the tumble of dyed blonde hair perched on top of her head, Francesca wanted to say that Medusa would be an easy option, but she felt that Dolly-Babe might not think that funny. Sally told her about Medea. Murdered children and all.

'Gawd help us! Isn't there someone more, well, you know, nice and attractive? A bit more glamorous – like me?'

'We could lend you a book if you want,' Sally offered. Then, seeing a pile of magazines on the table between them, she said, 'Are you into the psychic world, Mrs Fitzgerald?'

'Call me Liberty-Raquel, darlin', and, yes, I am. Are you?'

'Kind of.'

This was news to Francesca. She helped herself to one

of the magazines and flicked through it. 'Psychic Perception – All Your Financial Problems Solved', was the title of one of its main articles.

'So have you had any really weird experiences?' asked Sally. 'You know, like you knew what somebody was about to do or say? I get that a lot.'

Yes, thought Francesca, like you know exactly what I'm thinking of you right now and what I'll say to you later. But if she had thought her friend was teasing Dolly-Babe, she soon discovered she was wrong. Sally was in earnest. This was a whole new side to her friend that Francesca had not known existed. Amused, she continued flicking through the pages of the magazine. There was a big feature on 'Spiritual Astrology for a Better Sex Life', followed by a piece on 'The Truth Behind Spontaneous Human Combustion'. There was even a piece about casting love spells to push your potential partner in the right direction. Love, sex and money seemed to be the chief concerns of the magazine. So, no different from any other coffee-table glossy, you could say. Except that there seemed to be a lot of emphasis on money. An extraordinary number of clairvoyants, psychics, mediums and tarot readers were all willing to chat to you on the phone via your credit card.

'I went to a fortune-teller once,' she heard Sally say. 'It was a gang of us from school. We just did it for a laugh. But this woman who read my hand, she knew all about me. She knew things I'd never told anyone.'

'Ria's the same,' Dolly-Babe said, draining her glass and refilling it. She offered them the bottle, but they both refused. 'Ria's my personal psychic medium, and you know what? She told me I'd be going to a party while I was here.'

'She did?'

'Yes. She read the cards for me and the Eight of Cups was there.'

'What does that mean?'

'It signifies an expansion of social horizons. And I'll tell you something else. Ria says that your neighbour Mr St James is a part of my stay here. Ria says that he's going to play an integral part in my life. I just wish I knew what it was. It's so nerve-racking waiting to see what it's all about.'

Francesca felt as if she had escaped from the Land People Forgot when she and Sally finally got away. She said as much as they retraced their steps down to the beach, then on towards Villa Anna to see Theo.

'I don't know why you have such a closed mind to the psychic world,' Sally said huffily. 'It seems perfectly reasonable to me.'

'Well, coming from the girl who was unhinged enough to make a pass at my father, I'll take that with a handful of salt. I can't believe you're buying into all that rubbish.'

'It's the new rock and roll, didn't you know?'

'More like the new cash 'n' carry. I was checking out the classifieds in that magazine while you were chatting to Dolly-Babe, and it was page after page of "Most Credit Cards" accepted. It's a colossal con. It's for people too dumb to figure out that it's all a case of *que sera, sera*.' Then, seeing that she wasn't getting anywhere, she said, 'Did you see the expression on her face when I told her who her precious Mr St James was?'

'Sure did. Talk about the penny dropping.'

Both she and Sally had assumed that although Dolly-Babe did not know who Theo was, she knew who Mark was, so when they had made some reference to him being here to work on his latest book, she had shrieked, 'Well, Gawd bless us! You know, I kept thinking he was familiar, but for the life of me I couldn't put my finger on it.' It turned out that her husband had been taking one of Mark's novels to bed with him each night and a black and white photograph of the author had stared at her across their bed. Francesca thought this spoke volumes about a woman who had just been claiming to be intuitive and perceptive.

After their long, sweaty uphill climb, there was no one in at Villa Anna so they left the party invitation on a table on the terrace, weighting it down with a stone, and decided to go for a swim. They had had enough of playing Postman Pat. The remaining invitations could wait.

Chapter Twenty-Nine

Mark was giving himself a rare break from his strict writing routine and was spending the day in Corfu Town with Theo.

They had come into town for the memorial service to Theo's grandmother, Anna Vlamakis. She had been dead for eighteen years, but tradition was that on each anniversary of her death a special service of remembrance was held. Mark thought it a much more positive and substantial way to think of one's departed relations than leaving an occasional bunch of flowers on a grave in a windswept cemetery.

Here, courtesy of the Greek Orthodox Church, the friends and relatives who had gathered to remember Anna Vlamakis had now moved on from the spiritual words of comfort to what had been her favourite restaurant in the Listón, to celebrate her memory in gregarious Greek fashion.

Back in the late 1970s and early 1980s Mark had met the old lady several times on trips to Corfu, and had liked her immensely, despite the appalling way in which she indulged her only grandson. He had never been to Greece before he had met Theo, and when their unlikely friendship had developed, Theo had invited him to spend part of the 1978 summer vacation in Athens and Corfu.

Mark had been torn between the plans he had already made and the idea of actually allowing himself some fun. He had planned to stay on in Durham and work his way through the summer, serving behind the bar of a pub, and in his free time advance his grandiose theories that would one day save the world from itself. Going home to his parents, like his fellow students, and working for the family firm had not been a consideration. However, after a short tussle with his conscience, he threw some clothes into a rucksack and justified the trip by telling himself that travel broadened the mind. There was even a chance that he might get some writing done. In those days anger and the injustices of the world fuelled his work. His prose was then an outpouring of vitriolic loathing for the oppressors of the state. In other words, it was all hot air. But at the time, and in his youth, and in his hunger to make a difference to the world, it had been important to him. He was moderately successful at getting into print and had several articles published, mostly in a variety of home-spun rags that had a penchant for protest politics and the round-them-up-and-shoot-them genre of journalism. These were the people he hung out with, political activists whose main aim was to create a classless society.

So, not surprisingly, he kept his holiday plans to himself that particular summer when he flew off to Athens with a man who represented everything he opposed: wealth, privilege, and a set of handmade leather luggage that was as ostentatious as it was offensive to somebody who, in those days, was a zealous vegetarian and didn't even wear leather shoes.

Theo's parents, Christiana and Thanos Vlamakis, now living in Athens, had greeted him in their luxurious apartment overlooking the busy harbour with the same warmth and sincerity they had extended towards him in Durham. They were as effusive as they were hospitable and frequently embarrassed him by introducing him to their friends and neighbours as the man who had saved Theo's life, embellishing the tale with more drama each time they told it. 'Make them stop,' he had pleaded with

Theo. 'I can't stand it. Any more of it and I swear I'll turn back the clock and kill you myself!'

But Theo had laughed and told him to make the most of his hero status. 'Is it my fault that they have put you on a pedestal?'

'Cut the crap, Theo, and tell your parents to do the same.'

'Don't be so self-absorbed. Be generous enough to let them enjoy themselves at your expense.'

And the old maxim that a good story never goes away was perfectly true, for even now over lunch, Christiana was telling the myth once more to some elderly relatives who had flown in from Thessaloníki. Though she was talking in Greek, Mark could understand what she was saying by her body language and the way she kept smiling at him. He shot Theo a look that meant 'Distract her', but Theo merely smiled and carried on talking to a larger-than-life man on his right, who had the most extraordinarily shaggy eyebrows. He was the priest who had just conducted the service and, in his flowing black robes, complemented by a fuzzy white beard with nicotine stains around his mouth and a hearty, full-throated laugh, his presence gave the proceedings an air of robust jollity. There was no po-faced piety about him as he held out his wine-glass to be replenished and took a lip-smacking slurp.

Sitting on Mark's left was a quiet ghost of a man. He looked about a hundred and ten, and so frail that a gust of wind might blow him away. He was in a wheelchair pushed close to the table and was dressed in a suit that must once have fitted him properly. The same was true of his shirt; above a buttoned collar, a tightly knotted tie drooped mockingly at his neck, exposing loose, translucent flesh. Resting on his lap, like a curled-up cat, was an ancient Panama, poignantly shabby and knocked about. Its owner was Thomas Zika and Mark had met him on his first visit to Corfu when he and Theo had been staying with Anna. It was widely known within the family that Thomas Zika had been very much in love with Theo's grandmother and Mark had always thought it a great waste that in the autumn of their lives the pair had never married.

The skin on the old man's head was parched and taut across his skull and only a few wispy strands of white hair remained. His features, made delicate by the passing of time, were set in a face so pale and waxen it looked as if the sun might shine straight through it. His eyes were dim and watery, and uncomfortably red-rimmed, with just a few lashes. Poking out through gaping cuffs, trembling vein-streaked hands were trying to grip a knife and fork; no matter how hard he tried, the medallions of turbot kept slipping away from him.

Mark returned his attention to his plate. He had only taken a few mouthfuls when he felt a light touch on his elbow. 'I wonder, young man, if you would be so kind as to help me.' The voice, hushed and tremulous, was barely audible; Mark had to strain to catch it. 'I should hate to die of starvation,' Thomas Zika continued. 'At my age it would seem so very undignified.'

Mark smiled at him and discreetly took his cutlery.

'You have changed a great deal since I saw you last,' said Thomas Zika, when Mark had completed his task.

'With respect, Mr Zika, it's a long time since we last met. It must be more than twenty years.'

'Can it really be as long as that?'

'I'm afraid it is.'

'But you are happier now?'

The gaze from the watery, bloodshot eyes was as perceptive as the question. 'I like to think so,' Mark replied.

'The years have been good to you?'

'Some good, some not so good.'

The old man nodded slowly, thoughtfully. 'We always learn most from the bad times, the years of being in the wilderness. Would you agree?'

Mark smiled to himself. It was as if he was back in the rehab clinic with Bones.

'You find what I have said amusing?'

'I'm sorry, it's just that you reminded me of someone.'

'Ah, a wise old counsellor? Or perhaps a stupid old man, who should have learned by now to mind his own business?'

'You were right the first time.'

'Excellent. That is eminently better than the latter.'

After a long pause, Thomas Zika said, 'Would it be asking very much of you to help me further? It seems that my hands are determined to disobey my every command today. If you would harpoon the pieces, I think I could manage to steer them on a homeward course.'

It was a relief for Mark to help him, and unexpectedly he pictured himself doing the same for his father one day.

Time was when he couldn't have been in the same room as his father without wanting to strike him down. That was when he had used him as a focus for all the anger he had within him. His mother and two older brothers had come in for their share too, but irrationally it was his father he had most wanted to hurt. And, as a teenager, it had been so easy to rile him: the cutting sarcasm, the cruel home truth, the biting irony, and the withering contempt. Relentlessly he would goad his father, seeing him as nothing more than a moving target that was no match for his superior intellect. But the harder he pushed, the more his father withdrew. He kept up the pressure, just waiting for the day when his father would lose control. But it never came.

It was power he had wanted. Power over his father and his family. He craved it as much as he later craved drugs and alcohol. He was obstinate and ruthlessly antagonistic. An unlovable son who taunted his parents into sending him away to school – 'Go on, then, if you dare, prove how little you care.' And when at last they had reached the end of their tether and sent him away, he claimed a victory over them, awarding himself the moral high ground, asserting that he had been right all along. He was the most disruptive and obnoxiously offensive son any family could have been cursed with.

He was no easier at school. Sullen but volatile, he made few friends, the other children preferring to keep their distance from him. They were frightened of him: frightened of his anger; of what it could do to him, what it could do to them. And because his mood swings were so unpredictable, some of the older, braver boys called him Skitzy. He was twice suspended for smoking on school premises, and very nearly expelled just before O levels for turning the air blue with his language when a teacher caught him drinking in a nearby pub one lunchtime. His parents were summoned, and after they had begged the head to reconsider and an apology had been extracted from Mark, he was given a last chance. He watched them drive away afterwards, his mother holding a handkerchief to her face, his father tight-lipped and ashen.

It pained him now to think how close he had come to destroying his parents. But unleashing his anger had been his only source of comfort, his only means of survival: to reject his parents before they rejected him.

Making his peace with his family had been one of the many humbling experiences he had had to go through to complete the process of cleaning himself up. Bones had said that it was essential for his recovery that he underwent some family-therapy sessions. At first he had resisted the suggestion. Violently. 'No!' he had cried, leaping from his seat and nearly knocking it over. 'No,

I'm not ready for that.' His desperate voice had bounced off the bare walls of the austere room. From nowhere, his body was covered in a sheen of sweat. The white noise of his panic filled his head and his guts dissolved. Then the need for a drink flooded his system. A drink to drown the fear. Going over to the open window, he fought hard to resist his addiction by focusing on his breathing. He looked across the fields to the restored church spire, but his eyes took in none of it. His face was tight with recollection as he visualised the last time he had seen his parents.

He had let himself into their house late one night, using the key he had had for years, but until then had never used. This was no social call: he was there to steal from them. He had been out of work for nearly a year – employers are hard to come by when you're a full-time alcoholic and living in a squat permanently off your head. He had sold everything he owned, and scrounged from those who had anything worth scrounging.

His parents had discovered him in the dining room, clearing out a Georgian cabinet of silver knick-knacks. He was carelessly tipping them into a large bin-liner when the light was switched on. It was a toss-up as to who looked more shocked, him or them. His mother, standing a few inches behind his father, had gasped and clutched at the neck of her nightdress as if a blast of cold air had just swept in. His father, once he had gathered his wits together and realised what was going on, had said, 'At least have the decency to leave your mother the photographs.'

Looking down at what was in his hand, Mark had seen that he was about to add to his bag of booty a silver-framed picture of himself as a small boy. A smiling, untroubled face stared back at him; a happy child with a happy future ahead of him. Suddenly the awful reality of what he was doing hit him. With all the force of mainlining straight into his bloodstream, it made him hesitate. Made him wonder if there wasn't another way.

But it only lasted for a matter of seconds.

'I need money,' he said, and tossed the photograph into the bin-liner. He heard the glass break as it banged against another piece of silver. The threat he was making was so clear that he might just as well have been holding a gun to his parents' heads.

His father tightened the belt on his dressing-gown. 'How much . . . this time?'

'How much can you spare . . . this time?'

'Put the bag down and come with me.'

His father's flat voice had its usual effect on him, made him feel as though he was no more significant than one of his employees. Without looking at his mother, Mark followed his father the length of the house to his study, remembering a time when he had played here with his brothers, racing them up and down the long corridor and hallway, skidding to a halt on their knees as they flew across the polished wooden floor, rucking up rugs, bumping into panelled walls, their happy laughter filling the house while their mother gently rebuked them for their recklessness.

He stood in front of the walnut desk, and watched his father write a cheque. 'I'm giving you this on the understanding that, from now on, you leave us alone. You've done your damnedest to destroy yourself, I won't allow you to do the same to your mother. You're not to come here again.'

He snatched the cheque from his father's hand. 'I can live with that. I'm not too proud to know that I'm being paid off to safeguard your finer feelings.' He folded the crisp piece of paper in half and slipped it into his pocket, his mind already heading for the door to get out of the house, out of their lives. 'But satisfy my morbid curiosity, don't you care about me at all?'

The cool steely gaze – whose blueness matched Mark's own eyes – stared back at him, never wavering. 'No. I've had enough. I've done all that I possibly could for you. My conscience is clear.'

It was the longest conversation he had had with his father in years.

He was as good as his word and kept his side of the bargain by staying away. Until one day, coming round from a drinking binge that had lasted nearly a week – a week of which he had no recollection – he wrote his mother a letter. It was only a few melodramatic, disorientated lines saying that he was sorry for all the trouble he had caused and that he wished that he was dead.

Had it been a cry for help?

Almost certainly.

One instinctively knows when one has had enough. When it's time to come quietly.

Within two weeks Theo was helping him into a car and driving him through the night to a rehab clinic.

Bringing him out of his reverie, Bones had said, 'Mark, please sit down. You really have nothing to fear from such a meeting with your family, and everything to gain.'

Sinking into his chair, desperate now, he had begged, 'Please, I'm not ready. It's too soon. Give me more time.' Refusing to see his parents was the last line in his defence. Remove that and he would be vulnerable and exposed again.

But Bones was having none of his excuses. 'You have to learn to coexist, Mark. The new man you are becoming has to live alongside the man you once were. There must be no shame involved. There will never be a more perfect time to see your parents. Now, shall we say Monday afternoon for the first meeting?'

They had been through a similar process when Bones had suggested that it might be helpful and appropriate for Mark to see Theo. All the other 'guests' at the clinic had a regular time for meeting friends and family from the outside world but he hadn't wanted to see anyone: he had felt too raw and ashamed. But Bones was a persistent sod and arranged for Theo to come and see him.

'Is it very bad, this place I have brought you to?' Theo had asked, as they wandered the grounds in the bright spring sunshine shortly after they had been put through their paces by Bones.

'Let's just say it's growing on me.'

They sat on a wooden bench overlooking a small lake and watched a squadron of ducks swim by. 'I have known you all this time, Mark, and yet before this day you never told me about your friend drowning. I feel that I have let you down because you didn't feel able to confide in me. Have I been such a poor friend to you?'

'Hey, it's me on the guilt trip, okay? Don't go trying to steal my thunder.'

'But I do feel guilty. I'm disappointed with myself that I never saw through your subterfuge. Your act of wanting single-handedly to save the world should have alerted me to what you were really doing.'

'And what was that?'

'Trying to make an atonement for a young boy's death that you blamed yourself for. Oh, how very clever you were, I didn't ever suspect. Nor did I really understand just how successful you were at alienating yourself from everybody.'

'I wasn't entirely successful. I let you get close, didn't I?'

'And for that I feel truly honoured. But tell me what this strange little man whom you call Bones has taught you.'

'Oh, the usual half-baked theory that I have to learn to love myself.'

Looking stern, Theo said, 'Please, Mark, do not be so

flippant. Respecting oneself is crucial. Why can you not do that?'

'Who knows? By the time Bones has finished with me I might be able to.'

It was when it was time for Theo to leave that Mark felt his emotions slide out of control. Theo had hugged him goodbye, a fierce, heart-filled hug that had taken the breath out of his chest and made him cling to his friend like a frightened child standing with his mother at the school gate for the first time. He had never forgotten the compassion on Theo's face as he released his hold. Or his words: 'I will come back for you, Mark,' he had soothed, his eyes misting over, 'I won't let you down.'

Before the first meeting with his parents, he had had all weekend to stew in a ferment of anxiety and fear. How could he face them after everything he had done?

Would they come?

Perhaps his mother might, but his father? Would he feel that this was just one more aspect of his son's dismally weak character with which he didn't want to be associated?

Monday afternoon arrived, and in what was initially an excruciating ordeal, the last remaining spectres of his nightmare were finally laid to rest.

Bones started the proceedings by passing round a family-sized box of Maltesers and saying, in a carefully lowered voice that was clearly designed to draw them into a cosy circle of intimacy, 'Well, everyone, we live in a society that is only too keen to make us feel guilty. We can't throw away a shampoo bottle without thinking we should recycle it.'

Mark could see that Bones's unassuming manner was putting his mother at ease, but there wasn't a trace of a thaw in his father as he sat bolt upright in his chair, his face rigid with tension and disapproval. He was dressed for battle – suit, tie, shoes gleaming, eyes averted, defences bristling.

'What I thought we'd look at first,' Bones carried on, 'is how everyone likes to have a scapegoat. Nowadays we use the term quite lightly, but its true significance is based on the desire to get rid of the thing, or person, whom we consider to be the cause of all our problems. Even in our enlightened age, there's nothing better than to be able to blame something, or someone, for whatever is going wrong at a particular time. An unhappy husband will leave his wife for another woman because he believes the wife to be the one holding him back or not understanding him, for making him miserable. The truth is, he is holding himself back with his own misunderstanding of the many problems he refuses to acknowledge as his. Scapegoating goes on all the time. We blame the Russians or Michael Fish for bad weather. We blame politicians for the rising—'

'Are you saying that . . . that all this is our fault?' The question was barked with ferocious defensiveness.

'No, Mr St James, I am not blaming you. Far from it. I'm suggesting that you are blaming yourself for not being able to help Mark work through the unresolved anger of a tragic accident. But if I may be allowed to explain further. When Mark really began to get out of control, you soon found yourselves turning him into a scapegoat for your own feelings of inadequacy and failure. In some small measure it lessened the guilt for you, out of sight, out of mind. No, please, don't look so shocked. It was a position he deliberately forced you into. You had little choice in the matter. He already saw himself as the scapegoat for Niall's death and wanted to take things further by proving to those closest to him that he should be thoroughly punished for what he had done. So he bullied you into sending him away to school. I'm afraid he manipulated you perfectly by turning himself into the family's black sheep. Paradoxically he imagined it would make him feel confident and empowered to know that he was in charge of you all. By then there was no stopping him. He began to see himself as the superhuman carrier of collective guilt.' A smile passed over Bones's face. 'And I think you would both agree with me that he is certainly arrogant enough to believe that he was up to the job.'

And so it went on, Bones talking, his parents listening, as he gently guided them through the dark maze in which they had been trapped. He spoke of the need for them all to challenge the past, to look it right in the eye and see it for what it was – something that no longer existed. The atmosphere gradually became less charged. His mother said, 'What hurt me most was that he wouldn't let me touch him.' She looked at Mark, reached out to his hand. 'I so badly wanted to wrap you in love, to hold you, to make you realise that you were loved. But you pushed me away so many times that I gave up trying.'

Unable to speak, he squeezed her hand. He looked at his father, to see how he was coping, knowing that it wouldn't be easy for him. His father's body had gone slack, his head was bowed low, his chin almost touching his chest. With a shock, Mark realised his father was crying. In response he felt his throat constrict and the backs of his eyes prickle. He caught Bones gesturing to him to pass his father the box of tissues on the desk. But he couldn't. His body wouldn't move. It was paralysed by too much family history. Resentment. Bitterness. And a mutual fear of each other.

'Mark, I think your father might like a tissue. Would you pass him one, please?'

As cunning as ever, Bones had forced him to confront yet another ghost. He reached for a triple-strength Kleenex and, like a white flag of surrender, passed it to his father.

The head still bowed, there was an embarrassed murmur of thanks, followed by a loud trumpeting blow. But then the real tears flowed, and seeing his father's rock-hard exterior crumbling away, Mark lost it as well. For the first time since he had been a small boy he wept openly in front of his parents, the tears streaming down his cheeks. In response, a heavy weight magically rose from his shoulders. The relief was enormous. And, without disturbing them, Bones quietly left them to it.

He soon returned with a tray of civilising tea and a plate of custard creams, as well as a list of thought-provoking questions for each of them to consider for when they met the following day. 'What we'll need to address,' he said, dunking a biscuit into his tea and crossing one of his stumpy little legs over the other, 'is the concern that every parent feels in these situations. Where did we go wrong? My job is to convince you that you didn't.'

'But . . . but we should have done more,' Mark's father said, sounding as if he was having to squeeze the words through a throat that was tightly bunched. 'We should never have given up on him. I . . . I blame myself. If I had—'

Bones jumped on him from a great height.

'Fault is not being apportioned,' he said firmly, 'not today, tomorrow or any other day. Mark and I haven't invited you here to point the finger of blame at you, or accuse you of negligence. You're here because you have a shared history that, as painful as it is, needs explaining. Nobody, and I can't stress this enough, *nobody* is to blame. It is extremely important to remember that each of you was presented with an impossible no-win situation. You all did what came naturally to you. As parents you tried your best to help and understand him, but couldn't. He was beyond your reach. There's no shame in admitting that. No shame in admitting that you couldn't stop your son from hitting the self-destruct button. It was an impossible situation that you all dealt with in the only way you knew how.' He paused to offer them a second cup of tea. 'You know, the life we want,' he went on, tinkling his teaspoon against his cup, 'is rarely the life we have. All we can ever do is bridge the gap to the Promised Land.'

After that they were at least able to communicate with each other on a new, improved level. The resentment, bitterness and mutual fear he and his father had felt for each other gave way to tolerance and understanding, a glimmer of hope that life could be better.

And all these years on, they were still working at that bridge Bones had spoken of. Mark was a part of his parents' lives once again, and he suspected that they were just a little bit proud of him. His father, who normally didn't have time to read, never failed to get hold of his latest book the moment it was out – he always refused a free copy, saying that he wanted the pleasure of walking into their local bookshop and asking for his son's latest novel.

As for his brothers, Peter and Hugh – the clever bastards, he had always called them – he now had two sisters-in-law as well as three nieces and a nephew. He was a constant source of amusement to the children. They knew that their uncle Mark wasn't like other uncles. Last Christmas, his youngest niece had climbed on to his lap and asked him if all families had a skeleton like theirs hidden away in a cupboard. He had laughed and instantly made up a spine-tingling story about the one kept in the attic of his parents' house where they were all staying. He described how it came out of its box on the stroke of midnight and wandered around the house. The next morning, Peter had had a go at him for scaring Susie half to death and keeping her awake all night.

But there was one thing for which he was especially grateful to his brothers, and that was their enthusiasm for running the family business now that their father had retired: a business that had been in the family for three generations.

And what exactly was the family business?

It was, of all things, a brewery.

As Theo would say, 'How is that for a nice touch of your typically English irony?'

Chapter Thirty

They were the last to leave the restaurant. Thanos and
Christiana Vlamakis, along with the elderly relatives
from Thessaloníki, took a taxi to the airport to catch
their flights home, the priest went off in a haze of Metaxá
to the Esplanade to watch a cricket match and Theo and
Mark helped Thomas Zika back to his apartment on
Kapodistriou Street. They had only a short distance to
cover, but by the time Mark had pushed the old man's
wheelchair through the busy tourist-filled streets, he was
hot and perspiring.

Home for Mr Zika was on the fourth floor of a tall,
thin building that backed on to a maze of shadowy little
streets and tiny shops. From the front it looked out across
to the old fortress and the turquoise sea beyond.
Originally built for the old aristocracy of the town, the
Venetian-style house, with its elegant proportions,
wrought-iron balconies and shuttered windows must
have been a beautiful and impressive home in its glory
days; now it was just another example of faded grandeur.
Its yellow paintwork was dirty and peeling, its stonework
crumbling like blocks of salt. Split into goodness knows
how many apartments, it still had only one lift and they
had to wait patiently for it to descend to their level. It
was of the ancient metal-cage variety and clanked and
juddered slowly and disconcertingly, up to the fourth
floor. Taking Mr Zika's key Theo let them in. The first
thing that struck Mark as they entered the apartment was
the cool temperature. After the searing heat in the street,

it came as a welcome relief. He had read once that all old people's houses feel cold; it was the seeping away of the owner's lifeblood that made them like that. It was not the cheeriest theory.

Theo led the way, manoeuvring the wheelchair down a dim passage that was only just wide enough for it. They came to a high-ceilinged drawing room that smelt strongly of age and polish – years and years of polish that must have been assiduously applied to the delicate pieces of furniture that took up most of the available space in the large rectangular room. Burnished to a high gloss, tables, writing-desks, glass-fronted cabinets all vied for their own bit of space. Oriental rugs, some overlapping in places, covered the floor, marble-based lamps illuminated gloomy corners, and soft light bounced off glowing bronze statues and porcelain vases. A tapestry drooped on one of the walls, its colours muted, its silk surround ripped and sagging. It partially disguised a worrying crack in the plaster that had carved itself a forty-five-degree groove right up to the ornate cornice of the ceiling where a dusty chandelier hung. Faded drapes framed the tall, narrow windows and sunlight fought to penetrate the barrier of discoloured netting that looked as though it might turn to dust at a touch. The steady ticking of an ormolu clock on the mantelpiece added to the clutter of a room that made Mark feel uncomfortably on edge. But, then, turning to his right, he saw something that made him feel instantly at home.

Covering an entire wall, from floor to ceiling, were rows of leatherbound books. There were as many English titles as there were Greek ones and his hands twitched to reach out and touch them. 'You're a man after my own heart, Mr Zika,' he said, indicating the tightly packed shelves.

'Please, call me Thomas,' the old man said, as Theo helped him into a wing-backed armchair, where beside him was a small table with a chessboard on it; it looked as if a game was in progress. 'I think you have earned that right, after all the assistance you have given me. And go ahead, acquaint yourself with a few of my oldest friends.' He sank back into the seat and sighed deeply, a long, painful wheeze. He looked tired, as though he were only hanging on to life by a gossamer thread of strained will. 'If you would care to wait, Eleni, my housekeeper, will be here shortly and we could ask her to make us some coffee. But perhaps you are eager to be on your way.'

Stooping to tuck a blanket around the old man's legs, Theo murmured something that Mark didn't catch, but the gist of which became apparent when Theo went to make the coffee himself. While he was out of the room, Mark helped himself to a book from one of the shelves. The dusty smell of the mould-spotted leather reminded him of a thousand old bookshops in which he had browsed. He sat next to Thomas, showed him what he had picked out and fingered the pages with the greatest of care. After a while he sensed that tiredness was making Thomas vague and distracted. The lucid man with whom he had chatted in the restaurant was gone. Now he was murmuring indistinctly to himself, his eyelids drooping, his hands lying inert on his lap. It wasn't long before faint snoring added to the rhythmic ticking of the clock on the mantelpiece. Quietly replacing the book on the shelf, Mark went in search of Theo. 'I don't think Thomas will be wanting any coffee,' he said. 'He's asleep.'

The kitchen was small and dingy, with a free-standing cupboard against one wall and a fridge that vibrated noisily against the leg of a cumbersome old gas cooker. A pale blue Formica-topped table with chrome legs held an assortment of papers, unopened envelopes and a tin of pens and pencils. Above this was a thin shelf, on which a set of old pans was stacked. The poky room made a sharp contrast with the cluttered but opulent drawing room.

'I will make him some anyway,' Theo said, turning off the tap and looking for a cloth to dry the cups he had just washed. 'He never sleeps for long.'

'How old is he?'

'At the last count he was ninety-five. He does well for his age, eh?'

'Extraordinarily well. I can't imagine either of us still being around at that age. I'm not sure I'd want to go on for that long. What would be the point?'

'Ah, my friend, I would relish the thought that one day you would be as wise and as content as dear old Thomas, a man who needs only to play himself at chess and read his beloved books to be happy.'

'To hell with that, you'd just enjoy seeing me helpless.'

Theo narrowed his eyes and passed him a delicate bone-china cup of coffee, the gold line of its rim almost rubbed away. 'It was very kind what you did for Thomas over lunch,' he said. 'It isn't everyone who would have done that, and with such courteous compassion.'

'I suspect it was harder for Thomas to ask for my help than for me to give it.'

'But that is always the case. You of all people know that to be true.'

When they returned to Áyios Nikólaos, they found the party invitation that had been left for them on the terrace.

'And what excuse do you expect me to give my friends this time?' asked Theo, coming out from the house where he had changed to go for a swim. 'That you have a headache?'

Mark followed him to the pool. 'Why do you say that?'

'Because I know you so well. You would rather stay

here and bury yourself in the violent make-believe land of your imagination than show your face at a fancy-dress party and risk enjoying yourself in the real world.'

Watching Theo dive into the water and swim a length before coming up for air, Mark thought of Thomas Zika and how they had left him to the company of his books and the ticking of his clock, which cruelly echoed the long-drawn-out loneliness of what remained of his life. He said, 'Well, just to prove how wrong you are, Theodore Know-It-All Vlamakis, I will go.'

Theo turned over on to his back and laughed. 'Now this I have to see. Mark St James dressed up as a Greek god. Ha, ha, ha!'

His laughter continued long after Mark had left him to gloat over such an improbable notion.

Chapter Thirty-One

As it turned out Theo was denied a laugh at Mark's expense. On the morning of the party he received a phone call that had him changing his plans for the following week. Leaving his study, he went to look for Mark. He found him working on the terrace in the shade, his head bent over an A4 pad of paper, his hand moving steadily across the page. Reluctant to interrupt, Theo stood for a moment, marvelling at the creative process in which his friend was so absorbed. It was something he could never do. His brain was too restless to apply itself to just one task. He didn't have the single-minded determination, or the patience, to sit still long enough to be a writer. He bored easily and needed a variety of challenges if his attention was to be held.

Which was why he had spent most of life diversifying in the way that he had. When asked what he did for a living he usually said he did nothing more than dabble in property. But there were plenty of other things he got up to. He could never go anywhere without noticing a potential investment. It didn't matter how big or small it was, or how improbable; if he thought he could do something with it, he would immediately make enquiries and put forward an appropriate offer. Whether it was a run-down petrol station, a struggling taverna, or a large chain of shops that had lost its direction, he would bring in his own hand-picked management team and turn the business round. Once it was up and running, he would be looking for the next project to occupy him. And if he acted quickly, his next project was within his grasp.

Back in Athens a whisper of a rumour had started. It was in connection with the chain of hotels owned by the Karabourniotis family and, according to the word that had reached his office, the family was looking for an investor to help ease their growing financial difficulties. But Theo wasn't interested in putting money into anything that he didn't own outright, not when he knew he would have to stand back and watch his investment thrown away on yet more bad decisions and rising debts. If his fingers were going to delve into this particular pie, it would only be through a straight buy-out.

Not for a split second had it entered his head to leave it to his legal boys and accountants to meet with the Karabourniotis family, not when he believed in the personal approach. Besides, he knew them well, and knew just how proud old man Yiannis Karabourniotis was. Seeking help from outside his family was the last thing he would have wanted; it would have been his last desperate resort. Theo suspected that his greedy sons had driven him to this point, that they had been frittering away the profits on themselves rather than reinvesting in the hotels by modernising and expanding. This was another reason why Theo wanted to deal directly with Yiannis. Yiannis would never publicly criticise his sons, so the whole business would need careful handling and Theo trusted only himself to do that.

'How much longer are you going to stand there distracting me?' asked Mark, jolting him out of his thoughts.

'You will be relieved to know that I need to be in Athens again. I leave after lunch.'

Mark put down his pen and leaned back in his chair. 'How long will you be away this time?'

'I'm touched. You are missing me already?'

'Like a dog deprived of his fleas.'

'An unpleasant analogy, but in answer to your question, I don't know. A week seems probable.' He explained why he was going.

'So why the interest?' asked Mark. 'What's so special about these hotels that you feel you have to make another of your boardroom raids on them?'

'When I have so much already? Is that what you're getting at?'

'Yes. Exactly that.'

'Aha, the same old Mark. What a delight it is to know that despite your own success you still despise mine. It is quite simple. I want the hotels because they are there. They are available. If not me putting money on the table, it will be somebody else making a ruthless hostile bid. And, forgive my arrogance, but I believe I will offer Yiannis Karabourniotis the best deal.'

'What will you do with them?'

'Make them highly successful, of course.'

'But what makes you think you can succeed where he has failed?'

'I will not have two greedy sons milking my company. And if you have finished prosecuting me, I must go and pack. Then I shall wander next door and see Izzy.'

He had little to pack: running two households meant that he had everything he needed in both places. Each of his wardrobes was a mirror image of the other: suits, shirts, ties and shoes, as well as a selection of more casual clothes were duplicated. It was an extravagance – a bloody crime, as Mark frequently told him – but one he could easily justify. Packing consisted of a simple reorganisation of his briefcase for the week ahead. He then phoned his housekeeper in Athens to warn her that he would be arriving later that afternoon. Katina had worked for him for many years and knew his habits well. She lived close by so his unpredictable comings and goings were of little inconvenience to her. She assured him that she would have everything ready for his arrival. When he had put down the phone he changed into a suit and went next door.

It had been a curious week since he had told Izzy what he felt for her. Even more curious was that, during his busy week of travelling between Athens and Corfu, his feelings for her had not changed. She was never far from his thoughts. While she had been held captive at Villa Petros resting her ankle, the chance to see her alone had been non-existent. To his annoyance and frustration, there always seemed to be somebody about. He had thought of calling her from Athens on several occasions, but had known that there would have been people all around her making it impossible for them to have the kind of conversation he desired. The Fates, it seemed, were conspiring against them.

Or were they?

Surely if he really wanted to get her alone he would have made it happen. Wasn't that what he excelled at? Didn't he always make things happen according to his wishes? So why, then, had he not scooped up the lovely Izzy in his arms, carried her away and made love to her as he wanted to?

Was he frightened of doing that? Because in taking that step he might destroy what he had so carefully built up? She was so wary of him that he knew he still had a long way to go in gaining her confidence and her trust. If he moved in too fast he might jeopardise everything.

But there was another possibility to explain why he was treating her with such patience. It was a theory with which Mark had confronted him over supper one evening. 'You fancy yourself in the role of a disillusioned, soul-searching, worldly man wanting to be redeemed by the love of a sweet young girl. You see her as Jane Eyre to your Rochester, Rebecca to your Maxim de Winter, Fanny Price to—'

'Yes, Mark, I have grasped the subtlety of your words, you are not the only one to have trawled the pages of these fine books. But I'm afraid I think you are spending too much time in the world of fiction. You are so used to making things up, you don't know what is real and not real.'

'Oh, come on, own up to it. You're intrigued by the idea of harnessing a love as refreshing as the one you think Izzy can offer you. But what then? What will you do when you have succeeded in capturing her heart?'

'At the rate I'm going, I doubt that will ever happen.'

'Of course it will. You never fail at anything you're determined to have.'

'In business that might be true, but this is different. Izzy is not a commodity to be negotiated for.'

'I'm relieved to hear it.'

And this was what had started to worry Theo. With his sledgehammer comments, had Mark come close to what was really going on between him and Izzy? Had the division between his professional and his personal life become blurred? Did he view her as one of those must-have businesses? Was there a chance that his feelings for her were based purely on the desire always to have his own way? Was it the thrill of the chase that excited him? And if so, as Mark had said, 'What then?' Having won her heart, was there a danger that he would grow bored with it and search for another?

And wasn't that what he had always done?

But he didn't want to believe this. He wanted to believe that, at long last, the impossible had happened: Theodore Vlamakis had finally met the woman for whom he would forsake all others.

He was so deep in thought, his head bowed in concentration, that he let out a startled cry of surprise when he came face to face with the very woman he had been thinking about. 'Izzy,' he said when he had recovered himself, 'I was just on my way to see you.' Looking down at her ankle, he added, 'Should you be putting so much strain on it?'

She smiled. 'I'm testing it, but the others don't know, so please don't tell them. They'll be very cross with me.'

'And I, too, shall be very cross with you if you come to any more harm. Where are you going?'

'Down to the beach. I'm tired of just staring at it.' She indicated the bag on her shoulder. 'I wanted to find some driftwood to sketch. I feel like an escaped prisoner on the run.'

'May I join you?'

She looked at his clothes doubtfully. 'Won't you spoil your suit?'

'I promise I will be very careful with it.'

'You make a lot of promises, don't you?'

'But, I promise you, I keep them all.' He flashed her one of his best star-bright smiles. 'Now, I won't take any arguments, you must give me your hand.'

Why, thought Izzy as she slipped her hand through his, does he make everything sound so provocative? And why does he still scare me so much?

Laura had said it was because he made her reconsider everything she thought she knew about herself. 'He makes you wonder what it would be like to live a little dangerously. Instead of watching everyone else having a good time from behind the glow-white net curtains of your so-called respectable upbringing, Theo challenges you to dance naked in the street while kicking over the milk bottles and rattling the neighbours' dustbin lids.'

Maybe Laura was right.

When they were down on the beach, sitting on the stones, Theo, having removed his jacket and checked that his trousers wouldn't come to any harm, said, 'Do you realise this is my first opportunity to be with you on your own since you hurt your ankle? I might be forgiven for thinking that you have been hiding from me.'

Ignoring the implication of his words, she dug around in her bag for her sketchpad. Keeping her head down, she said, 'Up on the path you mentioned that you were coming to see me. Why?'

He selected a perfectly white stone the size of an egg from between his polished shoes and wrapped his fingers around it. 'I have to return to Athens again and I wanted to see you before I went. I am leaving in half an hour.'

'Will you be away for long?'

'A week. Perhaps longer. It depends how quickly I can get what I want.'

He threw the stone into the water and turned his head to fix his dark eyes on hers. There was a determination in his gaze that made her realise that no matter how hard she tried to have a normal conversation with him, he always had his own agenda. *It depends how quickly I can get what I want.* He never missed a trick, did he? 'You'll miss Max and Laura's party tonight,' she said, hunting through her bag again, this time for a pencil.

'I will miss more than that. I will miss you.'

'No, you won't,' she said brightly, 'you'll be far too busy.'

A hand came to rest on hers through the canvas of the bag. She glanced up to see a look of annoyance on his face. 'Please,' he said, 'do not take that oh-so-English mother-knows-best tone with me. If I say I will miss you, Izzy, I mean exactly that.'

He's just like a little boy, she thought. The moment he thinks he isn't being taken seriously, or there's a danger he can't get his own way, he takes offence. While she was pondering on this, he said, 'I have something for you.'

From the inside pocket of his jacket, he pulled out a mobile phone.

She looked at it, puzzled.

'It is so that I can speak to you in private while I am away. Switch it on late at night when you are no longer chaperoned and I will call you while you are in bed.' And as though to show her that his cross-little-boy act had gone, he grinned and said, 'Every night I will tell you a bedtime story.'

She laughed nervously. 'With a happy ending, I hope.'

'Well, Izzy, I would say that depends on you, doesn't it?' He leaned in and very gently kissed her. It was a small, brief kiss. Nothing to get too worked up over. But a tiny knot of panic tightened in her stomach. 'The ball,' he murmured, while stroking a finger the length of her jaw, 'as you English say, is in your court.'

Chapter Thirty-Two

Once Theo had left for the airport, Mark concentrated on the chapter he had started that morning. He was keen to finish it, and in view of the prolonged roll he was on, it seemed a shrewd move on his part to capitalise on his current good fortune.

It had been like this ever since he had overcome the problem of creating a credible will-they-won't-they love-interest scenario between his protagonist and the killer's next victim. He was feeling so confident about the way the book had developed a life of its own that he was beginning to think it was his best yet. And it was all down to one person. It was a shame, though, that he would never be able to give her the credit for inspiring him. That was out of the question. His actions might easily be misconstrued and he didn't want to cause any ructions. Least of all between himself and Theo.

As unexpected as it was, the source of his inspiration was none other than Izzy. Without her knowing it she had freed his imagination and enabled him to create a far more realistic sub-plot than he had hitherto put together.

Bones would have a field day with what he had done. 'You're nothing but a grave robber,' he could hear the man saying, 'stripping people of their lives for your own gratification.' And, yes, he supposed he was a bit of a Dr Frankenstein when it came down to it. He never thought twice about hoovering up snippets of other people's lives; it was simply part and parcel of being a writer. But in this instance, he had gone one step further. He had helped himself to a whole person; he had dropped Izzy into his novel. He didn't kid himself that she would be flattered by what he had done, not if she knew she had become his protagonist's lover, and certainly not if she knew she was next in line to get the chop at the hands of a psychotic killer. It was hardly the most honourable thing to do, or the best way to ingratiate himself with a fellow human being.

The idea had come to him the evening he had failed in his duty to get Izzy safely home – a point Theo had been at pains to labour when he had returned to Villa Anna. 'Did I ask you to chase her up the path and make her nearly break her neck? No! I asked you to make sure that she reached home in one piece.' He had been unable to sleep that night and as he lay tossing and turning, listening to the waves gently lapping against the rocks down in the bay, the solution had suddenly come to him. Switching on the bedside lamp, he had reached for his notebook and pen and feverishly scribbled the tumble of thoughts rushing to get out of his head. By the following morning he had the next three chapters planned and was eager to make a start.

Previously he had tended to echo the seriousness of the book's theme in his protagonist's sexual relationships, which meant that the bedroom scenes, in his view, lacked spontaneity. Graphic and raw, there was no tenderness, no love, not even a sense of euphoria when his protagonist finally got his leg over. It was sex to order. Sex in the name of duty. Just doing my job, ma'am.

But now he saw a way to change all that. Why not create a contrast of emotions within the book? Like the chiaroscuro effect of light and dark in a painting, could he not employ the same technique in his writing? And wouldn't the juxtaposition of some light-hearted sexual interaction make the evil undercurrents of the story appear even more threatening? It would surely add another dimension. The reader would be lulled into a false sense of security, making the outcome all the more shocking. Instinctively he had known it was the right course to follow and had got to work with renewed vigour.

As absurd as it was, it had been nothing more than the act of staggering up the hillside with Izzy in his arms and their shared laughter that had triggered off this new change of direction. But as simple and seemingly insignificant as this moment might have appeared to anybody else, for him it had allowed the chapters that had earlier floored him to flow effortlessly from his pen. When Theo had commented on the noticeable increase in his output and asked where the inspiration had come from, Mark had kept quiet, feeling slightly ashamed that he was using Izzy in such a dubious manner. He was acutely aware that it was wholesale exploitation and he didn't want Theo to know the depths to which he had sunk. Especially as during the last week or so Theo had shown all the signs of becoming possessively protective of Izzy. He didn't like to think of the outrage Theo would feel if he knew that the woman with whom he fancied himself in love was being vicariously exploited by his oldest friend.

But, this reservation aside, he was delighted with the way his work was going and wondered what his editor would make of it.

He also wondered what Bones would make of it. 'What's this, Mark? *You* writing about love and passion? Whatever next?'

No psychoanalyst worth his Freud and Gestalt can resist the temptation to dissect a client's sex life, and Bones had been no exception.

'Women,' he had said, opening a drawer and rustling a bag of jelly-babies at the start of one of their sessions, 'friend or foe?'

'That's a ludicrous statement,' Mark had countered. 'It can never be as simplistic as that.'

'Okay, let me come in from another angle. How many people have you ever really connected with, apart from Theo?'

'Why do you assume I have with Theo?'

'Are you afraid to admit that you have? Afraid to show that you're capable of caring for another person?'

He didn't answer Bones. Just stared him out. Then, to annoy him, Bones started whistling another of his tunes – 'Try A Little Tenderness'.

'Shut the hell up, will you?'

The whistling stopped and Bones popped a jelly-baby into his mouth. He chewed slowly, the sweet smell of artificial strawberry juice coming at Mark across the desk. 'And your answer?'

'As, no doubt, you've already concluded, apart from Theo I've never been really close to anyone.'

'Good.'

'It's good that I've never connected with anyone?'

'No, good that I extracted that confession from you without the use of thumbscrews.' He reached for another sweet. 'Now, then, back to you and women. How do you view them?'

'Have you ever thought that perhaps you have a serious sugar habit?'

'Deflecting the question and sending it off course by lobbing a personal criticism is neither original nor constructive, Mark. Does the idea of somebody ransacking your sexual history disturb you?'

'No.'

'Then try giving me an answer.'

'I don't think I can.'

'Perhaps you should allow me to do some of your thinking for you.'

'I thought therapists weren't supposed to do that. I thought—'

'Another attempt to deflect me? Really, Mark, why do you insist on doing this?'

'Because it's marginally more interesting than anything else going on here.'

'You're bored?'

'Out of my mind.'

'Talking of which, let's get back to it. Would you say that you were a success in bed? A sexual dynamo?'

'I've had my moments.'

'Mm ... As intrigued as I am by your so-called moments, let's think about the earth-moving pleasures you've given the women in your life. Were you good at that? A thrilling success?'

'Depends how one measures success.'

'And still you insist on shilly-shallying around with me. Which, you should have learned by now, only forces me to be more direct. Were you able to make your lovers climax?'

Watching Bones bite the head off a green jelly-baby, he said, 'Is any man really sure he's hitting the right buttons?'

The rest of the jelly-baby went the way of its head. 'I assure you, when the right buttons are pressed, you know all about it.'

This was the first time Mark had viewed Bones as a man who had a life outside the clinic. Was it possible that this little man with his insatiable sweet tooth was a super-stud in bed?

'Something amusing you?'

'Yes. You sounded as if you were boasting there for a minute.'

'Interesting that you should view it that way. But putting the question of my sexual prowess to one side,

309

shall we take a moment to hold yours up to the light and see how transparent it is?'

It didn't take Bones long to establish the obvious, that Mark's experience with women was pretty shallow. That he had interpreted emotional dependency as weakness. That he had been unable to commit himself. And that nothing lasted because nothing meant anything to him.

As Kim would have been the first to confirm.

Poor Kim. She really hadn't known what she was getting into when she had married him. It had been a disaster from the outset. Marrying solely to provide the necessary wings to fly in the face of his parents' disapproval was never going to be a solid foundation for a lasting relationship. Kim must have known what he had done, but perhaps, and if only to appease his conscience, he had always hoped that she had had her own game plan when she had agreed to go through with the marriage. After all, on paper he looked like he was worth the effort. As the youngest son and potential heir to a thriving family business, he must have seemed a good investment to a girl who had spent most of her childhood being shuffled from one foster family to another, and her young adult years camped out at Greenham Common, before going north to support the miners in her continued search for a sense of belonging.

It was during the miners' strike, and in a leaking, bone-shaking Bedford van on his way to help Arthur Scargill beat Ian MacGregor and *la* Thatcher, that Mark had met Kim. He had come upon her as she was trying to hitch a lift. Her hair was braided into rainbow-coloured dread-locks and she was dressed in dungarees several sizes too large for her with a donkey jacket turned up at the collar to keep out the rain. She was grateful to climb in alongside him to escape the downpour when he stopped to offer a lift, but street-wise enough to let him know she was no fool. 'Don't think you can try anything on with me,' she had warned him. 'I've got a knife and I'm not afraid to use it.'

'And good morning to you, fair maiden,' he had said.

'Oh, fancy yourself as a clever dick, do you?' she had responded. 'Well, like I say, make a move on me and I'll cut it off for you.'

Their whirlwind romance, as he had sarcastically described it for Bones's benefit, consisted of several months of communal living until the miners' strike came to an end. Then he wrote to his parents to inform them that he was getting married. 'The least you could do for me is be there at the register office,' he had written.

'That was really telling them, wasn't it, Mark?' Bones had said, when he recounted the scene of his marriage vows being witnessed by his stony-faced parents and brothers. Kim had dressed for the occasion by getting her nose pierced and wearing one of those multi-coloured, hand-knitted Peruvian hats with ear-flaps, while he had excelled himself with a pair of dirty combat trousers and a T-shirt with a picture of Lenin on the front. 'You badly wanted to rub their noses in the mire of your unhappiness, didn't you?' Bones remarked. 'What better way than to say, "Look, this is what you've driven me to do."?'

His parents gave him some money to put down on a small flat. Guilt-money, every penny of it, he had convinced himself, as he and Kim set up home and played at Mr and Mrs Domestic Harmony. But within a short while he had lost his job, his wife and the flat. Gone, too, was every scrap of his political ideology. There seemed no point in it. What difference did it make anyway? The void he was left with he filled with booze. When things got out of hand he tried a stint of going on the wagon, but it didn't help. He got the shakes and depression kicked in. And to beat the depression he upped the amount of cocaine he was taking to give him the lift he needed. But all that happened was that the drug used up what little energy he had so when the comedown hit him he felt worse than ever. His depression deepened, he became jittery and paranoid, and as panicky as hell. And though he was exhausted, he couldn't sleep, not with his brain racing at full tilt. He knew he needed help, but he was powerless to seek it. It was easiest just to keep on drinking.

'And where was Theo when all this was going on?' Bones had asked him. 'Wasn't he summoned to your wedding like your family?'

'No.'

'Why not?'

'I didn't want him there.'

'Didn't want him to see how fast you were sliding out of control?'

'Something like that.'

'And what was his reaction when you finally got round to bringing him up to date?'

'He asked me if I was happy.'

'And were you?'

'I told him I was.'

'That wasn't what I asked.'

'Well, of course I wasn't happy. I was having a blast of a time shoving corpses into cheap plywood coffins by day and avoiding my wife by night. A real recipe for joy.'

'I'll come back to your wife in a minute, but for now, tell me why you took a job surrounding yourself with the dead. Was that a satisfying career move, or a brilliant piece of macabre irony on your part? Or was it a mental reminder like one of those we stick on the fridge with a cute magnet – "Must remember to pay the television licence." Except in this case it was "Must remember what a dead body looks like, lest I forget the horror of Niall's death"?'

'I needed a job—'

'With a first-class honours degree in criminal psychology you could have got something more appropriate than working in a small-town undertaker's.'

'It seemed appropriate at the time.'

'Yes, I think you probably did see it as appropriate, particularly the element of macabre irony. A society dying on its feet, and you there to help bury it. Was that the big joke?'

'If you say so.'

'And who did you share this joke with? Kim?'

'No.'

'Theo?'

'No. No one.'

'So, it was a side-splitting laugh a minute with yourself? Except it wasn't funny, was it? It was, and please excuse the pun, a deadly serious affair. There was to be no escape from the spectre of your childhood. Rubbing shoulders with all those rotting corpses was your reward for failing Niall, wasn't it? Couldn't you have come up with something more subtle?'

'It was the best I could do in the circumstances.'

'Well, now, the sharpness in your voice tells me that you've had enough. But to finish with, let me leave you with this thought. You've never held down a job for more than seven months and your track record for staying in a lasting relationship is laughable. Is this a coincidence? Laziness? Or a fear of failure?'

It went without saying that every word uttered by Bones scored a bull's-eye. Since Kim had left him, when she couldn't put up with his drinking any longer, he had lost all interest in forming any kind of relationship, let alone a lasting one. He also felt disgusted with himself that he had treated Kim so badly, and the scant remains of any decency he still had held him back from doing the same to anyone else. As for work, he didn't want to do anything that might stretch him or give him a sense of achievement. By not accepting the challenge in the first place he could be sure not to fail. But it went a little deeper, as Bones took the trouble to point out to him.

'This is standard-issue stuff from the school of survival, Mark. Ever since Niall's death you allowed yourself nothing of any real worth, only the dregs of the barrel that nobody else was interested in having. It meant that if they were taken away, as Niall was, you wouldn't get hurt.'

It was a harsh summing-up of his brief marriage, but sadly it was true. If he hadn't been so self-absorbed he would have realised that Kim was chock full of her own emotional problems from her childhood, and that she needed his help, not his drunken black moods.

Looking back on those days – days and nights when she had stayed away from the flat because she had been terrified of what he might do next – it all felt like a terrible dream sequence. None of it seemed real. The shame of it was, he had never had the opportunity to say how sorry he was. Not long after their divorce he had read of her death in the local paper. She had got her life together far better than he had at that time, and was working in a supermarket, stacking shelves. She had finished her shift late one night, stepped out into the road to catch her bus home and was knocked down by a stolen car being driven by a fourteen-year-old boy. Death had been instantaneous. One minute she had probably been looking forward to her supper of beans on toast – one of her favourite meals, especially if the beans had those funny little sausages with them – and the next she was lying face down in the gutter, surrounded by a group of strangers checking her for any vital signs. Her untimely death should have given him food for thought, forced him to take stock. But no. What grief he had felt for her he obliterated by going on a three-day bender. As always, his response to anything that might touch him was to get drunk.

He let out his breath and leaned back in his chair. Yes. It was done. He had finished the chapter. Objective achieved.

He replaced the cap on his fountain pen – a gift from Theo when he had started work on his first novel – and stretched his arms up over his head. He could feel a day's worth of tension in his shoulders and neck, the muscles taut after sitting still for so many hours.

To help him unwind, he decided to go for a walk to the shop to buy another film for his camera. As he strolled along the hot, dusty road, he tried to decide what to do about the Sinclair party that evening.

Theo's parting shot when he had left for the airport had been, 'Fifty of your strong English pounds says that you are such a miserable killjoy you won't go to Max and Laura's tonight.'

It was tempting to let Theo have the last word and be done with it. A quiet evening alone would not be such a bad thing. He was used to his own company. But from nowhere a picture of Thomas Zika playing chess with himself to get through the long, lonely hours came into his mind.

It was as though he was being shown a glimpse of what the future held for him.

It was a future he didn't much care for.

Chapter Thirty-Three

While she was fetching a drink for Virginia Patterson and taking time out from her annoyingly overbearing manner, the roar of conversation and laughter told Laura that the party was a success. Not only had everybody made the effort to dress up, but they all seemed to be enjoying themselves. They made a curious gathering, and she didn't mind admitting that initially she had had misgivings about one or two of their guests getting on with each other. But it seemed that there was nothing like a change of identity, albeit a superficial one, to help lower the social mask one normally hid behind. And, looking at everyone on the terrace, who had come similarly wrapped in a white cotton sheet, she pictured the stripped beds they must have left behind in their villas.

Dressed as Hercules, Max was one of the few who wasn't wearing a sheet. He had plumped for shorts and a Lion King beach towel he had bought in Kassiópi. He had made a tail out of plaited string and sewn it to the bottom edge of the towel, which hung off him like a cloak; anyone who came near him, received a swish of his tail and a flash of his biceps.

Corky was dressed as Zeus, and to complete his sartorial sheeted elegance he had hung a lightbulb round his neck, stuck a three-foot-long cotton wool beard to his chin and fixed a lightning bolt made of cardboard to his chest. Olivia was stylishly decked out as Hera, Zeus's wife, and she had made herself a sceptre out of a garden cane borrowed from Angelos, which she had wrapped in cooking foil and used to keep Corky in line by poking him with it whenever the mood took her.

The girls had predictably gone for the not-wearing-very-much look. Francesca, dressed as Hebe, the goddess of youth, was barefoot, having laced her feet and lower legs with rose pink ribbons. The sheet she wore, or what there was of it – and Laura was sure that some of her precious bed linen had been sacrificed in the name of adornment – stopped a few inches below her bottom and was held in place by more of the rose pink ribbon to give her a perfect Playtex Cross-Your-Heart-bra outline. She was wearing her hair loose and her lips were heavily painted with red lipstick. Max had swished her with his tail and called her a pouting Botticelli tart.

Like Izzy, Sally had kept her costume a secret right up until the moment she made her entrance into the kitchen earlier that evening, before their guests had arrived. The look on Max's face when he saw her summed up their collective fear.

'Is that a muslin drape from your bedroom window that you're nearly wearing?' Laura had asked, wishing she had the body to do the same but fearing for every man's blood pressure.

'It is,' said Sally, performing a little twirl for them. 'Can you guess who I am?' She held up a makeshift bow and arrow, which action parted the folds in the diaphanous layers of muslin and exposed her breasts. When nobody answered – they were all too stunned – she said, 'I'm Artemis, the huntress.'

Francesca had laughed loudly. 'But she was a virgin.'

Sally grinned. 'Yeah, well, a little artistic licence goes a long way.'

'I'll say. Does it extend to wearing any knickers?'

'I'm wearing a flesh-coloured thong. Look, can't you see?'

It was an offer that had Max and his father averting their eyes and suggesting it was time for a drink.

Izzy appeared, then, dressed in what the girls called her Lara Croft khaki shorts and vest top. She was carrying a spear made from a garden cane and an impressive shield, made of cardboard and beautifully painted in shades of silver to match the spear. Though her ankle had more or less healed, this evening it was bandaged again and a toy arrow stuck out from her heel where a few drops of red paint had been dabbed on. 'Achilles,' she said, 'in case you were wondering.'

'My goodness, haven't we all been inventive?' said Olivia, 'How do you think our guests will fare? Will they pass muster?'

The guests, as Laura looked at them all now, had been equally creative, and the only repeat character was that of Hebe. While Francesca was more than qualified to play the part of the goddess of youth, Dolly-Babe was pushing the boundaries of belief a smidgen too far.

The Fitzgeralds had been the first to arrive and, just as Francesca and Sally had predicted, Bob's only concession to the theme of the party was a balloon at the end of a short length of string pinned to the shoulder of his shirt. It made him look as though he had two heads. It also made him conspicuously awkward, as it bobbed beside his right ear as though agreeing with his every word as he talked to Corky about problems with his business ventures on the island. He sounded more than a little put out that he wasn't finding things as straightforward as he had expected. He was full of conspiracy theories: of cartels that were freezing out honest men like him, and of red tape that magically appeared from nowhere if the locals didn't like the look of you. 'I had a neat little number all lined up with some old peasant who didn't have a clue what he was sitting on, and just as I was

318

about to get a contract organised, he refused to sell. Said he'd had a better offer. Better offer, my arse!'

Laura hadn't caught the rest of the conversation because Dolly-Babe had turned to her and said, 'Gawd, I wish he'd shut up. If I've heard him go on about losing that piece of land once, I've heard it a million times.' Laura suspected from the smell of Dolly-Babe and the way she swayed as she leaned into her that she had already had a head start on the drinking before she arrived. 'So what do you think of my costume?'

'Oh, very nice,' Laura had said, casting her eyes over a sparkly Spandex figure-hugging dress that Tina Turner would have been proud of, and a head of hair that was piled higher than normal and threaded through with sequin-covered ribbons.

'You know, I spent ages trying to decide who to come as, but then I thought, Come on, gal, who else could you be but Hebe, the goddess of youth?'

'Snap,' Francesca had said, joining them from across the terrace. 'I'm her as well.'

Barefoot confidence meets barefaced cheek, Laura had thought, with a private smile.

'Well, Gawd bless us,' Dolly-Babe had cried. 'You know, it was a close-run thing, it was her, or that Afro . . . Afro . . .' She had clicked her fingers as if to summon up the name. It had worked. Well, almost. 'You know, that one into love, Afrodykey.'

The Pattersons had arrived next.

Courtesy of the girls, everyone at Villa Petros had been given an advance-warning thumbnail sketch of Mr and Mrs Patterson and Laura wasn't at all sure that it had been a good idea to invite them, but having seen so much of their sons she had crossed her fingers and hoped for the best.

Within seconds of hearing and seeing Virginia Patterson, Laura had been plucked from the present and

319

dumped in the past of her schooldays and, in particular, on to the frozen hockey-field where a formidable games mistress had bullied the spirit out of her. Dressed in a crumpled white sheet, her plump feet pushed into flat Ecco sandals, Nick and Harry's mother had come as Athena, the goddess of wisdom and strength, and now, as she took the glass of Pimm's that Laura had just fetched for her, it sounded worryingly as if she was going to play her character a little too exact. 'Of course, if I'd had more warning I would have made a better job of my costume,' she said airily.

Yes, thought Laura, you might have taken the trouble to iron the sheet. And just as the horrible woman was getting into her stride, her words dried up and her eyes narrowed. Following her gaze, Laura saw that she had caught sight of Sally, who, it had to be said, looked as if she would be more at home in a soft-porn movie than at a holiday drinks party. Behind her large-framed glasses, Virginia's beady gaze immediately turned to her husband who was making no attempt to hide the fact that he was feasting his eyes on the gossamer vision as she drifted into the arms of his younger son. The good feeling Laura had enjoyed only moments earlier evaporated, to be replaced with concern, as if the mix of people here tonight was going to prove explosive.

But that was nonsense, she told herself. What could possibly go wrong? She looked around the terrace as though seeking confirmation that all would be well, that everyone was still enjoying themselves. Seeing nothing to alarm her, she thought what a shame it was that Theo had had to rush back to Athens that afternoon. 'I suppose that means Mark won't come,' Sally had said, when Izzy told them the bad news, and she crossed his name off the guest list along with Theo's. Giorgios' name already had a line through it: he was working in Kassiópi tonight.

'You sound disappointed,' Francesca had laughed.

'It's all right for you, you've got Harry. Now I'm definitely lumbered with Nick.'

Excusing herself from the circle of guests, Laura went inside the villa to fetch a tray of *mezéthes* that Sophia had prepared. When she came back out she saw Virginia Patterson being approached by Dolly-Babe. Feeling the need to intervene, or at least supervise the conversation between these two unlikely bedfellows, she quickly joined them and offered the tray of food.

'I shouldn't really,' said Dolly-Babe, her long-nailed hand playing eeny-meeny-miny-mo. 'Mm . . . they all look so delish. What are these?'

'I'm not really sure, I didn't make them, but they might be spinach pies.'

'*Spanakópita.*'

Dolly-Babe's hand hesitated and she looked up at Virginia. 'Spanky-what?'

'*Spanakópita,*' repeated Virginia, with an irritating tone of lofty supremacy. 'That's the correct Greek name for them.'

Oh, Lord, thought Laura. Was there going to be no let-up from this woman's need to feel superior to them all? But ever the polite hostess, she said, 'Nick and Harry were telling me that you live in London. Whereabouts?'

'Dulwich. You're from the north, aren't you?' She made it sound as if Laura came from the wrong side of the tracks.

Oh, go on, thought Laura, don't hold back, ask about our pigeons and whippets. 'Our families are both from Worcestershire,' she said lightly, 'but Max and I have lived in Cheshire for many years now.'

'Now there's a coincidence. My Bob and me, we lived in Cheshire for a while. In Alderley Edge.'

'I've heard of that,' said Virginia. 'Wasn't there a lot of talk recently on the radio about it being a den of pagans?'

'That was well out of order, all that stuff and

nonsense. Bob and me took great offence to being called pagans. Why, I'm the most spiritual person you'd ever meet.'

'Really? How interesting.' Virginia's voice was spectacularly condescending as she scanned the terrace for a kindred Dulwich soul, but found only her husband leaning in too close to Izzy and taking a peek down her front. Clearly annoyed, Virginia thrust her Pimm's to her lips and spiked her nose on the cocktail stick loaded with slices of fruit. Laura had to look away to hide a smirk. She saw Olivia coming towards them.

'Laura,' she said eagerly, 'you'll never believe what Nick's just been telling us. Apparently Christine and Mikey are here. He says he saw them on the beach this afternoon.'

'Friends from England?' asked Dolly-Babe.

Olivia laughed. 'Goodness me, no! Christine and Mikey are the runaway lovers. You know, the ones in the newspapers. Haven't you been following their story? We have. Avidly. Isn't that right, Laura?'

Laura cringed with hypocritical embarrassment. It was all very well showing a keen interest in private towards some racy tabloid titillation, but to admit it in public, and in front of a woman like Virginia Patterson who probably never sullied her mind with anything less worthy than a broadsheet, was too much.

'What? You mean that disgusting woman and the teenage boy? They're here?' Dolly-Babe's voice was shrill with disapproval. 'Gawd, it makes me sick every time I read about them. She's old enough to be his mother.'

'Talking about the runaway lovers?' asked Francesca with Sally, Nick and Harry in tow.

'Nick, I think you have some explaining to do,' said his mother. 'What's all this about you claiming to have seen—'

'Relax, Mum, I saw them all right.'

'So why didn't you mention it?'

He shrugged. 'Didn't think you'd be interested.'

'But are you sure it was them?' Laura asked Nick.

'I'm pretty sure. The age gap is a giveaway.'

'So if they really are here, where do you suppose they're staying?' asked Olivia.

Angelos and Sophia gave them the answer. The couple were staying in the villa owned by the German business-man from Frankfurt.

'But that's next door to us!' cried Dolly-Babe and Virginia Patterson together.

From across the terrace, Izzy was only half listening to Adrian Patterson. She was much more interested in what Laura and the others were discussing. She had already tried to give him the slip by saying she needed to go in search of a drink, only for him to follow her.

She had had more than enough of him with his sleazy smile and innuendo-loaded talk of what he did for a living. She had always wondered what kind of person made those dreadful TV programmes. Well, now she knew. The awful thing was, he probably thought she was impressed by what he did. She felt him pressing against her side as he stepped in closer still. 'You'll have to excuse me,' she said, her patience snapping, 'I promised Laura I'd help in the kitchen.' She walked away as fast as her ankle would let her.

Only when she was sure she was going to be left alone – when she saw Adrian Patterson talking to Silent Bob – did she slip outside again. She went and leaned against the wall at the edge of the terrace, away from where everyone else was gathered. Though it was dark now, with insects buzzing around the flaming torches that Max and Corky had lit, the night air fell warm and a soft breeze blew in from the sea. She closed her eyes and took a deep breath of contentment.

'I'm sorry to see that your ankle has taken a turn for the worse,' said a low voice from behind her. It was so distinctive, it could belong to no one else. 'Hello, Mark, we didn't expect to see you tonight. What a lovely surprise.'

Still looking at her *faux*-bloodstained bandage and toy arrow, he said, 'Yeah, well, I've surprised myself. Achilles, I presume?'

'How very astute.' Then over his shoulder, Izzy suddenly caught sight of Adrian Patterson heading towards her. 'There's somebody I'm trying to avoid,' she said, slipping behind Mark so that she was out of sight. 'I don't suppose you'd do me a favour by sticking around for a few minutes, would you?'

'Always happy to oblige. Who are you hiding from?'

'I'll point him out later.' When the coast was clear, she said, 'Do you want a drink? There's loads to choose from; wine, Pimm's, beer – she stopped. 'Oh, I'm sorry, I forgot, you don't, do you?' She felt herself colour.

'Hey, cut yourself some slack. It's my problem, not yours.'

'But it must be so awful for you in these situations.'

'Judging from the look on your face, it's worse for those who think they've put their foot in it.'

'So what can I get you? Coke? Fruit juice? Water? You're smiling. What's wrong? Have I said something stupid again?'

'Private joke. Some fizzy water would be fine. And when you come back, you can give me a run-down on everybody here and warn me of anyone I need to give a wide berth. Or should I come with you to keep you safe from whoever it is who's been bothering you?'

Seeing that Corky was now chatting to Adrian Patterson, she said, 'No, stay here, it looks as if I'll be okay for a while.'

Mark watched her go, then turned to look across the

water towards the twinkling lights of Albania and congratulated himself on having made it. While it was nowhere near as bad, he was reminded of his first AA meeting. It had taken all his courage to walk through that door that night and take his seat among the group, and he had had to employ the same sort of determination to get himself here tonight.

And it wasn't just about proving Theo wrong – though a bet was a bet, and this was one that he had clearly won – it had been more about convincing himself that he could change his life if he so wished. Once he had made the decision to be sociable, he had realised that he was looking forward to seeing Izzy again. He hadn't seen her since he had been so absorbed in his writing, and although he had spent great chunks of time with her in his imagination, he had missed the real Izzy, especially their chats down on the beach. As he waited for her to come back with his drink, he found himself thinking that she was the first woman he had ever bothered to get to know.

Women . . . friend or foe? Bones had once asked.

Well, the answer in this case was unequivocal: he viewed Izzy as a friend.

Hearing footsteps behind him, he turned round expectantly, assuming it would be Izzy. But it wasn't. It was Dolly-Babe, dressed up as the Queen of Spandex, and she was heading straight for him. Oh, Lord, it was true, there really was no peace for the wicked. Not for him anyway.

Chapter Thirty-Four

There was nowhere for him to hide, so he braced himself for another assault on his patience, which, as Theo would be only too quick to mention, was an attribute he didn't have in abundance. She sidled in very close, a skinny freckled arm reaching out to him. For a brief moment he felt the full weight of her – such as it was – as she steadied herself against him and slopped wine down the front of his shirt.

'Aha, Mr St James. I have a confession to make.' Her face, unlike her pale arms, was flushed and glowing, and her extraordinary hair looked as though it was on the verge of a landslide.

'Really?' Oh, great!

'Yes. I had no idea who you were until a few days ago.' She wagged a finger at him.

Looking at her unfocused eyes, he wondered if she was seeing two of him.

'But, you know, you could have said something.'

He edged discreetly away from her. 'I stand corrected,' he said, 'fully rebuked.'

She laughed loudly, and moved towards him again. 'But I always suspected that there was something, well, a bit different about you.'

'In what way?'

'You're like me, you see what's going on.' She gave a comically theatrical swivel of her eyes. 'You feel it, don't you? That's why you're a writer. You channel your powers into your books.'

It was tempting to enquire in which direction she thought her powers were channelled, but he refrained from doing so. It was child's play to make fun of somebody like Dolly-Babe.

'Any more news from your psychic friend back home?' he asked pleasantly. 'Looks as though she got it right about the party, didn't she?'

Her face lit up, which made him feel all the more sorry for her: how easily pleased she was. 'Ria's a gem,' she said. 'I don't know what I'd do without her. But you know what? My horoscope said something interesting today – except it was for yesterday, seeing that we get the papers a day late. I'm a Gemini. What star sign are you?'

'Aquarius.'

'I knew it! I just knew you had to be Aquarius.'

'Any reason why?'

She beamed a wide, garishly pink smile at him. 'It's obvious, darlin'. Aquarians are original, independent and creative. As a writer, that must be you to a T. Now, listen to this and tell me what you think. My horoscope said I've got to get out of the rut I've made for myself. "Why wait for fate to take its course?" was what it said.' She drained her glass of wine in a long, thirsty swig. 'What do you think it means?'

That you need to cut back on your drinking, was the answer screaming inside his head, but Mark knew better than anyone that a comment like that would only have Dolly-Babe reaching for another drink of denial. And talking of drinks, where was Izzy with his water? He looked over Dolly-Babe's shoulder and saw, to his relief, Izzy coming towards them.

'Sorry I was so long,' she said, giving him his glass and smiling at Dolly-Babe, 'but I was intercepted. Everyone's talking about our new neighbours.'

'Oh, who are they?' asked Mark.

Dolly-Babe's eyes flashed with a fury that seemed quite

out of place. 'Don't ask, it's too awful for words. The thought of that poor boy and that shameless woman makes my blood boil. And don't go giving me that argument that it's every young boy's fantasy to be seduced by an older woman. It's not natural. She's taking advantage of him. He's nothing but a child.' She shuddered.

Sharing a look of surprise with Mark at the vehemence behind Dolly-Babe's words, Izzy said, 'Have you been following the story in the papers about the mother of two running off with her teenage lover?'

'On and off.'

'Well, they're here in Áyios Nikólaos.'

'And staying in the villa next door to us!' cut in Dolly-Babe. 'I've a good mind to ring the papers myself and tell them where that dreadful woman is. She needs shooting, she does.' She raised her glass to her lips, saw that it was empty, and added, in a voice that sounded alarmingly bitter, 'I need a refill.'

They watched her move with exaggerated care through the chairs, tables and guests on the terrace. 'You know, I can't help feeling sorry for her,' said Izzy.

'I was thinking much the same myself a few moments ago.'

'You were?'

'Don't sound so thunderstruck. Didn't you have me down as the understanding, sensitive type?'

She looked at him hard. 'Not quite. I imagined you would be more interested in casting her as a victim in one of your novels – the ageing woman strangled by her blonde hair attachments, her long nails ripped off, her high heels—'

'Then you've got me all wrong. I choose my victims with much more care and thought.'

'So why do you suppose she's taking the moral high ground on the runaway lovers? I would have expected her to take the stance of more power to middle-aged women like herself.'

'I doubt that she sees herself as middle-aged. Show me a man or woman who claims they don't give a damn about growing old and I'll show you a liar.'

'I hadn't thought of that.'

'That's because you're fortunate enough still to have youth and beauty on your side.'

She smiled. 'You know that she's come as Hebe, don't you?' Then, casting an eye over his jeans and denim shirt with the sleeves rolled up to his elbows, she said, 'You're going to have to help me out with your costume. It's so subtle I must be missing it.'

He stood back from her, so she could see him better. 'I'm in disguise. Go on, guess which god I am.'

'Any clues?'

'Go for irony.'

'Mr Grecian 2000?'

'Do you mind? The hair's pure Bobby Shaftoe, not a wisp of grey. Try again.'

'Mm . . . Hercules?'

'And why would that be ironic? Don't you see me as a heroic hunk of masculinity?'

'Well, if you don't want me to insult you further, you'd better tell me who you're supposed to be.'

'I'm disappointed in you. I thought I could rely on you of all people. I'm Dionysus, god of wine. Who else could I possibly come as?'

In the far reaches of his mind, he heard Bones saying, 'It's always the same with you, Mark, isn't it? Go ahead, just throw another log of irony on the fire of your wretchedness.' And seeing that she didn't know what to say, and that the joke had fallen flat on its face, he said, 'It's a funny old thing, but we're a nation that simply doesn't cut the mustard when it comes to laughing at the afflicted.'

'It does leave us rather stranded.'

'But laughing at oneself is sometimes the best medicine of all.'

'When you were an alcoholic, could you laugh at yourself?'

Disconcerted by her directness, he took a thoughtful sip of his mineral water. 'No. In those days I wasn't capable of finding anything remotely funny.'

A sudden burst of loud bouzoúki music coming from behind them made them turn towards the villa, where on the veranda a space had been cleared and Angelos and Sophia were teaching Max and Laura some fancy Greek dancing; Laura had the hang of it, but Max was all over the place.

'Just as well you decided to join us here tonight,' said Izzy, 'or the noise would have disturbed you horribly. What made you come?'

Again he was surprised by her candour. 'Because I was invited.'

'You've turned down other invitations from Max and Laura. Why did you accept this one, and without Theo to hold your hand?'

'Goodness, you certainly know how to make a guy feel welcome, don't you?'

She smiled. 'Sorry, it's my curious nature getting the better of me. None of us expected you to come on your own.'

'Well, tell you what, help me become invisible and I'll think about satisfying that appalling curiosity of yours.'

'Invisible?'

'Her glass suitably refilled, Dolly-Babe is heading in our direction and, as sympathetic as I am towards her problems, I'm not in the mood to waste an entire evening on her. Fancy a walk on the beach?'

They slipped away unnoticed, but when Mark realised that Izzy's ankle still wasn't strong enough to negotiate the steep path at any real speed, he said, 'Theo would kill me with his bare hands if you hurt yourself again in my company, so there's nothing else for it, I'll have to carry you.'

'There's no need, I can manage. Really, I can.'

Ignoring her, he swung her off her feet and resumed their descent. 'Hold on tight, and no laughing. I said no laughing, Izzy! Don't you ever do as you're told?'

'Oh, all the time, just not when I'm with you.'

'Dear God, you're enough to drive a man to drink!'

'That's not funny, Mark.'

'Then behave yourself and stop wriggling, or you'll have my downfall on your conscience.'

'Has anyone ever told you you're a cruel and heartless man?'

'No, they wouldn't dare.'

They carried on down the hill in silence, the lively music from the villa growing more distant with every step.

'Mark?'

'Yes.'

'I know it's none of my business, but what made you become an alcoholic?'

He tightened his grip on her. 'You make it sound like a career choice. And you're right, it is none of your business.'

Another silence passed between them.

'I'm sorry. Was that a question too far?'

'Yes. What's got into you? You're not normally this nosy.'

'It's reading your novels. They've set me thinking. Made me wonder about the real you.'

'Well, don't bother. I'll give you fair warning, no good will come of it. Now, what d'yer know? We've made it in one piece.' He lowered her to the stones, faced the water's edge, and stretched out his arms dramatically.

'For your special delectation, Miss Jordan, I give you a romantically deserted moonlit beach. And a broken man into the bargain.' He rubbed his back meaningfully.

'But just think, you've got the return journey to look forward to.'

He groaned. 'Nothing else for it, I'll have to send for reinforcements.'

'Now, what was that you were saying about Hercules?'

'Hey, nice try, little lady, but if you want that kind of man, you're banging on the wrong door. I don't do heroics. Definitely not my call.'

'That's not what Theo says.'

'Oh, yes? And what has the mentally challenged Mr Theodore Vlamakis been saying about me?'

'He said you saved his life.'

'Did he now?'

'And did you?'

He frowned and rolled up one of his sleeves, which had come unfurled with all the exertion. 'Theo loves to exaggerate these things. It's the Greek way. Come on, let's walk. That's if your ankle's okay?'

'It's fine. And in case you're worried, I can manage the path perfectly well on my own. I just have to take it slowly.'

He smiled. 'Now you tell me.'

When they had got as far as the rocky outcrop, she said, 'Theo told me you were very brave to do what you did.'

'My, but you're a persistent little soul, aren't you?'

'No, just plain old-fashioned nosy.'

'So if I spin you a yarn of what a wonderfully brave chap I am, will you promise to shut up?'

'Hand on heart.'

'Okay, then, sit yourself down and when you're comfortable, I'll begin.' He settled beside her on the rock where they had first met. The tide was high, and the barely moving water was lapping softly at the stones beneath them. 'Now, what do you want to know first? Why I wasted a huge chunk of my life on drink, or why it was so easy for me to take on two thugs who were kicking the hell out of somebody I scarcely knew?'

'Um . . . you decide. You're the story-teller.'

'Okay. Here we go. Once upon a time, there was a small boy called Mark. There was nothing remotely unusual about him, he was pretty much your bog standard normal kid. Not particularly bright. Not particularly stupid. His parents were kind and loving, and he had two brothers who never gave him a moment's trouble, apart from being a lot smarter than he was, but, hey, you can't have everything. One day everything changed. At the age of twelve, Mark's best friend died and because he blamed himself, he turned into a monster who took out his anger and confused self-loathing on anyone within spitting distance. Especially his bewildered parents. Time passed and, much against the odds, he worked hard enough at school to get himself to college where he met a flash Greek upstart who represented everything this angry young man despised. You could say it was hate at first sight. Then, one very cold wintry night, he came across the aforementioned flash Greek upstart lying on the ground having his face rearranged by two lads who were interested in a redistribution of the contents of his wallet. With nearly a decade of anger stored up in this one skinny frame – a physique that never did improve with age, I might say – violence held no fear for our boy. Not even from a knife-wielding thug who stabbed him for his trouble.' He paused. 'You will say if I'm boring you, won't you?'

She shook her head, transfixed. 'No, please, carry on.'

'Well, the two young men paradoxically became good friends. They left college: one went on to become the disgustingly successful businessman you now know and love, and the other went from bad to worse. Still haunted by the death of his young friend, he opened his mouth and poured into it a magic brew called Instant Gratification, not seeing the label underneath that said "Danger and Self-delusion This Way". It was potent stuff. So long as he was full of the magic brew his world didn't seem so bad. But the more he drank, the more he wanted. Then one day, he was offered some better magic. Cocaine. Oh, how he loved this stuff. And how it loved him. They couldn't get enough of each other. They became inseparable. But before long, he realised he was in seriously deep shit. But, behold! Help was to hand. Theo, his fairy godmother, came to his rescue, carried him off to a clinic where a weird man called Bones with a sugar dependency waved a magic wand, and taught him to see the error of his ways. And surprisingly enough, from that point on, everybody lived happily ever after. Well, more or less.'

In the silence that followed, Izzy kept her eyes ahead of her on the curved disc of moon that was hanging in the clear night sky. She didn't trust herself to turn and look at Mark. She had found his story, despite his self-deprecating tone, so poignant that she was worried she might embarrass him by crying. She knew, though, that what she was feeling for him – for all the pain he must have suffered as a child – was mixed up with the confusion of emotions she had from her own childhood. Though their experiences were different, she could relate to him. She felt also that he might be one of the few people who would truly understand the sense of could-have-done-better that had always been with her. That dreadful sense of disappointment that had followed her all her life.

'Have I embarrassed you?' he asked, breaking into her thoughts. 'I'm sorry if I've made you feel uncomfortable.'

Hearing the touching concern in his soft husky voice did her no good. Her throat clenched and the tears started, and there seemed no way of stopping them. 'I'm sorry,' she mumbled, her head still turned from him, 'it's my own fault. I shouldn't have kept on at you. It serves me right.' And still the tears came. Oh, why wouldn't they stop? And why did she never have a tissue when she needed one? She sensed him moving beside her, then felt the firm but gentle pressure of his hand on hers.

'Do I detect a fellow-sufferer of self-recrimination?'

She sniffed as discreetly as she could and looked at him. 'I don't suppose you've got a tissue, have you?'

He dug around in his trouser pockets. '*Voilà!* You're in luck. An unused handkerchief.'

She took it from him and pressed it to her eyes.

'You can use it for your nose as well,' he said. 'I don't mind. There'll be no extra charge.'

She managed a small smile. 'Then you'd best cover your ears, this won't be very ladylike.'

'Don't mind me, just blast away.'

She did and felt much better for it. 'Sorry about that. I kept thinking of you as that young boy. It must have been so awful for you, blaming yourself like that. How did your friend die?'

'A boating accident. We didn't know what we were doing. He drowned and I survived, but wished I hadn't. As simple and as complicated as that.'

'Is that why you never go swimming, or out in Theo's boat with him?'

He nodded. 'Being in or on water freaks the hell out of me.'

She frowned. 'But didn't you say you live by the sea?'

'I didn't say I was sane, now, did I? It's a personal challenge I set myself a long time ago. Was I up to it? Could I cope with such a tangible reminder?'

'And can you?'

He seemed to hold this thought for a moment as he looked down at the dark water beneath them. He said,

'I'm sitting here, aren't I? So what's your story? What nerve did I inadvertently tweak? Theo hinted that you didn't have the Rebecca of Sunnybrook Farm childhood.'

'Something like that.'

'Care to be more specific? After forcing my sordid past out of me, I think it's the least you can do in return. Let's call it share-and-tell time.'

She gave him a tiny shrug. 'There's not much to tell.'

His hand moved back to hers. 'You sure about that?'

At his gentle persuasion, she told him about her mother, how terrified she had been of her, and of the death of the baby that had been such a destructive force within her family. She spoke about her father too. How she had quietly idolised him, and that it was only now that she realised just how angry she was that he hadn't done more to help, not just her but her mother as well. She said, 'I feel guilty that I feel so much anger towards him now that he's dead. It doesn't seem right.'

'Forget any thought of what you think is right or wrong. Just acknowledge what you feel or it will continue to hold you back from enjoying the life you're entitled to.'

'Is that how you see me? Somebody who's holding back?'

He gave her a reassuring smile. 'Honest answer?'

'Yes.'

'I see two Izzies. One who doubts her strengths and talents because they've never been encouraged and, as a consequence, settles for the status quo because it's safer that way. And then there's this other Izzy, the one who's perceptive, witty and just longing to break free and live dangerously. A woman who could do anything she wanted if she would only be generous enough to give herself the chance.'

'If she were to let go of the past, you mean?'

'Sounds easy enough, I know. But you're talking to a

man who knows better than most how much courage it takes to walk away from the only life you've ever allowed yourself . . . or felt that you deserved.'

When she didn't respond, Mark said, 'So you know what this means, don't you?'

'What?'

'It makes us a right couple of damaged goods sitting on the shelf of life's patched-together casualties. But one thing's for sure, we're quite normal. Despite what you might think, everybody has something niggling away inside them. As the old REM song goes, 'Everybody Hurts'.'

'Even Theo?'

'Well, maybe he's the exception. Though he does have one rather pressing problem at the moment.'

'Really? Is that why he's gone back to Athens again?'

He looked at her closely, trying to figure out whether she was being deliberately obtuse. He decided she wasn't. 'Izzy, you're his problem.'

'Me?'

'He's genuinely very fond of you and doesn't know how to convince you that he's serious.'

She said nothing but slid her gaze down and absorbed herself in examining the stitching on the hem of her shorts.

'Look, tell me to butt out if you want, but what do you feel for him?'

She raised her head. 'He's lovely, truly he is. He's funny, kind, and – and very attractive, but he . . .' Her voice trailed off.

'But what?'

'He frightens me.'

'Theo? He's as harmless as a wet sponge. He'd never hurt you, Izzy, I swear it. I'd stake my last Rolo on it.'

She shook her head. 'I didn't mean it in that way. It's difficult to explain, but I can't fully relax when I'm with him. I keep thinking that I could never make the grade with him. Take the time when he kissed me that night he took me out for dinner. It was hopeless. I was so tense, all I could think of while he was kissing me was a mental checklist: arms engaged, lips puckered, nose to the side. Stop laughing, it's true. That's exactly what I was doing.'

'I'm not laughing.'

'Then what's that tee-hee sound coming from your mouth?'

'It's disbelief.'

She gave him a shove and he shoved her back.

'You know, if you could get over this kissing problem, you'd see Theo in an altogether different light.'

'Don't tell me, all I need is an intensive course of kissing therapy. But believe me, I've had it with therapists, whatever their speciality.'

'How so?'

'When my boyfriend was trying to find a way to leave me, he insisted that we saw a therapist. She was very nice, but—'

'But you didn't trust her, right?'

'Correct. I didn't trust her at all. In fact I was convinced she was in cahoots with Alan. I was quite rude to her.'

'You couldn't have been as rude to her as I was to Bones. I threatened to kill him. There, I've shocked you. You'll think twice now about sitting on these rocks again with me late at night and all alone.'

She smiled. 'But shocking people is what you do best. Your books tell me that much.'

'I don't only live to shock people.'

'What else do you do, then?'

'Well, I'm a fair cook, so I tell myself. Chicken tikka masala on a Friday night being a locally acclaimed wonder of mine.'

'Mm . . . Anything else you're good at?'

'You want more? There's no satisfying some folk. Hey, but wait, I'm also great at kidnapping people from parties. Yeah, I can see you're impressed by that.'

'Well, close to it.'

'Do you want to go back and join the throng?'

'Not really. Not when there's a hairy-faced Pa Patterson trying to get a look down my front.'

'Ah, so he was the one you were keen to avoid, was he? I'm glad to have been of use. But if I'd known it was going to turn into an all-night session I would have thought to bring some food down with us.'

'Yes, for an expert kidnapper, that was a careless oversight on your part.'

'Are you always this picky?'

'Funnily enough, only with you.'

'Oh, shucks, now you're just trying to make me feel special.'

She laughed. 'Have you ever thought of writing comedy?'

'Is that a sneaky put-down?'

'No, I was being serious. You're very funny.'

'I've been accused of many things, but having a sense of humour is not one of them.'

'Well, I think you're funny. You make me laugh.'

'I also made you cry.'

'So you did. It would have to be bittersweet comedy in that case.'

'Okay, I'll ring my editor tomorrow and give her the good news. "Sorry," I'll tell her, "but I've taken expert advice and I'm scrapping the winning formula and going for cheap laughs. I'm going to be the new King of Comedy!"'

'You'd have to change the publicity shot of you on the back of the books and learn to lighten yourself up. No more scowling Prince of Darkness.'

'I'm beginning to go off the idea already.'

'I knew it. No staying power.'

'That's a bloke for you. First sign of a struggle and we're off.'

They laughed companionably, then sat in silence while a ferry passed on the horizon, its diamond white lights shining in the darkness, the throbbing sound of its powerful engine reverberating across the water. When it had disappeared, Mark said, 'What will you do about Theo?'

'I don't think I can do anything about him. I get the feeling he's a law unto himself. The cooler I play it with him, the harder he pursues me. I've given him no encouragement, really I haven't.'

'I know that sometimes it seems you'd have to shoehorn him out of that massive ego of his, but you mustn't be fooled by the exterior packaging. If you really got to know him you'd see that he's as normal and down-to-earth as you and me.'

'He wouldn't thank you for saying that.'

No, he wouldn't, thought Mark. She was quite right. If Theo had a fault it was his vanity. He had never seen himself as normal and down-to-earth. Back in Durham he had always liked being the one who stood out from the crowd. And in the intervening years nothing had changed: he still enjoyed his good looks, his expensive clothes, the choice of luxurious homes, the flashy cars and, of course, the attention they drew. 'So you don't see it ever working between the two of you? Not even as a holiday romance?'

She pulled the toy arrow from the bandage around her ankle, placed it between them, and swung her feet so that the backs of her boots tapped lightly against the rocks they were sitting on. 'No, I don't. I'm not his sort, not at all. You know that, deep down, don't you?'

'Whoa, there, don't go bringing me into this. This is between you and Theo.'

'But it's true. You must have seen him over the years with millions of girls, none of whom were like me.'

'Hundreds, not millions. He's not that good a catch.'

She gave him another playful shove and caught him with an elbow in the ribs.

He caught his breath, groaned and clasped his side. 'Watch it, Izzy, that's where I was stabbed.'

Her hands went to her face. 'Oh, Mark, I'm so sorry. Are you okay?'

He opened his eyes slowly and grinned. 'Had you going, there.'

'Don't ever do that to me again. You frightened me half to death.' She raised her hand again to give him a playful slap, but he caught her wrist and held it tightly.

'Oh, no, you don't,' he laughed, 'once is quite enough.' She laughed too, and in the soft moonlight, her face wreathed in smiles, it was the strangest thing, but he suddenly found himself entirely conscious of the moment. Without once raising his glance from Izzy's face, he knew that the sky above them was a glorious canopy of velvety darkness, that the stars were bright and shining, that the moon was a perfectly sculptured half-disc of light. He was aware, too, that the breeze that had blown all day had dropped, and that the sea was calm, soundless and glassy. His senses told him it really was the most beautiful night.

Yet more beautiful than any of this was the girl beside him. As motionless as he was, she was staring back at him with steady, unblinking eyes: eyes that earlier had been so sad but which were now bright with some new emotion he wasn't sure he recognised or understood. What he did understand, though, was his sudden desire to kiss her. Common sense told him not to do it. But when had he ever allowed common sense over the threshold of his intentions?

Loosening his grip on her slender arm, but still holding

it, he lowered his gaze to her lips and with the slightest of movements, inclined his head. His intent couldn't have been clearer. If she moves away, I shan't kiss her, he told himself, as though this would exonerate him of any wrongdoing. But if she stays where she is, I will.

Chapter Thirty-Five

It was an amazing kiss.

A clean sweep of a kiss that was silky and smooth.

Slow.

Gentle.

Intensely erotic.

With his hand on the nape of her neck he drew her closer, wanting more of the sweet warmth of her mouth, a mouth that was so deliciously inviting he couldn't think why she had ever doubted her ability to kiss Theo.

The thought of Theo invoked common sense. He should bring matters to an immediate close. He should clear his throat and mumble some kind of gentlemanly apology: 'Sorry, but I really don't know what came over me.'

But to hell with that! He knew exactly what he was doing and wanted to go on doing it for as long as he could.

As inevitably as night follows day, the moment came to an end, brought to a halt by the intrusive sound of a small fishing-boat crossing the water in front of them. He stroked her hair away from her face, tucked it behind her ear. 'I suppose one of us should say, "How did that happen?"'

'It was you,' she said, with a shy half-smile. 'You started it.'

'Not true. It was all down to you. You turned those lovely eyes on me. What was I supposed to do?'

'But it was you who lowered your head.'

'You didn't have to respond. In my mind I gave you the choice to back out. Look, I'll show you, this is all I did.'

He tilted his head and kissed her again. When she started to laugh, he stopped. She said, 'You tricked that one out of me.'

'So I did. But, in my defence, you make it so easy for me.'

'I'm not easy.'

She sounded cross, and realising his blunder, he reached out to her hand. 'I didn't mean it that way.'

The night air hung listlessly around them. The tide must have turned, for now the sea was sucking at the pebbly shore beneath their feet. 'But it's what it looks like,' she murmured. 'First Theo, now you.'

'What it looks like isn't what it is. I know that and so do you.'

She raised her eyes. 'I wouldn't want you to think that I'm the kind of girl who—'

'You made your feelings for Theo very clear when we were talking. I wouldn't have kissed you if I'd thought you were serious about him.' Though he spoke with conviction, Mark wasn't so sure that he was speaking the truth. Remembering the night he had seen Theo kissing Izzy, he understood now that it hadn't been disappointment he had felt as he'd stood on the beach looking up at them, it had been jealousy. The realisation confirmed what he had suspected about himself that day he had first met Izzy and took her back to Villa Anna to see Theo – he really had been jealous that his friend might find happiness and he might not. And not just any old happiness, but the chance to be loved by someone as special as Izzy. It was a disturbing conclusion that needed some thought. But now wasn't the time. Now he wanted to make Izzy feel comfortable with him again. He said, 'We could pretend it never happened, that we didn't kiss. Or make out that it was an act of impetuous madness.'

344

'We could . . . if that's what you wanted.'

'Doesn't it also depend on what you want?'

She looked up at him, her eyes wide and faintly troubled again. 'Why did you kiss me?'

'Because I wanted to. And because it felt entirely the right thing to do. Can I ask the same of you?'

'No.'

'Hey, I sense a degree of disparity going on here.' Her expression relaxed and he felt hopeful again. Hopeful. What an odd word to use. Hopeful of what? What did he expect to come out of all this? 'So who gets to have the final word on the subject? You or me?'

'Be my guest, take the floor.'

'Okay. Here goes. I'd like it going on record that you need have no worries about your kissing technique. Your fears are totally ill-founded. Not that I'm claiming to be an expert, you understand, but I reckon with a bit more encouragement you could really make a go of it.'

'Kissing for a living?'

'Mm . . . not quite what I had in mind.'

'And who would give me the necessary encouragement?'

He cleared his throat, slicked back his hair, and straightened an imaginary tie at his neck. 'I could make a start first thing in the morning.'

She laughed, picked up the arrow that was between them, turned it over in her hands and stroked the feathers. Impulsively, he took it from her and held it to his heart. 'Argh, you've got me right here, Izzy.'

She snatched it away from him. 'You're barmy. Completely barmy.'

'Actually, and just between you and me, this is the sanest I've ever felt.' He put his arm around her.

She relaxed into him, rested her head against his. 'Do you suppose after I've practised another kiss on you we ought to get back to the party?'

'Why, Sugar Lips, I do declare you're making me blush with your forward ways. But it's not a bad idea. Though if I don't think you're up to standard, you could be stuck here for a while.'

She gave him a nudge with her elbow. 'I thought you said I was good.'

'Easy there, Tiger, always room for improvement.'

Having insisted that Max and his parents had done more than their fair share of organising the party, Laura had packed them off to bed, and she and Izzy were in the kitchen, tidying up the last of the glasses.

Izzy knew that for the last hour Laura had been dying to get her on her own and subject her to an intensive question-and-answer session. When she and Mark had returned to the party, they had bumped into Laura as they had emerged from the path, so it was a foregone conclusion that she would want to know what Izzy had been up to with him.

'I thought it was strange when I couldn't find you anywhere,' Laura said now, as she opened the dishwasher and stood back to let the cloud of steam escape. 'It was Dolly-Babe who told me that she'd seen the pair of you sneaking away down the hillside like a couple of lovers in search of a smoochy hideaway. She was very put out. She was hoping to have Mark all to herself.'

'That's what he was afraid of.'

'Ah, so he used you as protection, did he? Very cunning of him. So, Izzy, how many holiday flings do you need?'

'It's not like that!' she cried indignantly. 'Despite what you all thought, I was never having a fling with Theo.'

'Calm down, I was only teasing. I think it's great that you're testing the water from more than one puddle, so to speak. And he is rather gorgeous with that dead sexy voice of his, I can quite see the attraction. But putting your string of conquests to one side, you'll never guess what went on here while you were enjoying your secret assignation down on the beach.'

Izzy couldn't believe her luck that so convenient a diversion was to hand and quickly grasped it. 'Don't tell me, Ma and Pa Patterson had a fight?'

'No, worse than that. Angelos was doing his best to teach Dolly-Babe to dance the light fantastic, and with more than a glass or two of oúzo inside of him, he let it slip who Theo really was. Not only that, it turns out the land that Bob was after was the olive grove here in Áyios Nikólaos that Theo bought. It all got very unpleasant with the pair of them thinking they'd been made fools of. They stomped off in a fearful fit of pique.'

'Goodness! Do you think Theo knew all along that it was Bob who had designs on the olive grove?'

'Of course he knew. Theo might like to give the impression of being a charming happy-go-lucky man for whom everything falls into his lap by haphazard chance, but to be as successful as he is it takes a ruthlessly sharp mind that's as astute as it is devious. With that land being right on his doorstep he would have known exactly who was behind the offer and what plans Bob had for it, so he had made certain that there was no likelihood that Bob could set them in motion.' She yawned hugely. 'Oh dear, that's it as far as I'm concerned, I'm going to bed. I'm all in. I'm definitely getting old, I can't take these late nights any more. I just hope the girls don't make too much noise when they get in – I could do with an uninterrupted night's sleep. You coming?'

But Izzy didn't follow Laura to bed. Her head was too full of that evening's events. She made herself a mug of tea and went and sat on the terrace. All the villa lights had been switched off and sitting in the darkness she felt the night wrap its cool aura of calm around her.

But the aura of calm didn't last for long.

A horribly familiar voice inside her head said, *And just what did you think you were doing down there on the beach, and for all the world to see?*

You know what, she answered her mother back, I was having the time of my life! There! What do you say to that? Mm . . . gone quiet on me, have you? Well, good. Because if ever there was a man worth disgracing myself for, this is the one.

She closed her eyes, defiantly shutting out her mother's unwanted presence, and relived every heart-stopping moment of that first kiss with Mark.

How it had happened was still a mystery to her. One minute they had been laughing and joking and the next, she had found herself wishing he would kiss her. And just as this thought had formed itself, he had lowered his eyes and tilted his head, and she had realised he was thinking the same. And the best thing was, there hadn't been a single attack of doubt or nerves throughout. It had felt so right between them. All she had been conscious of was the dreamy pleasure his soft warm lips were giving her. It had seemed so natural, so unforced and unhurried. And so sublimely wonderful.

Unlike the kiss she had had with Theo. How scared she had been that he would find her wanting. That he would think she was less of a woman than he was used to.

But Mark hadn't made her feel like that.

When eventually they had decided they ought to rejoin the party, Mark had offered to carry her up the path again, but she had put her foot down and said she could manage just fine. 'Am I allowed to hold the hand of Little Miss Independent, then?' he had asked.

'I think that would be okay.'

But, of course, he had done more than that. Half-way up the hillside, he had stopped and said, 'Do you remember? This is where you fell and hurt yourself. We'd better not take any chances, I'll take hold of both your hands.'

'But that would mean I couldn't walk.'

'True. But it would enable me to kiss you again, safe in the knowledge that those lethal hands and elbows of yours couldn't take another shot at me.' He had treated her to a repeat performance of that trick of slowly lowering his head. 'And would that be all right?' he had asked, holding back from her and making the moment all the more seductive and irresistible. 'I'd hate to be accused of presuming anything of you.'

The combination of his husky voice, little more than a whisper, the smell of his aftershave mingling with the heady scent of the cypress trees around them, and the heat of his body reaching out to her, all came together and hit her in the form of an all-consuming bolt of desire. It was a shockwave of pure lust that travelled at high speed the length and breadth of her. Tilting her head back, she closed her eyes and waited for him to kiss her.

But when a few seconds had passed and he hadn't, she opened her eyes. 'What's the hold-up?' she asked.

Holding her face in his long, smooth fingers, he said, 'I was just taking a good look at you. Committing you to memory.'

'Why?'

'Because I can't imagine a better way to remember this evening. Can I see you tomorrow?'

'Where?'

'On the rocks where we were just sitting . . . where I first met you.'

'Okay, I'll be there. Early, before everyone else is up.'

Thinking of the scene now, and looking at her watch, Izzy saw that it was only a matter of hours before she would be with Mark again. She hugged this happy thought to her, holding it tight, wanting to squeeze every delicious impetuous hope out of it. She didn't care a jot if she was crying for the moon, it was the best feeling in the world, and while it lasted, she was determined to enjoy it.

Further round the bay, at Villa Anna, Mark was also sitting in the dark. Staring at the sea, he was watching the outgoing tide breaking the surface of the water. Nearer to him, and down on the shore, he could hear the waves building in strength as they clawed at the sand and stones, dislodging what they could within their deceptively embracing touch.

The shifting tide echoed his own agitated state. And restless with a surfeit of energy he went and leaned against the low wall on the edge of the terrace. He suddenly wished that he had had the nerve to entice Izzy back here to spend the night with him.

He sighed heavily, ran his hands through his hair and told himself to think of something else. Something marginally less erotic than the thought of undressing Izzy and making love to her.

Think of Theo and what the hell you're going to say to him when you speak to him next! Oh, by the way, Theo, I've got this thing going with Izzy. No hard feelings, eh?

Chapter Thirty-Six

Francesca was regretting the amount she had had to drink. She was feeling sick and each time she closed her eyes the noisy packed-out bar they were squeezed into would spin round inside her head. She should never have knocked back all those tequila slammers. She had only done it to teach Harry a lesson. To show him that this was how you had a good time.

Earlier on, and already a bit tipsy, she had been boasting to Nick what a great kisser his brother was. She had then tried to kiss Harry in front of everyone, but he wouldn't let her. 'Don't, Francesca,' he had said, his face reddening, 'not here. Not like this.' But she had kept on until in the end he had unhooked her hands from around his neck and pushed her away. 'I'd rather kiss you when you were sober and knew what you were doing.' His voice had been as hard as steel. So had his eyes.

Humiliated right down to her varnished toenails, she had turned on him. 'Oh, lighten up,' she had shouted above the pounding beat of a disco anthem. But he had stood there looking down at her with that disapproving expression on his face.

'Yeah,' Nick had joined in, 'stop being such a pain, shape up or push off.'

He had done neither. He had simply remained where he was, watching her coolly, his brows drawn together, making her feel like a naughty child. In defiance, she had ordered another round of drinks. 'You're embarrassing me,' she had said, bumping against him as she slipped off her bar stool and spilled tequila down his trousers. 'This is adult time, why don't you just go?'

And he had. Without another word, he had gone.

Now she was wishing he hadn't. She hated herself for having treated him so badly. Feeling sick and miserable, she also wished she hadn't listened to Nick's suggestion that they leave her parents' party, get changed and head into Kassiópi. She had been enjoying herself up until then. She and Harry had been having a great laugh together – they had even joined in with all that Greek dancing with her parents. But it was Sally who had said, 'Oh, come on, don't be boring. Let's go.' She knew the real reason why Nick had wanted to come: he had wanted to meet up with that bloke from Glasgow, the one with the accent as thick as cold custard who had been supplying him with his wacky-baccy. According to Giorgios, it came across from Albania. Occasionally it would wash up on the shore; that was when a delivery went wrong, when the Corfiot coastguards would appear on the scene unexpectedly, and the terrified Albanians would shove the lot overboard. Some of the waiters they had got to know joked that they spent the winter months when all the tourists had gone home sampling what came ashore.

She was no prude, but Nick was a mug for smoking the stuff. God knows what was in it. A bloody fool, that's what he was. And it was all his fault that she was stuck here drunk, and that Harry had left her. She wanted to go home, wanted to be sick in the privacy of her own bathroom, then lie on the bed and crash out. But she wasn't so drunk that she was going to risk walking through the olive grove in the dark on her own. Dad would go mad if he discovered she had done that. Technically she might be a full-blown adult, but to him she was still his little girl. In her wretchedly self-pitying state she felt tears welling in her eyes. Blinking them away, she knew she had no choice but to wait for Nick and Sally to decide that they had had enough and were ready to leave. Though knowing how they liked to party, she was probably in for a long wait.

As it turned out, once Nick had found his Glaswegian friend and had got what he had come for, he didn't feel the need to hang about. 'Right then, girls,' he said, tucking an arm through theirs, 'shall we go?'

They made slow progress. Sally was in a worse state than Francesca, and leaving the bright lights of Kassiópi behind them, and propping themselves up on each other, they entered the darkness of the olive grove. None of them had a torch, and once again Francesca wished that Harry was with them.

'If Captain Sensible was here, we'd have no problem seeing where we were going,' said Nick, as if picking up on her thoughts. 'Wouldn't you know that he'd take the bloody torch with him?'

'Don't talk about him like that.'

'Oo-er, listen to her,' jeered Nick. 'She's really got the hots for him.'

'Shut up, Nick, and keep walking before I land one on you. Save your energy for your brain, what there is of it.'

'I think I'm going to be sick,' groaned Sally. She staggered away from them and vomited into the bushes. It had the effect of making Francesca follow suit. No more booze for the rest of the holiday, she promised herself, as she emptied the contents of her stomach. No more tequilas. And definitely no more nights out with Nick.

When they had finished, they found Nick slumped on the ground, his back resting against the trunk of an olive tree, his head tilted upwards. 'Something to clear the mind,' he said, waving a clumsily put-together reefer, its end glowing red in the darkness.

'You're an idiot, Nick, smoking that junk.'

'After what you've just deposited in the bushes, Frankie girl, I'll take that as a case of pots and kettles. You need to learn to chill out. You're getting to be as bad as my brother. Perhaps you're seeing too much of each other. Wish I knew what it is you see in a dork like him when you could have me.'

'I've told you before, don't call me Frankie! And if you really want to know, your brother's worth ten of you.'

'Oh, come on the pair of you, stop arguing,' said Sally. 'Let's get going. Give me a puff of that, Nick. It'll help me feel better.'

By the time they had reached the bay, Nick was laughing and joking. He insisted that they go down to the beach. 'It's a beautiful night, girls,' he said, staring up at the moon and slipping his arms around them once more. In his mellowed state he was all love and peace. So was Sally. 'Oh, yes, my cool sisters of swing,' he sang out expansively, 'it's a real beautiful night for catching the vibe. You know what we should do, we should go for a swim.'

It was a crazy idea and Francesca was having none of it. To her horror, Sally agreed with Nick, and giggling loudly, she flung her arms around him and kissed him. 'I never knew until now just how brilliant you were, Nick.'

'But you're both off your heads,' Francesca protested. 'You're mad even to think of it.'

They paid her no heed, slipped out of their clothes, held hands, and ran into the water.

Annoyed and resigned, Francesca watched them go. She was so tired and fed up, she was tempted to leave them to it, to climb the hill and go to bed. But something told her not to leave her friend. If Sally came to any harm, she would never forgive herself. Once again, she had no choice but to wait for Nick and Sally to get bored and come to their senses.

She sat down on the stones and instantly what little

energy she had drained out of her. Her head felt like a ball of lead wobbling on her neck and the need to sleep was so overwhelming that she lay back and closed her eyes.

As long as I can hear them, she told herself drowsily, everything will be okay.

Chapter Thirty-Seven

Mark was watching the scene below him with rising apprehension.

He had been on the verge of going to bed when he heard voices drifting up from the beach. Putting down the book he had been reading, he had gone to the edge of the terrace to see what was going on. Straining his eyes in the darkness, he had recognised Max and Laura's daughter, Francesca, and her friend, Sally. The younger of the Patterson boys – the shambling, feckless one with long hair – was with them. And by the look of them they were drunk, staggering about, laughing and joking, raising their voices more than was necessary. His blood had run cold when he had seen Sally and the boy strip off and throw themselves into the water.

An excess of alcohol and a late-night swim was not a wise combination, and as he stood now, rooted to the spot, he saw them swimming further and further away from the safety of the shore. Seeing Francesca lie back on the stones as though she was settling in for the night only added to his fears.

You're overreacting, he told himself, they'll be fine. Stop worrying. They're old enough to look after themselves. Just read your book and mind your own business.

He turned away from the sea and retraced his steps to his chair. He had taken no more than two paces when he heard a cry. A girl's cry. He spun on his heels and peered into the darkness.

Laughter drifted up to him on the gathering breeze. It

was the boy. Floating on his back, his arms stretched out either side of him, he seemed to be finding something hysterically funny in the sky above him.

The fear that had wedged itself in Mark's throat subsided and once again he told himself not to be such a fool. But then he realised something was wrong with the picture he was looking at. Something was missing.

The girl whose cry he had heard, where was she?

He strained his eyes to pick out the whiteness of her body in the water. Where the hell was she?

From the terrace of Villa Petros, Izzy had also observed what was going on. She, too, concluded that something was wrong and headed for the beach as fast as she could.

She found that Mark had got there a few seconds ahead of her. The look of alarm on his face, confirmed her fears. 'Sally,' she said breathlessly, 'where is she?'

'I don't know, I can't see her. The tide's going out, she must have drifted with it. You wake Francesca and I'll shout to the boy. What's his name?'

'Nick. It's Nick.'

Standing at the water's edge, and though he couldn't see the boy, Mark began shouting to him. 'Nick,' he bellowed, 'Nick, can you hear me?'

There was no answer.

He tried calling to Sally. But there was no answer from her either.

Nor could Izzy get any response from Francesca. No matter how hard she shook her, Francesca slept on. All she got from the girl was an incoherent mumbling before she turned on to her side and sank further into a deep state of blackout. Giving up on her, Izzy went and joined Mark.

'It's no good,' he said. 'They're not answering me.'

Then in the silence they both heard a cry.

Followed by another, and another.

Keeping the panic from his voice, and ignoring the nausea in the pit of his stomach, Mark kicked off his shoes. 'Go and get help. I'll swim out to them.'

'But, Mark, you can't, you—'

'Go! *Go on!*'

She watched him plunge into the water, before turning to race back up the hillside. But just as she reached the path, disaster struck. Her ankle gave way and she keeled over in pain.

In order to overcome the phobic instinct that had been with him for the last thirty years, Mark knew that he had to use the raw terror of those memories – of Niall's open-eyed death mask of a face – to strengthen his body. If he couldn't do that, if he let the memories overwhelm him, he would never survive.

In the distance, he saw what he thought was a head bobbing in the darkness. Pushing his arms through the water, kicking his legs as hard as he could, he heard the terrified shouts for help. But it was only one voice he could hear, and it was such a deep-throated cry of fear he couldn't decide whether it was Sally or the boy.

He swam on.

Harder.

Faster.

But the gap didn't seem to be closing. Now that he was so far from the shore, the waves were building, buffeting him relentlessly, and the effort just to stay afloat was harder to sustain. His stomach was cramping and the muscles in his legs were bunching. It was a struggle just to keep his breathing going. To keep the rhythm. To use the memories. Not to give in to them.

A sudden wave caught him off-guard and salty water hit the back of his throat. Panicked and choking, he swallowed it. And then his nerve went. It was all too terrifyingly familiar: the powerful swell of the sea, the sense of uselessness, the deep, deep, coldness.

His body was no longer responding to anything he told it to do: it had turned to stone. A wave covered him, then another, and as he slipped beneath the surface he knew it was over. He had cheated death as a child, but this time it would not be denied. It was futile to fight it. Why not let the Grim Reaper have his way? It would be over in seconds.

He opened his mouth and water flooded in. The searing and strangely echoing coldness of it filled his head and lungs, but suddenly his chest heaved with a desperate need for air, and he realised that although his leaden brain might have been fooled into admitting defeat, some other part of him wasn't prepared to give in.

A new strength rushed through him, and he propelled himself to the surface. Coughing and spluttering, he gasped for air, fought for his life as the waves continued to buffet him. Treading water, he got his breathing under control again and looked around for any sign of Nick or Sally, not holding out much hope of finding them, not now.

At first he thought he had imagined it, but then he heard it again. A faint cry for help. Straining his stinging eyes in the darkness, he saw a flash of movement scarcely twenty yards from him.

It was Sally trying to stay afloat.

Adrenaline pumped through him and he swam over to her. She saw him and the relief showed in her panic-stricken face. She sank into his arms, frightened and exhausted, but he wasn't prepared for her weight and they both went under. Down and down they went. Deeper and deeper. Her cold body slithered out of his grasp and he lost her. Kicking his feet, he swam to the surface, got his breath back, then dived down for her. It was so dark he couldn't see anything. The salt water was burning his eyes. Suddenly he felt a hand. He grabbed at it and, with a tremendous surge of energy, hauled her upwards. But she wasn't moving and her freezing cold body was a dead weight in his arms. A grotesquely distorted image of Niall's face flew into his mind.

Anger and despair ripped through him. *No!* It couldn't happen twice.

He held on tightly to Sally's motionless body, and with one arm around her chest, and treading water, he prayed that he had the strength to get them both back to the shore.

He turned to start the long, hard swim, but was momentarily dazzled by a flare of light. In his shocked, exhausted state, he didn't register what it was. But as the light grew nearer and brighter, and he heard the low throaty roar of an engine, he realised it was a boat coming to help.

'Whoever you are,' he murmured wretchedly, his mind plummeting back to that moment when the lifeboat had come for him and Niall, 'you're too late.'

Chapter Thirty-Eight

Izzy caught sight of Mark and Sally in the water and, her heart racing with relief, she pushed against the throttle, nearly knocking herself off her feet as the boat lurched forward in her haste to reach them. Ignoring the pain in her ankle as she tried to stand firm, she gunned the boat straight ahead. She came in close, cut her speed, and leaned over the side of the boat to Mark.

'I think she's dead,' was all he said as between them they heaved Sally's lifeless body into the boat.

Izzy's heart sank. Dead? No! Oh, please, no. Not this outrageous young girl who had made them all laugh. Not this fun-loving soul who was so bright and vivacious with everything before her. Leaving Mark to haul himself in, she felt for a pulse, determined to find one. He had to be wrong. Pressing her fingers against Sally's throat, she held her breath, blocked out everything else around her, willed the faintest flicker of life to reveal itself. Desperation made her think she had imagined it, and hardly trusting herself, she moved her fingers, then tried again. But yes. There it was. A pulse. No more than a flutter, but a sign of hope. Summoning all her first-aid knowledge, she started working at Sally's chest to expel the water that had tried to claim her, then tilting her head back and pinching her nose, she breathed into her cold mouth. The taste of salt, vomit and alcohol on Sally's lips made her want to retch, but she carried on relentlessly, filling her own lungs with air before steadily breathing it into Sally. She would not let her die. 'Come on, Sally,' she murmured, her hands pumping at the girl's chest, her brain fighting to chase away the fear that she might fail. 'Come on, Sally, you can do this. Come on.' A sudden gurgling sound, followed by a twitch of movement beneath her hands, instantly renewed Izzy's dwindling hopes. She turned Sally on to her side and said to Mark, 'Have a look in that seat cupboard. Laura sometimes keeps spare towels in there.'

After a brief fumble, Mark passed Izzy two large beach towels and helped her wrap Sally, who was now shaking violently. 'What about the boy?' he asked. His voice was a rasping whisper, his breathing heavy, and crouching beside her, water pooling on the deck from his dripping jeans and shirt, she could hear his teeth chattering. Shivering with cold, his hair plastered to his head, his eyes dark and wild against the paleness of his face, she knew he was in shock. 'He's okay,' she said, touching his arm to reassure him. 'He made it to the raft, that's where I left him.' And thinking it might help Mark to recover by having something to do, she added, 'Do you want to get us back?' He stared at her blankly, as though not understanding. Then he nodded and moved to the front of the boat. After studying the controls, he turned it round and headed for the raft. Above the sound of the engine and Sally's stifled sobs, Izzy could hear him cursing to himself. She had never heard such language: it was a furious litany of obscenities that made her wince as she cradled Sally in her arms.

Nick was waiting for them at the raft. He climbed in and took the towel Izzy offered him.

'Is she okay?' he asked, bending down to take a look at Sally. She was still crying and didn't seem aware of his presence.

'She'll be fine,' Izzy said, then, distracted by flashing beams of light on the shore by the jetty, she saw that Francesca was on her feet and that Max and Laura were with her. Corky was there too. The sound of the boat starting up must have disturbed them.

Pandemonium broke out when they got to the jetty. Everyone started talking at once. Max was beside himself with relief, thanking Mark and Izzy for what they had done, and Laura, who had been consoling Francesca, reached out to Sally and held her tightly. But there was anger too. Francesca's relief that Sally was all right made her turn on Nick. 'This is all your fault,' she yelled at him. 'It was your idea to go swimming. I told you not to, that you were both too drunk and too high. But you wouldn't listen.' She was screaming at him, tears running down her cheeks. 'If you hadn't been so keen to get off your head on dope none of this would have happened!'

Max's face turned white. 'Drugs?' he hissed. 'What drugs?' He flashed his torch on Nick's face.

'Nothing heavy,' said Nick, blinking in the light and clutching the towel around him. He was nothing like the cocky lad they were used to seeing. With his long hair clinging to his head and neck, and his thin legs poking out from beneath the towel, he looked pitifully young and vulnerable. 'It was only a joint, you know, just recreational.'

From behind Izzy, where he had been pulling on his boots, Mark stepped forward and squared himself up in front of Nick. He took hold of him, lifted him clean off his feet and shook him. Really shook him. 'You crazy little bastard,' he raged. Then throwing him to the ground, he shouted again: 'Spare us! Only a joint! Don't you get it? Don't you understand that because of you and your joint several people very nearly died here tonight? Can you live with that? Or maybe you're so arrogant you think you can.'

Without another word, he stalked away into the darkness, leaving them not knowing what to say or do next.

It was Corky who took command. He helped Nick to his feet, and said, 'Righty-ho, drama over. Let's get everyone up to the villa and into some dry clothes. Laura, you take Sally, Max, you look after Francesca, Izzy, you and I will bring up the rear with young Nick.'

'Um ... sorry to be a nuisance, Corky,' Izzy said, as everyone started to move, 'but I'm afraid I've turned my ankle again.' In view of what had happened she felt ridiculous bringing attention to herself but she knew she wouldn't be able to make the steep path without help. When she had decided that the best way to help Mark was to use Max and Laura's boat, every step she had taken to the jetty had made her cry out with pain. Now her calf was swelling and throbbing unbearably.

It had been a terrible risk she had taken, but it had been all she could think to do. Max had shown her how to handle the boat on one of their many trips out in it, but she wasn't sure how to start the engine. Then she remembered where Max kept a spare key and had been relieved to find that it was no more difficult than a car. The outboard motor had sprung into action first go. She had hauled in the anchor, untied the mooring rope, switched on the bow light and headed out into the bay to find Mark and the others.

Now, as Corky helped her and Nick up the path, a shiver went through her as she thought how differently it might all have ended if she hadn't been able to start the engine.

In the warm of the villa, and while Max phoned the emergency number for the local doctor's surgery, Laura made them tea. In the ensuing commotion Olivia was roused from her sleep and immediately fussed over Sally, wrapping her in Corky's dressing-gown, and when that proved insufficient to stop her shivering as she lay on the sofa, Francesca holding her hand, she instructed Corky to fetch a blanket.

Feeling sorry for Nick, who was being held responsible for the near tragedy, Izzy limped across the sitting room and sat next to him. He was fully dressed now, in the clothes that he had earlier stripped off, but he was still cold and a little shaky. She put a comforting arm around his shoulders.

'I think it would be best if I got going,' he murmured, his head bent down to the floor.

'No,' she said firmly. 'Have some tea first, then somebody will take you home.'

He shook his head dejectedly. 'It would have been better if I'd drowned out there. It would save my parents the job of killing me when they discover what I've done.'

'Don't ever say that,' she rebuked him. 'Treat this as a warning not to be so stupid again. You and Sally survived by the skin of your teeth. Be glad for that.'

He looked up at her. 'That bloke who saved Sally, why did he go berserk with me?'

'Let's just say he had his reasons. And if you've got any sense, you'll give what he said some thought.'

The next morning, sitting on the veranda in the shade of the pergola, everyone was subdued with shock and lack of sleep. The plans that had earlier been set in motion for the day had been dramatically altered. Max, Corky and Olivia wouldn't be the only ones flying back to England: understandably, Sally wanted to go home too, to be with her parents.

Max had phoned them after the doctor had confirmed that, though badly shaken, Sally was physically in good shape for somebody who had nearly drowned. Nobody had envied Max the job of explaining to Mr and Mrs Bartholomew what had happened, and his relief when he had handed the phone to Sally had been considerable. In the harsh brightness from the overhead spotlights in the kitchen where he sat at the table, his head bowed, he looked as if he had aged ten years in that one night.

With the decision made that Sally was to fly home, Laura had said that she would go too.

'But why?' Max had said, 'there's no need.'

'Yes, there is, I know what you'll do – you feel so bad about this, you'll take Sally home to her parents and accept the blame for what's happened.'

'We could make sure he doesn't do that,' Corky said, 'we'll go with him.'

'Thanks, but I'd rather be there myself.'

'In that case, I'm coming with you,' said Francesca.

Because it was clear that the holiday was now over for them all, Izzy said that perhaps she ought to return home as well.

But Max wouldn't hear of it. 'No, Izzy, with your ankle the way it is, you're not going anywhere. Besides, there's no reason for you to leave. Make the most of some quiet time on your own. Angelos and Sophia will take care of you. You won't have to do a thing.'

'Yes,' agreed Laura, 'please stay. It's not fair that your holiday should be cut short. Francesca and I will probably be back in a couple of days, with Max following on as soon as he's done what he needs to.'

'Are you sure?'

'Yes. Very sure,' said Max, getting up from his chair and coming over to where she was sitting, her ankle heavily strapped and resting on a low table. He kissed the top of her head. 'After what you did last night, this is the least we can do for you. If you and Mark hadn't seen what was going on, the telephone call I had to make to Sally's parents would have been very different.'

Just before lunch Max and Laura went to see Mark. They wanted to thank him for what he had done. They came back from Villa Anna a short while later, disappointed.

'He wasn't in,' Max said. 'I feel really bad that we haven't been able to thank him. It was quite a risk he took swimming that far out to save Sally and I want him to know how grateful we are.'

Izzy kept to herself just how big a risk it must have been for Mark. *Being in or on water freaks the hell out of me.* She wondered at his extraordinary courage in doing what he had. She also remembered that they had agreed to meet down on the beach that morning, but that had been before the events of last night had overtaken them all.

An hour before everyone had to leave for the airport, they had visitors.

It was Harry with his parents. There was no sign of Nick. The relaxed atmosphere on the terrace immediately evaporated, and under the pretext of some last-minute packing, Corky and Olivia made themselves scarce. When Izzy struggled to her feet to make her exit and join them inside the villa, Virginia Patterson said, 'Don't go on our account, not when it's you we need to thank.'

From her flat, unemotional tone, Francesca thought she had never heard gratitude so poorly expressed. Neither was there any evidence of it in the ghastly woman's face.

'It wasn't just me,' Izzy replied, settling down again. 'It's Mark you should really be talking to.'

'We've tried,' said Harry, 'but there's no answer. He must be out.' His gaze moved from Izzy and came to rest on Francesca where she was sitting between her parents, both of whom were suddenly bristling as if they needed to vent their feelings.

'Thank you, Harry,' said his mother, 'but I think your father and I are capable of handling this on our own.'

'Yes,' chipped in her husband, 'that's if you would allow us to get a word in.'

It was such an unnecessary put-down that Francesca coloured with indignation for Harry. How dare his parents treat him so offhandedly? But then she recalled how shamefully she had treated him last night, and knew she had to put things right between them before she left for home. In a voice loaded with contempt for his mother and father, she said, 'Seeing as you're not needed by your parents, Harry, perhaps you'd like to come and have a word with me. There's something I'd like to say to you.'

She led him to the far end of the terrace where she knew they wouldn't be heard or observed. Knowing she was short of time, she took the direct approach. 'Look, I just want to say that I know I behaved appallingly last night, and I'm really sorry. The minute you left I regretted what I'd said. God knows what I was fired up on, but I'm more sorry than I can say. Perhaps if I hadn't got so drunk . . .' she paused and stared down into the bay, 'none of this mess would have happened . . . I might have been able to stop Nick and Sally.'

'I think it was me who fired you up,' he said softly. 'Maybe if I hadn't humiliated you, you wouldn't have felt the need to get drunk.'

'When *you* humiliated *me*?'

'Yes. When I wouldn't kiss you.'

She looked shamefaced. 'I should never have tried to force you to do that. I knew you wouldn't want to, not in front of everyone, but I still went ahead and did it. I wanted to prove to you, and your brother, that you could knock the spots off him any day.'

He smiled shyly. 'Really?'

'Yes, really. You're miles more interesting than him. And it's about time you realised that. You should also stand up to your parents. They were bloody awful to you just now.'

'Anything else?'

'Yes, I'd like to kiss you goodbye, if it wouldn't be too horrible for you.'

'You're leaving?'

'Change of plan. I'm going back home today with Sally and my grandparents. Mum and Dad are going as well. It seems the right thing to do.'

'What time's your flight?'

'Soon.' She checked her watch. 'We've got to leave in three-quarters of an hour.

He moved in closer. 'So it had better be a proper goodbye kiss, then?'

She nodded. 'One to remember.'

Manoeuvring her up against a pillar, and taking off his glasses, he stroked the side of her face then kissed her for the longest and sweetest moment. When he stopped and drew away from her, he said, 'Do you think you'd like to keep in touch, back in England?'

She smiled. 'Now, what do you think?'

He replaced his glasses. 'I think the rest of my holiday is going to be extremely dull without you.'

The villa seemed very quiet when everyone had gone. Izzy had been alone in it before, when she had first hurt her ankle, but this time it was different. It was as if an unhappy spirit was lurking somewhere in the large house, following her about.

Sitting on the terrace, looking down on to the beach, she tried to occupy herself by reading *When Darkness Falls*. She had only four chapters left, which meant the tension was building to its climax, but despite the quality of the writing she couldn't keep her mind fixed on the plot. It kept wandering off, worried about the story's creator. Where was he? What was he doing? She had hoped he might come and see her, but of course he wasn't to know that she was immobile again. There hadn't been time last night for her to explain why she had disregarded his instruction to fetch the others.

Her mind wasn't put at ease when later that evening Sophia came to cook her a light supper. She was full of apologetic mutterings that she and her husband had not known of the drama that had taken place and been on hand to help. She was also furious that drugs had been involved.

'It is the Italians and Albanians,' she said, banging Laura's expensive Le Creuset frying-pan down on the cooker and cracking eggs into a bowl. 'They are bringing it here to our perfect island and ruining everything. If I ever got hold of them, they would know about it!'

Her angry outburst complete, she then went on to tell Izzy that Angelos had been to Villa Anna that afternoon to see to the pool and had reported back to his wife that there was no sign of anybody in or around the house. 'It is very strange,' Angelos had told her, 'the shutters are all across the windows, as if nobody is there. And Theo's guest rarely goes out during the day. Always he is working. Writing. Writing. Writing. He has his favourite spot in the shade where he sits every day. But not today. Perhaps he has finished his book?'

Izzy knew this couldn't be so. Mark had told her last night that he was only a third of the way through it.

She went to bed early that night but was soon woken by the sound of ringing. She fumbled for the bedside lamp, rubbed her eyes and tried to work out what had disturbed her. It was a while before she remembered the mobile phone Theo had given her. She leaped out of bed and, too late, remembered her ankle. Agonising pain shot through her and she limped over to the dressing-table. She looked at the compact little device wondering how to switch it on, then pressed a likely button and heard Theo's voice.

'Izzy,' he said, 'is that you?'

'Yes.'

'You sound sleepy. Were you in bed? It's very early. Are you unwell?'

'No, I'm not unwell, just tired. The last twenty-four hours have been rather hectic.' She told him about Nick and Sally.

'Dear God in heaven, that's terrible. And Mark actually went into the water to rescue Sally?'

'Theo,' she said, 'I might be being silly, but I'm worried about Mark. He told me last night of his fear of water, about the friend of his who drowned when he was a boy. And after he'd saved Sally, it was obvious he was in a state of shock, and since then nobody has seen him. Angelos called at the villa today and said there was no sign of him.'

'You're right to be worried, Izzy. I'll ring him now and call you back later.'

Within minutes the mobile was ringing again. 'I can't get an answer from him, Izzy. Now, please, it is a lot to ask of you, I know, but will you do me a favour? There is a key under a flowerpot by the door at the back of the house. I want you to go inside and make sure that my friend is all right. If he is angry that you have invaded his privacy, tell him it is his own fault. Tell him he should have answered the phone. But whatever the outcome, call me. My number is on my desk in my study.'

Chapter Thirty-Nine

Izzy hadn't told Theo the one important factor that was going to make her mission nigh on impossible – her re-injured ankle. The doctor who had checked out Sally had also taken a look at her and told her what she knew already: she was back to square one, and rest, plenty of it, was the only cure. Fortunately she still had the crutches and with these, she was now making slow progress down the path and along the hillside to Theo's house; concentrating hard on not missing her footing in the dark. Also, she was trying to suppress the fear that something terrible had happened to Mark. Without him having said as much, she knew that Theo's concern for him was the same as hers; that the shock of what he had made himself do last night might have had him knocking back a restorative drink. A restorative drink that might have done him untold harm.

Her daunting journey complete, she leaned against the gate to Theo's villa physically and mentally exhausted. Her whole body ached from the effort, and she stood for a moment to catch her breath, to rub away the tension in her shoulders and to rest her good leg. Ahead of her, and beneath a star-pricked sky, the low-roofed house was in darkness. The bushes around her stirred in the mild breeze, and far off in the distance she could hear a dog barking.

She pressed on to the door Theo had told her to use, flashed the torch over the steps and saw the pot he had mentioned. He hadn't thought to tell her how large it was, though, or that it contained a hydrangea that came up almost to her waist. Resting the crutches against the wall, she bent down and tried to rock the pot to one side. Angelos must have watered it that day for it was damp and even heavier than she expected. She gave it another shove and tilted it sufficiently to grab the key before letting it down with a heavy thud. Wiping the moist soil off her hands, she raised the key to the lock, then hesitated. Shouldn't she give Mark the opportunity to open the door rather than blunder in and perhaps embarrass him? He might have chosen to do nothing more worrying than shut himself away for the day to work.

The most rational explanation was that he wasn't in, that he was enjoying a late supper in Kassiópi. Or, like her, he had simply gone to bed early.

As plausible as these suggestions were, they didn't satisfy her.

She gave a gentle tap at first, then a more vigorous knock. 'Mark, are you in there? It's me, Izzy.' Not getting any response, she inserted the key and turned the handle. She stood in the dark, eerie silence, getting her bearings in a house she had only ever been inside twice before. Closing the door behind her, she thought she heard a noise, and suddenly she was scared, her heart in her mouth, her brain conjuring up chilling murder scenes from the books she had read of late. 'Irrational,' she muttered under her breath. 'Get a grip.' She crossed the stone floor of the sitting room and went towards the kitchen, where she thought the noise had come from.

She found him hunched over the kitchen table, his head clasped in his hands. He was so still, she thought for a moment that he was asleep. Then a worse thought hurtled into her head . . . that he was dead. 'Mark?'

He raised his head slowly and revealed a face of gaunt agony. His skin was grey and lined, his eyes dull and bloodshot, distant, unseeing. His hair was awry from where he must have been raking his hands through it, and it gave him a wild, almost manic appearance. He was dressed in the clothes he had worn last night; crinkled and patchy with salt, they smelled of stale sweat and vomit. But, thank God, there was no smell of alcohol on him. 'Mark,' she said, 'please, what can I do to help?'

He pressed the heels of his hands to his eyelids as if to clear his thoughts and summon the energy to speak to her. 'If you could bear it, would you hold me, please?' he murmured. His voice was thick, a faint husk of a whisper, and the pain in it made her react at once. Very gently, she took him in her arms, cradled his head against her and absorbed the tremor that was running through him. They stayed like that for an age, disconnected from time or their surroundings; it might have been for ten minutes, it might have been for ever.

The shrill ringing of the telephone made them both start.

'I know who it will be,' said Izzy, reluctantly releasing him. She moved across the kitchen on her crutches to the phone that hung on the wall beside the tall American-style fridge.

'I couldn't take the suspense,' said Theo. 'Is he all right? Please, God, say he's well and ready to abuse me with a tirade of foul language for my interference.'

'Yes and no,' she said truthfully. 'Hold on a moment.' She covered the receiver with her hand. 'It's Theo, Mark. Will you speak to him, please? Just put his mind at rest that you're okay. He knows about you rescuing Sally.'

He came stiffly to the phone and took it from her. 'It's okay, Theo,' he said tiredly, 'I haven't done anything silly. I'm just a bit out of it, that's all. Was it you who sent me the guardian angel? Well, how else would she have known about the key? And, no, of course I'm not mad with you. I'm more grateful than I can say. Look, I'll

374

speak to you tomorrow. Now isn't the time. Yeah, cheers, mate.'

He put the phone back on the wall and turned to Izzy.

'You're not cross I came, are you?' she asked nervously.

'How could I be?'

'Why didn't you open the door when I called to you?'

He dragged his hands over his face, distorting his features. 'I don't know. It was as if I was paralysed. I haven't been able to think straight all day . . . not since last night.' As if noticing the crutches for the first time, he said, 'What have you done to your ankle?'

Sensing that he wasn't ready yet to discuss what he had gone through, she told him. 'But that's not important. I'm more concerned about you. Have you eaten anything today?'

'No.' He looked down at himself and shook his head wearily. 'I'm sorry, I must look and smell pretty disgusting.'

'Nothing that a shower won't put right. Do you think you can manage that?'

While he was in the shower, Izzy put his clothes into the washing-machine and set it whirring. She made him some tea and took it through to his bedroom, doing her best not to spill it on Theo's expensive rugs as she made the precarious journey on one crutch from one end of the villa to the other, taking in a couple of steps and a narrow archway that she had to tackle sideways on.

His bedroom came as a surprise. It was meticulously tidy: there were no clothes lying around, no coins, pens or combs cluttering the surfaces, no book left face down with its spine cracked, no socks lurking in the corner of the room, not even a pair of shoes left haphazardly on the floor. The white cotton sheets on the bed were unwrinkled and the pillows perfectly placed – clearly Mark hadn't slept there the previous night. As she pulled the top sheet back in readiness for him, he appeared behind her in a clean pair of boxer shorts and a black REM T-shirt. He still looked tired and haggard, but there was a reassuring glimmer of light in his eyes now.

'I know this will sound like the worst chat-up line in the history of come-ons,' he said, smoothing back his hair and casting his gaze over the bed, 'but would you stay with me tonight?'

She tried to keep the shock from her face, but must have failed miserably, for he said, 'Slow down, Izzy, I don't mean it in the way you're thinking. I . . . I just don't want to be alone. I'd like to know that you were there.'

'Okay,' she said, 'if you think it would help.'

He gave her one of his T-shirts and she changed in the bathroom. He had already turned out the lamp when she joined him, but in the moonlight that peeped in through the shutters at the open window, she could see that his eyes were closed. She could also see the harsh contours of his ravaged face, which betrayed his suffering. He must have spent that day reliving an experience he would never be able to obliterate fully from his memory. It struck her then, as odd a thought as it was, that she had never come up with one of her silly celeb-lookalikes for him. It's because he's unique, she thought. He's a man like no other. And, thinking that he might already have dozed off, she slipped noiselessly under the sheet beside him. But he wasn't asleep and with his back to her, he said, 'Thank you for doing this, Izzy.' She moved a little closer and placed an arm tenderly around him. She felt his shoulder quiver and realised just how tense he still was. Gradually she sensed his thin, angular body relax, until finally he fell asleep.

She lay wide awake in the semi-darkness, listening to his uneven breathing, wondering at the extraordinary situation she had got herself into. Could this really be Izzy Jordan, that well-known shall-I-shan't-I ditherer; the proponent *par excellence* of 'Oh, I couldn't possibly do that'; the neurotic woman who listened to voices in her head for guidance? Come to think of it, Modern Woman and Prudence Jordan had been slacking recently.

Didn't her mother have anything to say about her scandalously immoral daughter, who was currently lying in bed with a former addict.

'Well, I don't care what you think,' she imagined herself saying to her mother. 'Mark might have had more than his fair share of problems, but he's the first man I feel truly comfortable with.'

She thought about this, and realised it was true. What's more, she trusted him, or more precisely, she had trusted herself to trust again. He was so honest, so direct. And so easy to be with. There was no chicanery to him. She never felt as though he was setting a trap for her.

With these thoughts running through her head, she soon fell asleep and dreamed that she was back in the children's home. She was standing anxiously at the window waiting for her father to appear through the snow. Except it wasn't her father who arrived to see her, it was Mark, and she wasn't a child, she was an adult. He was helping her to put away the box of Fuzzy-felt shapes, telling her that the tears always dry. No matter how many tears, they all dry in the end.

Beams of early-morning sunlight were penetrating the shutters, enabling Mark to watch Izzy as she slept next to him. With her hair swept back from her face, she looked so peaceful, and so very beautiful. But there was something different about her that he couldn't quite put his finger on. Then he understood what it was. He had never seen her with her hair pulled back from her forehead before. He noticed an ugly two-inch scar just into the hairline of her right temple and wondered how somebody so intrinsically cautious could have received such an injury. A car accident perhaps? He winced at the thought and dispelled it immediately. He didn't want to imagine her coming to any harm.

Last night on the phone with Theo, he had referred to Izzy as his guardian angel, and even now, this morning, when he was thinking straight at last, he could think of no better description. Goodness knows how much longer he would have remained sitting in that petrifyingly inert state if she hadn't turned up. The awful horror of being so vividly reminded of Niall's death had disarmed him of the power of reasoned thought. All his brain would allow him to focus on was that he had so very nearly failed again. And he would have failed if it hadn't been for Izzy: if she hadn't had the sense to use Max's boat that girl would have died. Him too, probably.

But that wasn't entirely why he had lost it yesterday. Coming up from the beach, after his explosive outburst at that idiot Patterson boy, he had come face to face with temptation for the first time in years. The craving for a drink had hit him so suddenly, had been so strong, it had completely freaked him out. Cold fear had made him nauseous and he had only just made it in time to the villa before he was violently ill. He was shaking, and sweat poured off him. Shocked at the strength of the craving, he hadn't trusted himself to move from the chair in the kitchen, terrified that just a single step might take him to where he knew Theo kept his hoard of oúzo and Metaxá. And, as he desperately fought to keep his nerve, his mind had swirled in the vortex of Niall's drowning and his funeral. Mark's parents hadn't wanted him to attend it, they had said he was too young, that he had already gone through enough, but he had insisted on going. Afterwards he had wished he hadn't. Niall's mother had been distraught with grief-stricken anguish. She sobbed throughout the service in the little church, loudly and without restraint, and later collapsed against her husband at the graveside. Mrs Percival's inconsolable sorrow had left an indelible impression on his tormented mind. Even so young he had felt the need to comfort these heart-broken people, to take their grief from them. But what could he offer them when he was a living reminder of all they had lost? They never said anything, but he could see it in their eyes, the bitter reproach – Why couldn't it have been you who drowned? And in that moment, as he had stared at them across the gaping hole in the ground, the body of his friend just feet away, Mark would have given anything to trade his life for their son's.

And, of course, for the best part of twenty years that was exactly what he tried to do. If it hadn't been for Theo, he might have succeeded.

What a lot he had to thank Theo for.

Then, gazing down at Izzy's sleeping face, he thought that he had a lot to thank her for too. He couldn't remember much about being on the boat with her, but he could recall the determined way in which she had worked to bring Sally back from the dead. To his shame, he had been convinced her efforts were in vain.

Turning his thoughts to last night, a flicker of a smile crossed his face as he thought of Izzy's endearingly prim expression when he had asked her to stay with him. Only twenty-four hours earlier he had been fantasising about getting her into bed, but last night all he had wanted was to feel her arms around him so that he would sleep, and surer still that she would keep him safe . . . safe from the weakness that would always be with him. To his amazement, she had trusted him enough to do as he asked.

Few people had ever really trusted him, and who would blame them? Not so long ago he had lied, cheated and stolen from his own family and friends, but here he was, lying next to this innately good person who trusted him implicitly.

And if Izzy trusted him so completely, what did he feel for her?

Difficult to say.

Or was it?

Didn't being with her make perfect sense? Hadn't he always, right from the start, felt comfortable with her? And hadn't he looked forward to their chats on the beach? And what of his writing? Wasn't it time now to be honest about his use of her in his book? Pretending that she was nothing but a lucky hit of inspiration was a classic example of deluded thinking that would fool no one. That was the real reason why he hadn't told Theo the truth behind his new-found roll of creativity. Theo would see straight through him.

So what did it all mean? That while he had been setting her up as the love interest for his protagonist in his novel he had been nurturing a whacking great desire to sleep with her?

Or did it go deeper than that?

Did he see something in her that was lasting and emotionally satisfying? The potential for a long-term relationship, perhaps?

It was a little after nine o'clock when Izzy woke. Her first thought was of Mark, and seeing that the other side of the bed was empty, she didn't bother to dress but went in search of him.

He was outside in the garden, sitting on the low white wall in the bright sunshine. Dressed and shaved, he was looking better than he had last night, much more his normal self. He smiled when he saw her and came to meet her in the shade of the terrace as she leaned on her crutches, wishing she could be rid of them and fling her arms around him.

'How are you feeling?' she asked.

He kissed her cheek. 'A little wobbly, but a lot better . . . thanks to you.'

'I didn't do very much. I only—'

He silenced her with a kiss, this time on the lips. 'You were there when I needed you. So do me the kindness of accepting my thanks with good grace. Breakfast?'

'Just a mug of tea would do.'

'Tea it is, then. And don't even think of following me. Sit down and allow yourself to be waited on.'

It was a beautiful day. The sky was vast and uncompromisingly clear, and beneath it the sea stretched away into a hazy infinity of shimmering blue. A delicate warm breeze fanned the leaves on the nearby olive tree, and down in the bay, the sound of waves breaking gently against the rocks accompanied the early-morning shift of cicadas, who were already in fine voice. It was a glorious morning and contrasted sharply with the disturbing events of the last couple of days.

During the night Izzy had heard Mark moaning in his sleep, as if caught in the grip of some deeply rooted terror. Once or twice she had reached out to him, tried to soothe him, but it had had no effect.

'I've made you some toast,' he said, reappearing sooner that she had expected, 'just in case you were being polite.'

She looked at the tray he was carrying. 'Toast as well as chicken tikka masala. You were holding back on me.'

'Doesn't do to give too much away too soon.' He sat opposite, picked up a mug of tea to pass to her, but paused with it mid-air. 'You know, I really am grateful for last night. If it hadn't been for you I might . . . Well, who knows what I might have been driven to do?'

She took the mug from him. 'It's Theo who deserves the thanks. He phoned me and when I told him how concerned I was because nobody had seen you he made me come and make sure you were okay.' She took a small sip of her tea and added, 'He's a very good friend to you.'

'I know. Which makes what I feel for you all the more complicated.'

Not looking at him, or asking what exactly it was that he felt for her, she said, 'I would never want to come between the two of you.'

'It wouldn't come to that.' And changing the subject, he said, 'So tell me, how's Sally?'

She told him that Sally had been given a clean bill of health by the doctor Max had called out, about the Pattersons coming to see them, and how everyone had left yesterday afternoon.

'Leaving you home alone?'

'I did suggest that maybe I should cut short my holiday, but Max and Laura wouldn't hear of it. They said they'd be back soon and that everything would return to how it was. Laura will probably come ahead of Max, so I shan't be on my own for too long.'

'I'm glad they persuaded you to stay on . . . and that you're alone.'

She raised her eyes and met his. They were the same colour as the sky above them, just as clear, just as breathtakingly beautiful. 'I'm glad too,' she murmured.

His lips twitched with a smile. 'Eat your toast and stop flirting with me, Izzy.'

She feigned indignation. 'I wasn't flirting with you. The very thought.'

'Yes you were, and unless you want to find yourself being carried off to bed, I'd advise you to go easy on any more direct eye-contact.'

'Are you threatening me?'

'No, merely propositioning you.'

'Oh, I don't think that's ever happened to me before. So, what you're saying is, if I behave myself we'll just carry on having a quiet breakfast together. Whereas if—'

Slowly rising from his chair, he came round to her side of the table. 'Whereas if you keep looking at me the way you are, I'll have no choice but to do something about it. It's entirely up to you.'

She pushed herself to her feet, smiled flirtatiously and hooked her hands around his neck. 'Well, in that case, ready when you are.'

Laughing, he picked her up, carried her inside and lowered her on to the bed where they had slept the night. He kissed her lovingly, but when she began to remove what little clothing she was wearing, he waved her hands aside. 'How about you let me handle that, Izzy? I think I can remember what to do.'

Chapter Forty

'So tell me again about this dunderhead Alan who didn't know a G-spot from his Air on a G-string?'

It was a week later and they were by the pool, following a failed attempt at taking an afternoon nap – a siesta seemed such a waste to Mark when there were other things he would much rather be doing with Izzy. Now, as he rubbed sun cream on to her back, he felt pretty damn smug with himself. More than once in the last few days he had thought of Bones's words about knowing when the right buttons had been pressed and, credit where credit was due, the man had known his stuff. Lying in the drowsy afterglow of their first time in bed together, Izzy had left him in no doubt that the buttons had been well and truly pressed. Not just once, but several times. 'Do it again, Mark,' she had sighed, her arms wrapped around him.

'I'm not as young as you, Izzy.' He had laughed. 'I need to rest up for a while.'

'No, you don't,' she had murmured, her lips brushing his ear, while one of her hands drifted across his chest, caressing his hot skin with light, sensual movements. She soon proved him wrong – that he was in no need of rest – and later, when they had refuelled on supplies brought in on a tray from the kitchen and they were sitting cross-legged on the bed, she had told him about her last boyfriend, who had convinced her that she was a non-starter when it came to sex.

'Well, if you'd like me to write him a letter disputing

that theory of his,' he had told her, as he trailed a finger over the smooth curve of her shoulder, 'I'd be more than pleased to do so.'

Taking his hand and kissing each of his fingertips, she said, 'You know what? I couldn't give a damn what he thought about me.'

'Tut tut, Miss Jordan, you're using language your mother wouldn't approve of.'

'I think I'm doing a lot more that my mother wouldn't approve of.'

'Time to extend the list, then. I'd hate to short-change her. What shall we play now?' And manoeuvring her on to her back, he had begun kissing her, working his mouth down the length of her body.

'No, Mark, not again.'

'You're only saying that.'

'Oh, go on, then.'

'A little more enthusiasm, if you wouldn't mind . . .'

'Why do you want to know so much about that rat?' she asked now, and in answer to his question.

'No reason.'

'You're lying, Mark.'

'Oh, gee, you're too smart for me, Izzy. But it's a guy thing, you wouldn't appreciate it.'

She turned over and sat up. 'Try me.'

He screwed the lid back on the sun-tan lotion. 'Okay,' he conceded, 'it makes me feel incredibly good about myself to know that where he couldn't cut the mustard I can. Makes me sound a bit of a rat as well, doesn't it?' he added.

She smiled. 'Like you said, it's a guy thing.'

'Not cross with me, then?'

'No, not cross with you.'

'Good, because I couldn't think of anything worse. I'd have to spend the rest of the day on my hands and knees grovelling to you. I'd have to raid every florist's on the

island and surround you with flowers of apology. I'd
have to dream up so many extravagant gestures of love
that you'd—'

'Throwing your money at me now, are you?'

'I might not look the part, but Theo's not the only one
with bags of gold under his mattress.'

'Is that so?'

He caught the edge of mockery to her voice. 'Hey, I'm
a household name, didn't you know?'

'What, like Andrex?'

He laughed. 'Phew, for a moment there I was running
the risk of being in awe of myself.'

Angelos paid them a visit later that afternoon while Mark
was working. He brought with him a carrier-bag of
home-grown tomatoes and cucumbers, and after checking the pool, he went round the garden watering Theo's
beloved plants. He hadn't said anything, but Mark knew
that Angelos and his wife must have guessed what was
going on between him and Izzy: they couldn't have failed
to notice that she was never at Villa Petros and that only
one bed at Villa Anna was being slept in. He hoped to
God that Theo had no cause to get in touch with either
Angelos or Sophia while he was in Athens: he didn't want
his friend to hear the news from anyone but him. Initially
he had thought that it would have to be done face to face
when Theo returned, but it was proving so difficult for
either of them to talk to Theo on the phone without
feeling guilty that this morning they had agreed they
couldn't keep lying to him, that they would have to break
it to him the next time he called.

They had gone to ridiculous lengths to keep the truth
from Theo, each of them chatting separately with him on
the phone – Izzy spoke to him on the mobile he had given
her, and Mark on one of the phones inside the house.
There had been no question of Mark staying with Izzy at

Max and Laura's place: after last week, when Mark hadn't answered the phone, Theo was now keeping a regular tab on him, calling most evenings when he had finished work and had returned to his apartment. 'You really don't have to do this, Theo,' Mark had told him, only last night.

'I know that, but I want to. It serves you right for frightening me so badly. I've just been talking to Izzy. She sounded odd to me. Is she lonely without Max and Laura, do you think?' And to make Mark feel even more of a conniving bastard, Theo had asked him to keep an eye on her. 'For some unaccountable reason she likes you, so maybe you could go and see her and cheer her up.'

'Yeah, I'll see what I can do.'

'So how is the work going? You are still writing at speed?'

'Like a rocket on high-octane fuel.'

'Excellent. I have a feeling this book will be your best, Mark. The muse is performing well for you, eh? Long may it continue.'

It was a sentiment he privately echoed. Izzy was the perfect muse. Though she was with him so much of the day and night, she was no distraction. When he wanted to work she was more than happy to sit reading quietly or go for a swim in Theo's pool. Often she would get out her drawing and painting things and sit for hours dabbling, as she modestly called it. Yesterday he had turned the page of his notepad and caught her sketching him. When he insisted that she showed him what she had done, he had been amazed by how well she had captured his likeness. 'You've made me look very serious,' he said. 'Couldn't you have given me a smile?'

'But you weren't smiling at the time, you were deep in concentration. That was what I was trying to show. And anyway, the Prince of Darkness can't wear a cheekychappy grin when he's exploring the dark night of the soul.'

It was then that he decided to come clean about using her for his novel.

'Do I die?' she asked, in that candid way she did sometimes.

'I haven't decided.'

'What? You don't know the outcome of the book?'

'Not in this instance.'

'Oh, well, if it's all the same to you, I'd prefer to live.'

'I'll see what I can do.'

Her only frustration was that he wouldn't let her go wandering off on her own. Her ankle was a lot stronger now – she no longer needed the crutches, and was able to go for short walks – but he wouldn't hear of her going far. 'Quit the wheedling and the pouty look, Izzy. What if you fell and couldn't make it back?'

'I'd rely on you coming to find me.'

'Forget it. I've done all the carrying up and down that bloody hillside I'm ever going to do. One more session like that and I'll give myself a hernia. And what use would I be to you, then? Satisfying your insatiable sexual appetite will be the last thing I'll be good for.'

Her mouth dropped open and the colour rushed to her face.

He loved the way he could still shock and embarrass her. 'Too late now to be feigning a chaste innocence, Izzy. Remember, it's in my arms that you show your true colours.'

Apart from Angelos and Sophia, and Izzy's chats with Max and Laura on the phone, they hadn't seen or spoken to anyone else. They had caught the odd glimpse of the Patterson boys on the beach, but had seen nothing of the runaway lovers – if it really was them staying here, and Mark had his doubts – or the Fitzgeralds, not that he expected Dolly-Babe to come calling. Not now. Izzy had told him about the olive grove Theo had bought from under Bob's nose and he had asked Theo on the phone why he hadn't thought to mention it to him.

'What was there to tell? I bought a piece of land. It is not the first or the last investment I will make without running it by you for your approval.'

'So there was nothing vindictive in what you did?'

'Vindictive? You think protecting my immediate environment from being developed into a cheap and nasty resort is an act of malicious intent on my part?'

'You're deliberately missing the point. Did you enjoy getting one over Dolly-Babe and Silent Bob because they treated you like an ignorant oik?'

'But, Mark, it is you who are deliberately missing the point. I stole nothing from them, they did not own the land, it was not theirs.'

'True, and now it's yours.'

'Yes, now it's mine. And as you so often say, once again I have had my own way.'

Angelos wound up the hose and put it back into the store cupboard where he kept the rest of his garden tools and the chemicals for the pool, then waved and was gone.

Izzy raised her arms above her head and stretched languidly. 'I suppose I ought to write to my mother.' She sighed.

Mark finished constructing the sentence he had in his head, got it down on paper and said, 'And tell her what?'

'That the weather is still hot and sunny and that I'm still having a wonderful time.'

'Nothing about meeting a devilishly attractive man who's fast developing a compulsive disorder to have sex with you every other hour.'

'Mm . . . Perhaps I'll keep that for the next missive.'

He smiled at her dead-pan expression, noting that she

was learning to parry his attempts to make her blush. 'How often do you write to your mother?'

'As often as my conscience gets the better of me.'

'So how many times since you've been here on holiday? To the nearest unit of ten will do.'

'You horrible man.'

'It's taken years of counselling to hone me down to this level of astuteness. But I reckon I could whittle you into shape by 2050.'

She pulled a face. 'I'll be an old woman by then. What a dreadful thought.'

'Spare a thought for me. In eight years' time I'll be eligible to go on a Saga holiday.'

She laughed, leaned over and kissed him. 'Now, that I'd like to see.'

He pulled her on to his lap. 'Then you'd best stick around, kidda.'

He worked steadily for the rest of that afternoon, his mind flying along with the plot. If there was any one thing he wanted to get across in his novels, it was that a society that underestimates the destructive nature within each and every one of its members was a society beyond help. By exploring man's most basic flaws – those of wanting to be in a position of power and the need for recognition – he wanted to prove that murderers aren't a different species, that they are *us*. That they do not, contrary to popular opinion, walk around giving off an unmistakable air of evil, enabling everybody else to give them a wide berth. More often than not, the most successful murderers are clever, charming and seductive, with a chameleon-like ability to switch from apparent good to abhorrent evil.

Creating a monster on the page was no problem to him; it came more easily than crafting the victims. He always found it perfectly straightforward to justify why somebody had committed a heinous crime. Essentially he saw his novels not so much as whodunits but as whydunits, which peeled away the layers of deceit, corruption and greed to get to the truth. He particularly liked the idea of shaking the reader out of any complacency he might harbour about his own safe little world. Yes, my friend, this really could be you! But for the grace of God, it might have been you who turned into the monster who murders, rapes and molests.

It had always intrigued him that, when studying the mind of a criminal, there was no denying the recognisable facets of one's own personality staring back at one. He had been talking to Izzy about this in bed the other night when she had asked him about the theme of his latest book – normally he hated to discuss what he was currently working on. 'It's about a man who survived a classroom massacre when he was a boy,' he had told her. 'By wrestling the killer to the floor, he saved the rest of his classmates from being butchered.'

'So he's the hero, the goodie?'

Smiling at her black-and-white simplification of good versus bad, he had said, 'Well, he was the hero then, but now he's the baddie.'

'But why?'

'He never truly recovered from the trauma. I mean, would any of us survive mentally unscathed from such an ordeal? Clinically speaking he's psychotic, out of touch with reality.'

'But what makes him want to kill?'

'Oh, the usual, voices in the head. Visions.'

She had chewed her lower lip. 'I have voices in my head.'

'I'll wager they're not on the scale I'm talking about.'

'So what's this book going to be called?'

'*Flashback Again*. And before you ask why, it's because the killer starts suffering from flashbacks to the time he survived the massacre. He believes it's a call for him to track down the other survivors and kill them.'

She had flinched, then rolled on top of him, and said, 'Just think, I'm in bed with the strange man who creates all this despicable horror.'

He had pulled the sheet over her head and growled in her ear, 'Be very afraid, Izzy. Be very afraid.'

The evening sky was a glorious infusion of indigo that had seeped into swathes of bright sapphire. Stars pricked at the darker patches and the moon, still quite low, spilled its light across the shimmering sea. Thinking how glad he was that he had accepted Theo's offer to spend the summer with him, Mark tried to recall when, if ever, he had been so relaxed and happy.

He had arrived here in June, as nervy and jumpy as hell, half frightened to death of his own shadow, but now look at him. It was ages since he had given his *Silent Footsteps* copy-cat stalker any thought, and now that he had successfully distanced himself from what had been going on at home, he felt he had been an idiot to let it get the better of him.

The only cloud hanging over him now was making his confession to Theo. During supper, he and Izzy had decided that tonight was definitely the night. Out of the corner of his eye, he caught Izzy glancing apprehensively at the mobile on the table between them. 'Let's not wait for him to ring us,' he said decisively, 'let's call him and get it over and done with.'

She checked her watch. 'Do you think he'd be home this early?'

'We could give it a try.' He reached for the phone and tapped in Theo's number. It rang and rang, and just as he was on the verge of giving up, he heard Theo's slightly breathless voice. This was it, then.

'Theo, it's Mark. Is it a good time to talk?'

'It's fine, but wait a moment while I pour myself a drink. I've just this minute got in. You would not believe how hot Athens is.' Hearing the clink of ice against glass, Mark could almost smell the oúzo Theo was pouring as he moved about his apartment carrying his cordless phone with him. 'There, that's better. Now I am sitting down and I am all yours. There is nothing wrong, I hope?'

'Why do you say that?'

'It's just that it is so rare for you to ring me. How is Izzy? Have you seen her today? Did you do as I asked? Have you cheered her up?'

'Um . . . yes, in a manner of speaking. And . . . and she's very well. Oh, hell, Theo, there's no easy way to tell you this, I just hope you can forgive me.'

'Why, what have you done?' Theo's tone was instantly wary.

'I'm sorry, Theo, but I've—' He stalled hopelessly. He cleared his throat, tried again. 'The thing is, Izzy and I . . . well, we've kind of been seeing each other.'

The silence said it all.

Mark's gaze locked with Izzy's and she squeezed his hand. 'Say something, Theo. I'm getting the feeling you could beat the hell out of me.'

Still nothing.

'Would it help if I got down on my knees and said I was sorry?'

'Oh, please, save the theatrical drama for your novels.'

'Look, you have to believe me, I didn't mean to do it. It wasn't deliberate, I couldn't help myself.'

'Or stop yourself, it would seem.'

Mark had never heard Theo's voice so cold. 'You're right,' he muttered, 'I couldn't.'

Another silence.

Until, 'How long have you been *kind of seeing* Izzy, as you so delicately put it?'

'Since the night of the party.' It was almost the hardest part of the confession, letting Theo know that the deceit had been going on for as long as it had.

'And . . . and do you think it is serious between the pair of you?'

Mark kept his gaze on Izzy's anxious face. 'Yes. Much to my amazement, I think it is.'

'Then it is settled. There is nothing more to be said.'

'Of course there is, and don't you dare try taking that line with me, Theo.'

'Which line would you prefer me to take?' The coldness had thawed, and in its place was dry cynicism.

'I don't know. But one that ensures our friendship isn't damaged.'

There was another lengthy pause, during which Mark heard the clink of ice again. In his mind's eye, he saw Theo swirling the glass round in his hand, tilting back his head and draining the drink in one. But then he heard the unexpected sound of laughter. 'Theo?'

'It is all right, my friend, I am just beginning to see the funny side of it.'

'You are?'

'Yes. You have never before coveted anything I had or aspired to anything I have accomplished, and yet here you are, stealing the prize that, quite possibly, I wanted most.'

'It wasn't like that.'

'I know, but let a defeated man have his pride. Is Izzy there with you?'

'Yes, she is.'

'If she will speak to me, put her on.'

Mark passed the phone to Izzy. 'It's okay,' he whispered, 'the worst is over.'

'Theo,' she said, 'I'm sorry, truly I am. We never intended—'

'Ah, Izzy, come on now. All is fair in love and war and,

besides, you were always honest with me, you did not deliberately mislead me. It is I who have misled myself. But to show you how magnanimous I can be, Mark is my best friend and, more than anyone, I know that he deserves somebody as special as you. Now take good care of one another. And, please, do try to have a civilising effect on him for me.'

'I'll do my best.'

They went to bed that night and lay in each other's arms with a clear conscience at last. But when they woke the following morning, a clear conscience was the last thing on their minds.

Chapter Forty-One

They were roused by the sound of insistent knocking.

'If that's Angelos with another bag of cucumbers, I'll swing for him,' fumed Mark. He pulled on a pair of shorts and stomped off to answer the door. Izzy hurried after him. If Angelos was about to get it in the neck from Mark she ought to be on hand to defuse the situation.

But it wasn't Angelos. It was two men they had never seen before. One was young and red-haired, in tight jeans and a black tank top, and the other was in shorts with hairy white legs; his face was hidden behind a camera – a camera that was making a fast, mechanical whirring sound.

'Mark St James?' enquired Carrot Top, a notebook and pen emerging from his back pocket. 'Didn't wake you, did we?' The camera whirred again.

'What the—' Then, changing tack, Mark hurriedly started to close the door. But he wasn't fast enough. A foot was already in place.

'Just a few words, that's all.' Another whirr from the camera.

'What about?'

'It's about your neighbours across the bay, Christine and Mikey. You did know they were staying here, didn't you?'

'What if I did?'

'Oh, come on,' urged Carrot Top, 'it's the story of the summer. Give us a break. You know what a tough business this is. A word or two is all I need.' Izzy guessed he had slipped into what he imagined was his congenial let's-be-mates-about-this routine. 'Bet your publisher wouldn't say no to a bit of free publicity for you, eh?'

'What my publisher wants doesn't necessarily correlate with what I want. But if it's my neighbours' story you're after, go and see them. I'm sure they'd be as delighted to see you as I am.'

'We can't get near them. They've barricaded themselves in.'

'You do surprise me.'

'So, then, how about it? Why not help us out?'

'Well, boys, I'd love to, but it's like this, I know damn all. Now, if it occurs to me that I could be of any assistance, I'll let you know. Now have a nice day, y'all.'

Izzy had to stop herself laughing at the tone Mark was using. If he put any more syrupy sarcasm into his words they'd be able to make flapjacks with them!

'This your girlfriend, then?' asked Carrot Top, his tactics changing abruptly.

'That's none of your business.'

'Like to say a few words?' Carrot Top leaned in towards Izzy. She backed away. Suddenly it didn't seem so funny. 'Oh, go on, don't be shy. It's . . .' he flicked through his notebook '. . . Izzy Jordan, isn't it? Surely you've got a view that you'd like to share with us. And if not that, what about you and Mr St James saving the lives of that young girl and her boyfriend? Not just drunk apparently, they'd been smoking something a bit dodgy, hadn't they? Nasty combination. Lucky for them you were around. I'm sure you don't need me to tell you it's a great story. So, how about it?'

'I think the expression she's hunting for is "no comment",' said Mark firmly. 'So if you'd be so good as to remove your foot from my threshold, I'd be eternally grateful. And if you don't, I'll have to slam the door on it very hard, very painfully. Now, are we through with the small-talk?'

Reluctantly Carrot Top and his sidekick went on their way, leaving Izzy and Mark to speculate on how they had discovered the runaway lovers' hiding place.

'Do you suppose Dolly-Babe actually carried out her threat?' Izzy asked, when they were sure that the coast was clear and they had taken their breakfast outside. 'I would never have had her down as the type to interfere like that. It seems so vindictive and mean-spirited. What's it got to do with her?'

'No doubt she was as keen as the next person to have her fifteen minutes of fame. And, don't forget, one of the tabloids was offering a reward for anyone who could lead them to the star-crossed lovers.'

'Yes, but surely the Fitzgeralds aren't short of money.'

Mark shrugged. 'Who knows? Things aren't always what they seem.' Then, raising Theo's binoculars to his eyes and sweeping them across the bay, he let out a whistle. 'Take a look.' He passed her the glasses.

'I don't believe it,' she said, after she had focused on what he had seen. Squeezed into the garden at the front of the villa the runaway lovers were renting, there was a cluster of men and women. The cans of lager and cameras were a dead giveaway. Tabloid bounty-hunters without a doubt. And, just as Carrot Top had said, it looked as if Christine and Mikey had barricaded themselves in. The villa's bottle-green shutters were resolutely in place providing an impenetrable barrier for the zoom lenses that were trained on the windows for the first sign of movement from within.

Moving her field of vision further up the hillside, Izzy focused on the villa where Dolly-Babe and Silent Bob were staying. 'Oh, my goodness,' she exclaimed.

'What?'

'It's Dolly-Babe. She's posing for the cameras in a

rhinestone-encrusted swimsuit. Lord, you'd think it was *Hello!* taking pictures of her. Here, see for yourself.'

Mark took the binoculars. 'And, if I'm not mistaken, she's being interviewed.' Shifting the glasses a couple of inches to the left, he said, 'Hey, guess what, the same's going on down at the Pattersons' place.'

'What? Ma Patterson in a rhinestone swimsuit?'

'Now, wouldn't that be a sight? No, there's no sign of her. It's your personal cleavage inspector, Pa Patterson, being interviewed.'

As she picked at the bread roll on the table in front of her, Izzy's face was solemn. 'It's not funny, really, is it? And how did that journalist know my name?'

Mark put the binoculars down. 'Odds on that Dolly-Babe has shared more than is necessary. After all, it would be simplicity itself to inveigle any amount of gossip out of her.'

'But why bring us into it? What have we got to do with it?'

'Damn all. But that would never stop a seasoned hack from gathering as much colour and gossip as he could to bulk up a story. You've got to keep in mind that there's no real news back home so they'll get what they can elsewhere. A cheap flight to the sun for a day or two and a nice little scoop for their editor. What do you say to us getting out of here for the day?'

'I'd say let's do it. Let's go somewhere quiet and free of nosy-parkers. How do you fancy Old Períthia?' Old Períthia was the deserted village high in the hills behind Áyios Nikólaos. Max and Laura had taken Corky and Olivia to see it during their visit, but Izzy had missed out on that excursion because she had been resting her ankle.

'Sounds good to me,' said Mark, 'but how will we get there? Is there a bus?'

'We could take Max and Laura's Jeep. She keeps

telling me on the phone that we can use it any time we want.'

'There's just one small snag. Will you be able to drive?' He cast his eyes doubtfully to her ankle.

'I don't see why not. But don't you want to drive? I thought men hated being a passenger when there was an opportunity to get their hands on a steering-wheel.'

'Part of my sordid past, I'm afraid. I was disqualified after smashing into a tree while chemically enhanced. I was lucky to walk away. Cowardice has made me reluctant to reapply for my licence.' He looked uncomfortable, his eyes fixed on some far-off point on the horizon.

'Goodness, you've really lived, haven't you?'

He gave a short laugh. 'Why is it that I can never shock you with my past deeds, Izzy? You're supposed to shake your head and tut with disapproval at my wicked recklessness.'

'Mm . . . would it help if I did?'

But before Mark had a chance to reply, a movement in the oleander bushes to their right distracted him. His glance froze. A figure was slipping away down the hillside; a flash of red hair told them it was Carrot Top.

'Definitely time to get the hell out of here,' Mark said grimly.

The wind snatched at the map in Mark's hands as Izzy drove along the road towards Kassiópi. She had only driven the Jeep a couple of times so she took it slowly, especially when they had passed Kassiópi and Mark instructed her to take the next left towards the village of Loútses. The road narrowed and instantly became steeper. The higher they climbed the fewer cars they saw and, following the twists and turns through the terraced hillside, they eventually came to an open stretch of road that looked back towards Kassiópi and the stark, yellow-ish-brown mountains of Albania across the glimmering sea. It was a magnificent view and Izzy stopped the car so that they could take a look. They stood in the breathless heat and, without the noise of the engine, it was blissfully quiet, save for a faraway church bell that was clanging softly, its mellow timbre blending harmoniously with the sweet soprano trill of birdsong. She reached for her camera from the back seat and took several pictures. When she turned round, Mark snapped his own camera at her. 'Not fair,' she grumbled. 'I wasn't ready.'

'Tough.' He smiled and tapped her head, dislodging her baseball cap.

They drove on, climbing ever higher. The increase in altitude made her ears pop and, not long afterwards, they saw a row of cars parked neatly to one side of the road. But she didn't stop. She was determined to park as near as she could to the deserted village. There was no point in pushing it with her ankle, the less walking she had to do the better. Luck was with her. There was a space at the top of the line of cars, into which she managed to squeeze the Jeep.

They followed the well-trodden path and soon came to the first of the ruins. The small single-storey house had lost its door, but had retained its old wooden shutters. Devoid of paint, and now the colour of ash, they hung crookedly from twisted hinges. Through gaps in the stonework, bushy plants grew in wild abundance. Roof tiles lay scattered on the ground, broken and chipped, some ground to dust. They stepped into the gloomy interior. It was unexpectedly dank and chilly. A musty smell of age and decay mingled with the more forceful stench of cat pee. Izzy tried to imagine what it must have been like when a large, boisterous family had lived here, but she couldn't. This soulless, crumbling little house with its dungeon atmosphere was too far removed from the pretty whitewashed homes she had glimpsed during her holiday, with their starched white lace curtains at sparkling clean windows and beaded curtains at the swept and polished doorways.

She slipped her hand through Mark's. 'It's sad, isn't it,' she murmured, 'to see something so uncared-for?'

He didn't reply but led her back out into the bright sunshine where a young German couple were studying their guidebooks. Exchanging smiles, they went on further towards the centre of the village where there was supposed to be a taverna that served lunches. But instead of heading straight for it, they took a path through yet more ruins, walking at a slow, leisurely pace, perfectly in step with each other. When they came to a low wall, where a large, ancient olive tree lowered its silvery-leafed branches and provided a welcome canopy of shade in the baking heat of the midday sun, they climbed over the wall and lay on the parched grass. Nobody else had ventured this far and they were alone. Breathing in the smell of wild garlic and listening to the persistent thrum of the cicadas, which in the secluded, deserted place seemed even louder than usual, Izzy closed her eyes and wondered how the crazy media circus was getting on back in Áyios Nikólaos.

Was it really possible that Dolly-Babe had blown the whistle, just as she had threatened at the party? And if it had been her who was responsible, why had it taken a week for the press to arrive? And just how much extra gossip was Dolly-Babe being persuaded to part with? She decided she would ring Max and Laura that evening. If there was any danger of those journalists printing the story about Nick and Sally, it would be better if they knew about it in advance. As for old Ma Patterson, she would probably die on the spot at the thought of her cultured Dulwich friends reading about her younger son's holiday escapade.

While Izzy hoped that Nick had learned something from the near tragedy, she also hoped he wouldn't beat himself up over it too much. The anger that had made Mark lash out at the boy that night had shocked her at the time, but given what he had just forced himself to do, she could fully understand it.

During their first day together, Mark had apologised for his loss of control. Not quite meeting her eye, he had said, 'I'm sorry you had to see me like that, but I lost it. If I'd had the strength, God alone knows what I would have done to that boy.' He had gone on to say how impressed he had been with her life-saving skills. 'You were straight into it. When did you learn how to do that?'

'At school. We have to do regular first-aid refresher courses.'

'Just as well you were such a diligent student. Any chance of you practising some more mouth-to-mouth on me?'

They were in bed and leaning on top of her, he had kissed her long and lingeringly, working his tongue deep into her mouth. Lifting his head, he had said, 'And just why the hell did you let that fool of a boyfriend convince you that you were hopeless in bed, Izzy? Take it from me, you're dynamite.' Holding her close, he had swept away the hair from her face and planted a soft kiss on her forehead. Seeing the scar on her temple, he had said 'How did you get that?'

He had made no comment when she had finishing telling him, but kissed her with such gentle tenderness that her body had ached with desire for him.

'What are you thinking of?'

She opened her eyes, turned her head and saw that Mark was looking at her. 'You've a smile on your face that could melt cheese,' he said.

'I was just contemplating the effect your finely tuned bedroom technique has on me.'

'So, I'm good, am I?'

She sighed, 'Oh, more than good. A supreme artist.' But, wanting to tease him, she added, 'Well, not bad for an old guy.'

He groaned. 'It's a terrible thought, but when you were curled up on the sofa watching *Blue Peter*, I was at university.'

'And what were you doing when *I* was at university?'

He thought about this, as though doing the sums on the eleven-year gap between them. He said, 'Hitting the bottle with a vengeance.' He raised himself up on an elbow. 'And what about your own talent in the bedroom? The King of Comedy can only do his best when he's working with the classiest material.'

Without answering, she plucked at a long piece of grass and used it to trace the outline of his jaw and mouth. His lips twitched and he took the grass from her hand and did the same to her. It tickled and she started to laugh. 'No,' he said, when she pushed him away, 'what's sauce for the goose is good for the gander.' But she ignored him, rolled on to his chest, and snatched the piece of grass out of his grasp. 'You're playing with fire, Miss Jordan,' he warned, and suddenly she was on her back and he was lying on top of her and one of his hands was undoing the button on her shorts.

'Mark, *no!*'

'This one's on me, Izzy, treat yourself. Go with it.' His fingers began to move, slowly, expertly.

'But someone might see,' she whimpered, trying desperately to hang on to reason, but already her body was betraying her and responding swiftly to his touch.

'Who cares? Live a little. Have some fun.'

And she did.

Again and again.

Wave after wave of exquisite pleasure.

She lay in stunned silence afterwards, languid and

limp, staring up at the silver leaves dancing in the breeze above them, shocked that he could arouse her so effortlessly. 'That must be an all-time record,' he said, brushing his lips over hers. 'You were over the finishing line before I'd fired the starting gun.'

'It's you. You have this terrible effect on me.'

'I'm glad to hear it, but face facts, my darling, you're a hussy.'

'Oh, Lord, am I?'

'Yes, shamelessly so. But don't ever change, that's just how I like you.'

She closed her eyes. Hussy. It was official; she was a hussy. That's what this gorgeous man with his husky voice and extraordinary life had turned her into. She was a woman who now lay on the sun-baked earth in the scorching heat, experiencing the fastest orgasm known to mankind. She smiled to herself, feeling like the cat who had got more than the cream. How's that for living dangerously? she thought. How's that for dancing naked in the street and kicking over the milk bottles and rattling the dustbin lids? Opening her eyes, she said, 'With Alan I used to fake it, just to hurry things along.'

He lay on his back and laughed loudly. 'Oh, please, keep those confessions coming. I just love to hear them.'

'And what about your previous lovers? Did you have the same effect on them?' She could tell from his silence that she had surprised him.

'Bones asked me much the same question in the clinic,' he said eventually.

'And your answer?'

He shifted his position so that he was sitting with his shoulders resting against the wall. 'As humiliating as it was I had to admit that I made a lousy lover. Probably on a par with your Alan.'

She sat up next to him, her legs stretched out alongside his. Touching the inner side of his thin wrist, she lightly trailed a finger the length of a vein. 'So it was more than just a guy thing, the interest in Alan?'

'Shucks, Izzy, you've caught me out again.'

'So what was the problem?'

'I hadn't met you.'

'No, seriously.'

'I *was* being serious.' He stroked her hand. 'Low self-esteem also played its part, of course. That and the drugs.'

'I thought they kind of buoyed you up, you know, made you want to do it all the more.'

'For some people they do. Maybe in the early stages. But mix it with a barrel-sized cocktail of whisky and vodka and you're lucky if you can walk straight, never mind impress the girls. Cocaine made me feel invincible, as if I was running like the wind, but all I was doing was running on the spot. I was going nowhere.'

'Did no one try to stop you?'

'In the beginning, yes. But you have to remember, I didn't have many friends. Relationships don't last when you're abusing yourself, not when you're self-absorbed and insensitive to anybody else's problems. And, anyway, the few people I knew put my behaviour down to the fact that I'd always been a difficult bastard. Though once I suspected people were looking out for me, I became cunning. I drank on my own, kept things hidden.'

'Even from Theo?'

'Especially from Theo. I couldn't bear to see the disappointment in his face whenever he saw me drunk. He didn't bother with censure, he just tolerated me as though I was a badly behaved child who was letting him down. I'm relieved in a way that he never saw me at my worst, when I thought I could drink myself sober.'

'And what were you like at your worst?'

He let go of her hand and plucked at the parched grass between them. 'Oh, mood swings that covered everything from violent rage to weeping self-pity. A restless and paranoid concern only for myself. A need to put others down before they did it to me. And, most importantly, a hard-nosed determination never to admit I was out of control. I was like the Grand Old Duke of York: when I was up, I was very up and when I was down, I was down on my knees, head in the gutter. I did some pretty awful things and I can't dignify any of them. There are no excuses I can offer.'

Sliding her palm under his hand, she slipped her fingers between his and squeezed them gently. And thinking of the night she had found him all alone in the darkness at Villa Anna, she said, 'Mark, what would happen if you did have a drink?'

'It would probably kill me.' He spoke the words quite calmly, as if he had told her nothing more significant than what time it was. 'I have to accept that I have an addictive personality, and that the programme of recovery I embarked upon all those years ago is with me for life. I'm still in touch with Bones by phone and letter, and once a year I pay him a visit so that he can ask me a lot of absurd questions. He calls it my MOT – Mark's Ongoing Therapy.' He gave her a wry smile. 'Of course, I only go to humour him.'

She smiled too. 'Of course.'

A tiny sparrow flew down from the olive tree above them and landed a few yards from their feet. Keeping very still, they watched it hop towards them as it pecked hopefully, but in vain, at the dusty ground. It soon gave up and flew off in search of more promising pastures.

'So tell me, Izzy. Have I put you off?'

'Put me off what?'

'Getting involved with me.'

'I think I'm already involved with you,' she said softly, and even more faintly, 'heart, body and soul involved.'

'Heart, body and soul,' he echoed, staring straight ahead of him. 'Would that be the same as love?'

Caught between wanting to tear out her heart with her bare hands to give him, and protecting herself from being hurt again, she said, 'I'm not sure. You tell me.'

He turned his head, held her face in his hands, and kissed her lightly. 'We'll have to see, won't we?

That evening back in Áyios Nikólaos, where the bay was now empty of journalists and photographers, Izzy phoned Laura. She was mortified to learn that Max and Laura had already had several newspapers contact them about Sally nearly drowning.

'All we can do is wait and see what they come up with,' Laura said. 'If there's anything to report, we'll fax you a copy first thing in the morning.'

They spent the night at Villa Petros and early the next morning, when they opened the door of Max's den, Izzy and Mark were horrified at what they found: a long roll of printed fax paper stretched right across Max's desk and cascaded down on to the white-tiled floor.

Chapter Forty-Two

It was all there in hideous black and white.

The exposure of Christine and Mikey's whereabouts in Corfu had been thoroughly detailed, including their subsequent return to England, where, and in the words and pictures of the *Sun*, the *Mirror* and the *News of the World*, Mikey had been reunited with his open-armed parents. Most photographs showed a smiling, cocky lad who looked about twenty and who had clearly had the time of his life. In contrast, the *Mail* showed a picture of Christine, her head bent, her shoulders sagging, her eyes hidden behind sunglasses. For her, the fun was over. Not only was she going to have to face her husband and children but, at the insistence of Mikey's parents, the police had every intention of pressing charges. Izzy felt sorry for her: whatever dream she had been chasing, it had now become a fully fledged nightmare.

With the tawdry details of the runaway lovers exhaustively dealt with – and Mikey had not been shy in giving the tabloid boys what they wanted, though one suspected that any moment his canny parents might get Max Clifford involved – the journalists had gone on to fill up the pages with an exposé of what they called, the Jag-and-gin crowd who holidayed in this idyllic part of Corfu and who were apparently abusing local kindness and hospitality with their careless middle-class arrogance.

Not even the fuzzy reproduction quality of the fax machine could take the edge off the disreputable savagery of the journalists' self-righteous knives. Headline after headline, paragraph after paragraph gave a wildly distorted version of who they all were and what they had been up to. Max and Laura were shown to be wealthy, uncaring parents who had slept on while their drunken daughter's drug-taking friend had nearly drowned. Mr and Mrs Patterson were portrayed as parents who had a lax attitude towards the taking of recreational drugs by their out-of-control junkie sons, with Mr Patterson caricatured as a sixties throw-back hippie who made sleazy low-budget documentaries. And the Fitzgeralds – the ex-croupier and the self-made man – were held up as paragons of moral decency for blowing the cover of an evil woman leading an impressionable young boy astray.

Mark had been similarly misrepresented. 'Bestselling Novelist and One-time Addict Mark St James in Drugs Drowning Drama' was one headline.

Izzy could feel Mark's growing annoyance as together they scanned the long roll of paper. There were several photographs of him; one she recognised from the covers of his books, and another of the pair of them standing wide-eyed and startled in the doorway of Theo's villa – she in just a T-shirt, which mercifully covered everything, and him bare-chested and in his shorts. There was a caption describing her as 'Mr St James's Holiday Companion'. It made her sound as though he had found her through an escort agency. But the paragraph that incensed her most was the one that had been put together as a result of Carrot Top eavesdropping on a private conversation. Mark was portrayed as having a cavalier attitude towards his previous problems, that smashing a car into a tree when off his head was an everyday occurrence for him. Furious, Izzy wondered at Carrot Top's nerve. 'It's so wrong,' was all she could say. 'How dare they do this to you?'

'It's how it works.' He threw the paper on to Max's desk and walked away. She didn't go after him, sensing that perhaps he wanted to be alone. Carefully folding the long piece of paper, she placed it neatly on the desk and phoned Max and Laura.

Within seconds Laura had answered. She sounded upset and told Izzy Max was so angry that he had already been in touch with the company lawyer to see if anything could be done. 'I've never seen him so cross,' she said. Izzy could hear that she was close to tears. 'And we've had Sally's parents on the phone. They're livid and blaming us for what happened. They've called us irresponsible.'

'But that's ridiculous. Sally's an adult. It was down to her what she drank or smoked. You mustn't blame yourself, Laura. Promise me that. Do you want me to come back?'

'No, there's no need. Stay there. We'll be joining you as soon as we can next week. We'd come sooner only I've got a doctor's appointment arranged.'

'Nothing wrong, is there?'

'I doubt it, but Max is insisting I get checked out. You know what a worrier he can be. I keep telling him it's my age, but he won't listen. I think he's anxious that it could be something serious. And wouldn't that be the last thing we need on top of all this? How's Mark?'

'Angry.'

'He needn't be. I thought he came out of it a lot better than the rest of us.'

'Yes, but I get the feeling he doesn't like his past being dredged up in such lurid detail.'

'Well, if you get the opportunity go and see that ghastly Dolly-Babe and tell her she ought to be ashamed of herself for what she's done. And to think I almost felt sorry for her at the party. Now all I feel like doing is wringing her scrawny old neck! My only consolation is that she looks such a tart in the photographs of her

411

sprawled on a sun-lounger with all that cellulite on show!'

'You haven't sent any of those pictures. Why not?'

'Oh, didn't I? Well, I certainly meant to. I'll do it when we've finished talking.'

A short while later, the fax machine sprang into life again and Izzy ripped off the length of paper. Laura was right. Dolly-Babe hadn't fared at all well – not so much *Hello!* as *Oh, My Gawd!*

The following morning, because his father couldn't resist reading about himself, Harry was dispatched to the supermarket to buy a copy of every English paper that had arrived in Kassiópi bearing yesterday's news. When he got back to the villa the rest of his family were waiting for him. They each grabbed a paper from him and soon found what they were looking for. Even his mother was eagerly flicking through the pages, despite her earlier protestations that she wouldn't be reduced to such vulgarity.

'I don't believe it,' his father cried. 'They've got my age wrong! How could they think I was sixty?'

'Because you look sixty,' said Virginia. Her tone was cruel and bitter. 'That dreadful Fitzgerald woman has implied that since we're neighbours here, it makes us friends.' Shuddering at the thought, she returned her attention to the paper.

'But sixty!'

'I don't think your age is the issue here, Dad,' snapped Harry. He folded the paper he had been reading and put it aside. 'They've made complete jerks of us.'

'I don't know what you're so worried about, they've barely mentioned you. Probably because you're so boring.'

Harry turned to his brother, tempted, just this once, to put the advantage of his height and weight to good use.

Predictably Nick's subdued sackcloth-and-ashes routine had been all too brief; now he was well on the road to reverting back to his old irritating self. It had been too much to expect that the novelty of the reformed character he had sworn to become would last more than a week. 'Blame by association is enough to be going on with, Nick,' he said. He stood up. 'And if you've got any sense, you'll all realise that what's printed here about our family isn't far off the mark.'

He left them arguing among themselves and headed down to the beach where he sat on the pebbles and stared out at the sea. They were returning home in three days' time and he couldn't wait to leave. Spending the summer with his parents had been a crazy idea. He should never have agreed to it. He should have stuck to his guns and gone backpacking round Turkey.

But if he had done that he would never have met Francesca.

He threw a stone into the water and watched the ripples extend further and further in the calm sea. Nothing happens in isolation, he thought. Everything is connected.

He got to his feet and decided to walk into Kassiópi and ring Francesca from one of the public phones in the harbour. He had held off until now, not wanting to push it with her, but after reading all that stuff in the papers he wanted to see how she and her family were taking it.

Mark said goodbye to his agent and rang off. He had phoned Julian to make sure that his wish to keep his private life out of the press would be respected.

He stood at the kitchen window that overlooked the terrace and wondered whether Izzy would mind if they went back to Theo's villa. They had spent the night here at Max and Laura's so that they could be on hand for the first of the faxes, but now he wanted to get on with some work. He was about to interrupt her shower to ask her this when the phone rang. Though he knew it couldn't be for him, he picked it up anyway. Without preamble, a shrill voice demanded to speak to Isobel Jordan. 'I'm afraid she's busy at the moment,' he said.

'Nothing new in that. She's always too busy to speak to her mother.'

Ah, so here was the infamous Prudence Jordan. He leaned back against the wall and settled in for a chat. 'She's in the shower, Mrs Jordan. Can I get her to return your call?'

'A shower at this time of day? But it's nearly lunchtime.'

'Maybe for you but for us it's well past lunchtime. But, then, we don't have any restrictions on the use of bathrooms here.' He couldn't resist tossing in that final comment just to see how she would react. He heard a sharp intake of breath, and sensed her uncurling herself, like a coiled snake.

'To whom am I speaking?'

He smiled to himself. Now the fun would start. 'My name's Mark, and I'm a friend of your daughter.'

He caught another sharp inhalation of breath. 'You're the one in the newspaper, aren't you? You're the drunk she's hitched herself up with.'

He'd had worse, but as opening accusations went, it wasn't bad. 'She may well have hitched up with me, Mrs Jordan, but as for being a drunk—'

'Oh, don't think you can be clever with me, young man. Just because you're a writer, don't imagine for one moment you can twist my words round to make me look silly.'

'I wouldn't dream of it, not when you're so capable of doing that all on your own.'

He missed her reply as, out of the corner of his eye, he saw Izzy come into the kitchen. Fresh from the shower, she was still wet and wearing only a towel, her hair pulled back sleekly from her face. It made her look even younger. He beckoned her over.

'Who is it?' she mouthed.

'Your mother,' he whispered. 'We're getting along like a house on fire.'

Her eyes opened wide and she clutched at the towel. 'Give it to me, let me speak to her.'

After a brief tussle, he passed her the receiver, and in a voice that he knew was loud enough for Izzy's mother to hear, said, 'Say goodbye to the old witch from me, won't you?'

Izzy visibly paled as she took the receiver. 'No, Mum, he was joking. Of course he didn't mean it.'

'Says who?'

'Please, Mark,' she begged.

He put his head next to hers so that he could hear what was being said.

'What's wrong, Mum? Why have you phoned?'

'I might have known you would try and take the innocent approach, but I suppose you're proud of yourself, aren't you, parading your reputation in the papers for all the world to see? Did you stop to think what people would think? Or how it would make me look? It was your aunt who showed me. She rushed straight here soon as she could to have a gloat at my expense. A drunk and a drug addict, the paper says. How could you, Isobel? He'll be totally unreliable. He'll probably get you hooked as well. He'll lie to you and steal from you, they do that. They can't stop themselves.'

'*Mother!* This is ridiculous. Mark's put all that behind—'

'Well, he would tell you that, wouldn't he? But you know what they say, once a drunk, always a drunk. And he'll have brought all his problems on himself, see if I'm not wrong. Weak-willed, that's what he'll be. But be it on your own head. Don't come crying to me when he's used and abused you. Though God knows what he sees in a simpleton like you. Or perhaps that's the appeal.'

This was too much for Mark, and he wrenched the phone out of Izzy's hand. 'I'm well aware, Mrs Jordan, that you've had problems of your own over the years, but the only one who's using and abusing your daughter is *you*! Now, if you don't mind, I'm going to cut you off so that I can try and undo some of the harm you've caused.'

'Well, really—'

But that was as far as Mark allowed her to go. He slammed the phone down and took Izzy in his arms. Tears were filling her eyes and he stroked them away. He kissed her forehead. 'She's going to make a formidable mother-in-law for some poor sod,' he said, lifting her chin and willing a smile back on to her face.

'Only a very stupid man would want to marry me,' she murmured faintly.

'Or how about a very stupid man who was wildly in love with you?'

Chapter Forty-Three

A week later, and with the furore caused by the invasion of bounty-hunters for the British press now behind them, Angelos brought Izzy and Mark the news that somebody new had come to stay in what had been the Pattersons' villa – they had gone home to Dulwich. He also told them that the Fitzgeralds were vacating Villa Mimosa in the next couple of days. With his ear pressed so firmly to the grape-vine, Angelos was able to tell them that Silent Bob had at last got himself a foothold in the property market on the island. He had joined forces with a Norwegian businessman, and between them they were providing the financial backing for a holiday village to be built in the south of Corfu, which would unashamedly appeal to the young crowd. With the contract signed, he was now keen to pack up, return home and see to his other business interests.

Nothing had been seen of the pair, not on the beach, not up at the supermarket, not even in Kassiópi in one of the tavernas. But, then, as Mark had said, the embarrassment of seeing herself in the papers as others saw her was probably keeping Dolly-Babe firmly indoors, away from prying eyes.

The news that the Fitzgeralds would soon be leaving had Izzy suddenly wanting to see Dolly-Babe for one last time: there were questions she wanted answering. She wanted to know how the journalists had unearthed so much about Nick and Sally's near-drowning accident. Details had been printed that Dolly-Babe just couldn't have known. She hadn't been there, so how had she known that Nick and Sally had been drunk, or that they had been smoking an illegal substance? It was possible that Nick might have told the journalists what had happened, but Izzy couldn't imagine Mrs Patterson letting her son speak so unguardedly.

Determined to have her answer, and fired up on curiosity that just wouldn't go away, she decided to go and have it out with Dolly-Babe before it was too late and she lost her chance. Sitting on the terrace with Mark she told him what she had in mind.

Hardly raising his head from his notepad, he said, 'Fine by me, just so long as you don't expect me to come with you.'

'That's okay, I'll go on my own. I'd rather not witness her fawning all over you.'

Now he did look at her. 'Pumpkin pie, you're not jealous of the thing I've got going with that woman, are you?'

She waved his comment aside. 'You're welcome to her, Mark. Just say the word and I'll be on my way.'

He sucked on the end of his pen. 'It's a hard choice, you or Dolly-Babe. You'll have to let me sleep on it. What do you intend saying to her?'

'I haven't decided yet. But one thing I will get out of her is a promise that she'll apologise to Max and Laura tomorrow afternoon when they arrive. It's the least she could do in the circumstances for acting so maliciously. She may have felt slighted over that silliness with Theo, but she went too far in her desire to get her own back.'

'My, my, what a fierce little tiger you've turned into.'

Walking up the hillside in the hot sunshine towards her prey, Izzy did indeed feel as though she had turned into a different person. Not only was she a hussy – a shameless one at that – she was now a predatory cat preparing to pounce on somebody who had hurt her friends.

Well, maybe that wasn't entirely true. It was perhaps only a thin veneer of courage that she had acquired. Not thick enough yet to deal with her mother, she suspected.

After that terrible phone conversation, Izzy had dreaded the telephone ringing again and her mother hurling more words of bitterness at her. Mark's solution was to return to Theo's villa where there would be no danger of Prudence Jordan tracking her down. 'But I'm running away from her, aren't I? I should be able to stand my ground. I should face up to—'

'Ssh,' he had said, holding her tight, 'It'll come. When you're ready, it'll come.'

She hadn't even been brave enough to check the answerphone when she went back each day to make sure that the villa hadn't been broken into overnight. Again, Mark had helped. He had come with her to shield her from the task of listening to any potentially poisonous outbursts from her mother. To her relief, there were no furious messages left for her, only a much friendlier one from Laura giving Izzy their flight details. Tagged on to the end of it was: 'I suppose you're not there because you're with that gorgeous tortured soul again. I hope you're not indulging in unprotected sex, Izzy. See you soon.'

Mark had looked at her with cool amusement. 'Perhaps you ought to ring her and put her mind at rest, tell her that we're being eminently sensible and grown up.'

In bed that night as Mark lay staring up at the ceiling, his hands laced behind his head, he had said, 'What would you do if you did find you were pregnant? After all, condoms do have a failure rate.'

She had frozen into a rigid block of uncertainty. How had he sneaked that up on her so stealthily? And why? When a man asked a question like that it usually meant one thing: that he was getting cold feet. He had never actually said *I love you*, but was he now worrying that he had implied it by his actions? Was he now searching for an escape route? Her mother's triumphant face swam before her: *That's what you get for being so quick to leap into his bed! It's only ever about sex.*

'Um . . . I don't know.'

'But you must.'

Oh, heavens, what could she say? There was no right answer. Tell him she would want to keep the baby and he would think she would use it as a bargaining tool to trap him – *See, now you'll have to marry me.* But say she would get rid of it and he would think she was callous and cold-hearted: a wicked woman quite prepared to throw away his child. It was hopeless, she couldn't win.

In the silence that was stretching uncomfortably between them, he said, 'Let me put it to you this way, would it be so very bad if you were pregnant?'

'But I'm not, am I?' she sidestepped.

He turned to face her. 'What's wrong? It's a simple enough question. Nail it for me, Izzy.'

She swallowed. 'But it isn't that simple. There's more going on behind your words than you're admitting to.'

'Really. Such as?'

'You're . . . you're setting a trap for me.'

He rolled on to his side and kissed her. 'Stop trying to make me feel cheap, Izzy.' Pushing back the sheet, he placed a warm hand over her stomach. It was the most loving and tender of acts. 'Do you think I'd make a good father?' There was a look in his eyes and a depth of emotion in his voice she had never seen or heard before.

'No,' she said lightly, the sensual warmth of his palm spreading through her, 'you'd frighten your children to death with your horrific bedtime stories.'

'And if I promised to stick to the Brothers Grimm for their bedtime tales?'

'Mm . . . maybe then you'd be okay.'

He lowered his head and pressed his lips to where his hand had been. 'So what's your answer?'

'It depends what you're really asking me.'

'I think you know what I'm getting at. I'm asking how you'd feel, one day, having my children within the context of a death-do-us-part situation.'

Half laughing, but half terrified, she looked at him nervously. Was he serious? 'But, Mark, you scarcely know me. You – you . . .' But the words fizzled out. What could she say? As crazy as it was, especially in view of the short space of time they had known each other, she knew that, given the opportunity, and as reckless as it was, she would happily run off into the sunset with Mark, and on any day he cared to name. But was it really possible that he felt the same for her?

'I know what you're thinking,' he said, 'that we haven't known each other for long, but you must feel what I do, that it feels so right when we're together. These last two weeks have been the best of my life. This is more than just a holiday romance between us, Izzy.'

'But supposing it only feels right between us because we're here? Maybe back in England, when it's cold and raining and we're trudging round Tesco's bickering over biological versus non-biological washing powder, the magic won't be there.'

'Then we'll wait and see. I'm not saying that we should rush into anything, I just want us to plan to be together.'

He sounded so sure.

So very intense.

Slipping her arms around his neck, she kissed him. 'By the way,' she said, 'it would have to be non-biological. I have sensitive skin.'

A slow, sexy smile passed across his face. 'Now there's a coincidence. So have I.'

*

Dolly-Babe was all contrition. 'I can't apologise enough,' she kept saying, as she led Izzy towards the shade of a large candy-striped awning and invited her to sit down. 'I wanted to come and see you all to say I was sorry, but Bob wouldn't let me, and I didn't dare go behind his back. He's so very angry about losing that olive grove, and losing it to a man who tricked us. Though I don't suppose you would have wanted to see me anyway.' Her words were hurried and a little too joined together, her gaze anywhere but on Izzy, and her hands busy with the animal-print sarong that matched her swimsuit, straightening it this way, then that way.

'Is Bob here?' asked Izzy, looking towards the villa, and hoping he wasn't.

'No. He's gone down to Kávos where he's investing in some kind of holiday village. He won't be back till late. It's work, work, work for him. Never stops. But that's my Bob. Never happy unless he's a-wheeling and a-dealing. It's how he's got to be so successful. Millionaire by the age of twenty-eight – did I ever tell you that? Caravan park. Who'd have thought there was any *gelt* in caravans? Can't stand them myself. Horrible things. Give me claustrophobia. Fancy a drink?'

'No, thanks.'

There was a well-sampled bottle of red wine on the table between them and an empty under Dolly-Babe's chair. With shaking hands, she topped up her glass then clattered the bottle down on the table. 'Sure you won't join me?'

Izzy shook her head and wondered if this was what Dolly-Babe's life was like back in England: Silent Bob away all the time, leaving his wife bored and alone, day after day. It made her think of one of Mark's casual throwaway lines about the loneliness of the long-distance drinker. It caused her to see Dolly-Babe quite differently. She saw a determined pride in the older woman's face, a sad need to preserve the façade of her fading youth. She probably thought it was all she had left.

'I suppose you've come here to find out why I got in touch with the papers?'

Izzy nodded. 'Yes, I am. I don't understand why you interfered.'

Dolly-Babe slipped on her sunglasses, and got busy with her sarong again. She was pleating it now. 'How old do you reckon I am?' she asked finally.

Goodness! How on earth was she to answer that? 'Ooh . . . um . . . I don't know.'

'It's okay. I know I'm a figure of fun to young girls like you. But you wait until your only true gift starts to let you down.' Bitterness poured out from her.

'Youth isn't our only asset.'

'It is when you haven't got anything else to offer, such as a brain. Unlike you, I haven't had a fancy education. My learning's been done at the school of hard knocks.' She drank from her glass in a long thirsty gulp. 'I'm fifty-one, and sixteen years ago I proved beyond all doubt that I was a brainless fool.' She fell silent, contemplating the glass in her hand.

Izzy said, 'We've all done things we regret, and it certainly doesn't mean we're any more stupid than the next person.'

Dolly-Babe looked at her sharply. 'How about getting pregnant and giving up the baby? How does that rate on the stupidity stakes? Because that's what I did.'

Izzy was at a loss what to say. She had come here wanting retribution on behalf of Mark and her friends and now she was feeling sorry for Dolly-Babe. 'I don't think that was a mark of stupidity,' she said, finding her voice at last, 'more an act of great courage. It couldn't have been easy for you. What happened?'

Taking another swallow of wine, Dolly-Babe said, 'It was before I'd met Bob. I'd just started work on a cruise ship as a croupier. It was a great life. I was earning good money, travelling the world, and meeting any number of men. Then I got pregnant. There was no way I could keep the baby, and with no one to turn to for help, I had to give it up. I know you're thinking I was being selfish, and probably I was, but at the time having kids wasn't what I wanted. I was having too much fun. So I had the baby, gave it away and went back to my old job. Not long after that I met Bob. But as the years have gone on, I've . . . well, you know . . . I've wondered about him. Yeah, I didn't mention that, did I, that he was a boy? Nice-looking little lad, thatch of black hair like you wouldn't believe, and a cute little nose.' She turned her head, stared down into the bay, her thoughts obviously on that tiny baby she had known for so short a time. 'Gawd, just listen to me!' she said suddenly, with false brightness. 'It's confession time at the OK Corral.' She sniffed loudly and reached for another drink.

'Did you never think of finding him?'

She shook her head violently. 'Bob doesn't know anything about it. He's got very strong views on matters like that. Likes things to be proper, no nasty secrets. The irony is, he's always wanted children, especially a son, but we haven't been able to have any. How's that for a cruel trick on nature's behalf? Punishment or what?'

'You could have adopted?'

'No, like I said, Bob's got strong views, his own, or not at all. And, besides, we were too old by then. We were in our early forties by the time we sussed that he was firing blanks. The adoption agencies would have laughed in our faces.'

'So, the thing with Christine and Mikey was all about your son?' ventured Izzy.

'I know it sounds dumb, but yes, yes, it was. I kept thinking that it could have been my son being seduced by that dreadful woman. Not that I'm saying Mikey's the child I gave away. Gawd, no, I'm not that daft. No, it was just the connection I'd made in my head. It was the age, you know, him being the same as my lad. It seems crazy now, hearing myself say all this. To be honest, it's a bit of a relief.'

'Don't you have anyone at home you can talk to?'

'No. Once I got married that was it. The life I'd led before was wrapped up and put away the moment Bob put this ring on my finger.'

Izzy eyed the impressive cluster of diamonds on Dolly-Babe's hand and wondered sadly if it had been worth it.

Hearing the phone ring, Mark hurried inside to answer it.

'Good and bad news for you,' Theo greeted him, his former good humour completely reinstated, as it had been for some days – to his shame, Mark wasn't so sure that he would have been able to forgive Theo so easily had the tables been turned.

He said, 'Go on, then, give it to me.'

'The good news is that the lengthy discussions I've had with old man Karabourniotis have not been for nothing. I have, at last, acquired the hotels I wanted.'

'Oh, I get it, and the bad news is that you're coming back?'

'Aha, always the step ahead of me, Mark. Yes, that is the bad news, so please, tidy up the love-nest the pair of you have created for yourselves. As from tomorrow you will have to keep the noise down at bedtime. Hearing Izzy's cries as you have her spiralling into a state of ecstasy will be too much of a torment for me.'

'I'll see what I can do.'

They talked some more. Theo wanted to know if there had been any more excitement in Áyios Nikólaos during his extended absence. 'No, it's all gone quiet. The Pattersons left with their tails firmly wedged between their legs. Harry, the only decent one among them, came to say goodbye and to thank Izzy and me for even thinking of saving his brother from drowning.'

'And Dolly-Babe and Silent Bob? What of them?'

'According to Angelos, they'll be leaving pretty soon. In fact, that's where Izzy is right now. She went marching off to extract an apology from Dolly-Babe for Max and Laura who, by the way, are also returning tomorrow afternoon.'

'Ah, that's good. I look forward to seeing Laura. I will be able to resume my flirting with her, now that I am no longer forcing myself to behave in front of Izzy. It will be just like old times. And to celebrate such happiness I will cook us all a meal.'

Finishing their call, Mark went back outside. He blinked in the bright sunlight, and awarded himself a short break from work. He decided to go for a walk along the beach. He didn't bother locking up as he would only be gone a few minutes and, besides, Corfu was the safest place he had ever known. Wasn't that what Theo had said when he had been urging him to come and spend the summer in Áyios Nikólaos?

Less than half an hour later, he was retracing his steps and enjoying a lightness of heart that was becoming familiar to him. Life had taken on a whole new dimension. There was a serene calmness to his days, which gave him a wonderful clarity of thought and hope for the future. Hell, he'd even started talking long-term plans with Izzy. Who'd have thought it?

For so much of his life he had worn bullet-proof armour to protect himself from any attack on his emotions, and now here he was fully exposed and loving every minute of it. What he had with Izzy, he had never known before. The funny thing was it didn't surprise him. There had been no earth-shattering moment of realisation that he loved her, not even a seismic jolt of his heart. It had slowly but surely crept up on him ever since their first meeting back in June.

He would never have believed that in less than two months he could have formed a relationship that had moved on to such a profoundly satisfying level of companionship. He knew, though, that he would do everything in his power to keep it that way. He had experienced very little real peace of mind in his life, and now that Izzy had given it to him, and in such abundance, he'd be damned if he let it slip out of his grasp. Being so perfectly connected with Izzy made him realise how narrow and one-tracked his life had been before. She truly touched the best in him, revealed a side of his personality he hadn't known existed.

And what would Bones make of it all? Would he warn him that there was a danger he might become too dependent on Izzy? Or would he just sit there looking all benign and whistling one of his blasted tunes? What would it be? 'Love Changes Everything' perhaps?

He pushed open the gate to Theo's garden and wandered over to the terrace, wanting to get out of the blistering August heat. He stood with relief in the cool shade of the pergola. He was just thinking of getting himself a drink when he stopped in his tracks. There on the table, where he had been working earlier, was an envelope with his name on it.

The writing was unmistakable – small, cramped and slanting to the left.

It was just like all the other letters he had received back in England.

Chapter Forty-Four

Mark sat down to read the letter.

It didn't take long.

All it said was: ARE YOU READY?

He crumpled the piece of white A4 in his hand, crushing it so hard he half expected to see it disintegrate into a pile of dust. He dropped it to the ground.

He bent forward, clasped his head. It was madness. How could this be happening? How had the stalker found him?

The answer came to him in a sickening bolt of comprehension.

How had Izzy's mother known about the pair of them?

She had read it in the newspapers back home, that's how. Even his parents had got in touch after reading about him at their Buckinghamshire breakfast table.

So, thanks to Dolly-Babe and those bloodsucking journalists, his whereabouts had been handed on a plate to whoever was stalking him.

ARE YOU READY?

They were the very same words he had written in *Silent Footsteps*. It was the last communication the stalker made before he killed his victim.

He closed his eyes, rubbed at his temples. This couldn't be for real. Whoever had done this, surely they didn't really want to kill him. Wasn't it just a sick joke that had slipped beyond the usual boundaries of loony-tune behaviour?

He let out his breath, realising that he had been

holding it in. A coldness was gripping his insides. His heart was racing, thumping painfully in his chest. His every instinct shouted that this was no joke. Somebody was playing with him in deadly earnest. This was serious. Somebody had a grudge against him and was determined to make him pay for some imagined crime he had committed.

But who?

Who had he ever crossed – and to the extent that they had been prepared to track him down half-way across Europe so they could extract their revenge?

No, it was no joke. For somebody to have come this far, they meant business.

He thought of everyone he knew – or thought he knew – back in Robin Hood's Bay. He pictured the small writers' group he taught in the village hall, seeing their faces one by one. Okay, some pretty off-the-wall folk attended the weekly get-togethers, but not one of them seemed so kooky as to want him dead. Not even Lionel Bridges, whom he had had to take aside one night when the class was over and ask him to ease off the pornography he insisted on writing and reading aloud to the group. Lionel wrote under the ridiculous pseudonym of Shona Mercy, and caused no end of offence and embarrassment to some of the more genteel lady members, including Deirdre, a grey-haired spinster who cleaned for Mark once a week.

Deirdre had full and frequent access to his home and correspondence, which gave her plenty of opportunity and the means to stalk him, but he simply couldn't accept that she had a malicious bone in her body. Since her retirement as a school secretary, she took care of her elderly mother, who was in her nineties and whose health was failing, and now spent her free time writing what he called chintzy poetry.

No, not even the most far-fetched Agatha Christie plot

would have her down as a potential killer: she was much too delicate and refined for such rough work. When she had applied for the job as his cleaner he had been so surprised he had asked her why she wanted to do it – he couldn't imagine her baby pink little hands scrubbing out his bath. 'It's not the money, pet,' she had told him, 'I just need to be out from under Mother's feet occasionally.'

Then there was Dale, the young garage mechanic who wrote bloodcurdling Gothic horror *à la* Bram Stoker and Anne Rice. In fact, he lived and breathed Gothic horror, spending his weekends and holidays working at the Dracula Experience in Whitby – the one-time home of his hero Bram Stoker. With the aid of a pair of fangs and a black cape lined with red silk, his job was to scare the punters, which he said he loved doing. But had the ghoulish world of vampires worn thin for Dale? Had he looked around and seen a more satisfying way to thrill himself?

He went through the other members of the group, but could find no reason for any of them to want to terrorise him, let alone kill him.

He cast his mind further, beyond Robin Hood's Bay to London. Had he offended some writer at one of the countless literary dinners he was invited to? Someone from the Crime Writers' Association perhaps? Someone who felt aggrieved that he had got the award that they had thought was theirs. But that was madness. Okay, the priesthood of crime writers was known for attracting a weird and cranky old bunch who took themselves too seriously, but not your actual real-life murderer, surely?

No, the probable culprit was one of his readers. Somebody he didn't know. An obsessed fan who was psychotically at the mercy of a controlling inner voice. He let his thoughts wander down this more convincing path, recalling any number of strange incidents he had encountered at his book signings, which invariably brought out the anorak crowd. Once, in Leeds, a woman had turned up purely to tear him off a strip for using such foul language in his novels, calling him an affront to the English language. Another time, down in Plymouth, there had been a man dressed in black biker gear with a stark skull of a face. He wouldn't speak but silently, almost menacingly, he had pulled the latest Terry Pratchett book out of a carrier-bag and thrust it at him to sign. Mark had tried to explain that he wasn't Mr Pratchett, cracking a joke that he wished he was, but the man had deepened the scowl on his gaunt face and pushed the book further towards him. He had signed it just to be rid of the screwball.

But no amount of recollection was helping Mark. It was an exercise he had been through before, anyway. He had got nowhere then, and he was getting nowhere now. With a bitter sense of irony, he thought that maybe it was the publicity department at his publisher's who were behind the letters; after all they had every reason to hate him. Perhaps they had decided to get their own back on him for being such an awkward bugger.

So lost in his thoughts was he that he didn't hear the slow footsteps approaching. Nor did he sense the hands raised behind his head. Not until they were covering his eyes.

'Guess who?'

He leaped in the air so violently he nearly knocked Izzy off her feet. 'Holy shit, Izzy!' he cried, his voice ringing out with raw nervous energy. 'What the hell do you think you're doing?' He fell back into the chair, his whole body flooded with the electricity of so much adrenaline pumping through it. 'You scared me half to death.'

She sat beside him, her face pale with shock.

'I'm sorry,' she murmured, 'it was meant to be a joke. I didn't mean to frighten you.'

He heard the anxious concern in her voice and saw her distress. He forced a smile. 'Hey, it's okay. It's me. My fault. I shouldn't be such a nervous wreck.' And, straining to add some normality to the situation, he said, 'How'd you get on with Dolly-Babe? Did you take her to task?' He took a surreptitious kick at the ball of paper by his foot, knocking it under the table out of Izzy's line of sight.

That evening, and while soaking up the quiet cool of the night and watching the stars come out, Izzy was positive she wasn't imagining it: Mark was acting strangely.

He had spent most of the evening ignoring her, glancing frequently at the growing shadows in the garden as the sky darkened and the trees grew taller and more solid. Restless and uptight, he was withdrawn and uncommunicative. She had asked him several times if he was okay.

'Sure I am,' he had said. 'Why wouldn't I be?' He had spoken easily enough, but his jaw tightened and there was a darkness in his eyes, which were alert beneath the fine sun-bleached fringe.

To gain his interest, she had tried telling him about Dolly-Babe and the baby she had given away all those years ago. But his attention had soon wavered. For something to talk about now, she returned to the subject once more. 'You were right all along,' she said. 'Poor Dolly-Babe certainly has had her problems to deal with, hasn't she?'

'Yeah, I guess it would explain her obsession with the psychic world,' he said absentmindedly, fingers picking at a shoelace, his gaze skimming the top of Izzy's head. 'There's nothing like diverting one's thoughts from the past by trying to predict the future.'

'I asked her how she knew so much about Nick and Sally, and she said she'd got it from Sophia. Apparently

Laura had told Sophia everything, so at least my curiosity is settled on that account. And the reason it was a week before the journalists turned up was that at first they didn't believe her. They thought she was just another crackpot, but then they got a tip-off from somebody at the airport.' Izzy could see that she had lost him again, that his mind wasn't even half on their conversation – so where on earth was it? 'And later I thought I'd tie you to the bed and tickle you with a feather duster,' she added.

'Yeah, that makes sense.' His gaze had switched to the far end of the garden and his fingers were drumming an irritating tattoo on the table.

'Or would you prefer a wet kipper?'

'Whatever you think. I'll leave it to you.'

After a long pause, his fingers stopped moving. He turned sharply. 'A wet what?'

'Ah, I've got your attention now, have I? Come on, Mark, tell me what's wrong. Ever since I got back from Dolly-Babe's you've been acting oddly.' She saw him hesitate and knew then with certainty that something had happened when she had been away from him. 'Did someone phone you with bad news? It's not Theo, is it?'

He shook his head. 'It's nothing. Nothing that you need worry about.' His tone was casual but not convincing.

'But if something's bothering you—'

'Please, Izzy, just leave it. I don't want you involved. In fact you're the last—' But he stopped himself short. 'Forget it, it was . . . it was my publisher, that's all. They always rattle me like this.'

As Izzy slept, Mark lay wide awake beside her. The room was unbearably hot. It was the hottest and muggiest night he had known, but nothing would persuade him to open a window. While Izzy had been in the bathroom getting ready for bed, he had checked all the doors and windows, making doubly sure that they were locked. Coming out of the bathroom Izzy had commented on the stuffiness of the bedroom and had suggested she open a window to let some air in, but he had told her not to, that he was fed up with being bitten in the night by all the mosquitoes that made straight for him. Accepting this without argument, she had climbed into bed and fallen asleep almost immediately, her head resting against his shoulder.

As sleep continued to elude him, he thought of what he had said to Izzy outside on the terrace, or what he had very nearly said – *I don't want you involved. In fact you're the last* . . . What he had been going on to say was that Izzy was the last person he wanted anywhere near him right now.

If a crazy psycho had come here to Áyios Nikólaos to satisfy an inner voice that was telling him to kill Mark St James, then what was to stop him having a go at Izzy as well?

He didn't know what to do for the best.

Should he get Izzy the hell out of here and on a plane back to England – frightening her silly in the process – or should he keep quiet and go on watching their backs until the threat had passed?

But the threat might not pass.

If the stalker was going to stick to the script of *Silent Footsteps*, an attempt would be made on his life.

He had never felt surer about anything.

Chapter Forty-Five

The day started as idyllically as any other morning Izzy had woken to during her holiday – the sky was a faultless blue, the sun dazzling, the air fragrant with the scent of pine, and the sea glimmering peacefully in the bay below – but a cloud of tension hung over her, and it just wouldn't go away.

It emanated from Mark, and nothing he said or did helped to lift the bad feeling that had descended upon her since yesterday evening. Every time she looked at him she could see that he was unreachable, that his distracted thoughts were elsewhere. His troubled face and distant eyes only confirmed her belief that something was terribly wrong. Though he had sat at the table in his usual working spot in the shade, she knew he hadn't written a single word all morning. She had frequently caught him staring at her, his expression dark and puzzling. It was as if he was worried about her. But why? Or had she got it wrong? Had she annoyed him? Had she said or done something?

She had tried wheedling the truth out of him, but had got nowhere. He was a firmly closed book to her. He didn't seem to want her near him, preferring to sit in remote silence, yet neither did he want her where he couldn't see her. When she had said she was going down to the beach for a swim, he had asked her what was wrong with Theo's pool.

'Nothing,' she had said. 'I just fancied a dip in the sea. It'll be cooler.'

'Then I'll come with you. I could do with a change of scene.' He was on his feet before he had even got the words out.

Now, and while she swam in the refreshing water, he was sitting on the shore, tense and watchful, his hand shielding his eyes from the glare of the sun as he scrutinised her every movement. And scrutinised everybody else's movements on the beach. Especially anyone who came near her.

'Paranoid' was the word that kept going through her head.

It was as if a switch had been flicked inside him and he had become a different man. A man who jumped at the slightest movement or sudden noise; a man who suspected trouble at every turn.

What on earth had got into him?

She was so concerned, she wished that Theo was here already. He was arriving later that afternoon, but for Izzy his arrival couldn't come fast enough. She felt sure that if anyone could get Mark to relax and open up, it would be Theo.

Not in any particular hurry to get home, Theo ignored the turning for Áyios Nikólaos and drove on to Kassiópi so that he could buy what he wanted to cook for dinner that evening. Parking his car between two open-topped Jeeps, he strolled round the harbour to his favourite bar for a drink before he went shopping. He greeted its owner, Michalis, with a warm handshake and asked how business was.

Michalis gave the obligatory could-be-better shrug and said, '*Étsi kyétsi.*'

Theo smiled, knowing that business was always good for Michalis. As well as this popular harbour bar, he also owned several apartments in Kassiópi, another bar up in Róda, and a villa in Majorca, where he and his wife spent their winters once the olives had been harvested from their highly productive olive groves. '*Étsi kyétsi*' meant that Michalis was confident he would be banking enough money this season to extend his interest further on the island, ready for next spring. 'And your mother?' Theo enquired. 'The last I heard of her from Sophia and Angelos was that she had been unwell.'

'Ah, plenty of life in her yet,' Michalis said, with a hearty laugh, 'Eighty-five and still able to lift a shovel. She was helping my son, Andonis, to repair a drain only the other day.'

'You work her too hard,' remonstrated Theo.

Michalis threw his hands in the air. 'It is her, not me, she is not happy unless she is busy. You know how it is.'

Theo knew exactly how it was. Greek women: the older they got, the more determined and fiercely independent they became. His grandmother had been the same. Despite advice and warnings from her doctor to slow down, she had continued to live her life just as she had always lived it: to the fullest. Taking it easy had been anathema to her.

Waiting for Michalis to bring him his drink, Theo watched a brightly painted caïque disgorge a group of noisy, sunburnt tourists, most of whom started heading towards Michalis' bar. Still dressed in his expensive handmade suit, and despite having removed his tie and unbuttoned his collar, Theo knew that the contrast between his appearance and that of this crowd of scruffy holidaymakers could not have been greater. One man, wearing only shiny football shorts and trainers and a pair of boxer shorts on his shaved head – was this the ultimate in sun protection? – was staring at him as though he were mad. One of us has a problem with his mental faculties, thought Theo, as he removed his jacket and hung it carefully on the back of his chair, but it is not me.

Michalis brought him his oúzo and ice, and after a

further exchange of words, he left Theo alone so that he could tend to the needs of the rest of his customers – the Full English Breakfast Plonkers, as he called them, the ones who thought plates of chips and mushy peas were sold the world over. 'What? No mushy peas, mate? Are you having me on?' But in spite of their ridiculous foibles, the British punters were well liked here: their plump wallets were open all hours when they were on holiday. Unlike those of the Scandinavians, who, according to Michalis, were so tight they preferred to stay in self-catering accommodation and cook for themselves.

Sipping his drink, and his thoughts turning closer to home, Theo wondered if he would be successful in hiding his feelings of envy and disappointment when he saw Mark and Izzy together. Though he had gone to great lengths to convince Mark that he held no grudge towards him, he hadn't been able to pretend to himself that he was happy with the way things had worked out. The trick was to make light of the matter, he knew, which so far he had managed to do. But that had been on the telephone when there had been no danger of his expression betraying him. He had deliberately lied to Mark about the necessity of prolonging his stay in Athens – he had acquired the chain of hotels early on – but he had not had the courage to return home immediately. So he had stayed and immersed himself in work; routine stuff he could easily have organised by phone, fax or e-mail from the comfort of his villa here on Corfu. From somewhere he had found the strength to tease Mark that it was so good and generous of him to let the eager lovers have their time together. Not a word had he said about his own cowardly need to keep away because he didn't trust himself to behave in a reasonable manner.

He had always viewed Mark as the brother he had never had. Well, now he felt like calling in a brother's privilege, that of knocking Mark's teeth out for stealing his girl!

He drained his glass, left what he owed Michalis on the table, and crossed the harbour to the shops. It was time to get on. Time to stop feeling sorry for himself and maybe even admit that, on this occasion, he had lost to a better man.

Izzy was in the shower after her swim and, knowing she would be there for some time yet, Mark went outside. Taking a deep breath, he steeled himself and pulled an envelope from his pocket.

It had been waiting for him when they came up from the beach, casually left on the doorstep for anyone to see. Luckily Izzy hadn't spotted it – she had been hanging her towel over the line between the two olive trees at the side of the house, and he had stuffed it into his pocket before she reappeared.

Glancing over his shoulder to check that she hadn't cut short her shower, he ripped open the envelope.

I'VE CHANGED MY MIND. IT WON'T BE YOU.

That was it.

It might not appear much, but in essence it paved the way for a whole new nightmare. The stalker was writing his own script now.

I'VE CHANGED MY MIND. IT WON'T BE YOU.

It could mean only one thing. The deranged person had changed his mind over his choice of victim.

With shaking hands he slid the note back inside the envelope. What the hell was he going to do? The intent of the threat could not be clearer. Whoever it was must have been spying on him and Izzy and decided to hurt him in the worst possible way. He was going for Izzy, he just knew it.

How could he protect her?

He paced the terrace, his thoughts tumultuous and

439

chaotic. He forced his brain to think straight, to conjure up a credible solution.

Home.

That was it.

Get Izzy home to England.

Hide her.

Keep her safe.

But as fast as these thoughts flitted through his head, he knew it wouldn't work.

Hiding, running, how long could that go on? How long could he live with the uncertainty? He suddenly thought of the day he had confessed to Izzy about using her in his latest novel, when he had also admitted that he didn't know what would ultimately happen to her character. He remembered her smiling and saying, 'Oh, well, if it's all the same to you, I'd prefer to live.' He recalled too, his response: 'I'll see what I can do.'

The memory of those glibly spoken words made him feel physically sick. Sick, because when confronted with the real thing he didn't know how the hell he was going to protect her.

As if realising he was still pacing the terrace, and that it served no purpose, he came to an abrupt stop, spun on his heel and bolted inside the villa, fear and despair driving him to make sure Izzy was all right. He banged on the bathroom door and called to her, 'You okay in there?'

The door opened almost instantly. 'Yes, why, have you come to soap my shoulders for me?' She smiled at him as she wrapped herself in a towel. 'Because if so, you're too late. Or maybe there was a certain scene from *Psycho* you wanted to run through with me?'

He couldn't think of anything to say, so he forced himself to smile and pulled her hot damp body to him. He squeezed his eyes shut, blocking out the gruesome image to which she had just alluded and the indisputable and painful truth in all this mess: if anything happened to Izzy, he would never know peace of mind again.

Theo had been in the villa only a short while – he had scarcely exchanged his suit for a pair of shorts to go swimming – before he knew that something was wrong.

At first he had put it down to the three of them feeling uncomfortable with each other and, given the circumstances, it was perhaps to be expected. But he had soon realised that he was picking up on a much greater problem. Had the happy couple had a falling-out already?

'You are acting the part of a genuinely possessive lover, eh?' he said to Mark, when they were alone by the pool, and alone only because Izzy had insisted that she returned to Max and Laura's villa to be there to greet them when they arrived from the airport. Theo had been surprised at the strength of Mark's vehement objection to her going, but had said nothing, watching instead the agitated manner in which he had tried to dissuade her. He had even suggested that he go with her.

'No,' she had laughed, 'that's not fair to Theo. You stay here and chat while I make sure everything's ready for Max and Laura.'

'But Sophia and Angelos have seen to that. They were there this morning. What else needs doing, for pity's sake?'

But his words hadn't detained her and she had gone with an assurance that they would all be together that evening for supper.

Getting no response from Mark about him being a possessive lover, Theo said, 'You will scare her off if you continue to treat her like a caged bird.' He floated on his back, stared up at the cloudless blue sky and waited for Mark to say something. A tiny, wholly unworthy part of him was pleased that all was not well between him and Izzy.

'When you've finished your swim, I want to show you something,' Mark said.

Theo rolled over on to his front and swam to the shallow end of the pool where Mark was looking down at him. 'You sound serious. What is it?'

'Finish your swim, then I'll tell you.'

He raised himself out of the water, shook the water from his hair, and wrapped a towel around his waist. 'It is finished. I am at your disposal.'

Mark led him across the garden, up the steps of the terrace and inside the villa. To Theo's surprise, Mark took him into his study where he opened one of his desk drawers. 'I hope you don't mind me hiding these here, but I didn't want Izzy to see them. You'll understand why. The first came yesterday, the other today.'

Theo took a crumpled piece of paper from Mark's outstretched hand, a neatly folded one too. 'Tell me this is a coincidence, Mark,' he said, after he had read the two letters. 'Or, better still, convince me that all authors get strange mail like this when they're on holiday.'

'I wish I could. I wish, too, that I didn't feel so genuinely scared by whoever is behind them. He must have seen me in the newspapers back in England and come out here straight away. I might just as well have mailed him your address. God, Theo, if this lunatic's intention is to frighten me, he's doing a bloody good job of it.'

All the petty, rancorous thoughts of a few moments earlier were gone as Theo stared at the letters. Now he felt nothing but protective concern. 'His actions prove beyond doubt that he is serious, Mark, and I'm afraid I don't believe that he only wants to frighten you. My instinct says that his intentions go further than that.' Theo understood now, all too clearly, that what he had thought were the actions of a possessive lover had been a rational man's attempts to keep the woman he cared for safe, and without alarming her. 'Mark, if this person really wanted to hurt you, how do you think he would go about it?'

There was no hesitation to Mark's reply. 'You know the answer to that as well as I do. He would try to harm somebody who mattered to me.'

'Then we have to act. We must go to the police.'

'Other than providing us with a round-the-clock guard to catch our stalker red-handed as he plays Mr Postman again, I don't think they can do anything.'

'If that is what it takes, then that is what I shall insist upon. You must bear in mind, Mark, that the Greek police are not the same as your soft English bobbies. Here on Corfu they take a firm line with anyone they consider to be having a detrimental effect on another person's well-being. They enjoy a very real sense of power, and because they carry a gun they have a bark that is as fierce as any bite, believe me.'

'Okay, if you think there's a chance of them helping, then so be it.'

'Good. Tomorrow morning we will go together into Kassiópi and show this stalker that he has made a gross error of judgement by coming here to play his sadistic games. This man has to be found, he has to be confronted once and for all, or this madness could carry on for ever. If he is allowed to, he will keep you dangling by threatening to kill those closest to you until he has driven you insane.'

'Thanks for making it such a stark reality for me.'

'I am only saying aloud what you must have already thought. Now, why don't we go and see how Izzy is getting on? She should not be out of our sight. We need to ensure that somebody is always with her. I would suggest also that you do your best to settle her mind. I could tell from her manner and the way she was looking at you that she is worried about you. Try to make light of the fact that you have been acting strangely. And while the police are hunting your stalker, I think it would be a wise precaution if I take you both to stay with me in Athens.'

'But won't that alert Izzy and make her think something is wrong?'

'I will word my invitation so beautifully she will not be at all suspicious of our motives. Come, Mark, trust me, have I not always taken good care of you?'

Chapter Forty-Six

Darkness had closed in around them and in the soft glow of candlelight Izzy could feel the anxiety of the last twenty-four hours gradually loosen its hold on her. Max and Laura were in wonderfully high spirits, laughing and joking throughout dinner, bouncing their good humour off Theo, and making it impossible for the rest of them not to respond with equal ebullience. Even Mark seemed more relaxed. She glanced at him over a flickering candle; his eyes no longer held the tense, distracted look they had worn earlier. She wondered if Theo's arrival had helped him resolve whatever problem had been bothering him, because since Theo's return he had been a lot less edgy. He caught her watching him and, giving her a small smile, he extended a hand across the table. She reached out and touched just the ends of his fingers with the tips of hers. It was a deliberately discreet and intimate gesture, which Izzy had thought would go unnoticed by the others. But she was wrong.

'No, no, *no*!' cried Theo from her left. His voice was so loud, so sudden, it made her start, and without any warning, he slapped his own hand down on top of theirs. 'I will not allow it,' he said sternly. 'I refuse to sit here playing the hairy green gooseberry. Is it not bad enough that I have to put up with watching Max and Laura acting like a couple of young teenagers? Must I endure your mishy behaviour as well?'

'It's *mushy* behaviour,' laughed Max, putting an arm around Laura's shoulders. 'And, anyway, a man can't help loving his wife, especially one as beautiful as mine.' He kissed her cheek, then with his lips against her ear he whispered something. Laura gave him a small nod, and Izzy noticed a particular smile on her lips that she now realised had been there ever since her friends had arrived at the villa that afternoon. Except now it was bigger.

'We only found out yesterday,' said Max, his face breaking into a grin that widened by the second, 'and it just goes to show that you're never too old. Laura and I are doing a Tony and Cherie Blair, we're going to be parents all over again. And just so that you know how to react, we're both as pleased as punch. Well, now that the shock's wearing off, we are,' he added.

Izzy went straight to Laura and hugged her. 'That's such amazing news. Congratulations. I suppose that explains why you were so tired all the time. Did you have any idea?'

'None whatsoever. At my age pregnancy isn't the first thing that springs to mind when you're feeling under the weather, especially as I've been taking the pill all these years, if a little slapdashly at times. I thought perhaps the heat was getting the better of me. Or, worse, that I was entering the twilight zone of hot flushes and dizzy moments. But Max insisted I saw a doctor when we were in England and, hey presto, one pregnant geriatric mother diagnosed.'

Shaking Max's hand and smiling broadly, Theo said, 'You old dog, Max, it seems I have thoroughly underestimated you!' Then he leaned across the table and kissed Laura. 'Congratulations, my darling, I'm so pleased for you. It is indeed heart-warming news.'

Laura smiled. 'You don't think we're too old?'

'Heavens, no!' said Izzy. 'Though Max might have to start his training sooner rather than later if he isn't going to bring shame on the family name at all those school sports days you've got to look forward to now.'

Max groaned. 'Oh, thanks, Izzy. But I'm hoping by then they'll have invented the three-legged zimmer-frame race.'

'And what does Francesca have to say to this good news?' asked Theo.

'Her exact words were: "Well, Dad, I always wanted a baby brother or sister to boss around, so I guess this is better late than never."'

'And Corky and Olivia, what do they think of you two rascals?'

'They're delighted. As are my parents. My mother is thinking that perhaps she could go in for some kind of fertility treatment and get in on the act.'

'Well, I think it is quite brilliant what you have done,' said Theo, 'and I look forward to next year when you spend your summer here with little Sinclair junior.' He suddenly clapped his hands. 'This is definitely something to celebrate. Champagne it is! We must drink to your good health and for a baby boy as even-tempered as his beautiful mother.'

'You wouldn't by any chance be ignoring the possibility that it might be a girl?' suggested Mark.

Theo shook his head decisively. 'No. My intuition says that it will be a sturdy little boy to keep his father on his toes.' He rose from his chair.

'Would you like some help, Theo?' asked Izzy, also rising to her feet and hoping he would say yes. It seemed an ideal chance to get him on his own and talk about Mark: until now there had been no such opportunity.

'Thank you, Izzy, that's very kind of you.'

But they were alone only for a few moments, and before Izzy had so much as decided on her opening gambit, Mark appeared in the kitchen with a stack of dirty plates.

'I thought I'd bring these in,' he said, opening the dishwasher and bending down to it.

447

'You see, Izzy?' said Theo, as he pulled out a bottle of Veuve Clicquot from the bottom of the fridge. 'You see how he doesn't trust me for a single minute to be alone with you. He comes in here under the pretext of being helpful, but really he wants to be very sure I will not push you down on to the kitchen table and kiss you long and hard. I pose an interesting threat to him, eh?'

'The day I feel threatened by you, Theo, is the day the sun stops shining. Now, shall we just get on with serving the champagne? Laura says she only wants a small glass and I'd like some more water.'

'Oh, Izzy, can you hear the harsh quality to his words? Are you sure you would not like to reconsider what you have got yourself into? It isn't too late to change your mind. A lady is allowed to do so.'

'But this one has no intention of doing so,' said Izzy, glad to hear the familiar put-downs between Mark and Theo. After the stilted conversations she had had with Mark since yesterday, it came as a refreshing change to listen to their customary rivalry. 'And if I could get a word in between you two,' she added, 'you're going to have to give me a clue where you keep your glasses, Theo.'

He pointed to a cupboard, gave her a tray, then said to Mark, 'She is insolent as well as stubborn, that girl, you will need to watch her.'

'Something I have every intention of doing,' replied Mark, as Theo went ahead with the bottle, which he was going to open outside. And, wanting to assure Izzy that all was well – just as Theo had instructed him to do earlier that afternoon – Mark took the tray of glasses she had just arranged and set it on the dresser behind them. 'I'm sorry I've been so preoccupied lately,' he said, holding her hands, 'I should have warned you that I get like that sometimes. I hope I haven't upset you.'

She looked at him as though carefully considering his

words. He thought for a nasty moment that she didn't believe him, that she had guessed the truth. 'But you're okay now?' she asked.

Relieved that she didn't seem to have rumbled him, he rested his hands on her shoulders, drew her closer. 'Right now at this very minute I'm more than okay. What man in his right senses wouldn't feel completely okay if he were standing here in my shoes?' He kissed her deeply. Then he slipped his hands around her waist, determined to convince her that he was his old self, and said, 'Now what exactly was it Theo had in mind for you on the table?'

She laughed and laced her fingers behind his neck. 'Never mind Theo, what do *you* have in mind?'

'Why, Sugar Lips, you're doing it again. You're leading me astray.'

'Only following your lead, Mark. Nothing more.'

He kissed her once more. But only briefly. 'Come on, we'd better get back out there or we'll never get any peace from Theo.'

'So there you are,' said Max, when they reappeared on the terrace, 'We were just debating whether we'd have to resort to glugging the bubbly straight from the bottle.'

'And don't tell me that would be a first for you,' laughed Izzy.

Taking the tray of glasses from Izzy, Theo poured them their drinks, and while everyone entered into the spirit of out-toasting one another, Mark once again let the conversation go over his head. He was finding it an impossible strain to pretend that everything was fine. Staring into the dark night sky, he noticed that a strong warm breeze had sprung up and was sending eerie patches of thick cloud scudding across the moon. In front of him, just a few inches away, the candles on the table were flickering as the wind almost blew them out. He wished with all his heart that the wind was strong enough to blow away the weight of worry and fear that was dragging him down. Despite Theo's confident assurances that all would be well – that they could disappear to Athens leaving the local police to track down the stalker – he simply didn't believe that matters could be so easily resolved. His lack of faith in Theo's unshakeable convictions reminded him of the waking-in-the-middle-of-the-night sensation he occasionally experienced when his subconscious was working overtime on a plot that wouldn't come together as he wanted it to. It was as if there was an important detail he and Theo were both overlooking; a fatal flaw in their logical reasoning.

He tuned back into the conversation just in time to hear Theo hotly defending his nation. 'Believe me, Greece's domestic economic health is better than you English like to think it is,' he was saying, 'its international standing in the wider community is—'

'Hey, there's no need to get so defensive, Theo,' Mark cut in irritably, 'Everyone sitting round this table knows the contribution you make towards keeping the domestic economy afloat here, and we're all very proud of you. So give it a rest, will you? I thought this was a party and that we were meant to be enjoying ourselves.'

'Hear, hear,' agreed Max.

Theo rolled his eyes. 'Please, the pair of you, take your patronising sarcasm and stick it up your anally retentive English jacksies!'

'But that's where we keep your precious Elgin Marbles.'

'Max Sinclair, now you are just playing dirty with me. How did I ever get involved with such a disreputable bunch of people? What have I ever done to you to deserve this cruel treatment? Truly, sitting here with you, I cannot think of anything worse. Hand on heart, you are my worst nightmare.'

They all laughed, but then, and in the midst of the

light-hearted moment, a disembodied voice said, 'None of you has any idea of what a worst nightmare is. But after tonight, well, maybe you just might.'

Their laughter died instantly. Coming towards them in the shadowy darkness was the figure of a man, and though Mark could make out little more than a silhouetted outline, he saw all too clearly that the man was holding a gun, and that he was pointing it straight at him.

Chapter Forty-Seven

Mark's first thought was: this is it.

His second thought was to take charge and make sure no one fancied himself a hero.

'Nobody move,' he whispered, scarcely opening his mouth to speak when the initial gasps of alarm had passed and silence had fallen on them. 'It's me he's come to see, so just sit tight.'

He sounded so much calmer than he felt. Gooseflesh was running amok all over him and the rush of adrenaline coursing through his body was greater than any chemically induced hit he had ever experienced: his heart was pounding as if it would burst clean out of his ribcage. Squinting, he tried to get a better look at the man.

Whoever he had imagined to be behind the letters, it was not this thin, ageing, insignificant little man hiding in the shadows. It was tempting to think that they could easily outfight him. But though they undoubtedly had size and numbers on their side, this lunatic sure as hell had the upper hand: he had a gun.

Rising slowly from his seat, so slowly it was hurting the muscles in the backs of his legs, he tried to move a little nearer. His movements were too obvious, though, and the man started waving the gun, acting every inch the madman who wouldn't think twice about using it. But then he probably was a madman, wasn't he, and thinking twice was an occupational hazard he would avoid at all costs?

'*Sit down!*' They all jumped at the voice that screeched crazily out of control. Laura clutched at Max who had his arm around her, and Izzy, her eyes frantic with terror, reached out to Theo. 'I said sit down!'

'Do as he says, Mark,' urged Theo, his expression pleading with him not to do anything that would endanger their lives.

But ignoring both his friend's words and those of his stalker, Mark calmly held up his hands in a see-no-tricks-up-my-sleeves gesture. 'It's okay,' he said. 'It's me you want, and it's me you've got. Let's talk.' He moved a few inches further forward, his main concern now to shield Izzy. Her place at the table meant that she was nearest to this nutter. The man might be pointing the gun at Mark, but that last letter had said, I'VE CHANGED MY MIND. IT WON'T BE YOU.

'Who says I want to talk?' The question was defiant, the tone level.

'If you've come here to kill me, I think the least you can do is explain why.' From his side, Mark heard Izzy let out a small cry of disbelief. He willed her not to say anything. Please, God, don't let her move. Make her invisible. 'So how about it?' he continued, stealing another small step on his pursuer. 'After all, it's a condemned man's right to have one last request.' How reasonable he was making it sound. He could have been negotiating with a salesman in a car showroom, asking for alloy wheels to be thrown in for free.

'I know what you're doing,' the man said, 'I'm not a fool. You think a bit of negotiating will solve this. It won't. Though if it's talk you want, then, yes, I'll go along with you. But you stay right where you are. No nearer, do you hear?'

Knowing that it might be his last chance, Mark gave an exaggerated shrug of agreement and stepped neatly in front of Izzy; the first part of his mission accomplished.

Now all he had to do was play for sufficient time for a miracle to happen. 'So who are you?' he asked.

The man's response was to tilt back his head and laugh. It was a horrible, twisted laugh. The sign of a man who had slipped into that dark place of the soul where right and wrong had crossed over. 'I'm disappointed in you,' he sneered. 'I know it's been a long time, but I would have thought your powers of deduction would have made the connection by now.' And, as if it had been planned right down to the exact second, he moved forward, the clouds that had been covering the moon slid by and a shaft of silvery light shone down on the terrace. The man's face was suddenly, and shockingly, visible.

Recognition hit Mark with a sickening bolt of horror. Take away the wilderness of grey hair, the pallid skin that was wrinkled and loose, the stoop of the wire-thin shoulders and it was Mr Percival . . . Niall's father. 'But . . . but why?' he murmured, finally finding his voice. 'Why are you doing this?'

There was another burst of hideous laughter, and a look of pure malice in the eyes that stared back at Mark. 'Because I hate you. I've hated you for thirty years. You as good as murdered our only child. It was your fault he died.'

'But I was a child myself.' The defensiveness in his words made Mark feel as if he had never moved on from being that frightened boy of twelve who had clung to an upturned hull of a boat while the waves had crashed over him.

'You were a devil child. You were always making Niall do things he didn't want to do. You were a wicked, malignant influence on him. It should have been you who died, not Niall.'

'Don't you think that there were times when all I wanted to do was to turn back the clock? Didn't you ever

454

consider that I'd spent most of my life wishing it had been me who had drowned?'

'Easy words now when you're trying to save your own skin. But I know you're incapable of feeling any real emotion. Real emotion was living with that nightmare every day, coming home from work and knowing my son wouldn't be there. Waking up in the morning and knowing—' His voice broke, but he quickly carried on again. 'It was too much for his mother. She never recovered, never had a happy thought in her head. Because of what you did, grief drove her mad. She spent most of her time shut away in a psychiatric hospital, not knowing what day of the week it was, not knowing who I was. As surely as you killed Niall, you destroyed her. Thanks to you, she took her own life eight months, one week and two days ago. So, tell me, how does it feel to be accountable for two deaths?'

Numb with the realisation that this man had suffered so much, was so desperate to square the account, and that the evening could only have one tragic outcome, Mark couldn't speak. He couldn't even shake his head to deny what he was being accused of. And, despite the intense warmth of the night, he felt chilled to the bone. Sweat was pouring off him, running down his back, trickling between his shoulder-blades. He tried to think straight. Tried to concentrate on what Niall's father had just told him, to make sense of it.

Eight months ago when his wife had killed herself, that was January . . . in February *Silent Footsteps* had been published . . . A week later he had received the first of the letters. He forced himself to speak, to wrench the words out of his parched throat. 'So you want revenge for both those deaths? Is that what you've come here for?'

'Doesn't that seem reasonable?'

'No. I'm sorry, it doesn't.' For a surreal moment they

were back in the car showroom and he was haggling over those bloody alloy wheels again.

'And I am sorry too, but this has gone on for long enough. It is time for this madness to stop.' It was Theo, up on his feet and standing next to Mark.

Swinging his arm, Niall's father pointed the gun at Theo. '*I* will decide when this comes to an end. Not unless you want to die first.' His eyes had turned glassy and his face glistened with a sheen of sweat. His expression was that of a frenzied killer.

'Please, Theo,' Mark murmured, 'no heroics. Sit down and let him say what he needs to say.' Keeping his gaze steadfastly on the gun, he sensed, rather than watched, Theo reluctantly sit down. He took a deep, steadying breath, and knowing all too well that negotiating their way through this was their only hope, the dialogue, such as it was, had to be kept going. He said, 'If you'd hated me for so long, why didn't you kill me before? Why wait?'

'Oh, don't get me wrong, I thought about killing you all those years ago. Night after night when I couldn't sleep, I saw myself taking you out in a boat and leaving you to drown. Some nights I would imagine myself holding you under the water, watching you flail your legs and arms just as Niall must have done. It didn't help with the insomnia, but it was better than counting sheep.'

'Oh, God help us, you're one sick bastard.'

It was Max who had spoken, and Niall's father's eyes hovered maniacally over him. Terrified that he might just go ahead and squeeze the trigger for the sheer hell of it, Mark distracted him by saying, 'So what stopped you?'

The unhinged gaze swivelled back to him. 'I wanted you to suffer. And I knew that, in a small way, you already were.'

'You knew about my addiction?'

'Oh, yes. I knew all about that. I knew everything you were doing. I made it my business to shadow you.'

'You were stalking me even then?'

'Every step. I saw what you were doing to your family, how you were making your parents suffer. How you were throwing everything they had given you right back in their faces. You were destroying them as much as you were destroying yourself. If it hadn't been such sweet justice, I might have felt sorry for them. But I didn't. I didn't want to waste a single emotion on people who had looked down their noses at us. They never thought our Niall was good enough to be a friend for their precious son. I was only an employee and what right did my son have to fraternise with the likes of you? Whereas the truth was, Niall was too good for you.'

The mind-deforming bitterness that this man had harboured for all these years was so strong that Mark could feel it coming out of him like a poisonous cloud of evil. It must have consumed him for so long that it was as much a part of him as his legs and arms were. 'So what was the plan? I assume you had one?'

'You assume correctly. I decided that I wanted to wait until you had recovered and had something worth taking, a life you enjoyed and would want to preserve. I watched you become a success, making something of yourself at last.' He paused and swallowed hard. 'Do you have any idea how painful that was? To see you succeeding and knowing that my son had been denied that right. That all he had was twelve pitifully short years before he was left to rot in the ground.'

'But surely my miserable life wasn't ever worth taking?'

'To an extent, I'd agree with you. Which is why I've got something better in mind for you. I knew you'd hand it to me on a plate in the end. And reading about your so-called bravery in the newspapers, how you and your

457

girlfriend had saved that girl's life, well, I saw then that the moment had come. I'm right, aren't I?'

It was just as Mark had suspected. 'Yes,' he said simply, and seeing the hand tighten its grip on the gun, he knew that time was running out. He had to think of a new direction in which to take Niall's father; he had to channel his thoughts somewhere different. He thought of Bones – calm, detached Bones – and how he would deal with this situation. Steeling himself, he said, 'How did you feel when you read about me saving that girl?'

There was a flicker of some new emotion in the crazed face before him. But there was no answer to the question.

He pressed on. 'Did it make you think about the unfairness of our world? The indiscriminate giving and taking of life? Did it make you want to scream to whoever would listen that it wasn't fair?'

'*No!* It made me hate you even more.'

'Why? Because I'd proved myself where once I had failed? Don't you think that I tried my damnedest to save your son? That I would have wanted to save my friend? But you never wanted to believe that, did you? At the mercy of your own guilt for not being there when Niall needed you most, you turned me into your personal scapegoat, didn't you? Somebody had to take the blame for you failing your son . . . and then your wife, so why not me?'

Tears suddenly sprang into the old man's eyes. 'That's a lie! It was you. *You!* You didn't try hard enough. You didn't care enough. If you had, you would have saved Niall. But your kind doesn't care. They don't care about anyone but themselves.' His voice was cracking up and the strength of his grip on the gun had lessened; the slim barrel was drooping so low, it was pointing at Mark's feet. For a split second Mark thought of taking his chance and hurling himself forward to seize the gun. But he knew the gap between them was too great. He would

458

never make it in time. There was nothing else for it but to keep the dialogue going and inch his way forward. He took the smallest of imperceptible steps, but got no further. The gun was back into position and aimed squarely at his chest.

'I warned you. No nearer. You think I won't do it, don't you? You think I'm just a crazy old fool who hasn't got the guts.'

Tears were streaming down the old man's cheeks, his hands, mottled and stringy with veins, were shaking. Mark could see that he was dangerously close to the edge, which meant that anything might happen. 'I don't think anything of the kind,' he said soothingly. 'It's taken a lot of courage to get this far. A lot of smart planning too.' He was acting out a classic talk-them-down trick – convince them you thought they were a genius and they loved nothing more than to prove it to you; he had used it several times in his books.

Wiping his face on the back of a hand, Niall's father pulled himself together, seemed to hold himself firm. 'Smarter than you'd ever know.'

'Clever of you to use the sequence of events in *Silent Footsteps*. A nice touch, that.'

'I thought you'd appreciate it. Just as you'll appreciate that I have absolutely nothing to lose by what I'm about to do. I've lost my son and my wife, I have nothing left. So here's one more nice touch for you. You have two seconds to choose who I kill. Your closest and oldest friend. Or your girlfriend. Sorry, you weren't fast enough, time's up. I'll choose for you.' And with an agility that took Mark completely off-guard, he moved so that he now had a clear view of Izzy and was aiming the gun straight at her, his fingers already squeezing the trigger.

'*No!*'

It was a scream so loud and violent, Mark felt his jaw

snap, and in an explosion of energy he threw himself in front of Izzy.

He heard the shot and the cries, but most of all felt the massive jolt of agonising pain rip through him. From then on he was conscious only of a blurred sense of pandemonium breaking out, and as his legs crumpled beneath him, he dropped to the ground and another jolt of pain hit him.

He heard and felt nothing more.

Chapter Forty-Eight

Theo's recollection of what had happened was already taking on a vagueness that was the result of acute shock. It was fortunate that he had given his statement to the policemen from Kassiópi several hours ago, because if he was asked now for the details he might not be so lucid. Certain elements of the night were already jumbled in his head.

At the time he had been fully in control, organising everything, the ambulance, the police, and, with Max's help, trying to stem the flow of blood, of which there had been so much. A pool of it had formed on the terrace, and in the panic one of them had stepped into it and made macabre red footsteps on the stone paving.

Now, as he stood alone at the window, his haunted reflection staring back at him while trying once again to recall the sequence of events, he found that he could not picture that dreadful moment when the gun had gone off. He could not bring himself to focus on what he had seen, knowing only that in those last insane seconds he had been powerless to help his friend.

Before that, he could remember the wind blowing the candles, hot wax splashing on to the table, the sound of the sea breaking on the rocks below and thinking: This can't go on. We have to stop it. All the talking in the world is not going to stop this man from killing each and every one of us.

And just as he had thought this, the crazy little man had started saying that Mark had to choose whom he was going to kill. It was at this point that his memory was now distorting the picture. He could see and feel himself wanting to move. Wanting to push Izzy out of the way, but he hadn't been able to. Fear had immobilised him. Just as now the after-shock was immobilising his brain. All it would allow him to remember were the moments before the first shot was fired and everything that happened immediately after the second.

He was on the ground beside Izzy. She was shaking and screaming as she knelt over Mark's blood-soaked body – his head was covered with it, as was his chest and back. It had taken both Max and Laura to pull her off so that he could see if there was any chance of saving him. 'He's dead,' she kept crying. 'He's dead. He's dead.' Laura had held her tight, doing her best to soothe and comfort her, but was unable to find the words to deny what they could see for themselves.

But Mark had defied them. He wasn't dead. And that was when Theo had taken control. If Mark was going to survive, they needed to act immediately: they had to get him to hospital.

By the time the ambulance arrived, Mark still hadn't regained consciousness and his pulse was faint, barely there at all. The amount of blood he had lost seemed so great that Theo was convinced the long journey to Corfu Town would be futile. He would never make it that far.

He should have had more faith in his friend's tenacity to live, though. Mark did make it to the clinic that Theo insisted he be taken to and it was here, right now, that he was being operated on. All Theo knew at this point was that Mark had been shot in the chest and that he had cracked his head badly when he had fallen to the ground. He had no idea how critical his injuries were, or what his chances of recovery were.

Max and Laura had stayed behind at the villa, but Izzy had insisted on coming with Theo. Now they could do nothing but wait for someone to come and tell them the news. Although they never actually voiced their fears to each other, Theo knew that Izzy was preparing herself for the worst. Just as he was.

He turned at the sound of a door opening and saw that she was back from the bathroom. White-faced and hollow-eyed, her clothes still stained with Mark's blood, she said, 'Any news?'

He shook his head.

She came and stood next to him at the window. 'Why didn't he tell me he was being stalked?'

'He didn't want to frighten you. Especially when he realised you might be in danger.' He felt her shiver beside him and put his arm around her.

'I knew there was something wrong, but he wouldn't talk to me.'

'You mustn't be cross with him. It shows the depth of his feelings for you. He was trying to protect you.'

'That man . . . Niall's father. He was very ill, wasn't he?'

'Yes. He was truly sick at heart. There would have been nothing anyone could have done for him. It's a hard truth, but I believe it's best that he killed himself.'

'Did you explain everything to the police?'

'Everything. But I expect there will be more questions to answer tomorrow. Or, rather, later today.' He glanced at his watch, and as he did so, the door behind them opened. They both turned to see who it was, knowing that this was what they had been waiting for. Holding Izzy's hand, Theo spoke in Greek to the doctor, wanting to protect her for as long as he could, to be the one to break it to her. He could at least do that much for Mark.

But there was no need to protect Izzy. The news was good. Mark was going to be all right. Though his right lung had been punctured by the bullet, which had gone clean through his chest and out of his back, the doctor was matter-of-fact about the operation he had just performed.

'It's a routine procedure,' he assured them. 'We've re-inflated the lung and sewn it up, nothing to worry about, really.' He went on to say that Mark had one of the toughest skulls he had come across and it had saved him from any damage to his brain when he had collapsed and hit his head. 'Given the severity of the cut to his head, another skull might have crushed like an egg, but not this one.' There had been a slight cause for concern at the length of time Mark had been unconscious, as a result of the fall, but all the tests showed so far that he was going to be just fine.

It was generally agreed between Izzy and Theo that Mark made a lousy patient. They told him so, three days later during one of his griping sessions about the constant prodding and poking that went on whenever he tried to sleep. 'It's like they think I'm a laboratory experiment for them to play with in moments of boredom,' he complained.

'An expensive laboratory experiment that I am paying for,' Theo corrected him over his shoulder, as he left the room to give Izzy and Mark some time alone.

It was a comment that provoked a snarl of such ferocity from Mark that Izzy burst out laughing. 'You have no idea how good it is to hear you whingeing like this,' she said.

'I'm not whingeing,' he snapped.

'You are. You're behaving atrociously.'

'Then get me out of here.'

She looked at his gaunt face, the blackened arcs beneath his sunken eyes, the dressing that was stuck to the side of his head – and where a large patch of his hair had been shaved off – and at the layers of bandages strapped around his chest. 'According to the doctor you're not going anywhere for at least another three days,' she said firmly.

'Don't try bossing me about,' he scowled, while trying to suppress a yawn, 'you're not at school now, Miss Jordan.'

He fell asleep shortly afterwards. He slept a lot, but lightly, and only for brief periods of time. Leaning back in the chair by the side of his bed, Izzy closed her eyes. She wasn't sleeping properly either; her nights were filled with chaotic, exhausting nightmares. Recurrently she would hear Mark's cry that fateful night. *'No!'* It clung to her, a whorl of a scream that went on for ever, wailing its siren of terror and desperation. She frequently dreamed of Mark being shot, of holding him in her arms, watching helplessly as his life ebbed away, taking with it her every hope of happiness. Usually the dreams were a replay of what had really happened – including Niall's father holding the gun to his own head and ending his life, just as he had on the terrace. But last night she had dreamed that Niall's father was alive, that they were all back in England, that having killed Mark he was now stalking her. 'There's no one to protect you now, Izzy,' he was saying, as he crept up behind her, 'no one to die in your place.'

Max, Laura and Theo had commented this morning on how tired and drained she looked. She had tried to make light of it, insisting that she was fine. 'A few sleepless nights never hurt anyone,' she had said, keeping to herself the depth of her shock at what had happened. She couldn't come to terms with the fact that she had come so close to dying, that if it hadn't been for Mark's selfless act of courage she would probably be dead.

Though she was desperate for rest, Izzy found the corridor outside Mark's room too noisy for her to sleep. There was a constant squeak of shoes on the polished floor, a steady hum of voices, a persistent ringing of telephones. Giving up on the idea of snatching a nap while he slept, she went to look at the cards and flowers grouped together on the table at the end of his bed. His parents and brothers had been the first to get in touch after Theo had called them to explain what had happened. They had then phoned Mark to make sure he really was okay, as had his agent and publisher who had read of the incident in the papers back home. Max and Laura had visited several times, bringing with them newspapers and chocolates, neither of which he had so much as glanced at. The largest bunch of flowers, and easily the most ostentatious, was from Dolly-Babe and Silent Bob. Their card wished him a speedy recovery and contained a postscript of their home address – they had left for England yesterday morning – 'Just in case you're ever passing our way,' Dolly-Babe had scribbled.

'About as likely as me being left alone in this hell-hole,' had been Mark's muttered response, when he had read it.

As the days progressed, Izzy grew concerned. Far from making a steady recovery as they had been told he would, Mark seemed to be slipping into a decline. The doctor said he thought Mark was depressed.

'It's as if he's given up,' the doctor told her and Theo, 'as though he doesn't care one way or the other if he gets better.'

'Would it help if he was discharged and nursed where he felt more relaxed?' asked Theo.

The doctor shook his head. 'No. He's not to be moved. Not yet. Not until I'm happy with his mental state.'

A little over a week after he had been admitted, Mark told Izzy that he thought it would be better if she stopped coming to see him.

She was devastated, and felt as though the air had been knocked out of her. 'But why? What have I done?' She had to steady herself against the back of a chair.

He looked straight at her and, with not an ounce of emotion in his voice or expression, he said, 'Let's face it, Izzy, it was never going to work between us. It was nothing more than a holiday fling with a few extra excitements on the side. It's over. Please don't make a drama of it. I'm tired, I'd like to sleep now. To be left alone.'

Mark watched her go for the last time, turned his head into the pillow and buried it as far as it would go.

Early next morning he had a visitor.

A furious visitor.

Theo.

He marched in and, for a good five minutes, ranted and raved at Mark. Then he paced the room and ranted some more, resorting to his native tongue when he ran out of English. The attack was as thorough as it was vociferous.

'Have you quite finished?' Mark asked him, when at last the room fell quiet.

But clearly Theo hadn't. 'Do you have any idea what you have done to that poor girl?' he demanded. 'She is distraught with what you have told her. Inconsolable.'

'She'll get over it.' He made his voice sound far away, distant, uncaring. Just as he had yesterday with Izzy, when he had hoped that the carefully added note of irritation in his final words would hasten her departure and bring about an end to the pain of seeing the heart-shattering destruction he was wreaking. Outwardly he might have given a convincing performance of indifference, but inwardly he had been a broken man. He had never felt so sure about a decision, yet so hurt by it.

Theo wheeled round on him, glared angrily. 'I doubt that. She feels more for you than anyone else ever will.'

'Maybe now she does, but when she gets back to England she'll put this summer behind her. Put it down to

467

experience and think of it as an interesting holiday romance.'

'And will you? Will you return to your sad, lonely little world and imagine that she didn't storm the castle to reach your heart and touch you in some beautiful, lasting way?'

'Don't start getting sentimental on me, Theo. Keep the purple prose for some other mug who'll listen.'

'I would rather be sentimental than afraid to grab the chance of enjoying the life I was meant to live.'

'I'm afraid I don't possess your giddy, optimistic approach. For some of us, the real world can only ever be a disappointment.'

As though he had used up all his anger, Theo came and sat in the chair next to the bed. He leaned forward, his hands clasped between his legs. 'Just explain to me why. What has changed your feelings for her?'

Mark had known that it would come to this, that he would have to give Theo a reasonable explanation. An act of cold indifference was never going to satisfy him. 'I have to end it, Theo,' he said quietly. 'I'm not doing this out of self-interest. I'm doing this for Izzy. Surely you can see that. Everything I touch I either spoil or destroy. Izzy was very nearly killed because of me. I simply won't let myself put her at risk again.'

Theo stared at him in astonishment. 'But, Mark, that is nonsense. It is irrational beyond belief. You do not spoil everything you come in contact with. Far from it.'

'Really? What about Niall, and his parents? All three of them dead at the last count. And what about the pain I caused my family? And even you, days after meeting me you wind up mugged.'

'And what of all the good things that have occurred because of you, eh? Any other man would be satisfied with saving just the one life, but no, you have to score a hat-trick of saving three: mine, Sally's and Izzy's. A super-human feat, a record to be proud of, perhaps.'

'Well, you know what Scott Fitzgerald said: "Show me a hero and I will write you a tragedy." Now please, Theo, don't make this any harder for me. Tell Izzy whatever you think will make her feel better, but don't waste your breath trying to make me change my mind. It won't work.'

Chapter Forty-Nine

The holiday was over.

Despite what Max and Laura thought.

They were keen for Izzy to stay on for another week, to leave when they did. But she had told them several times already that it would be better if she went home as originally arranged. 'You deserve to have some time alone before you have to go back as well,' she said now, as they tried once again to dissuade her from going.

'Just a few more days,' Laura implored, passing her a plate. 'It would do you good.'

Izzy settled the plate on the table in front of her. 'But my flight's booked,' she said wearily. She was tired of having to defend her decision.

'And can be changed just like that,' said Max, snapping his thumb and middle finger together. 'Really, Izzy, we don't want you to leave, not yet. Not like this. It's too soon after everything that's happened.'

'Max is right,' Theo joined in. 'It's much too soon.'

'It's nearly a fortnight. And, anyway, school starts next week. I have to go home. There are things I have to organise.'

Nobody said anything more, and in the silence Izzy watched Theo open the box of pastries he had brought with him, his fingers working at the knot in the ribbon, his brow furrowed. Wretchedness was making her irritable and impatient, and she suddenly wanted to snatch the box out of his hands and slash at the ribbon with a pair of scissors.

Since the night of the shooting, and when he hadn't been at the hospital visiting Mark, Theo had spent even more of his time at Villa Petros. It was as if he had formed a pact with Max and Laura, as though the three of them couldn't get through a single day without a conversation about the shooting, as if one more conversation would exorcise the painful memories. She couldn't bring herself to tell them that she didn't want to keep going over the same well-trodden ground. She didn't want to be reminded of how lucky she was to be alive, not when she felt so numb and miserable. For that reason alone, she needed to get away. She was banking on going home to get back to normality. To put the summer behind her.

To put Mark behind her.

But she knew that would never happen. She would never forget him. They might not have known one another for very long, but the distance she and Mark had covered together was greater and more meaningful than anything else she had known. She had trusted him completely . . . had given herself, heart, body and soul, to him.

Theo had explained to her what lay behind Mark's apparent dismissal, and while it didn't change matters, it at least gave her the reason why he had suddenly, and inexplicably, rejected her. As Theo had been at pains to point out, Mark's reasoning might be irrational and misguided, but it meant that she could accept that there wasn't anything more she could have done. Unlike her break-up with Alan, Mark hadn't left her feeling humiliated and used, or guilty.

And wasn't this exactly what Laura had wanted for her? A holiday fling to prove to herself that she was up for a bit of fun with no strings attached? No broken hearts. No recriminations. Only a wonderful sense of empowerment.

471

But it wasn't that simple.

Her heart was hanging in there by the sheerest of threads. Which was why everybody was treating her so carefully. They had turned her into a fragile ornament that they weren't quite sure where to place for the best. She loved them for their kindness, but wished they would stop. A little rough handling would be so much better. A rap on the knuckles and a stern word or two telling her to pull herself together would be easier to cope with. Her mother's uncaring approach would be perfect. *So, he had his fun and dumped you, did he? I warned you. You've only yourself to blame. How very foolish you've been. Here, make yourself useful and dry the dishes.* Modern Woman would help too. She would stand with her hands on her hips: *Hey, lighten up, sister, and count yourself lucky you got out while you still could. He was always going to be trouble.*

As they sat on the terrace enjoying the late-afternoon sun, Izzy sensed the conversation bouncing over and around the only subject she was interested in.

Mark.

How was he?

Had his depression lifted?

Had he asked after her?

Did he, like her, lie awake at night reliving those days they had spent together?

He had been discharged from the hospital at the weekend and Theo had come to see Izzy the morning after, just as he had promised he would. 'He is better for being with me,' he had told her, 'but only because he is more comfortable cursing my interference and ineptitude than that of a pretty young nurse.'

'He will be all right, though, won't he?'

'Don't worry, Izzy, I will see to it that he makes a full recovery. As to the confused workings of his mind, which is governing his heart, well, that I cannot speak for. I wish it were different. Truly I do. I had such high hopes for you both.'

'So did I,' she murmured . . .

Now unable to wait another moment to ask the question she most wanted answered, she interrupted Theo, who was telling Max and Laura some story about Angelos over-watering his flowers. 'How's Mark?' she said. Instantly three wary faces stared back at her. If I were a grief-stricken widow, this is how they would treat me, she thought. 'How is he?' she repeated.

Theo put down the pastry he was eating. He licked the crumbs from his fingers. 'He is getting stronger. Putting on a little weight also.'

'Is he writing?'

'In the morning, yes, for a couple of hours. But by the afternoon he is too tired, which, as you can imagine, frustrates him. Not to put too fine a point on it, he is a raging pain by about three o'clock. I have to go back to Athens the day after tomorrow, so I am taking him with me. I hope the change of scenery may do him good. If not, I will put him on the first available plane for England and let him fend for himself.'

'No, you won't.' Laura smiled. 'You're too kind-hearted to do that.'

He sighed. 'Maybe that's true, but I swear he is testing my patience to its outer limits.' Then changing the subject, he said, 'How quiet it is going to be for you and Max with us all gone. It might even feel like a proper holiday for you.' He picked up the remains of his cake and smiled one of his charming but infinitely roguish smiles. 'But promise me you will rest your legs during this pregnancy, Laura. I don't want to see you next summer with varicose veins.'

Both Max and Laura laughed at his irrepressible warmth and good humour.

This is how I must try and remember my holiday, Izzy

thought, as she made herself join in with the laughter; a happy and carefree time.

Early next morning, as arranged, Theo came to take Izzy to the airport. 'I have business in town to attend to,' he had told Max yesterday, 'so I might as well save you the journey.'

The goodbyes were as tearful as Izzy had dreaded. Although she knew she would be seeing her friends in a week's time, it felt so final. This really was the end of a magical dream. Even if she came back again – and everybody said she must – it could never be the same.

The airport was horribly crowded with hundreds of holidaymakers queuing to check in their luggage. Theo waited with her and she was conscious of people staring at him as though they thought they should recognise him. Dressed in one of his immaculate lightweight suits with a pale blue shirt and tie, and dark glasses, there was a flamboyant film-star quality about him. She thought back to the first time she had met him and how like George Clooney she had thought he was. 'Do you get this trouble wherever you go?' she asked, after a woman had stopped her trolley to have a better look at him.

He lowered his sunglasses and smiled. 'It's you they are staring at, not me.'

'Mm . . . they're probably wondering what I'm doing with such a gorgeous man.'

He laughed. And laughed loudly. 'My God, Izzy. At last, you have paid me a compliment. I have waited all summer to hear you say something pleasant about me. No, no, don't start crying. Not here, or people will get entirely the wrong idea.'

'Am I allowed to shed a tear now?' she asked, when she had checked in her luggage and had joined the queue to go through passport control.

'A very small one. I don't want my suit to be ruined by

a flood of tears. It might shrink and that would never do.'
He hugged her tightly. 'Okay, that's enough emotion,' he
said, releasing her from his arms. 'Too much and I will
let the side down with you. Take good care of yourself,
Izzy, and keep in touch. I want to know how you get on
with your dreadful headmistress, what cunning revenge
you have in store for her. Max and Laura are bullying me
to visit them in England, so we will meet again quite
soon, I'm sure. And, of course, next year you will come
to Corfu again. No, don't look so doubtful, Izzy, you will
come again, I know you will. This place suits you. The
island has its regular visitors who just can't keep away.
Mark my words, you will be one of them.'

She smiled extra hard at his words.

'There, you see how brave you have become? What
inner strength you have found here on holiday?' He
kissed her cheeks and then, 'And lastly, this.' He pressed
his lips firmly to hers. 'Be lucky, Izzy. Be happy.'

With her head leaning against the small window of the
aeroplane, she watched the landscape beneath her. When
the island had disappeared completely she felt a sharp tug
on the thread that was holding her heart together. No
more tears, she told herself sternly. Just accept that once
again Chance has played its little game with you. Now
you have happiness, now you don't.

She slept through most of the flight, dreaming of the
coming autumn term at school and discovering on her
first day back that she had a child protégé in the new
intake: a small blond-haired boy who could knock
Picasso into a Cubist cocked hat.

Home had never looked more dreary or unwelcoming. It
had all the cheer of the Arctic tundra.

She had chosen this ground-floor flat after her split
with Alan because she had thought it had such a warm,

475

cosy feel to it, but now as she pushed open the front door and lugged her bag into the hall, then gathered up the mountain of mail from the mat, she thought it cursed with gloom. Nothing could have matched more appropriately the sense of desolation she had come home with. She was reminded of the abandoned house she and Mark had looked at in Old Períthia.

It's the rain, she told herself, as she stood in the middle of the sitting room staring out through the window on to the communal lawn she shared with the rest of the residents of the converted house.

That and the grey sky.

And the sub-zero temperature of a typically English summer's day.

It's not the flat, she chided her flagging spirits. The flat is fine. It's your home. Your only home, so you'd better get used to being in it again.

There, that was telling her.

To soften the lacklustre light from outside, she switched on two small lamps and set to with her unpacking.

Thanks to Laura insisting that anything that needed washing she throw into the machine yesterday morning, everything was clean and neatly folded, so it took her no time at all to put it away.

Dealing with the backlog of mail was rather different, however. It took her over an hour to sort it into piles: action needed sometime in the future, and action required first thing in the morning. There was one letter, though, that she had deliberately left till last. She had recognised the stark white envelope the moment she had seen it and had put it aside to be dealt with when she was feeling stronger. It was from school and could mean only one thing: she was being given a mealy-mouthed redundancy package.

A perfect and fitting end to her holiday.

*

476

She didn't know whether she was disappointed or relieved when she opened the letter in bed that night and read that she hadn't been given the elbow after all.

Amazingly, she had been promoted.

In real terms it wouldn't amount to much. She would be working longer hours with greater responsibility and for not much more money.

Still, it would look good on her CV when she got round to looking for a new job.

Switching off the bedside lamp, she thought, Oh, well, business as usual, then. Nothing turns out the way I think it will.

When would she ever learn?

Chapter Fifty

'I have to go,' Mark said, 'you know I do. It's time.'

'But are you sure you're ready?'

'Come on, Theo, you were there when the doctor gave me the all-clear.'

Theo shook his head doubtfully. 'To travel on your own, though . . . Supposing you feel unwell? What if—'

'We could play the What-if game for ever and a day,' cut in Mark. 'No, like I say, I'm ready to go home.' He picked up a small white pebble and hurled it into the sea. Too late he realised his mistake and winced at the pain. To his disgust he had been advised to wear a sling to restrict his arm movements and protect the damaged muscles in his chest and shoulder, but he had dispensed with it at the first opportunity, claiming he no longer needed it, that he didn't want the fuss or bother of it. Nothing would make him admit otherwise that a punctured lung, even if it had made a full recovery, hurt like hell if he coughed or breathed too deeply. And if he moved too sharply, as he just had, his body declared payback time.

Sitting beside him, Theo must have noticed him wince. He flashed Mark a look of impatience. 'You see? I'm right, you are still in pain, you are not ready to go home yet. And with that dreadful haircut you look like a half-starved refugee. They'll stop you at the airport, accuse you of being an illegal immigrant.'

With a rueful smile, Mark ran his left hand – the one that didn't pull on his weakened muscles – through the stubble on his head. Three days ago, while still in Athens with Theo, he had acquired the mother of all haircuts. Fed up with looking in the mirror each morning and seeing the bare patch on his scalp where it had been stitched back together, he had decided to go for the buzz-cut look to even things out. He had walked into the nearest barber's and had the lot as good as shaved off. When Theo had got back from work late that night, he had taken one look at him and dropped his jaw to the floor. 'That, my friend, is going to take some getting used to!'

Just as Theo had said it would, the change of scene had been good for Mark. The sense of having been-there-done-that was not lost on him. It was, after all, in Athens, that he had stayed while getting his head together after he had left the rehab clinic and tried to decide what to do next with his life.

While Theo was at his office, an elegant, stately, refurbished town-house in a quiet square a short walk from his apartment, Mark had spent the mornings writing. But it hadn't gone well. Slow and tortuous, it was like pulling teeth. Another change of environment and associated disruption to his routine hadn't helped. In the afternoon he tried to rest, as he had been advised. When he couldn't sleep, despite being so tired, he would tune out by flicking through the channels on Theo's state-of-the-art television, but the sheer awfulness of Greek daytime viewing was in a class of its own and had had him riveted. Greek soaps, he had decided, were produced, directed and acted by comic geniuses, only they didn't know it. There were more gasps of surprise, rivers of tears and shock-horror scenes in one half-hour slot than in a month's worth of British and Aussie soaps combined. But it hadn't induced sleep, and resorting to the old standby of Sky and CNN to help him nod off, he kept wondering why Theo bothered with such an expensive piece of kit when the home-grown programmes available to him were so bad. The answer was in the stash of videos and DVDs he found in an elegant cabinet in the corner of the marble-floored sitting room. Since his last visit to Theo in Athens, it was apparent his friend had developed a taste for his own little bit of Merry Olde England in the form of *Only Fools and Horses*, *Monty Python* and *Blackadder*. There was even a shelf dedicated to some of the BBC's best costume drama over the last twenty years. It was an extraordinary hoard that made Mark smile and had him wondering if this was how his friend kept his English up to scratch.

In the evenings, when he had a resurgence of energy, he and Theo would go out for a meal. They went for walks too, strolling round Theo's favourite areas of the city, invariably finishing up in the Pláka district and watching the world go by. They had had dinner with Theo's parents several times and, as ever, Christiana Vlamakis had lavished an excess of concern on him.

'Oh!' she had cried, patting his arm when Theo told her the details of the shooting. 'You are not a safe man to be around.'

He must have flinched when she had said this, as Theo had hurriedly gabbled something to her that was incomprehensible to his ears but which had the effect of making Christiana cluck around him for the rest of the evening.

'It was a figure of speech my mother used,' Theo said, during the drive back to his apartment that night. 'I don't want you brooding on those words of hers.'

'She's right, though, isn't she?'

'You know my view on that subject, so please do not bait me. I think you are mad to give any credence to such a tomfoolish theory.'

'Credence to such *tomfoolery* is the expression, you want.'

'Pah!'

It was the nearest they got to discussing Izzy. And, for that, Mark was grateful. There was nothing more to be said. She had gone back to England to get on with her life without him. That was the end of the story he had written for them.

Yet, as he sat here on the beach in Áyios Nikólaos with Theo towelling himself off after his swim, and recalling the many times he had enjoyed Izzy's company in this same spot, he didn't try to kid himself that he was better off without her. He knew very well that having Izzy in his life was infinitely better than not having her in it. But that was a luxury of thought he would not allow himself to dwell on. She was better off without him. Safer, too.

He knew Theo would disagree with him, which was why there was no point in discussing it with his friend, but he was convinced that he wasn't destined to live a normal life. The happy-ever-after scenario that others enjoyed would always elude him.

Two days later, his return to England went as smoothly as he could have hoped for, apart from Theo making a fuss at the airport and insisting that he be helped on to the plane and met at the other end. 'You are not to lift that heavy luggage. You must lose that appalling pride of yours and ask for help.'

'Sure you wouldn't prefer me to be pushed about in a wheelchair?'

Theo had slapped his forehead with his hands. 'Now, why had I not thought of that?'

'No, Theo, *don't*!'

'Okay, I'll let it go for fear of you turning nasty. Now prepare yourself, I am about to thoroughly embarrass and annoy you.'

Which he did, embracing Mark and smacking two great big kisses on either side of his face.

*

While listening to the lunchtime news on the radio and waiting for the kettle to boil, Mark realised that it was one of those rare moments since his return, three days ago, when the phone wasn't ringing and he had the house to himself.

Once word had gone round the village that he was home, everybody wanted to come and see him. The shooting had found its way into a number of the British papers, including the local rag, the *Whitby Gazette*. Coming so soon after the near-drowning accident it must have been a story too good to pass up. As a consequence, there was a fascination on the part of those he knew, even vaguely, to hear the grisly details straight from the horse's mouth.

Deirdre had been the first to call round, bringing with her a Victoria sponge cake, some gingerbread and scones, a pot of home-made lemon curd and a cheese and onion quiche. 'Well, pet,' she had said, settling the stack of Tupperware boxes on the worktop, removing her shoes and stepping into her slippers, 'you've been having a time and a half of it, haven't you?'

Lionel Bridges had been next to pay him a visit, followed swiftly by Dale, who brought with him his latest girlfriend: a raven-haired oddity, who also worked part-time at the Dracula Experience in Whitby. They told him they were moving in together, renting a tiny terraced house called Karma Cottage. He had had to stop himself smiling at the thought of them ever having children: they'd be straight out of the Addams Family! The rest of the writers' group soon made an appearance, and it was as well that Deirdre had been so thoughtful and kind as everyone who called on him with offers of help – did he need a lift to the hospital, the doctor's, or the supermarket? – was hungry. And while they happily tucked into the cakes and scones they took it in turns to ask him the questions that were burning holes in their tongues. Lionel

– always a man for detail – had been straight off the starting block, wanting to know what sort of gun had been used. Mark had had to admit that he didn't know. 'Sorry, Lionel,' he had said, 'not my instrument of death. Wouldn't know a Bren gun from a tommy-gun.' It was true. He had never used them in his novels; he preferred his killers to be more ingenious. For some peculiar reason he had the idea that there was something horribly prosaic about a life being ended by a mere bullet.

But now that the initial interest in him had been satiated, he was being allowed time on his own. With the exception of the nightly phone calls from Theo and the early-morning ones from his family, he had been left, at last, to catch some much-needed breath.

He made himself a mug of tea and took it up to the first floor, to his study, which stretched from the front of the house to the back. He had chosen this room to work in because it had such great views: out across the cliff edge and the boundless sea, or to the rolling hills of the north Yorkshire moors. Sitting in his sea captain's chair – another of his self-deprecating sick jokes – he put his feet on his desk and sipped his tea thoughtfully. He had been looking forward to this moment, hoping that the familiar would ground him. He let his eyes roam the neatly organised shelves at either side of the chimney-breast where a potted history of his life could be put together from the books, records and CDs he had collected over the years.

Above the fireplace was a Victorian watercolour. It was a beautiful, restful landscape, all fading light and muted shades of colour, painted by a highly thought-of artist who had lived in the village at the turn of the century. Oddly enough, it had been the first present he had bought himself with his first advance from his publisher. Whenever Theo saw it, he said it represented the lesser-spotted St James's underbelly of sentimentality.

It also provoked him to make fun of Mark's inability to spend the money he earned. 'You are useless with money,' he would say. 'You don't have a clue what it can do for you.'

'That's because I don't have the imagination for it,' he would protest.

'Rubbish! It's guilt. You spent so many years lecturing the world on the perils of capitalism you can't bring yourself to enjoy it.'

Swivelling his seat, Mark switched his gaze to the blank screen of his computer. It reminded him that he hadn't got round to checking his e-mails. He decided that as they had made it this far without his attention, they could wait a while longer.

His tea finished, it was time to get started on some work. What with all the visitors and interruptions he had had, he hadn't had a chance to get anything written, and when he didn't write he got twitchy. And twitchy was bad. Twitchy encouraged doubts to rise to the surface of his brain, nagging little maggots of anxiety that crawled around hinting that he was way off-course with the plot, the narrative, the dialogue.

He set out his things.

Notepad.

Pens.

Pencils.

Next he inserted a CD into the hi-fi, switched it on, reread the last few pages of what he had written and held the fountain pen poised over the blank page.

And that was as far as he got.

Two hours later, and discounting the words, 'Chapter Forty-Eight', not another word had appeared on the page.

Everything was in order, just as it should be: the ambience was right, the tools were right, so what the hell was the problem?

He had no answer.

He changed the CD. Replaced U2's *The Joshua Tree* with Bob Dylan's 'Blowin' in the Wind' and sat down again, pen poised.

Nothing.

He resharpened his pencils, fitted a new ink cartridge into his pen, ripped out the top page of the A4 pad of paper – well, it might be jinxed – reheaded it, gave Bob Dylan his marching orders and slipped in his lucky CD, REM's *Up* – fingers crossed, it had always worked well for him in the past.

But still nothing.

The page was blank.

And remained so for the rest of that day and the following week.

It was a disaster.

How could this have happened? How could that old enemy of every author, the dreaded writer's block, have worked such a perfect number on him? No matter what he did, there was a complete absence of creative thought going on inside his head. Nothing would come to him. He was all out of words and ideas. It was a catastrophe.

Uncannily he recalled his thoughts while sitting in Theo's garden at the start of his visit, when he had laughed at himself for being so wrapped up in the futility of ritual and joked that he would get so used to writing with a musical backdrop of cicadas that he wouldn't be able to work without it.

No more than coincidence, he told himself firmly. Don't give it another thought.

But without the collusion of his book to work on, he knew that he was being forced into a corner. His brain was denying him the one thing he had used as a defence mechanism to ward off the terror of that night when Niall's father had tried to shoot Izzy. By focusing his thoughts on the plot of his book, continually readjusting pages of dialogue in his mind, mentally checking that every I was dotted and every T crossed, that no stone of narrative was unturned, it had, until now, successfully kept him busy. Kept him from dwelling on Izzy . . . what she meant to him. Without that vital weapon of defence, he was now at the mercy of his imagination. He had started having long-drawn-out dream sequences in which he was repeatedly trying to save Izzy from being shot. He usually managed to wake himself before the real terror set in, but in the early hours of this morning he had woken in a sweat-drenched tangle of sheets, screaming Izzy's name – he hadn't reached her in time and she was dying.

Now, as he stood in the kitchen making himself some breakfast, he shuddered at the rawness of the memory. He slapped two pieces of buttered toast together and went outside to the small garden that overlooked the cliff edge and the sea. He listened to the screech of seagulls wheeling overhead and watched a group descend on the rooftops of his neighbours' houses. On the other side of the low wooden fence, he heard his immediate neighbour open his back door. Bill Watkins was a sprightly octogenarian who, notoriously, was as deaf as a post, but after a brief exchange of smiles while the old man threw a bag of rubbish into his dustbin, Mark turned away embarrassed, convinced that Bill must have heard him screaming like a banshee through the wall.

So what's next on the agenda of madness? he asked himself.

Another week of being unable to write?

More nightmares?

Or are you going to do something about it?

I could ring Theo and talk it over with him, he answered the contentious voice of his conscience.

Yeah, and you could be as evasive with him as you always are.

In the end, though, he did ring Theo. But his own problems were pushed aside when Theo said, 'What a coincidence, I was going to call you. But I'm afraid it's not—'

'You're not coming over, are you?' interrupted Mark, slipping effortlessly into their usual line of derogatory banter and finding some relief in it.

'No, you're quite safe. But it saddens me to tell you that poor old Thomas Zika died in his sleep last night.'

'I'm sorry, Theo. He didn't have any family left, did he? Who will arrange the funeral?'

'Oh, I will see to that. It is to be a very small affair. My parents are flying over. They were very fond of him. As I was.'

Me too, thought Mark, when later he put down the phone and remembered how protective he had felt towards Thomas on the day of Anna's memorial service. He felt sad. Sad because Thomas had lived so very long and never truly had what he wanted in life. He had contented himself to love Theo's grandmother from afar, but wouldn't he have preferred to be married to her? Why had he been so prepared to compromise his own wishes and desires? Why hadn't he pursued Anna more determinedly?

These thoughts stayed with him for the rest of that day – another day of not being able to write – and he knew it was no coincidence that whenever he pictured Thomas Zika in that restaurant, unable to feed himself, he transferred himself into Thomas's place. Would he end up the same, never knowing what it might have been like with Izzy, never taking that risk to find out just how fulfilling a life they might have shared?

He ran a tired hand over his jaw, pressed the heels of his palms against his closed eyes, imagining all too clearly the solitary games of chess that awaited him.

And what if his current mental state continued and he could never write again?

It was a terrifying thought.

Previously his writing had been his point of reference. It had compensated in some way for not having a relationship, but now he had neither.

So what or who are you afraid of? asked the voice that had questioned him in the garden earlier that morning.

He suddenly smiled to himself, thinking of Izzy and how she had admitted to hearing voices in her head.

Going upstairs to his study, he realised that he had actually thought of her without it hurting. It was progress. It made him wonder if he could face looking at the photographs he had just had developed. He hadn't looked at them yet, unsure whether he wanted to be reminded so vividly of what he had jettisoned. His fingers hesitated over the package on his desk, but he rejected the temptation. Not yet. It was too soon.

He sat down and toyed with the idea of sneaking up on his notepad and seeing if he could get some words written.

But fear of failing again made him switch on his computer to check his e-mails instead. There were the usual messages from his publisher keeping him informed of stuff they thought he gave a monkey's for; a message from his father who had recently joined the ranks of the Silver Surfers and now spent an obsessive number of hours browsing the Internet; a note from Lionel asking if he could drop round with some chapters from the steamy pen of Shona Mercy for him to read – top-shelf eroticism was not what Mark needed right now – and lastly, and this one had him leaning forward in his seat, a message from Bones, who was just back from a brief working secondment in California. His message said that on his return to work at the clinic, he had been shown the newspapers regarding Mark's latest exploits – a colleague had kept them for him thinking he might be interested.

Five minutes later as he was dialling Bones's home number, Mark was aware of yet another voice banging on inside his head.

It was Dolly-Babe, jangling her bangles and telling him Bones's e-mail was a SIGN.

Yeah, he thought, a sign that I'm desperate.

'It's not a bad time to call, is it?' he asked, when Bones picked up.

'Hello, Mark. Now, would that be bad in the sense of—'

'Don't you ever cut yourself some slack?'

'Just a little joke. You know, I was thinking of having an answerphone message that said: "Sorry, none of my multiple personalities are here to listen to you, but I'll deal with you just as soon as I've found myself."'

'I wouldn't bother.'

'So, what can I do for you? I was wondering when I'd hear from you.'

'Why do you assume I want something?'

'Well, for one thing it's nearly midnight and for another you've recently flirted with death again. Not once, but twice. How am I doing?'

'You're slipping, you missed out on the girl.'

'On the contrary, I was saving her. And that wasn't meant to be a pun on your fine heroic deeds. Now tell me everything. It's late, so no games of mental hide and seek. Do that and I'll put the phone down on you.'

He did as Bones instructed.

When he fell quiet, Bones said, 'Good. So where shall we dive in first?'

'Anywhere you like. Why I can't write. Why I've started having nightmares about the shooting and why I told the woman I love to get the hell out of it and leave me alone because she'd be better off without me, that I'd only bring her bad luck.'

There was a long pause, during which Mark half expected to hear the familiar, almost reassuring rustle of a sweet wrapper. 'Well?' he said irritably. 'I thought there were to be no games.'

'Mm . . . There's a word I'm looking for. A word that covers your last point. Now what is it? It begins with a C. Help me, Mark, you're the one who's good with words.'

'Hell! I didn't think I'd have to play Twenty Questions!'

'Come on. You can do it.'

'Okay, how about Conditioning?'

'No.'

'Convergent thinking?'

'No. And that's two words. I said one.'

'Causal attribution?'

'Are you listening to me?'

'God, not one of Freud's old cookies, Castration anxiety?'

'Now you're just showing off. No, the word I was thinking of begins with a C, followed by an R, an A and finally a P.'

'Crap?'

'Yes. Your head must be full of it, Mark, if you're arrogant enough to think that the world revolves around your petty little actions. How many times do I have to tell you, it is not your job to save mankind from itself?'

'But—'

'No buts, this is where I get tough with you. You've phoned me at this ridiculously late hour, not to seek my advice but to have me confirm and sanction what was already in your mind, hoping I'd give you the necessary permission and blessing to go ahead. Don't interrupt, I haven't finished! It's bloody obvious why you're having nightmares and even more obvious why you can't write, even to a swollen-headed fool like you. But, as usual, you're deliberately hiding from the truth. I bet you've even told yourself you don't deserve this lucky break. I'm right, aren't I?'

'Maybe.'

'And after everything I've taught you, you still come up with a hare-brained thought such as that! Will you never learn? By the way, you say that you love this woman, have you by any chance been brave enough to tell her you love her?'

'Er . . . not in so many words.'

'I thought not. The same old Mark. Scared of being vulnerable. Scared of a committed relationship. But I notice you didn't use the word in the past tense, which means that subconsciously you haven't consigned the relationship to the wastepaper basket, so I would suggest that you do something about it. Go and tell her that you love her. I guarantee your nightmares will stop and your writing will flow. If I'm wrong I shan't charge you for this consultation. How's that?'

'Oh, go suck a Murraymint!'

'That's my boy!'

'But what if she doesn't love me? She's never actually said she does.'

'That's a risk you'll just have to take. My guess is she's worth the gamble. Or would you rather you never found out? Now listen to me, and listen well.'

'You're not going to start whistling one of your bloody awful tunes, are you?'

'I was tempted a few minutes ago, Genesis's 'Throwing It All Away' struck me as fitting. But, no, I was going to ask if you consider yourself to be a success in bed with this woman?'

Mark laughed, then winced. His chest still wasn't up to it. 'If you really want to know, I'd say we were a corona of excellence.'

Bones laughed too. 'I said you were good with words, Mark. I like that. You see her as the heavenly body and you as the halo of light. A sparkling image on which to end our conversation. Keep me posted, won't you? Think happy thoughts, Mark. Goodnight.'

Chapter Fifty-One

By the second week of the autumn term, Izzy knew she didn't have a child protégé lurking among the new intake, despite what the parents might like to believe of their offspring. 'He's so artistic, so amazingly good with his hands,' was a boast she had frequently heard since she had trained to be a teacher. And Mrs Claremont, an insipid mother of the oh-don't-do-that-darling variety, who had already bestowed on the school a generous offering of three ready-made, badly-behaved boys had felt the need to make the same proud boast of her latest, hopefully last, contribution. 'He likes nothing more than to really get stuck in,' she had gushed on the first day of term, when she had presented a moon-faced child of five to Izzy. Claremont number four looked more like a bruising seven-year-old, and at eight thirty-five in the morning, with his tie already askew, and his shirt bubbling over the top of his grey shorts, he had certainly looked the type to want to get stuck into anything and everything. The muckier the better, probably. The more annoying the better.

Two weeks on and Claremont number four had lived up to Izzy's predictions. He was an utter menace in the art room, lacking the ability to concentrate for more than three minutes at a time and wrecking anything he touched. He was also a bully, picking on nearly everybody in the class, terrorising them with his bigger build and strength. He took special pleasure in making fun of a timid little girl called Gemma, who spent most of their art lessons sniffing back the threat of tears and twisting a prettily embroidered handkerchief around her fingers. She was such an unhappy child that Izzy had sat down with her at the end of Friday afternoon's lesson, just before last break, and asked her if she was all right. A tiny nod was all she received for an answer.

'Have you made any friends?' she asked, suspecting not: the child was new to the school and hadn't come up from the kindergarten like most of the others had.

A sideways shake of her head confirmed Izzy's suspicions.

'That's a shame. Friends are important. Do you know what would make you lots of friends?'

Another sideways shake of her head.

Izzy leaned in close to her and whispered into her ear. Then, with a reassuring smile, she said, 'Do you think you could do that?'

'I think so.'

'Good. So why don't you practise getting that voice a little louder over the weekend and then give it a go in our next art lesson on Monday afternoon?'

It was now Monday afternoon, first period after lunch and Izzy had the staffroom all to herself. Not having a lesson to teach, she was supposed to be genning up on the latest edict from the headmistress about the new report system she was implementing. Computerised report cards were replacing the out-of-date A4 sheets of paper upon which teachers with handwriting as poor as any GP's could disguise the unpalatable truth behind scribbled lines of false praise.

But computerised report cards, or whatever else the headmistress wanted to introduce, held no interest for Izzy. Looking out of the window, down on to the playing-fields where on one side a group of boys in muddy shorts were being taught to run headlong into an enormous battering ram, and on the other, girls were chasing each other with hockey sticks and showing scant regard for anybody's safety, she knew that soon none of this would matter to her. Some time in the new year she would be gone.

No one knew of her plans to leave, not even Max and Laura with whom she had spent Saturday evening. They had come to her for supper; it was her small, rather inadequate way of thanking them for such a wonderful holiday. Laura was looking fabulously well on her pregnancy and was clearly going through the blooming stage. Snuggled up on the sofa with Max, she was a picture of health and happiness, and bursting with energy and enthusiasm. As was Max. Much to Izzy's surprise he had told her that evening that he was thinking of selling his hugely successful management consultancy.

'Are you serious?' Izzy had asked him.

'Very. I've even got somebody sniffing round wanting to make an offer. It's a good one too. I'd be a fool not to take it.'

'But what will you do?'

'That's what I want to know, Izzy.' Laura had laughed. 'I have visions of him wearing a zip-up cardie and following me round the supermarket like Victor Meldrew, saying, "How much? I don't believe it!"'

'I'm not sure what I'll do,' Max had said, shrugging off Laura's joke. 'Something new, something different. Small-scale consultancy work on my own terms would be tempting. I missed so much of Francesca's early years, I'll be darned if I'm going to make that mistake again. So we'll just have to see.'

It was Izzy's view exactly about her own future, except while Max wouldn't have to worry where his next penny was coming from as he waited for something new and different to land in his lap, she would have worry in spades over the coming months.

Discovering that she was pregnant had seen to that.

Misfortune couldn't ever just rain on Izzy Jordan with a soft pitter-patter, oh, no! She had to be swept away on a tidal wave of rotten luck.

Not that the baby was bad luck. The baby was wonderful, but it was a frightening prospect. She would be entitled to maternity leave, of course, but what then? How would she be able to afford decent childcare on her salary and run her flat? She would probably have to sell it, buy something smaller, live in a cheaper area.

And how would she ever live down the shame her mother would make her feel?

A child born out of wedlock in the Jordan family!

A single-parent family!

A government statistic!

Scandalous!

Still, there was always the hope that her mother would be so appalled she would never speak to her again.

There was also the shame she would bring on school to consider. Once it became impossible to hide the bump under her power suit – yes, as absurd as it was she had succumbed to the horror of wearing a skirt and jacket – the head would never stand for anything as sordid as an unmarried mother-to-be on the staff. What sort of a message would that give the youngsters, to say nothing of the awkwardness of explaining her situation to the board of governors?

And what about Mark?

When she had used the pregnancy-testing kit yesterday evening and had seen that she had hit the jackpot, her first thought was of the expression in Mark's eyes that night in bed when he had asked her if she thought he would make a good father. She would have to tell him, of course. It was only fair. And even if she did keep it from him – and the thought had occurred to her – when Max and Laura found out she was pregnant they would be sure to tell Theo, and in turn, Theo would be bound to let Mark know. But what mustn't happen was for Mark to think she was using the baby as a bargaining tool. She would never do that.

But for all the chaos ahead, she was really quite calm. Surprisingly so. She had no idea what she was going to do, how she was going to juggle the consequences of her summer away, but some inner force of optimism was gently leading her by the hand. It was as if the tiny baby inside her knew best. 'Hey,' it was saying, 'trust me on this, I've got it all worked out.'

The children were coming in from the playing-fields now. She looked at her watch. Ten minutes and the bell would summon her for her next class.

It wasn't until she saw Gemma looking anxiously over her shoulder to where Claremont number four was preparing to take aim with a bit of spit-soggy tissue that she remembered her chat with the shy little girl on Friday afternoon. 'Gemma,' she said, standing in front of her desk, 'I'd like you to be my personal helper this lesson. You can start by passing round the sheets of paper we need.' She watched the child move nervously round the two large squares of desks, sliding a piece of orange A3 to everyone as they laughed, chatted, scraped chair legs on the tiled floor, slipped on their art overalls and rummaged noisily through their pencil cases. In contrast to their happy, relaxed faces, Gemma's was a study of fixed concentration. Poor child, thought Izzy, recognising the expression she had worn most of her school days when she had been terrified of making a mistake. Just as she had been all her childhood, frightened to death of dropping the responsibility she had been given but wanting so much to prove that she could do it.

When Gemma was two boys away from David Claremont, Izzy saw him raise his fingers to flick his revolting handmade missile at her. Gemma saw it too.

497

She looked him straight in the eye and said, 'David Claremont, you're nothing but a silly baby and if you can't behave, you should go back to being in the kindergarten class where you belong with all the other silly babies.'

She was word-perfect, had remembered every word Izzy had whispered into her ear. Not only that, her diction had been as clear as a bell, as authoritative as any teacher's, and from the expression on her face, she was suddenly walking on air. She didn't seem at all bothered that she was now the focus of everybody's attention, that everyone had stopped what they were doing and were staring at her, wondering, no doubt, where this new, assertive Gemma had come from. Izzy noticed a few smiles of admiration around the classroom, as well as the frown on Claremont number four's face. There was even a hint of a trembling lower lip.

If it was the only lesson Izzy ever taught a child, she knew it would be the best one. She was going out on a high, if nothing else.

But, meanwhile, she had a lesson of doing creative things with pasta tubes and lentils to make the most of. Not even the thought of clearing up the floor afterwards lowered her spirits as she saw the dramatic change she had wrought in Gemma. Gone was the threat of tears, gone was the twisted handkerchief, and in place was a smile of heady achievement as she continued to help Izzy, handing out what was needed.

Forty minutes later when it was a toss-up between describing the nearly finished pieces of work as art or have done with it and call it a pasta and lentil bake bound with glue, the shadowy figure of the headmistress appeared at the half-glass-panelled door. Izzy hoped that it was nothing more than one of her regular patrols to make sure that everybody was where they were supposed to be and that they weren't enjoying themselves too much. But the handle turned and in she came.

Oh, Lord, what did this mean? Had she got wind of her pregnancy? But how? Nobody knew, she had told no one. Her panicky thoughts were abruptly distracted by a cry of 'Oh, Miss, look at what David's done! He's got glue everywhere!'

Perfect! Just what she needed. This would really impress the head.

She turned to see what the dreadful child had done now and groaned at the sight of him. He was covered in white PVA glue. The stupid boy must have lifted the pot over his head and poured it over himself. It was a wickedly tempting thought to roll his chubby body round the floor and cover him in pasta and lentils, then staple him by his ears to the display wall. From behind her she could hear the head muttering about it being an inappropriate moment, that perhaps they would call back a little later when Miss Jordan wasn't quite so busy.

Izzy groaned to herself again. Oh, this was really bad. A prospective parent was being shown round the school and had just witnessed the art teacher's singular lack of talent for keeping a class of five-year-olds under control. But then she heard a man say, presumably the prospective father, 'How refreshing to see such a hands-on technique being employed. Do you mind if we don't rush away?'

Oh, thanks, buddy, she thought, stooping to untie the knot of Claremont number four's art overall. Brilliant. She had caught herself one of those sly parents, who wanted to see how she was going to handle things. But then she stopped what she was doing. That had been no prospective parent. Not with that voice.

Slowly, hardly daring to believe what she had heard, she straightened up and turned round.

It *was* him.

It really was Mark.

He looked different somehow. Smarter than she had ever seen him, as if he had tried to dress the part of a prospective parent. The baseball cap was a mistake, though.

'I think it would be better, Mr St James, if we came back later,' the head insisted, looking pointedly at Izzy. 'We're extremely proud of the new science laboratories we had built last autumn. Mr Weston is our head of—'

His gaze on Izzy, Mark said, 'I'm not interested in science. Science is for geeks. Art and literature, that's what does it for me.'

His words, together with his forthright tone, brought an instant hush to all the children, as well as a cold glint to the headmistress's eyes. Izzy recognised it as the look of a headmistress who had decided that this parent would be trouble, that no matter how strapped for cash the school was, she could do without his money. 'Perhaps the library would be of more interest to you,' she said briskly. 'This way.' She held open the door, and gave him space to pass.

'In a minute,' he said, making no attempt to move and keeping his gaze on Izzy. 'I want to see more of this classroom. Why don't you deal with the sticky problem child while Miss Jordan gives me the low-down on what goes on in here?'

Izzy was almost quaking at his sheer nerve. She hid her face by trying to untie the wretched knot on Claremont number four's overall, but she knew that the head had to do as Mark had suggested or appear grossly discourteous and unprofessional. She felt a pang of sympathy for the moon-faced child as he was hauled from his seat and all but dragged outside to his awaiting punishment.

The classroom was still unnaturally quiet as Mark approached her, his boots crunching twirls of pasta with each step he took.

'Well, Miss Jordan, how about it?'

She forced herself to look at him. 'How about what?' How could he do this? How could he just wander in here without warning her? And why?

He came within a few inches of her. His voice was so low she had to strain to catch it. 'Is that the power suit you told me about? It makes you look different. Very high maintenance.'

'I'm afraid I haven't really got an awful lot to show you, what with it being the start of a new term,' she said, for the benefit of all ten pairs of ears that were listening; she had never known a class to be so attentive. Then, in a frantic whisper, 'What on earth are you doing here, Mark? Why have you come?'

'To apologise. I've undergone a reality check. I've been a complete fool.'

She led him to the back of the classroom, towards the big cupboard in the alcove where she hoped they could speak without being overheard. 'The theme we'll be covering this term,' she said, as he followed closely behind, 'is autumn. We'll be using as many media as we can to capture the spirit of the season.' She slowed her step, lowered her voice. 'And when you've apologised, what then?'

What then? was the million-dollar question that had plagued Mark every mile he had covered by taxi and train since first thing that morning. During the long journey he kept thinking of his conversation with Bones, and how easily Bones had shaken the truth out of him. Until that moment, he hadn't said out loud that he loved Izzy. When he had been with her, he had skirted every which way around the simple phrase – I love you – never quite committing himself to it, never letting her know the extent of his feelings. The truth was, he had been scared of what his love for Izzy meant to him. When he had come close to losing her that night in Corfu, it had frightened him to know just how painfully vulnerable his love for her made him. But all those days and weeks without her had taken their toll, and he had known that he couldn't go on pretending to himself that he was protecting her by ending their relationship. The only person he had been protecting was himself. And, as usual, Bones had been the one to cut straight to the heart of the matter, forcing him to see things clearly.

Getting off the train at Manchester and finding himself a taxi for the remainder of his journey, he had worried that Izzy would refuse to speak to him – after what he had done to her, she had every right to turn him away. Which was why he had engineered their meeting as he had. Coward that he was, he had hoped that by seeing her like this, so publicly, she would be at a disadvantage and less likely to be angry with him. It had been simplicity itself convincing that money-grabbing snob of a headmistress over the phone that he was interested in sending his non-existent children to her school – he had made out he had four all under the age of eight – and an appointment had been instantly made. And, as public venues went, this fitted the bill perfectly: all these goggling children couldn't keep their eyes off them.

'It's the *what then* that I've come here to resolve,' he said, his voice still low, 'I could get poetic and talk about how much I miss you. I could say how the sky was dark without you, how the sun never shone, and that the stars had dropped out of the heavens, but there'd be a danger you'd laugh at me. I could also confess that I can't write without you in my life. But that might make it appear as though I have a cheap ulterior motive in coming here, so I'd better not mention that. Which leaves me just the one option to prove I'm being sincere.'

They were standing in the shelter of a large alcove now, facing an open cupboard, their backs to the class of children who had started up a rumble of activity; chairs were being scraped across the floor and voices were raised. It was probably going to be the only moment of privacy they got before some nosy child came to see what was going on, so seizing his chance, Mark lifted Izzy's chin with his hand, bent his head and kissed her. It was the lightest of kisses, their lips barely touching. 'Do you remember that day at Old Períthia,' he murmured, still kissing her, 'when I asked you if being involved with somebody, heart, body and soul, was the same as being in love?'

She nodded.

'Well, I'm here to say that it is the same. I love you with all my heart, with all my unattractive body and with all my ragged, unworthy soul.' He pulled away, looked into her face. 'Tell me that being an irreplaceable part of my life is enough for you, Izzy. Tell me that you love me.'

'Oh, Mark, it's more than enough. And, yes, of course I love you, how could you ask? But please, we have to stop this. You'll get me the sack.'

'Wouldn't I be doing you a favour, getting you away from that awful headmistress?'

'Not if she refuses to give me a good reference.'

'I'll write you all the references you'll ever need. Come on, Izzy, make a break for it, let's get out of here. I don't mind getting you the sack for a furtive kiss, but I draw the line at young minds being perverted by the sight of their teacher being made love to in the art cupboard, which is what we'll end up doing if we stay here a minute longer.'

'But I can't possibly leave them.'

'Yes, you can. It's easy. You just give me your hand.'

His madness took her as far as the doorway, where, having crunched across the floor, they found their escape thwarted by a partially scrubbed Claremont number four and a furious-looking headmistress. Izzy's nerve ran out on her, went and hid in the furthest corner of the room.

Now sanity and reason would step in and make her realise it couldn't be that simple.

'Mr St James,' said the head, looking none too pleased, 'if you feel you've quite exhausted the delights of the art room, perhaps we could—'

'Sorry,' he said, pushing rudely past her, 'I'd love to stop and chat, but Miss Jordan has a pressing engagement I'm rather keen for her to fulfil. And as for the delights of the art room, believe me, I'm bowled over by them.'

Oh, my goodness, Izzy thought, as they raced to the front of the school to where her Triumph Herald was parked, it really is going to be as simple as he says.

Hardly aware of the short drive back to her flat, or of the speed at which they had tumbled into bed and made love, Izzy sank into the softness of the pillows behind her and looked across the room to the framed sketch she had drawn of Mark when she had first set eyes on him. How intensely serious he had seemed that day on the rocks as he looked out across the water, not at all the witty, unpredictable and loving man she had come to know.

'By the way,' she said, 'I just want you to know that you are totally and utterly mad, Mr St James.'

He lay with his head half on her chest and half on her stomach. 'I suspected that might be the case,' he responded, without looking up.

'Why didn't you phone or at least write to me?'

'I thought about it but decided a personal appearance was more appropriate. I'll never forget the expression on your face when you saw it was me.'

She stroked his spiky hair, what there was of it, understanding now why he had worn the baseball cap. One look at his brutally cut hair and the terrible scar, complete with stitch marks, on the side of his head and he would have been refused entry to the school; the headmistress would probably have called the police saying an escaped convict was on the loose. 'You realise, thanks to you, that I'm going to be the talk of the staffroom,' she said. 'For days and weeks to come I'll be the only topic of conversation.'

'I'd hoped to turn you into a legend at the very least. I want you to become known as the reckless art teacher who abandoned her pupils to run off home to have sex with a complete stranger in the middle of the afternoon.'

Reckless, she repeated to herself. Well, she had certainly become that. She closed her eyes and wondered how he would react if she told him she was pregnant, that right now, he was just a few inches from the heartbeat of his child. Feeling his weight lift from her, she opened her eyes. He had raised himself up on an elbow and was staring at her.

'You've got a strange look on your face,' he said, 'one that says you know the punchline that nobody else knows.'

She smiled hesitantly. 'Maybe I do. Maybe I don't.'

Kissing her forehead, he said, 'Well, I'll leave you to your secrets, then. I need a shower.'

'Help yourself. But you'll have to make do with girlie shower gel. It's all I have.'

He grinned. 'Who knows? It might bring out my feminine side.'

She had almost fallen asleep when she sensed she wasn't alone. Turning over, she saw that Mark was standing at the foot of the bed. He smelt of Timotei shower gel and was wearing her lilac bathrobe, the sleeves of which were hopelessly too short for his long thin arms. But it was what he had in his hands that really caught her attention. It was the box containing the pregnancy testing kit she had thrown into the bin in the bathroom last night. Oops.

'Is this the punchline?' he asked, holding out the package for her to see.

She searched his face for a clue to his thoughts. But his expression was unreadable. Scared, she suddenly wondered if she had got it wrong about him wanting to be a father. Or maybe he did fancy it, but not just yet. She sat up straight, held the duvet against her. 'We weren't as careful as we thought we were. Does it . . . does it change anything?'

A silence passed, his eyes not on her, but on the pregnancy-testing kit. At last he looked at her. 'Too damned right it does!'

Chapter Fifty-Two

The combined christening party for Maximilian Corne-
lius Lewis Sinclair and Beth St James – Mark had been
adamant there would be no fancy names for a child of his
– was a suitably joyous occasion.

It was a warm summer's day in the middle of June, the
party of close friends and family had spilled out into Max
and Laura's pretty garden, and as Theo held Beth in his
arms and posed with Mark while Izzy took their
photograph, he felt it was the proudest moment of his
life.

'You are the luckiest man alive,' he said to Mark, when
Izzy had left them to photograph somebody else, 'I hope
you appreciate everything you have.'

'Including my mother-in-law?'

'Ah, well, you win some, you lose some. But at least
she is here and on speaking terms with you.'

'Oh, she's on speaking terms all right, she never stops
speaking to us. She phones every other day to check that
Beth is sleeping in the right position, that Izzy isn't
feeding her too often, or too little, and that we're using
the correct nappies, not the ones she's just read are
carcinogenic.'

Theo chuckled. 'It's a fair price to pay for your good
fortune. And your own parents? How do they feel
towards their latest grandchild?'

Both men looked across the lawn, to where Izzy was
patiently trying to line up the St James family – including
a host of children who wouldn't keep still – to have their

picture taken. The scene reminded Theo of Mark and Izzy's wedding day earlier that year in Robin Hood's Bay. They had married on a bitter winter's morning and the photographer had had less than five minutes to take his pictures outside the small Methodist chapel before they died of hypothermia. The reception had been a modest affair back at the house, and because no cars were allowed into the quaint little village, they had to walk down the main street in a flurry of snow before cutting through a criss-cross of sheltered narrow passageways. But at least they had had the pleasure of thawing out in front of a roaring log fire while drinking mugs of life-saving hot chocolate. Serving hot chocolate instead of alcohol as a welcome for their guests had been Izzy's inspired idea. 'So much more practical than champagne on a day like this,' she had said, as they warmed their frozen hands gratefully on the mugs of reviving sweetness. It had been particularly good to see Mark's parents in such happy circumstances, their obvious love for and pride in their youngest son, who had taken such a long and tortuous route to happiness.

In answer to Theo's question, Mark said, 'They're delighted with Beth. You'd think she was their first grandchild.'

Refraining from saying that perhaps Beth was special because she was the one grandchild they had thought they would never have, Theo said, 'And judging from their faces, it looks as if they're just as delighted with Izzy.'

Mark smiled. 'Yeah, she's worked her magic on them as well. Shall I have Beth now so that you can get yourself a drink?'

Theo held on to the tiny sleeping child possessively. 'No need, I am quite happy as I am. It's a shame your old mentor, Bones, isn't here. I would have liked the opportunity to meet him again after all these years. He missed your wedding also.'

'It's his way of keeping his professional distance, I guess.'

'If it had been me I would have jumped at the chance to rejoice over one of my biggest success stories. And talking of stories, what's the latest news of *Flashback Again*?'

'The general opinion is that it's my finest hour. "Popular while remaining literate," is what the literati are saying. As if they know anything. There's even talk of a film.'

'Aha! Didn't I tell you? Didn't I say that I had a good feeling about this one? You should listen to your old friend more often. He knows what he is talking about.' The loudness of his voice stirred the sleeping baby in his arms. Two little feet kicked from under the silk christening gown, then a pair of eyes opened wide: they were grey and solemn, just like Izzy's. 'She is quite adorable,' sighed Theo, 'and so very like her mother.'

'Really? I hadn't noticed.' Bending down to take a closer look, Mark stroked his daughter's delicate cheek, 'Can't see it myself.'

'Oh, surely you cannot be so blind that you—' Theo stopped short, realising that Mark was teasing him. 'Oh, he of so little heart and soul.'

'That's not what Izzy says about me. In fact when we're in bed she—'

'Please,' cried Theo, clasping Beth closer to him to cover her ears, 'spare the child your saucy bedroom tales! Now, behave yourself and tell me when you are coming to stay. You will be coming, won't you? You'll both need a holiday after the year you've had. Max and Laura are flying over in a couple of weeks. Why don't you join them?'

Mark shook his head. 'Not a chance. Last summer was a little too action-packed for us. We've decided to go somewhere else. We thought walking in the Himalayas would suit us better.'

'What? Are you mad? How could you be thinking of taking my precious little goddaughter to the Himalayas?'

'He's not, Theo,' said Izzy from behind him. 'He's winding you up. Shall I have Beth for you? Give your arms a rest. I know she's only a few weeks old but she gets heavier by the minute.'

Again Theo held on tight. 'No, I am fine. And I shall not part with her until you have told me when you are coming to stay.'

'We were going to talk to you about that. Go on, Mark, you ask him, it was your idea.'

Theo detected an air of discomfort in his friend.

'It's no big deal,' Mark said, 'but we wondered if you would help find us a house to buy. With all the tourists that descend on the village in the summer, it gets so busy, we thought—'

'No, Mark,' corrected Izzy, with a smile, '*you* thought.'

He scowled and pushed at his hair, which had mercifully recovered from the savage attack on it last year. 'Yeah, okay,' he said. '*I* thought that if we had our own place in Áyios Nikólaos I'd be able to get more work done during the summer months. There'd be fewer distractions.'

A small smile appeared on Theo's face. Then it widened into a ridiculously huge grin. He lifted Beth so that her little yawning face was inches away from his. 'You hear that, Beth?' he said, planting a kiss on the end of her nose. 'That was your father speaking. Now I know he is everything he was meant to be. A happily married middle-aged man with a beautiful wife and daughter and fast becoming a fat, capitalist pig. Ah, ah, ah, Johnny Two Homes St James! He'll be renewing his driving licence next just so that he can own a flashy car like your uncle Theo.'

'If you weren't holding my child, I'd ram this fist right where I've always wanted to shove it!'

'Oh, admit it, Mark! Admit, just this once, that you have undergone a wonderfully radical shift of perspective on what is important in your life.'

Laughing to herself, Izzy took Beth from Theo and left them to it. She wandered across the lawn to where Max had fixed a rope swing to the branch of an old apple tree for when his son was old enough to play on it. 'He's planning ahead with everything,' Laura had told Izzy on the phone, during one of their long catch-up sessions. 'I'm just glad he saw sense and didn't sell the business and become a part-time house-husband or he would have been fussing around with Lord knows what else.'

After testing the swing to see if it would take her weight, Izzy lowered herself on to the wooden seat. She shifted Beth in her arms so that she was comfortable and gazed at her lovingly. 'You were right,' she murmured softly. 'You told me you had everything worked out. You just didn't tell me how well you'd got it sorted.'

Since Mark had made his extraordinary appearance in her classroom that day last autumn, her life had changed beyond recognition. She had never been so happy, or felt so self-assured. She knew now that the two were inextricably linked, for how else would she have found the nerve to do what she did last September?

Before the headmistress had had a chance to demand an explanation for her appalling behaviour and consequently sack her, Izzy had marched into her office the following morning to carry out a pre-emptive strike. Disappointed not to find the head skulking in her lair, she had caught sight of an offensively insipid calendar of Anne Hathaway-style cottages on the wall. Taking a pen from the head's mahogany desk tidy, she flipped September over and sketched in a man urinating down the smoking chimney-pot of October's half-timbered thatched cottage. 'How's that for putting your fire out, you horrible old dragon?' she muttered. Hearing footsteps on the wooden floor outside, she hurriedly turned back the page, replaced the pen in the desk tidy, and greeted the headmistress with a polite smile. 'I've brought you this,' she said, dropping an envelope on to the desk. 'It's my resignation. I'm leaving, as of now, this very minute. Not very professional, I know, but under the circumstances I'm sure you won't want me to stay.'

Later that morning, and after phoning Laura to tell her what was going on, she locked the door to her flat and set out with Mark on the long drive to her new home. 'No doubts?' Mark had asked, when they stopped for petrol and a bite to eat at a Little Chef on the A1. 'After all, Miss Jordan, this is a little rash for you, very out of character.'

Kissing him, she had said, 'My only doubt is whether my poor old car will make the journey. Now buckle up and tell me how much further we have to go.'

'It's all the way or nothing, Izzy.'

'Would there be any other way with you?'

And that, she knew, would always be the case. Her life with Mark would never be boring; it would never contain anything as dull as a half-measure. It would always be an exhilarating roller-coaster ride of extremes. When he had fully taken in the fact that she was pregnant, he had swung through every emotion. From euphoria that he was going to be a father, to maudlin concern that she might not have told him. 'How did you think you were going to manage on your own?' he had asked, his eyes moist, his voice thick.

'How any other single mother would manage.'

'But you would have told me, wouldn't you?'

'Yes,' she had said firmly. 'I was always going to tell you. I just didn't know when or how. I didn't want you to think I was forcing your hand.'

'You know your trouble, Izzy, you're too bloody considerate.'

'Sweet of you to say.'

They had stayed up all night, discussing what they would do next.

'I want you to come and live with me,' he had said. He was adamant. 'Tell that headmistress to go shove her job where the sun don't shine, and become a kept woman.' Her doubtful expression provoked him to add, 'What scares you most? Standing up to that despotic she-devil, or accepting the position of being my live-in lover?'

'Oh, definitely the latter.'

'So what exactly is it that you're not sure about?'

'I'd need to know if it was a permanent position. I couldn't—'

'Bloody hell, Izzy! I don't believe you. Of course it's permanent.'

'You never said.'

'Well, I'm saying it now. And if needs be I'll get you a ring first thing tomorrow morning to convince you.'

'Is that a proposal?'

He frowned. 'Yeah, okay. I could have put it better, but will it do for now?'

'Why? Will you have something better up your sleeve at a later date?'

Pushing her back on to the bed, he had said, 'You'll have to wait and see.'

A month later he proposed 'properly' when he took her on a midnight walk on the beach in Robin Hood's Bay. Despite the cold, it was a beautiful night, with a full moon pinned to the cloudless sky like a sheriff's badge, its silvery light tiptoeing across the waves behind them. 'Now, would you say this was romantic enough for you?'

he had asked, getting down on one knee in the damp sand and rummaging through his coat pockets. 'Damn it, where the hell did I put it? I had it a moment ago.' He was suddenly a mass of volatile nerves. He cursed some more, then eventually found the ring in his jeans pocket. 'Oh, for heaven's sake, Izzy, stop laughing! This is supposed to be one of those perfect moments you'll never forget.'

She grabbed hold of his collar, pulled him to his feet and kissed his cold lips. 'Believe me, I'll never forget it. It'll stay with me for the rest of my life. I'll always love you, Mark, but promise you'll never go mainstream on me. I'm not sure I could handle you being normal. And, by the way, the answer's yes.'

'Yes?'

'Among all that cursing and fumbling I'm assuming there was a proposal of marriage.'

The sound of laughter made Izzy look up. Nearer the house Corky was telling Laura's parents something that had them laughing loudly. To the left of them, Max and Harry were deep in conversation – Harry had recently graduated and much to Francesca's horror there was talk of him joining her father's firm. Laura's horror was that there might be a danger of Ma and Pa Patterson becoming a part of their family. 'Imagine having to be nice to them on a permanent basis,' she had told Izzy. A scary prospect indeed.

Sitting in the shade of the house, and showing Francesca how she should be holding her baby brother, was Izzy's mother. How poignant the sight of Beth and little Max must be for her, Izzy thought sadly. Having given birth to her own child and experienced the bond of motherhood, she couldn't think how she would cope if Beth was suddenly snatched from her. If five weeks was all she was allowed to have with her child, what desperate depths of depression might she sink to? She held Beth tightly and watched her mother across the garden.

When she had summoned the courage to take Mark home to meet her mother, Prudence had been perfectly vile to him. In that hateful little bungalow with its ghastly memories, her mother had asked Mark why he thought she would be remotely interested in meeting him. 'After the way you spoke to me on the telephone, you should consider yourself lucky that I've let you over the threshold.'

'I thought you would want to meet the man who was going to marry your daughter,' he said lightly.

'Marry? Who said anything about you marrying?'

'I just did. It's why we've come to see you. We're planning on getting married in January. We thought you'd want to know.'

Pouring herself another cup of tea, her cold eyes appraising him, she said, 'A tawdry affair in a dreadful register office, no doubt. You needn't waste an invitation on me, I shan't be there.'

Turning to Izzy, he said, 'Well, I should think that comes as quite a relief to you, Izzy, doesn't it? At least now we'll be able to enjoy the day.'

How could he have said that? How could he have been so brazen? But if she had thought Mark had been blunt in what he had said so far, she was well off-beam. His worst was yet to come.

'Are you going to just sit there and let this monstrously rude man speak to me in that way?' her mother demanded.

'Look, Mum, it doesn't have to be like this between us. Why don't you—'

'Like what precisely? What are you getting at? And why is this tea so weak? How many bags did you put in the pot? I knew I should have done it myself. I never could trust you to do anything right, not even something as simple as making the tea. You know how I prefer it to be—'

'Quite honestly, Mrs Jordan,' interrupted Mark, and in a voice that was sublimely cordial, 'I don't give a flying fuck how you prefer your tea. We've come here today to tell you we're getting married and that you're going to be a grandmother sometime at the beginning of May. Now, that may be of interest to you or it may not. But while Izzy and I go for a walk to rid ourselves of your choking bitterness, why don't you mull over those details and see what you really think of them. But get this, when we return I expect you to be civil. Is that clear? One foot wrong, and I promise you will never *ever* see your grandchild. Nod if you understand what I have just said.'

If every staring statue in that room had shattered in the awesome silence that followed as her mother gave an imperceptible nod, Izzy wouldn't have been surprised. They left her sitting in her chair, speechless, her tea-cup wobbling in its saucer. When they returned an hour later, resigned to driving straight back up to Yorkshire instead of staying the night, as planned, they found Prudence in the kitchen, at the sink, peeling a mound of potatoes and listening to *Sing Something Simple* on the radio.

'Which would you prefer,' she asked, as they joined her, 'roast or mashed potatoes with your chicken? I thought we'd eat at six, I'm not one for eating late. Izzy, you'd better sit down and rest. Too much running around won't do the baby any good. Are you taking any iron supplements?'

It was extraordinary. Like the ECT treatment she had all those years ago, it was as if the shock of Mark's words had erased all the earlier unpleasantness from her mother's mind. She cooked them supper, and while they ate, she enquired politely after Mark's writing, offered to knit a selection of matinée jackets for the baby, and when it was bedtime, she even allowed them to sleep together.

So had that been the answer, then? Would years of misery have been avoided if only Izzy had had the guts to fire off a round or two of Anglo-Saxon at her mother as Mark had?

She would never know, and maybe it didn't matter. What they had now between them, as new and fragile as it was, was more important than what might have been. The pink jackets and mittens her mother had made for Beth – and there were plenty of them – might be hopelessly too large for her, but it was a heart-warming and reassuring sign that they were moving in the right direction. The fraught tension that had gone into those horribly distorted squares for the cold and hungry in some faraway African village had been replaced with garments that were beautifully made, if a little old-fashioned. 'So long as she doesn't start knitting me a Val Doonican sweater, I don't care how many things she knits or how grim they are,' Mark had said, when yet another parcel arrived in the post revealing a further addition to their unborn baby's wardrobe.

In that same delivery, there had been a letter from Dolly-Babe. Unbeknown to Izzy, when Mark had returned home last summer, he had penned a note to Dolly-Babe thanking her for the flowers she had sent him while he had been in hospital in Corfu. He had also mentioned that drinking wasn't going to help her forget the past – he had tried it himself. Izzy had no idea how he had had the nerve to write such a letter, or how he had actually worded it, but the response, when it finally came months later, was to thank him for his advice:

I was that angry with you when I first read your letter that I threw it in the bin. Bloody awful cheek, I thought. That girlfriend of yours must have been shooting her big mouth off to you, telling you stuff that was confidential. But all that day when Bob was out, I couldn't stop thinking about what you'd written, and what Ria had said about you changing my life. Anyway, to cut a long story short, I've been attending one of those groups you suggested, you know the kind of thing – 'My name is Liberty-Raquel and I'm an alcoholic.' Not that I am, of course, but you've got to meet them half-way, haven't you? Well, you don't need me to tell you that, I'm sure. There are people in the group much worse than me. Drink, you wouldn't believe it! Or what they knock back. Last week a woman admitted to drinking nail-varnish remover, said she couldn't get enough of it! But for all that, they're not a bad crowd and it does get me out of the house, so I'd just like to say thanks – thanks for giving me a kick up the backside.

'So you did help change her life in the end, didn't you?' Izzy had said to Mark, when she had finished reading the letter.

With typical bad grace, he had growled, 'Say so much as one word of my having fulfilled a psychic's prediction and I'll invite her to stay with us!'

Beth wriggled restlessly in her arms and Izzy nudged at the grass beneath her feet and set the swing moving to and fro. The rocking motion instantly settled the baby and Izzy smiled at the thought of Mark carrying out his threat. He might be one of the most unpredictable and daring people she knew, but she doubted that even he would go that far to prove he was as good as his word.

'And what, pray, Mrs St James, are you thinking of to make you smile like the proverbial Cheshire cat?'

'Really, Mr St James, creeping up behind me like that and cross-examining me with your impertinent questions!

Isn't a wife allowed to have a few secrets from her husband?'

Coming round to stand in front of her, Mark placed his hands at shoulder height on the ropes of the swing and looked down at her. 'I knew marriage would be a mistake. I liked you better when you were a scarlet woman lying in the sun, baring and confessing your all.'

'Ssh, you'll make your daughter blush.'

'Just like her mother, then.' He reached out to take Beth so that Izzy could get to her feet. 'So what were you smiling about?'

'You, of course. You know how funny I think you are.'

'Mm . . . I keep forgetting what a highly twisted sense of humour you have.'

She laughed. 'If I have, it's only developed since I met you.'

Slipping a hand around her waist, he drew her close. 'Are you up for a full-frontal kiss right under your mother's nose?'

'Oh, I think I could manage that.'

'My, how you've changed your tune. Now brace yourself, Izzy, this is going to be a big one.'

From across the garden, Theo watched his friend kiss the woman he had once hoped would feel for him what she so clearly felt for Mark. He felt no envy, just a deep, satisfying sense of contentment.

'Well, Theo, it isn't quite what you had in mind almost a year ago when you thought you might sweep Izzy off her feet, is it?'

He turned to see Laura at his side. He took the glass of wine she had brought for him. 'How very unkind of you to remind me of my arrogance that day on the terrace with you. But I'm not too proud to admit that it's been a good lesson for me.' Then, looking back at Mark and Izzy, he said, 'They've done an excellent job of sweeping each other off their feet, haven't they? They truly bring out the best in one another.'

She squeezed his arm. 'Cheer up, Theo, you'll find your Miss Right one day. Just when you're least expecting it, there she'll be, all gorgeous and utterly in love with you.'

'And in the meantime, do I have your permission to flirt with you?'

'What? With my awful legs?'

'Oh, my darling Laura, please don't tell me you've let yourself go. Did I not warn you about those varicose veins? Did I not tell you to rest your legs during your pregnancy? What you need is a good holiday to recuperate, and I know just the place, where the sun shines all day and the pace of life comes to a grinding stop.'

She burst out laughing. 'The pace of life comes to a grinding stop? You must be joking!'

He grinned. 'Well, excluding the everyday drama of a middle-aged mother and her schoolboy lover turning up in the bay, a near-fatal drowning, a tragic shooting, people falling in love and the careless conception of a couple of charming babies, I think you'll agree that the pace was pretty slow and made for the perfect holiday.'

She raised her glass against his. 'And let's not forget our perfect friend and neighbour, Mr Theodore Vlamakis who made it all possible. Thank you Theo. You're an exceptional man.'

'Now that's something I won't dispute. Cheers!'